Their Christmas Knights

Two handsome heroes are ready to save these damsels in distress—and make Christmas *extra* special this year!

We're proud to present

SILHOUETTE SPOTLIGHT

a second chance to enjoy two bestselling novels by favourite authors every month— they're back by popular demand!

December 2004
Their Christmas Knights
featuring
Holly and Mistletoe by Susan Mallery
One Christmas Knight by Kathleen Creighton

January 2005
Their New Year Babies
featuring
Same Time, Next Year by Debbie Macomber
Happy New Year—Baby! by Marie Ferrarella

February 2005
Say 'I do'
featuring
The Sheriff's Proposal by Karen Rose Smith
The Cowboy's Seductive Proposal by Sara Orwig

Their Christmas Knights

Susan Mallery

Kathleen Creighton

 **SILHOUETTE**®

*First published in Great Britain 2004
Silhouette Books, Eton House, 18-24 Paradise Road,
Richmond, Surrey TW9 1SR*

THEIR CHRISTMAS KNIGHTS © Harlequin Books S.A. 2004

The publisher acknowledges the copyright holders of the individual works as follows:

Holly and Mistletoe © Susan W Macias 1996
One Christmas Knight © Kathleen Modrovich 1997

ISBN 0 373 04970 6

64-1204

*Printed and bound in Spain
by Litografia Rosés S.A., Barcelona*

Holly and Mistletoe

SUSAN MALLERY

SUSAN MALLERY

is the *USA TODAY* bestselling author of nearly fifty books. Frequently appearing on bestseller lists, she makes her home in the Pacific Northwest with her handsome prince of a husband and her two adorable-but-not-bright cats.

To Barbara Zieger. I was determined to give
you a second fire fighter to fall in love with,
and here he is. Enjoy! With love and thanks for
all the years of friendship

Chapter One

The woman sitting next to him clung to his hand as if she were afraid he would bolt. Her eyes were closed, and her lips moved in silent conversation. Long blond hair tumbled over her shoulders and brushed against their joined fingers.

Jordan Haynes recognized the sights and smells of the hospital. He recognized that the faint blurring at the edges of his mind meant he'd been given a strong painkiller. But he didn't recognize the woman. Still, it was damn nice of her to be so concerned, whoever she was.

She dropped her head slightly, and her hair slipped onto his wrist. Cool silk, he thought, wishing he had the strength to raise his free hand and touch the pale strands. His arm felt as if it had been pinned down by an elephant, although he knew it was just weakness that made him unable to move. So instead of touching her hair, he turned his attention to her face.

She had freckles across the tops of her cheeks and on her nose. Freckles. He grimaced. Her wide mouth tilted up at the corners. Except for the mascara darkening her lashes, she didn't wear makeup. He would bet fifty bucks that her eyes were blue and that she'd been a cheerleader in high school. She looked wholesome enough to be in a milk commercial. So what was she doing in his hospital room?

Her hair continued to stroke his skin. The soft, erotic touch had his mind producing fantasies his weakened body had no chance of fulfilling. At least not any time in the near future.

He tugged his hand free of her grasp. Instantly her eyes opened. Yup. Dark blue. He owed himself fifty bucks. As soon as he got out of here, he would pay up.

The woman smiled. Her pink lips parted, exposing white teeth and a smile so pleased, she might have just won the lottery.

"You're awake," she said, then took hold of his fingers again. The smile broadened. "I'm thrilled. The nurse said you were going to be fine, but I was worried. How do you feel? Any pain? Do you want some water?"

He tried to speak and realized his throat was scratchy. He coughed. Before he was done, the woman had stood up, reached for a small plastic pitcher and poured some water into a glass. She slipped one arm behind his shoulders, then raised the glass to his lips.

"Sip slowly," she said.

He obliged. When he'd finished half the cup, he nodded to indicate he was done. She set the glass on the table beside his bed, then returned to her seat. This time she clasped his hand in both of hers. Before he could extricate himself, she leaned forward and pressed their joined hands against her chest.

That got his attention. While she'd been standing, he'd

gathered a quick impression of curves. Awe-inspiring curves. She had the kind of breasts that made up every adolescent boy's fantasies. Right now his wrist nestled between them while the knuckle of his index finger brushed against the base of her throat. It didn't matter that her loose sweatshirt was hardly seductive. As far as he was concerned, they could spend the rest of the day in this position.

Then he noticed her blue eyes darkening with emotion, and he had the uncomfortable feeling she might be fighting tears. Dear God, anything but that.

"Who *are* you?" he asked gruffly.

The woman stopped blinking and smiled again. "I'm Holly Garrett." She made the announcement as if that cleared up everything.

He didn't know any Holly Garrett, although judging by the way she was staring at him—as if he'd single-handedly saved the world—she obviously knew him.

Great. Either the painkillers were doing strange things to him, or he was losing his mind.

"And?" he prompted.

She stared blankly for a moment, then laughed. He felt the vibration of the sound against the back of his hand, which was still pressed against her chest. Friendly, he thought. A charming trait in an attractive woman.

"There was a storm," she said. "You saved my cat."

The memories flooded him, and he groaned. The high winds had blown over a tree, sending it crashing through a single apartment above a detached garage. Not only had the unit been partially crushed, but the pipes had broken and flooded the place. When his men had arrived, there hadn't been much left to save. He recalled a frantic woman trying to get through a stuck door. Water had been everywhere. The two-story structure looked as if it was about to collapse. Jordan had grabbed her around the waist and hauled her to safety. She'd been screaming about her damn cat. Like a fool he'd gone after the animal. And look what it had gotten him. He'd been back in Glenwood less than six months, and already he was in the hospital. Damn.

"You were wonderful," Holly said, her voice thick with emotion. "I don't know what I would have done if something had happened t-to..." Her voice gave out.

"Ah, yeah, well, nothing did, right?"

She sniffed. "Thank you," she murmured, and squeezed his fingers.

"Just doing my job," he muttered. And a poor job at that. He was going to take some well-deserved teasing when he went back to the station.

Judging from the throbbing in his legs and back, he wouldn't be returning to work any time soon. Everyone had seen what had happened, too. He'd found the cat and had made it safely out of the apartment, clutching the squirming furball under his coat. Once they were out on the balcony, the cat had tried to get away. Jordan had been afraid the animal would be injured by the fire trucks or lost in the crowd, so he'd hung on to the cat from hell. They'd wrestled each other, and the cat had nearly won. But in the end Jordan had prevailed and grabbed it by the scruff of its neck. Unfortunately in the process he'd lost his footing on the wet wooden balcony above the garage and had fallen off the side.

In front of everyone. He swore silently.

"Anything broken?" he asked, eyeing his leg under the sheet and blanket. He couldn't tell if he was in a cast or not.

Holly shook her head. "No. I took Mistletoe to the vet, and she's just fine."

"I wasn't asking about the cat," he said dryly.

She stared at him a moment, then blushed. Color

climbed from her neck to her face, covering her cheeks, then moving up to her hairline. Her mouth formed a perfect circle.

"Oh."

She glanced down, seemed to realize she was clutching his hand to her bosom and released him. "Oh, sorry. You meant *your* injuries. I don't have specifics. The nurse said you would be going home tomorrow, if that helps." She gave him a quick glance. "I'm sorry we were so much trouble."

The hand she'd abandoned felt cold. He missed her heat and the faint thudding of her heartbeat. Not to mention the close proximity to her impressive breasts.

"Just doing my job," he said again.

She shook her head. "No, you did more than that. One of the other fire fighters told me it was dangerous for you to go back for Mistletoe. There was some question about the structural integrity of the apartment. And now you're injured. I feel so horrible. If there's anything I can do, please tell me."

He thought about asking her to hold his hand again, but before he could form the question, the door opened and a half-dozen people poured into the room.

His younger brother, Kyle, was first. "Heard you fell off a building," Kyle said, grinning. "Anything to be a hero."

Two of his sisters-in-law pushed Kyle out of the way. Elizabeth and Rebecca rushed to his side. "How do you feel?" Elizabeth asked.

"You can stay with us," Rebecca offered. "There's plenty of room."

His third sister-in-law, Sandy, asked, "Anything broken?"

"I'm still not sure," he said, but was drowned out by

his older brothers, Travis and Craig, who offered their expert medical opinions on his condition.

Austin Lucas, a friend of the family, stepped to the other side of the bed and shook hands with him. "Glad you're going to be okay."

"Me, too," Jordan answered, then realized Holly was gone. Somehow she'd slipped out of the room as his family had entered.

He looked at the concerned group of people surrounding him. They talked to each other about his condition and argued over who was going to have him stay with them while he convalesced. The conversation washed over him, a warm, loving blanket of concern. He knew everyone in the room cared just as he cared about them. He loved them, but he wasn't always one of them. Like Austin, Jordan spent much of his life on the fringes, watching the rest of the world connect in a way he couldn't understand.

So he let them argue, because he knew in the end he would do what he wanted. He would go home and be alone, because that was the way he preferred it.

"Yes, yes, it's very macho, but I'm not impressed." Elizabeth Haynes stood with her hands on her hips. Although her husband wasn't the oldest of the Haynes brothers, Travis had been the first of them to marry, so Elizabeth was the leader of the women. Right now she was speaking for all of them, and Jordan didn't like what she was saying.

"I'm staying in my house," he said, and glared at her defiantly. The fact that he was flat on his back diluted some of his power, but he wasn't going to acknowledge that.

"Fine. Stay here. Just not alone."

He raised his hand to his face and rubbed his eyes. Everything hurt. His legs, his chest, his back, even his hair.

He'd stopped taking painkillers that morning. Maybe it had been a mistake.

Elizabeth sat on the edge of the bed and took one of his hands. It reminded him of another woman who had recently done the same.

He couldn't get Holly Garrett out of his mind. As a rule he avoided romantic entanglements. This time he was tempted to break his rule. Fortunately his physical limitations prevented him from acting on impulse. With a little luck, by the time he was healed, he would have forgotten all about her. In the meantime he had to get everyone to stop treating him like an invalid.

"You have two choices," Elizabeth said. "Come home with one of us, or…"

"I'll take the 'or,'" he said.

She ignored him. "Or have Louise stay here and look after you."

He scowled.

"I know," she said. "You hate Louise. No one knows why. Not even Louise. Over the years you've made your feelings about her very clear. However, you're out of options. The doctor said you have to stay in bed for two weeks. So someone has to be here to look after you. It's up to you, Jordan. Stay here with Louise or come home with one of your brothers."

Jordan turned his head toward the window. He could see bright blue sky and a few puffy clouds. Late fall in northern California could be rainy, but today the weather welcomed him home.

Stay here with Louise or go live with one of his brothers. The latter wasn't a problem. He got along with all of them. But it was only about a month until the holidays. Everyone would be busy with preparations. He would be in the way.

Louise. He swore silently. No one understood why he

didn't like her. But he knew the truth. Her guilty secret. He'd carried it around with him for seventeen years. Everyone accepted her as a de facto member of the Haynes family. Everyone but Jordan. He questioned her motives for getting close to the brothers.

"Well?" Elizabeth prompted.

"You're not leaving me with much of a choice."

"That's the point."

He drew in a deep breath. He'd bought the old Victorian mansion less than two months ago. So far, he hadn't made much of a dent in restoration. Maybe he could get some work done while he was convalescing. He wouldn't be allowed back at the fire station until after the first of the year.

"I want to stay here," he said, then regretted his decision.

"If you're sure." Elizabeth leaned close and kissed his cheek. "Be nice to her, okay? She's doing you a favor."

"No problem."

She smiled. "Liar. You're going to make her life hell. I'd better go warn her." She rose and started out of the room. When she reached the doorway, she glanced back at him. "None of this would be a problem if you'd found yourself a wife."

He smiled at the familiarity of this conversation. Elizabeth was forever trying to get him married off. "I like being single."

She didn't return his smile. "That's twice you've lied to me, Jordan. It's a good thing I love you as much as I do. Maybe I'll have my husband beat some sense into you."

"I could take him."

She raised her eyebrows.

"Well, maybe not today, but by the end of the week, for sure."

She stared at him for a moment. "Maybe this is a good thing—lying flat on your back will give you time to think about your life."

"I like my life just fine."

"You've got your brothers fooled, but we females know better. You need a woman."

"I'm a wounded hero. Leave me in peace."

"You're a stubborn pain in the rear, but I still adore you. Take care of yourself and be nice to Louise."

She gave a quick wave and disappeared into the hallway. Jordan listened to the sound of her footsteps on the hard-wood floor until they faded into silence. Then he was alone.

It was how he preferred to spend his life. Alone. He was used to the solitude. But for the next few days he was going to have company. Louise. Elizabeth had admonished him to be nice. He grimaced. If she knew the truth, she wouldn't be so eager to have Louise around. But Elizabeth didn't know. No one did. He wasn't sure why he'd been so diligent in guarding Louise's secret. Probably some use-less sense of honor. It didn't matter that he owed her noth-ing or that she'd destroyed his family. He couldn't bring himself to betray her.

He heard footsteps again, but these weren't his sister-in-law's. Louise Carberry entered the room and stared at him. She was of average height with short blond hair and blue eyes. He guessed she had to be in her midforties, although she looked younger. A bright, long-sleeved fuchsia blouse hung loosely over purple pants. Louise dressed as if she were color-blind. She folded her arms over her chest and stared at him. He stared back.

The moment reminded him of wrestling with the damn

cat on the landing. He'd won the battle but lost the war
when he'd gone over the side of the balcony and fallen to
the hard ground below. His gaze narrowed, and he wondered if he would end this encounter equally battered.

Holly parked her car in front of the large Victorian mansion. It was barely after six in the evening, but already it
was dark. The sun set before five in the late fall. She could
see the faint outline of the beautiful old house. The peaked
roof, the oddly shaped windows.

Years ago this part of Glenwood had been home to the
rich and powerful families who made their fortunes in tim-
ber, mining and the railroads. By the Second World War
most of them had left the small community for San Francisco or Los Angeles, but their houses remained. Some had
been torn down, and some had been converted to offices.
A few were being restored.

Holly stared up at the building and wished she had the
money to buy one herself. She would turn the downstairs
into a showroom and live upstairs. She smiled. It was a
lovely dream but had no basis in reality. Still, her fingers
itched to feel the original wood molding and trace the
shape of the stained-glass windows above the double-wide
front door.

She opened the car door, collected the pink bakery box,
then got out. The early evening was still. Only the faint
call of a night bird disturbed the silence. She drew in a
deep breath and inhaled the scent of trees and the faint hint
of some distant fire. The homey scent reminded her she'd
lost *her* home three days ago. Everything she owned had
either been crushed or soaked beyond repair. At least Mistletoe was safe.

Holly clutched the bakery box firmly and started up the
stairs. Store-bought cookies wouldn't begin to repay the

debt she owed Fire Captain Jordan Haynes, but they were the best she could do right now. She didn't have access to a kitchen. As soon as she could afford to get a new place, she would bake something wonderful.

She climbed the three stairs leading to the front porch. The wide wooden deck was bare. A single light burned by the front door. It wasn't difficult to imagine what the porch would look like in the summer with sunlight spilling onto the refinished floor. There would be a swing at one end, by the large window on her right. Maybe a white wrought-iron table-and-chair set at the other end. She could see ladies in long dresses and gentlemen in tall hats. Children would play on the lawn, their laughter a happy background noise to the adults' polite conversation.

"You are the most stubborn man it's ever been my misfortune to know."

The loud voice startled Holly, and she jumped back. She stared at the front door. She'd been about to knock, but obviously this wasn't a good time.

A low male voice rumbled, answering the woman's claim, but Holly couldn't make out the words.

"If I didn't care about the rest of your family, I'd leave you here to starve," the woman continued. "It would serve you right, too. Even my Alfred, God rest his soul, wasn't this fussy about his food."

More male rumbling.

"Fine. Be insulted. You don't like anything else about me, why should I be surprised that you resent being compared to a dog? Oh, and Alfred was better looking than you, too."

Before Holly could step back, the front door flew open. A woman stood in the doorway and stared at her. "I thought I heard a car pull up."

Holly didn't know what to do. She was poised awkwardly on the porch, with one foot behind her as she tried to make her escape.

"I…" she said, then paused. "I've come to see Captain Haynes, but I'll come back. This obviously isn't a good time."

The woman grimaced. "There's never a good time with that one. He's the most stubborn, pigheaded, difficult man I've ever met." She paused and shook her head. "Why you'd want to see him is beyond me, but you might as well come in. Maybe you can talk some sense into him. Oh, by the way, I'm Louise."

She held the door open. Holly forced herself to walk forward. Once in the house, she shifted her weight from foot to foot and stared at her hostess.

The woman wore a bright yellow long-sleeved shirt tucked into cobalt blue slacks. The silver belt around her trim waist matched the moon-and-star silver earrings she wore. The two women were about the same height, although Holly had come straight from work and still wore two-inch heels.

"What are you doing now?" a male voice inquired. The tone of the question implied the woman was doing something he wouldn't like.

"Answering the door. Quit being such a baby. You don't want me in the room with you, but you yell at me if I go away. Make up your mind, Jordan."

"Who is it?" he asked.

Louise rolled her eyes. "One of your women."

"Oh, no," Holly said quickly. "I'm not—"

"Which one?"

Louise glanced at her. "What's your name?"

"Holly, but I'm not—"

"Holly," she yelled toward the back of the house.

Jordan was silent. Holly figured he was trying to place her.

"I'm not one of Captain Haynes's women," she said.

Louise smiled. "Then that makes you a smart girl. That boy is nothing but a difficult toad." She shouted the last part of the sentence, aiming the words in the direction of what must be his room. After drawing in a deep breath, she released it slowly. "I'm real sorry I ever agreed to this. He's going to be the death of me. And Lord knows I'm far too young to die." She paused and drew her eyebrows together. "Who are you, then?"

"I'm Holly Garrett." Holly shifted her package to the other arm and held out her hand. "My apartment was destroyed in that big storm earlier in the week. Captain Haynes went back inside to save my cat." She shook Louise's hand. "I'm the reason he was injured. Actually Mistletoe is, but I feel responsible."

"Mistletoe?"

"My cat. She got scared once they were out of the apartment and tried to get away. Captain Haynes managed to hold on to her, but in the process he lost his footing on the balcony and fell over the side. I feel terrible about what happened."

Louise's lips started to twitch. She chuckled for a moment. "Felled by a cat. Serves him right."

"I brought cookies," Holly said, holding out the box. "They're not much. I couldn't make them myself. I don't have a kitchen right now. I wish I did. I really like to cook and bake."

"Louise!" Jordan yelled.

"Wait a minute," she yelled back, then lowered her voice. "He's going to be flat on his back for two weeks. I don't think I'm going to last here."

"You're his…?"

"Housekeeper. It's a temporary job. Very temporary. You want some coffee?" Louise didn't wait for an answer. She just headed for the rear of the house.

Holly trailed after her. As they passed through the foyer, she noticed the stunning chandelier hanging down from the ceiling two stories up. The tiny crystal teardrops were original. They caught light and created rainbows. The banister was hand carved, the floors in great shape. In her mind's eye she saw the house as it had once been and what it would be like again, given enough time, money and love.

"He's through there," Louise said, pointing to a half-closed door.

Holly saw a library and beyond that the foot of a bed in what had once probably been the study.

"How is he?"

Louise snorted. "If his foul temper is anything to go by, he's improving every hour."

They entered the large kitchen. A tray sat on the table in the center of the room. Louise motioned to it. "Says he won't eat it. Can you imagine? I've been cooking all my life, but Mr. High-and-Mighty doesn't like it."

Holly glanced at the plate filled with meat loaf, mashed potatoes and vegetables. It smelled wonderful. Her stomach growled. She hadn't had anything since breakfast, and suddenly she was starving.

Louise smiled. "Help yourself."

"Oh, I couldn't."

"Louise!" Jordan called again. He sounded furious.

Holly looked at the tray, then in the direction of the makeshift bedroom. She owed Jordan Haynes a big debt. He'd saved her cat. Mistletoe had been her mother's gift to her the Christmas before she died. A single dinner wouldn't do much to repay what she owed him, but it could be a start. She didn't know much about men, but she was intimately familiar with a sick room.

"Maybe I could help," she said cautiously.

Louise planted her hands on her hips. "Honey, you're welcome to try." She glanced at the clock over the stove. "My evening college class starts in forty minutes. I don't have the time to fix Jordan something else. Why don't you go introduce yourself and if he takes to you, then be my guest."

"Thank you," Holly said, then headed back the way she'd come. She knew several dishes specially designed to tempt an invalid's appetite. She'd taken care of her mother for years.

"Oh, and Holly?"

She paused, then glanced over her shoulder. "Yes?"

"Tell the boy to put some clothes on."

Chapter Two

Tell Jordan to put some clothes on? Holly blinked several times. "You mean he's—" She couldn't even say the word, but she could sure think it loudly. Naked?

Louise winked. "You'll just have to go see for yourself, won't you? Don't worry. He hasn't got anything you haven't seen a dozen times before."

Holly gave a weak smile, then headed for the study. Actually Louise was wrong. Jordan *did* have something she had never seen before. At least he did if he was naked.

As she walked through the library, one part of her mind noted the hand-fitted floor-to-ceiling bookshelves and the large crystal light fixtures hanging in each corner. In front of her she could see the bottom of a bed. Her steps slowed. Naked? No, Louise wouldn't do that to her.

She stopped on the library side of the doorway and cleared her throat. Maybe she should warn him that she was about to enter his room. So if he was, well, naked, he could cover up.

Still, she hesitated before speaking. She didn't know what to say. Just thinking about the handsome fire fighter made her nervous. At the hospital she'd been so concerned about his condition, she'd barely had time to notice his looks at all. But once he woke up and they spoke, she hadn't been able to think about anything else. Her stomach had gotten all sort of quivery, and she'd barely been able to form whole sentences. Thank goodness his family had shown up and she'd been able to escape before she made a complete fool of herself.

Now here she was, about to enter his bedroom. Well, not *really* his bedroom. He had been put downstairs because it was more convenient and would make it easier for him to get around without having to worry about stairs. She remembered when they'd first moved her mother to the downstairs family room. Holly sighed at the memory. She might not know a single thing about men, but she knew how to take care of someone. That's why she was here. Because Jordan Haynes was injured. If she remembered that and forgot how he looked, then everything would be fine.

"Captain Haynes?" she said softly as she stared at the scarred hardwood floors. "Hi, I'm Holly Garrett. We met in the hospital. May I come in?"

"Sure."

She paused, waiting to hear the rustle of bed sheets as he covered himself. There was only silence. She reminded herself that sick and injured people had a lot of similarities. They got frustrated, bored, tired of the pain and isolation. And if she was worried about him being naked, she wouldn't look at anything below his neck.

She drew in a deep breath, smiled broadly and stepped into the converted study.

Thick drapes had been pulled over two sets of windows. In the daylight the room would get morning sun. A hospital bed had been set up in the center of the room. She was familiar with the model. The electric motor allowed the occupant to raise and lower both the head and the foot to find the most comfortable position. A low table had been pushed to one side, and there was a straight-back chair nearby.

Holly ignored the patient for as long as she could, then gave a quick prayer for courage and turned her attention to him.

He wasn't naked. Not completely. Still, her breath caught in her throat, her heart started pounding and she had the uncomfortable feeling that she was turning bright red.

Jordan had raised the back of the bed so he was in a nearly sitting position. Dark hair tumbled onto his forehead. Equally dark eyes studied her in return. She wasn't sure if it was the shape of his masculine features, the set of his jaw or just a perception problem on her part, but she knew he was the best-looking man she'd ever seen. The muscles in her legs felt funny. It took her a moment to figure out they were shaking.

Her gaze dipped to his bare chest and the sheet bunched around his waist. She swallowed, resisting the urge to run for cover. Sculpted muscles defined his shoulders, arms and the hard, flat region of his belly. He looked as if he were posing for a provocative calendar.

"Searching for visible proof of my injuries?" he asked.

Holly realized she'd been staring at him for several seconds. This time she didn't have to guess about blushing.

The heat climbed quickly from the edge of her collar to her cheeks. She ducked her head.

"I..." What was she supposed to say?

"Have a seat."

She sank into the straight-back chair and folded her hands on her lap.

"You're the lady with the cat," he said.

She risked a glance. He didn't look annoyed. "Yes. You saved her. I stopped by to see how you were doing. I don't mean to intrude."

He studied her as intently as she had studied him. His attention made her uncomfortable, but she didn't feel she had the right to protest. Fair was fair.

She smoothed a hand over her skirt and wondered what he saw when he looked at her. Blond hair and blue eyes, which sounded more exciting than they were. Curves, she thought grimly, knowing her five-year battle against an extra fifteen pounds had ended in an uneasy truce. The pounds didn't multiply, and she stopped trying to make them go away. So her breasts and hips were a little larger than fashion dictated. She would survive.

"Did you bring the cat to finish me off?" he asked at last.

It took her a moment to realize he was teasing. She smiled. "Mistletoe is very sweet. I'm sure she didn't mean to hurt you. She was just scared."

"Yeah, right. I saw the look in her eyes. She was glad I went over the side." His gaze brushed across her face. "What happened to your hair?"

"My hair?" She reached behind her head and touched her braid. "Nothing. I'm wearing it back."

"Let me see."

She half turned in her seat and tilted her head so he

could see the French braid. She'd pinned the end up by the nape of her neck to form a loop.

"I like it loose," he said. "You've got beautiful hair."

"Oh." She blinked. "Ah, thank you."

Had he just paid her a compliment? Holly figured he had. Why? Is that what men and women did? Was he flirting? No. Not with her. She wasn't his type. Actually she didn't know what his type would be, but she was pretty sure she was the furthest female from it. He was injured, that was all. Or possibly delirious.

She cleared her throat and wished she'd had more experience with this kind of situation. The problem was she'd never spent any time with a man and his bare chest before.

"I brought cookies," she said. "They're from the bakery. I don't have a working kitchen yet, but when I do, I'll make something from scratch. That is, if it wouldn't be too inconvenient."

"I think I can handle the inconvenience of you baking me something," he said, then smiled.

The smile caught her unaware. Lines crinkled by his dark eyes. His teeth were white, and his handsome face became almost painfully beautiful. Everything inside her bubbled so much, she thought she might start floating around the room. Wow. She needed to get out more.

"I'm pretty hungry," he said. "Would you mind bringing me a couple of those cookies now? I'd get them myself, but I'm—" He motioned to the sheets.

"Naked," she said without thinking.

"What? No. I'm not supposed to get up for a couple of days. I'm not naked."

Naked? Had she actually said *naked*? Holly covered her face with her hands and made a whimpering noise. "No," she said. "I didn't mean… That is, I…"

"Holly?"

He said her name softly. She thought about just running from the room, but her legs were too shaky to cooperate. "I didn't mean that," she murmured. "Louise said for me to tell you to put some clothes on, so I just sort of thought—"

"It's okay."

She risked sliding her hands down so they just covered her mouth, then she glanced at him. He wasn't smiling, but he didn't look mad. She breathed a sigh of relief and dropped her hands to her lap. "Sorry. Look, I'll go get those cookies for you."

She rose to her feet and reminded herself of his injuries, which were, indirectly, her fault. Act like a nurse, she told herself. She knew how.

"Are you on any medication?" she asked. "Pills you have to take with food?"

"Nope."

She thought about testing for fever but knew she couldn't disconnect enough to touch his forehead without swooning. She consoled herself with the thought that he didn't look hot.

She fought a giggle. Okay, yes, he looked hot, but sexy hot, not fever hot.

Her body continued to tremble, but she tried to ignore it. After taking a couple of steps toward the door, she paused. "I'm a pretty good cook," she said, not looking at him but instead staring at the library in front of her. "If you don't like what Louise prepared for dinner, I could make something else." She swallowed. "No, it's a dumb idea. Never mind."

Just as well. She had to get out of his house before she embarrassed herself again. She wanted to tell Jordan it wasn't her fault. Except for a couple of her mother's doctors, she'd never spent any time around men. They were as foreign to her as space aliens.

"I'd like that very much," he said.

She whirled around to face him. "You would?"

"Sounds great. But only if you keep me company. I've been home for two days without anyone to talk to. I'm about to go crazy." Then he gave her that smile again.

Despite the shaking and the way her heart was slamming against her ribs, she forced herself to smile back. "Okay. I'll make something fast."

"I can't wait."

Holly didn't remember leaving the room or walking through the library and down the hall. The next thing she knew, she practically floated into the kitchen. Louise was leaning against the sink. She raised her blond eyebrows.

"Well?" the older woman asked.

"I offered to cook him something, and he said yes."

Louise shook her head. "He's the most stubborn man I've ever met. You're welcome to him." She walked over to the refrigerator and pulled out two steaks.

Holly eyed the meat. "Can he really eat that much?"

Louise grinned. "Only one of them is for him. The other is for you. I heard your stomach growling. You've been at work all day, haven't you? Barely stopped for lunch."

Holly thought of the half sandwich she'd never had time to get back to. It had been a busy afternoon. Still, she would much rather be busy and go without food than sit alone in an empty store, wishing for customers.

Before she could comment, Louise continued, "I know what it's like to be young. Thinking about everything but being healthy." She opened the refrigerator and pointed to the bottom bin. "There's plenty of fresh vegetables. He likes them steamed. Of course, not when I steam them."

"Why doesn't he like *you?*" Holly asked.

The housekeeper shrugged. She crossed the worn lino-leum floor and grabbed a denim jacket hanging from a hook by the back door. "I don't know. He's always been this way. I've been working on and off for the Haynes family for years. There's four brothers, five if you count Austin, who isn't technically family but might as well be. I've helped when they've had new babies, cooked for the bachelors, nursed them through illness—" she tilted her head toward the study "—and injury." She smiled. "They're a wonderful group of people. Except that one."

"Then why are you here?"

Louise slipped on her jacket. There was a backpack on a second hook. She reached for that and slung it over her shoulder. "Because I care about the family. I told them I would look after him, and the good Lord willing, I'll sur-vive. But that Jordan has a chip on his shoulder. Don't ask me why. He's never said, and I haven't bothered to ask. Maybe I will one of these days."

Louise opened the back door. "My class starts at seven. I'll be home around ten-thirty."

"Oh, I'll be long gone," Holly said. "I'm just going to cook his dinner, then leave."

"I appreciate this. I would have gone to my class no matter what, but I would have spent the whole time feeling guilty." Louise gave a quick grin, then left.

Holly turned to the old-fashioned kitchen and realized she hadn't asked where anything was. She was going to have to fumble around to find pots and pans. She didn't really mind. She was in one of the beautiful Victorian man-sions she'd admired since coming to town. Jordan Haynes might not get along with his housekeeper, but Holly thought he was nice. Best of all, she was taking the first step in repaying her debt to him.

                              * * *

Jordan watched Holly carrying in a laden tray. She'd found an apron and slipped it over the white frilly blouse and long, soft-looking blue skirt she wore. Her wide eyes shone with excitement, and her mouth quivered on the verge of smiling.

"Are you hungry?" she asked.

He inhaled the savory aroma of steak, baked potato and broccoli. "Starved."

She set the tray on the table he'd pulled next to the bed. Like the bed, the table had been rented from a hospital-supply center. He'd figured if he had to be restricted for a couple of weeks, he might as well be comfortable. The table slid around easily and could be raised and lowered to fit across his bed.

Holly reached for the bed controls. "Can you sit up a little more? It will be easier to eat."

"Sure."

She worked the controls like an expert. Next she raised the table two inches and slid it close. She unfolded a napkin and handed it to him. She played nurse very well. Interesting.

He glanced at the tray and saw it was set with two plates. "Thanks for joining me," he said. "Sometimes I get tired of eating alone."

Holly sank into the chair next to him. "I'm glad you don't mind. Louise suggested I join you. I was going to ask, but…" Her voice trailed off.

The all-business persona faded as quickly as it had arrived. She looked at him out of the corner of her eye, as if she didn't dare stare directly. Quite a contrast of personalities. Deliberate or unconscious? Then he reminded himself he'd spent nearly three days staring at the same four walls. His family had stopped by to visit, but it wasn't enough to fill the hours. He didn't care if Holly was a serial killer. He was grateful for her company, whatever her motives.

She took her plate and set it on her lap. He cut a piece of steak and tasted it. The meat was cooked perfectly.

"Great," he said when he'd swallowed, then leaned back. "So, Holly Garrett, cat owner, how'd you find me?"

"I went to the fire station. I thought I could leave the cookies with one of the men there and they would deliver them."

"Fat chance. They would have been devoured in thirty seconds."

She smiled. "That's what the captain on duty told me. He gave me your address. I hope you don't mind."

"It's fine. Glenwood is a small town. Everyone knows everyone. That's why I moved back."

"Where did you move from?"

"Sacramento. I'd grown up in Glenwood. When I decided to become a fire fighter, I left."

She cut some broccoli and speared it with her fork. "Don't they have a training academy here?"

"The county does. But that wasn't the problem. My father was the sheriff. His father was a cop, all my uncles are cops. I'm one of four boys, and the other three are all cops."

"You were expected to be a policeman, too." It wasn't a question.

"Exactly." He remembered the fights he'd had with his old man. His brothers had teased him about his choice, but they'd supported his decision. Not Earl Haynes. His father had threatened to disown him. By that time Jordan hadn't cared much about his father's opinion. Not after everything the old man had done.

Holly tilted her head slightly. "Are you happy with what you do?"

"Yes. But I didn't like being away from my brothers and their families. So I put in an application here. When a position for fire captain opened up, I got the job." He grinned. "One of my brothers, Travis, is the sheriff. He never said anything, but I suspect he put in a good word for me."

Holly laughed softly. The sweet sound penetrated his chest and, for a moment, thawed some of the cold he felt there. Then the laughter faded, and her eyes darkened with an emotion he could only label as sadness.

Don't be a fool, Haynes, he told himself. He didn't know this woman well enough to be reading her emotions.

"Your family sounds wonderful," Holly said, the tone of her voice confirming his guess. "I can understand why you would move back to be near them. How long have you been here?"

"About six months."

"That's when I got here, too."

"What brought you to Glenwood? It's not exactly a bustling metropolis."

"My mother and I inherited a store."

So she wasn't a nurse. "Which one?"

"An antique store across from the park. Now it's called A Victorian Parlor."

He remembered seeing the shop after it had opened. "When I'm feeling better, I'm going to be working on restoring this old place. Maybe I should come by."

"Definitely." She leaned forward. "The store specializes in Victorian pieces, with a whole section on restoration. There are books of wallpaper, both reproductions of old prints, as well as Victorian inspired. I can order fixtures, faucets, even disguised switch covers. As far as the restoration books go, a few are for sale, but mostly I loan them out. That's one of the things I like about Glenwood. There are so many old homes that people are restoring.''

She hung on to her plate with one hand and gestured with the other. Enthusiasm filled her voice.

''You like your work,'' he said.

''I love it.''

''Then I'll come into the store and get your help.''

''I'd like that.''

Their eyes met. She bit her lower lip and turned away. Jordan studied her. Part of him wanted her to be as shy and innocent as she seemed; another part of him hoped it was an act. If she was playing a role, then he wouldn't like her—and that would be easier for him. Mostly because he didn't want to admit being attracted to Holly Garrett.

''I remember that place being empty for a long time. When did you and your mother inherit the store?''

''My mom's aunt passed away about five years ago. She's the one who left it to us.'' She toyed with the last piece of steak, then pushed it away and set the plate on the floor. ''My mother was ill for several years. She had breast cancer that kept coming back. We talked about the antique store. It was our joint dream.'' Holly leaned back in the chair and folded her hands on her lap. ''After she died three years ago, I paid off the rest of the medical bills, then saved money. When I had enough, I moved up here.''

She told the story simply. Jordan knew there were many details she'd left out. He wondered about family. Was she an only child? Where was her father in all this? But he didn't like questions, and he wasn't about to force her to answer his. At least part of the mystery was explained. If her mother had been ill for a long time, Holly would have become familiar with hospitals. No wonder she could do a great nurse imitation.

''Do you like owning your own business?'' he asked.

"I love it. When I was still in high school, I had a part-time job working in an antique store. After I graduated, I worked there full-time. I know a lot about antiques, restoration. One day I want to buy an old place like this and restore it from the ground up."

"Two of my brothers have houses like this. Travis has finished his. Kyle and Sandy are still wrestling with plumbing upgrades. When I'm up and around, I can show you the houses if you'd like."

"That would be wonderful. What are you going to do with this house?"

"I'm not sure. In some of the rooms I'm stripping paint off the original molding. You wouldn't believe what people do to beautiful wood."

"Tell me about it. I've seen some horrible things. It should be illegal." She moved her chair a little closer to his bed. "Once I went to an estate sale. A woman had covered every piece of furniture with gold paint. It was appalling."

Holly continued with her story, but Jordan was having trouble concentrating. He stared at her face. When she'd visited him in the hospital, he'd noticed her freckles and the fact that she didn't wear much makeup. Today was the same. Her lashes were darkened with mascara, but other than that, she was as clean scrubbed as a ten-year-old.

He watched her full lips move as she spoke. Enthusiasm made her eyes sparkle. Her arms moved, and with them, her body. His gaze was drawn to her chest. She was definitely this side of curvy. Her breasts would spill out of his hands, but he didn't think he would mind all that much.

He fought down a grin. His family and friends considered him reclusive and brooding. Occasionally he bordered on surly. So what the hell was this woman doing in his house? And why was he so pleased to be in her company?

"When you're ready to strip wallpaper, let me know," she said. "I have a steamer that works like magic." She glanced at the high ceilings. "Even with that, in some of the rooms it's going to take days."

"I'll get my brothers to help me," he said. "I've helped them enough times."

"You're one of four, right?"

He nodded.

"That's nice." She sighed. "I always wanted a big family, but it was just my mom and me."

Holly was alone. Jordan didn't know what that felt like. Many times he found himself standing on the outside of family activities. Watching rather than participating. But that was about him, not about the family. He always had a place to go where he was welcome. He couldn't imagine a world where no one cared about him.

"There's no husband lurking in the background? Or a jealous boyfriend? I'm not in a position to have to defend myself."

She blushed. "Hardly. I haven't really had time for that sort of thing."

What sort of thing had she had time for?

Leave it alone, Haynes, he told himself. She wasn't the woman for him. He'd wondered if the innocent act was real. Now he had a bad feeling it was. Wholesome. Just as he'd first thought.

"How old are you?" he asked.

"Twenty-eight."

Twenty-eight and never been kissed. He pushed the rolling table to one side. That was unlikely. Holly had been kissed. How could she look the way she did and not have been kissed? She probably had a trail of men drooling after her everywhere she went.

"Have you met a lot of people in Glenwood?" he asked.

He meant men, of course, but asking that directly would be rude. Not to mention the fact that it would imply an interest he didn't have.

Liar, a voice in his head yelled. He ignored it.

"Some. People who come into my store are nice. I know my landlord, of course. I've made a couple of friends."

She looked away from him as he spoke, and he knew in that instant she was lying. She hadn't made a lot of friends, but she didn't want him feeling sorry for her.

He thought about the women his brothers had married. All of them were terrific and friendly. He had a feeling if he mentioned Holly to them, they would take her under their wings and draw her into the group. Or at least help her feel less alone. But Holly might not want him interfering.

Before he could ask or offer, she rose and collected their dinner plates. "Would you like some coffee?" she asked.

"That would be great. Oh, and some of those cookies you brought."

She gave him a quick smile, then headed out of the room. He watched the sway of her hips as she walked, and felt a stirring deep inside. He ignored it, just as he ignored the flicker of interest and the sensation of being intrigued. It had been a long time since a woman had caught his attention.

He reminded himself there was a price to be paid for getting involved. A price for caring. He wasn't willing to pay that again. But that wasn't what this was about. Holly was keeping him company. Nothing more. Soon she would leave, and he wouldn't have to see her again. Bad enough to risk getting involved with any woman. Worse to risk the heart of an innocent.

Chapter Three

Holly brought in coffee and a plate of cookies. While she'd been in the kitchen, she'd removed her apron. Jordan tried to ignore her curves and his body's natural reaction to them. Aside from the fact that they were strangers, he was in no condition to act on any impulses, however pleasant the fantasy.

"I didn't know how you liked it," she said as she set the tray on the table across his bed. "There's milk and sugar." She motioned to the small containers next to the plate of cookies.

"Black is fine."

She picked up her cup, added milk, stirred, then took her seat. "How do you feel?" she asked.

He shrugged, then grimaced as muscles in his back protested. "Like I was thrown off the side of a building."

Instead of smiling, she grew solemn with concern. "I'm so sorry."

"It's not your fault."

"Yes, it is." She leaned toward him and placed her cup on the table. "I shouldn't have asked you to go back and rescue Mistletoe. When I think about it now…" She swallowed. Her blue eyes darkened with an emotion he couldn't read. "You could have been killed."

"I wouldn't have gone in if I'd been in that much danger."

"Really?"

He nodded. "I like what I do for a living, but I don't have a death wish."

She gave him a faint smile. "She's all I have left from my mother. Mistletoe was a gift to me the Christmas before Mom died. I'm very grateful for what you did." Her voice was husky.

Somehow, in all the moving around, her chair had slid closer to the bed. Now, if she leaned forward as she was doing now, her hands rested on the edge of the mattress. A single strand of blond hair hung down by her cheek. The wisp brushed against her skin, but she didn't seem to notice. His gut clenched as he wondered if she was going to cry. He freely admitted he was a typical male, completely knocked off balance by female tears.

"Just doing my job," he said lightly.

She responded with a smile. "What made you want to do that rather than become a police officer like the rest of your family?"

He pushed the controls and lowered the bed a little, then tucked one hand behind his head. "When I was about eight or nine, a house in the neighborhood caught fire. I watched the fire department at work. I'd never really understood what my father and uncles did. I knew from television they were supposed to catch the bad guys, but Glenwood isn't a hotbed of criminal activity. The sheriff's department acts more as a deterrent than a crime-solving organization. But I could see what the fire fighters did, and I was impressed. That stayed with me.''

He reached for his coffee. That wasn't the only reason. Growing up, he'd also watched his old man. By the time he was twelve, he knew he didn't want to be anything like his father. Earl Haynes had a reputation for being a ladies' man.

Jordan swore silently. It wasn't just the women his father flaunted. It was the disrespect for everyone else. No one mattered, and nothing was important but Earl's pleasures. He often hit the boys for no reason, then told them to consider themselves punished in advance of their next mistake. Jordan's brothers had been able to look past the man and carry on the family tradition of law enforcement, but not Jordan.

He could feel his anger building. Even after all this time, his father still got to him. He wondered if that would ever change.

''Jordan? Are you feeling all right?'' Holly's voice was concerned. She rose and touched her palm to his forehead. With her other hand she took his wrist and felt his pulse. ''Slightly elevated,'' she murmured, ''but you don't feel hot.''

She pressed the back of her hand against his cheek, then touched his earlobe. He figured if she kept that up much longer, he could really show her an elevated pulse.

''Do you want a painkiller or are you due for some other medication?''

''I'm fine,'' he said. ''Relax.''

He *was* fine. Since getting out of the hospital, he'd grown used to the dull ache in his body. He'd wanted to give up his prescriptions altogether, but he needed the medication to sleep at night. During the day he did without.

She released his hand, sank back in her chair and continued to study him. Gone was the blushing innocent. He liked the contrast of competence and shyness almost as much as he liked her freckles.

She gave him a half smile. "I should leave so you can get some rest."

"I'd prefer that you kept me company. It gets pretty boring lying here all day."

"You've got Louise."

Rather than answer that, he reached for his coffee.

Holly opened her mouth to speak, but before she could say anything, there was a noise from the kitchen. She stood up and turned toward the sound.

"I'm back," Louise called.

Figures, Jordan grumbled to himself.

Holly glanced at her watch. "Goodness. I didn't realize how long I'd been here. You must be exhausted. I'm so sorry. You should have said something." She twisted her fingers together. "My only excuse is that I've been spending too much time on my own. Mistletoe is a sweetie, but she's not much for conversation."

She was babbling. He liked it. It meant she was nervous and unsure of herself. Better than that, it meant she liked him. He wanted her to like him.

He heard footsteps in the hallway, then Louise stepped into the room. Her eyebrows arched in surprise.

"You two seem to be getting along. Everything all right?"

"It's my fault," Holly said quickly. "After dinner I—"

Jordan didn't know how else to shut her up. He reached out and grabbed her hand. She turned and stared at him. He ignored her.

"Everything is fine," he told the housekeeper. "How was your class?"

Now both women were staring at him. He figured he had Holly's attention because of the incredibly hot sparks arcing between their clasped hands. He'd never felt anything like it before, and he sure as hell didn't know what it meant. He also wasn't going to let go, because he had a feeling if he did, she would bolt. He wanted to make sure she was going to come back and see him again.

Louise stared at him because his question was the first civil comment he'd spoken since she arrived. For a moment he wondered if it was really so necessary to be such a bastard around her. Then he reminded himself of all she'd done and how many lives she'd torn apart, and he knew she deserved all that and more. The fact that she was doing a nice thing by looking after him was something he would have to learn to ignore.

"The professor barely looks old enough to have to shave every day, but he lectures real nice," Louise said cautiously.

"I should go," Holly said, tugging her fingers free.

Jordan didn't want to let her go. For one incredibly stupid moment he wished he could stand up and kiss her. If he'd been on medication, he would have said it was the drugs talking, but he hadn't had anything since the previous evening. So it was the boredom or the pain. Or maybe it was the fact that outside his family, he didn't have many friends. He liked Holly. She was someone he could be friends with.

Even as he thought the statement, he half expected to be zapped by lightning. Sure, he wanted to be friends with her. That's why he'd spent half the evening staring at her curves.

"Come back tomorrow," he said without thinking.

Holly's full lips turned up at the corners. "I'd like that," she said softly.

He smiled. Her reaction was instant. Her mouth parted, and her breathing increased. He saw the faint tremor that rippled through her body. He'd never much wanted it, but apparently he still had it. The infamous whatever that made Haynes men popular with the ladies. Years before he'd used it to get whatever he wanted, but he'd grown up and the game had lost its appeal.

He turned off the smile, and Holly blinked, as if she were awakening from a spell. She gave him a quick wave and walked from the room. Louise followed. Jordan was left alone in the silence.

He would have to be careful. Despite his preoccupation with her curves, he liked Holly and he would be grateful for her company. But only as his friend. He didn't want anything more. He knew the truth about romantic entanglements. He'd learned it from an expert. Despite all the songs and movies about the joys of falling in love, the truth was that love hurt.

Holly walked into the kitchen to collect her purse.

"I'm impressed," Louise said, strolling behind her. "You worked a miracle."

"It wasn't very difficult." Holly smiled at the housekeeper and hoped her trembling wasn't obvious. Touching Jordan to see if he had a fever was one thing. She could ignore the fact that he was handsome, charming and very close to naked. But when he'd taken her hand and smiled at her, she'd thought she was going to faint.

She drew in a deep breath. It wasn't fair that one man should have so many good qualities. They should be spread around among several men. Then she wouldn't have to worry about making a fool of herself in his presence.

"Maybe it wasn't hard for you," Louise said, "but I can't get a lick of cooperation out of that boy. I don't suppose you'd consider coming here full-time until he's healed.''

Holly grinned. ''Sorry, I've got a business to run.''

''Just my luck. Guess I'm stuck with him.'' She rolled her eyes. ''He forgot himself and was nearly pleasant to me tonight. I'm sure I'll pay for that in the morning.''

''I don't understand why he acts like that.''

Louise touched her right earring, separating the dangling silver moon and stars. ''Could be any number of things. He's never come out and said. Glenwood is a small town. People know each other's business. But he's carried his anger for a long time. I suppose one day I'll have to have it out with him, but not tonight.'' She smiled brightly. ''You coming back tomorrow?''

''You really think I should?''

''Of course. If nothing else, I could use a break from his bad temper.''

''I know it's difficult. My mother was sick for nearly ten years. When she was feeling good, she was fun and easy to be around, but after days of being in pain she got—'' Holly hesitated.

''Cranky?'' Louise offered.

Holly smiled. ''That's as good a word as any.''

She glanced back toward the study. Jordan *had* asked her to come back, and she really would like to spend some more time with him. Tonight had been great fun. Talking with another person was much better than spending the evening alone.

''So you'll be here?'' Louise asked.

Holly started toward the front door with the housekeeper following behind. ''Yes. I'd like that very much.''

''Good. I look forward to it, and I'm sure Jordan does, too.'' She held the door open.

Holly stepped onto the porch and waved. ''Good night.''

It was just dinner and conversation, she reasoned as she started her car and backed down the driveway. It wasn't really like a date. So what if Jordan was funny, charming and handsome? She was being neighborly. Besides, she'd been so busy getting her business started, she hadn't had time to meet anyone. Jordan could be her first friend. And Louise, too, although the thought of seeing Louise again wasn't quite as exciting.

If nothing else, the visit would get her out of the store. Since she'd lost her apartment, she'd been sleeping in the shop. There were plenty of sofas to bunk on. They weren't that comfortable—but it was only for a few weeks. Stocking her store with inventory for Christmas had taken every last penny she had. When the storm had struck, she'd lost all her furniture and most of her clothes. She couldn't afford to replace everything, let alone come up with first and last months' rent. But if she had a good holiday season, she would be fine come January first. Then she would find a new apartment and buy a few things. In the meantime she had the store, and that was enough.

That night, as she stretched out in her sleeping bag on one of the more comfortable sofas, she thought about her evening with Jordan and smiled in the darkness. Her pleasure wasn't just about how he looked, even though his smile took her breath away. It was that he really took the time to listen to her. No one had ever done that before. She shifted, and Mistletoe meowed in protest. The cat was using her feet as a pillow. Holly could feel the vibration of Mistletoe's purring through the sleeping bag. The familiar sensation relaxed her.

"Maybe I'll take you to meet him," she murmured. "Then you can thank him in person."

Mistletoe yawned, obviously not impressed.

* * *

Three days later Louise opened the front door as Holly climbed the stairs.

"Right on time," Louise said.

"There weren't any customers in the store, so I closed exactly at five." She stepped inside, then set the large basket she was carrying on the floor. "I hope you don't mind, but I brought Mistletoe."

Louise eyed the basket. "Is she the cat responsible for Jordan's injuries?"

"Yes. She's really very sweet, but she got scared by everything going on."

"Don't make excuses. I like her already." Louise bent down and opened the basket. Mistletoe was curled up inside. Her long gray fur fluffed out around her. Big green eyes stared at Louise. The housekeeper let Mistletoe smell her hand, then scratched behind her ears. The cat purred in ecstasy.

"She's beautiful," Louise said.

"A purebred Persian, and she doesn't hesitate to remind people that she's special."

Louise stood up. Mistletoe sniffed the air, then stepped out of the basket. Her round belly hung low.

"Has she been eating too many table scraps or is she pregnant?"

"Pregnant," Holly said. "It's only a couple of weeks until she's due. I've been coming here every night, and I didn't want to keep leaving her alone. You're not allergic, are you?"

"Not at all." Louise bent over and petted the cat. "Aren't you a pretty girl? Now, you go bother Jordan. There's a sweet cat. Yes, you go shed cat hair all over his sheets." Mistletoe arched into the caresses. When Louise straightened, the animal began to explore the foyer.

Holly took a deep breath. "Something smells wonderful. What is it tonight?"

"Spaghetti. I had some frozen sauce. I just defrosted it in the refrigerator, then started heating it about twenty minutes ago."

In the past three days they'd settled into a routine. For some reason Jordan continued to complain about Louise's cooking. So Holly took credit for the evening meal, even though she didn't prepare it. It made Jordan happy, and Louise didn't mind.

The housekeeper disappeared each evening. Some nights she was at the local college taking courses. Other times she was baby-sitting or studying in the library. Holly privately thought she simply left to get away from Jordan.

"I don't understand why he's so stubborn," Holly said as she followed Louise into the kitchen.

As usual the housekeeper dressed to attract attention. This evening she wore a brilliant orange long-sleeved silk blouse tucked into black jeans. A gold belt circled her small waist. Her dangling earrings—a teapot twirling from one ear, a cup and saucer hanging from the other—swayed with her movements.

Holly admired her sense of style even if it wasn't what she would have chosen for herself. For the shop Holly favored ruffly blouses and long, flowing skirts. They reflected the era of the store but allowed her to be mobile. Fortunately she'd kept her work clothes at the store, preferring to change into jeans before she went home. She'd lost a lot of casual wear but could still be dressed appropriately at work.

"You really don't think he's caught on?" she asked as she leaned against the kitchen counter. The old-fashioned room hadn't been updated since the early fifties. The counter tiles were alternating light and dark green. The big stove had rounded corners and a storage area on one side. The only modern appliance was the microwave on the counter.

"Even if he has, why would he want to admit it?" Louise bent over and pulled out a large pot. "This should do for the pasta. The sauce is simmering on that back burner. Just give it a stir every fifteen minutes or so. The longer it cooks, the tastier it will be."

She motioned to a loaf of bread by the sink. "I picked that up fresh this afternoon." She winked at Holly. "I think he suspects I'm doing the cooking, but he likes pretending you're doing it instead. He gets to growl at me and have you keep him company every night. What's not to like?"

"I suppose. I guess I feel a little guilty claiming credit for all your wonderful meals."

"If it makes him feel better to think he's eating your food and not mine, let him. The faster he's feeling better, the quicker I can get out of here."

"How's he doing today?"

Louise grimaced. "Pretty bad. The fool got up this morning. The doctor told him to relax. Anyway, he overdid it and spiked a fever this afternoon. I finally convinced him to take an over-the-counter painkiller, and last time I checked, he was sleeping. You might want to look in on him. I think he'll wake up on his own in an hour or so."

"That's fine." Holly brushed her hands against her skirt, then stared at Louise. "I have another favor to ask."

"Sure, what?"

She cleared her throat. "Could I use the shower?" She felt her cheeks getting hot, but plunged on before she lost her nerve. "I've been living at the store since the fire. There's a bathroom with a sink but no shower. I've been bathing piecemeal, and I really want to be able to wash my hair without having to bend over that tiny sink.''

Louise stared at her for several seconds. ''Child, you don't even have to ask. Why didn't you say something sooner? There's five bathrooms in this house, and Jordan's only using one of them. Come right this way.''

Louise marched out of the kitchen. Holly followed on her heels. She was quickly shown the downstairs bathroom, the closet with fresh towels, then handed a thick terry-cloth robe.

''The boy never uses it, so it's practically new.''

Holly hugged the robe to her chest. She'd brought shampoo and other toiletries, but she hadn't thought of a robe. ''Thanks. I appreciate this.''

Louise shook her blond head. ''I'm the one in your debt. You're giving me a break by staying with him.'' She glanced at her watch. ''I've got to get going or I'll be late. I can't have a tardy on my attendance record. I've never been late once this whole semester. Oh, and I might not get home right on time. Several of us are going out to coffee with the professor after class.''

Holly stared at her. ''The one so young he doesn't have to shave every day?''

Louise shrugged. ''Oh, Richard isn't all that young. He's nearly thirty-five. He just looks young.''

''You call him Richard?''

Louise cleared her throat. ''Did I say Richard? I meant Professor Wilson. That's his name. I'm out of here. Have fun.''

With that, the housekeeper left the bathroom and walked down the hall. Holly stared after her and shook her head. Too much had happened too fast.

She set the robe on a hook behind the bathroom door, then went to collect her toiletries. Once in the foyer, she moved Mistletoe's basket to one side and picked up her oversize purse. Her cat raced down the stairs and came over to be petted.

"Are you enjoying all this new stuff to sniff?" Holly asked.

Mistletoe purred in response.

When Holly straightened, the cat took off to explore another part of the house. Holly moved through the library, then tiptoed into the study.

Jordan was sprawled out on the rented hospital bed. One dark lock of hair tumbled across his forehead. While he was asleep, he appeared a little younger, although just as good-looking. Her heart did its usual rapid patter against her ribs, but she was learning to accept the fluttery sensation. It was just part of the price she paid to spend time with him.

She reached out and touched his face. He was warm but not hot. If he'd spiked a fever, it seemed to have faded. Also, he was sleeping soundly without the restlessness that accompanies fever.

She studied him for a few minutes, examining the strong line of his jaw, his straight nose, the faint stubble on his chin. Sometimes while they were talking, she had the oddest sensation of being part of a play or a movie. It didn't feel real. What was she doing here?

But she didn't dare question her good fortune. Even though she'd never had much opportunity to spend time with men, she'd always dreamed about what it would be like to know one. Jordan was everything she'd imagined the perfect man would be. He was kind, funny, charming and when he looked at her a certain way, she could feel her bones melting. It would be easy to have a crush on him...or worse.

But she wouldn't. First of all, she'd heard a little about

the Haynes brothers from people in town. They had a reputation for being heartbreakers. She might as well try to learn ice skating at a U.S. Olympic team workout. She was completely out of her league. Not only was she a virgin, but she hadn't kissed a single male since she was fifteen. Talk about being out of the loop.

The second reason she wouldn't dare fall for Jordan Haynes was that as much as she might daydream about a man, even marriage, she knew it wasn't in the cards for her. Not because no one would love her. She liked to think that one or two people might think she was special. The real reason was that love required trust, and she'd been let down too many times. She couldn't imagine ever trusting anyone again.

She pulled the sheet higher up his bare chest, then left the room and hurried down the hallway toward the bathroom. She'd spent the past three days longing for a shower and she was going to enjoy every minute of this one.

A hideous howling broke through Jordan's dream and jerked him into consciousness. He sat up in bed, then groaned as pain ripped through his muscles. He shouldn't have gotten up earlier, as Louise had told him gleefully.

He shook his head and tried to figure out what was wrong. His brain was fuzzy, and he couldn't focus on anything. There'd been a sound. A—

The howling came again. Someone or some *thing* was being tortured. He threw back the sheet and tried to rise to his feet. The floor shifted. Or maybe it was him. He gripped the nightstand with one hand and the table by his bed with the other, then pushed up. As he locked his muscles, he realized he'd made one fatal error of judgment. He'd forgotten the hospital table had wheels.

It shot out from under him and went flying across the

room. Jordan lost his balance and tumbled toward the floor. He braced one arm to save himself, but it gave way and he hit the hardwood on his already bruised shoulder.

Footsteps sounded in the hallway.

"Jordan?"

It was Holly. She would be relieved to find out he wasn't naked under his sheet but instead wore shorts over his briefs. Then his eyes closed, and he couldn't think about anything but the pain.

"Jordan, what happened?"

"I heard something. Howling. Tried to get up."

"You fell. Are you hurt?"

He hurt like a son of a bitch. She raised his head to her lap, then stroked his face. He opened his eyes.

For a moment he stared at her, then he blinked, certain he must have hit his head when he fell. She was wearing a white robe and nothing underneath. He knew because the robe had parted, exposing the curve of one breast and the first hint of the rosy skin around her nipple.

He sucked in a breath. Her hair was wet and tumbling around her shoulders. Her eyes darkened with concern, and the fingers on his face were gentle and comforting.

Maybe he was dead. If this was heaven, who was he to complain?

Chapter Four

"Jordan?" Holly said, her voice laced with concern. "Please say something. Are you hurt?"

"I'm okay." He forced the words through the pain and awareness battling in his body. He couldn't remember hurting this bad before, nor could he remember being this instantly aroused. It was an odd combination that again made him wonder if he *had* clipped his head on his way down.

"Do you think you can get back into bed?" she asked, then glanced from him to the mattress. "I doubt I can lift you by myself."

"I can manage. Just give me a minute." He continued to stare up at her face. She smelled like shampoo and soap. Her pale skin almost glowed in the early-evening lamplight. Her chest rose and fell with each breath, and the edge of the robe slipped open a little more, exposing a taut nipple and the underside of her breast.

Heat coiled low in his belly. The pain from his injuries

and the ache from his groin set up a low-frequency hum that had him holding in a moan. He couldn't continue to torture himself this way, he thought grimly.

He rolled to his side, then started to push himself up to his knees. Holly scrambled to her feet and bent over, grabbing him around his chest and adding her strength to his. Together they moved slowly to the bed. Jordan dragged himself onto the mattress. Holly lifted his legs into place, then bent over and smoothed the sheet over him.

"Better?" she asked. "Do you want a painkiller?"

He shook his head, which surprisingly only hurt a little. "I'll be fine."

"You sure?" She sat on the bed next to him. Her hip bumped his.

"Yeah," he murmured, trying not to notice that now he could see her other breast.

She bent close and touched his forehead. "You feel a little warm."

"I'm sure it will pass."

She frowned. "I hope you're not spiking another fever."

He glanced at the deep V exposed by the oversize robe. "I'm sure that's not it."

She was so intent on his condition, she didn't notice she was flashing him. He wasn't sure if he should be pleased or insulted. While he appreciated the concern, no man wanted to be considered as sexually interesting as a eunuch.

"How did you end up on the floor?" she asked.

He'd almost forgotten the circumstances that had brought Holly rushing to his side. He rubbed his temple as he tried to remember. "I heard a noise."

"What was it?"

"I can't remember. I was asleep and something woke me. I got up to see what it was."

"Maybe you were dreaming."

"Maybe." He stared at her for a moment, for the first time really taking in the oversize robe and her wet hair. He reached out and fingered a damp strand. "What have you been up to?"

Holly blushed, then turned her head away. "I, ah, was sort of using your shower. I hope you don't mind."

He wanted to say she could use it anytime, but only on the condition he got to watch. Though he figured she wouldn't know he was kidding. Then he realized he wasn't kidding. Had it been that long since he'd been with a woman, or was it specifically that Holly Garrett intrigued him?

Dangerous question, Haynes, he told himself, and decided to ignore it.

"I don't mind," he said. "Is there a problem with the plumbing at your new apartment?"

She drew in a deep breath. The edges of the robe trembled slightly but didn't part any more. Staring at them was screwing up his concentration, so he lowered his gaze to her lap, where she rested her hands.

"Plumbing? Oh!" She seemed to realize how she was dressed. She touched her wet hair, then pulled the collar of the robe together and held it tight. "I, um, I don't really have an apartment."

He drew his eyebrows together and stared at her. "Where are you living?"

"At the shop." She gave him a quick smile. "It's really very nice. There's plenty of furniture. Some of the sofas are very comfy. I have a sleeping bag, a hot plate and a small refrigerator. There's even a bathroom, but it doesn't have a shower. So I asked Louise if it was all right for me to use the shower here. You were sleeping, or I would have asked you."

"You can't live there," he said.

"Why not? It's perfectly safe. I didn't have renter's insurance, and right now I can't afford to replace everything I lost, let alone come up with first and last months' rent. But right after the holidays everything should be fine. It's only for a few weeks."

She was talking quickly, and he wondered if it was to cover her nervousness. He figured it was. Now that she was no longer acting as his nurse, she was shy and embarrassed.

As he watched, the fingers at her collar tightened. "Go get dressed," he said gruffly, then closed his eyes as she scurried from the room.

When she was gone, he raised his arm to cover his eyes. He didn't want to think about Holly Garrett living alone in her store. After six the shopping district was deserted. She could get into trouble, and no one would be around to call for help. To make matters worse, thinking about her living there made him think about her not having access to a shower and instead using his.

She'd been so soft and tempting in his robe. His mind filled with a hundred different ways he could take them both to breathlessness and back. But he wasn't going to act on any of them. He was too old and cynical for a woman like her.

For a moment a flicker of regret raced through him. Regret for all he'd never experienced and for all he would never have. If he were someone else, if circumstances were different, he could pursue his interest in Holly. He could woo her slowly, risk caring about her and being cared about in return.

A fantasy, he told himself, even as he acknowledged the fantasy was a hell of a lot better than reality. It wasn't that he didn't believe in love; he just didn't like the consequences.

Seconds later the noise that had awakened him returned. It was a low-pitched yowl. Before he could make up his mind about the risk of trying to get out of bed again, Holly returned carrying a large gray cat.

He eyed the beast distastefully. He recognized the face. That cat was responsible for him being laid up. He thought about grabbing the creature and expressing his feelings, but in his weakened condition he didn't dare. The cat stared back at him, dislike gleaming from its bright green eyes. He figured the cat had gotten the best of him once, and that had been while he was healthy. God knows what it could do to him now.

Holly shifted the massive feline in her arms and smiled. "This is Mistletoe. Mistletoe, this is the brave man who saved your life."

Man and cat glared at each other. Neither was impressed.

"Mistletoe is a pedigreed Persian," Holly said, then set the animal on the floor. "I hope you don't mind that I brought her over. She's very special to me."

At the sound of her name, the cat glanced up at Holly, then purred and rubbed against her legs. When the feline completed the circle, she looked at Jordan and flattened her ears.

He stared back. "She's pretty fat."

"She's pregnant."

He had a moment of guilt for thinking evil thoughts about an expectant mother, then realized Mistletoe would probably pass her bad temper on to her offspring.

"I don't like to leave her alone at night," Holly said. "She's very well behaved. She won't be any trouble."

"Yeah, right," he muttered.

Holly picked up the cat and walked toward the bed. "Maybe you should pet her and get acquainted."

Mistletoe began to squirm. Holly set her on the foot of the bed. The cat glared at him. He glared back. She arched her back, gave a sharp *pftt*, then jumped down and stalked away.

Holly stared after her. "I don't understand. She's really very sweet and loves everyone."

"Uh-huh," Jordan said, knowing he'd just been insulted by a twenty-pound monster.

"I'm sure she'll adore you once she gets to know you."

Mistletoe had already sent him off the balcony of a building. He would hate to see what the cat was capable of when she put her mind to something.

Holly curled up in the chair Louise had brought into Jordan's temporary bedroom. The overhead light was off. The only illumination came from two floor lamps in opposite corners.

Jordan sat up in bed with the sheet bunched around his waist. They'd finished dinner and were sipping coffee. Holly was pleased with how far she'd come. Despite being in the same room with a good-looking man *and* his handsome chest, she was able to talk like a normal person. Definitely an improvement over the first day. Jordan still had the power to make her blush, but that was getting better, too.

She studied his face and eyes, searching for signs of fever or pain. "How do you feel?"

"That's the third time you've asked me, Holly. I'm fine." Then he smiled.

She bit back a sigh. Okay, she was able to survive the bare chest and witty conversation, but the smile... That smile could still reduce her legs to the consistency of whipped cream. She leaned forward and set her coffee mug on the nightstand before she did something stupid like dropping it.

"I'm concerned about that fever coming back." She rose to her feet and leaned over the bed. She touched his forehead, then his cheeks. "You're cool to the touch."

"You do that very well." He raised his eyebrows. "Lots of practice?"

"With my mom."

"How long was she sick?"

Holly settled back in her chair. "Ten years. I was fifteen when she found a lump in her breast. It was cancer. At first they just took the lump out, but then the cancer came back." She closed her eyes, recalling the terror of that time. Her mother had been her only parent. Because it was just the two of them, they were very close. She'd tried to be strong, but all she could think about was what was going to happen to her when her mother died.

"That's a lot to handle when you're fifteen," he said.

She nodded. "She had the usual treatments, but she was really sick. I guess some people tolerate them better. There were a lot of times I missed school to be with her."

"What else did you miss?" he asked, his voice low and concerned.

She opened her eyes and stared at him. "What do you mean?"

"You were a teenager. Most kids have a hard enough time dealing with school and growing up. You had your mother to worry about. You must have missed out on a lot."

Her eyes burned, and for a brief second she was afraid she was going to cry. Then she sat up straighter and blinked several times until the burning went away.

"Thank you," she said.

"For what?"

"For saying that. No one really noticed before. I was just a teenager, but I was expected to act like an adult. There wasn't anyone else to take charge. My mom couldn't do it. The doctors and nurses were busy. Mom had a few friends, but she didn't want them to know how sick she was. And my friends were young like me."

His dark gaze met hers. "You must have been scared."

"I was. I didn't want her to die. It was hard because I'd just started high school and I was involved in a lot of activities. I had to give them up. There was even this boy. Jimmy. We sort of dated. As much as one dates at fifteen." Holly stared down at her hands and realized she was twisting her fingers together. Consciously she stilled the movement. "He dumped me because I had to spend too much time taking care of my mom."

"Tell me his last name. As soon as I'm better, I'll find him and beat him up for you."

She smiled. "That's sweet, but no thanks. It was ages ago. It doesn't matter anymore."

"Sure it does. Some of those hurts never go away."

They stared at each other for a long time. Something in Jordan's eyes convinced her that he really did understand what she was talking about. She wondered what hurts he carried around from his past.

"Did your mother go into remission?" he asked.

"For a couple of years. I got through high school. After I graduated, I went to work full-time. I'd wanted to go to college, but there were medical bills. Then the same week we got the news that we'd inherited the antique shop up here, Mom found a lump in her other breast."

Holly's breath caught in her throat. She remembered hearing the sobs through the thin walls of their bathroom. She'd rushed inside and found her mother crouched down on the floor, crying and rocking. At that moment Holly had known the cancer had returned.

"Mom was strong. She had another remission, but this one was shorter. Then they found the cancer had spread everywhere. She hung on for a couple of years. It was hard on her, but she was very brave."

"Sounds like you were, too."

"I didn't do anything."

"You took care of her, didn't you?"

"I was her daughter. What else was I going to do? I was all she had."

She shifted in the chair and pulled her knees up to her chest. "Enough about this. I'm supposed to be entertaining you, not getting your spirits down. Let's talk about something more lighthearted."

Jordan thought for a moment. "If you could have gone to college, what would you have studied?"

"That's easy. Business. I want to do a good job running the shop, but I don't have all the education I need. I admire Louise for going back to school. That's what I want to do. Next question."

"You never mention your father."

"I don't have any contact with him." She thought about the single conversation she'd shared with her father six years ago. She could remember everything about it, right down to the sound of the rain on the windows. "He had an affair with my mother. When she got pregnant, he disappeared."

She said the words matter-of-factly. Jordan stared at her and wondered how she'd managed to stay so giving and innocent in the face of so much tragedy.

Holly had been abandoned by one parent and lost the other, yet she'd survived. More than that, she was happy and successful.

"I know about fathers like that," he said. "My dad stuck around, but I often think it would have been better if he'd left."

"Why?"

She looked at him intently. After her shower she'd dressed in jeans and a dark blue sweatshirt. The soft fabric deepened the color of her eyes. Her hair was long and loose over her shoulders. He wanted to pull her close and bury his hands in the long silky strands. He wanted to kiss her and make love to her until she forgot the past and its pain. He could make her forget. He could even seduce her. But if he did, he would break her heart, and that was one thing he wouldn't allow himself to do. So instead, he told the truth. If that didn't drive her away, nothing would.

"Haven't you heard about the infamous Haynes brothers?" he asked.

She shrugged. "Rumors, really. Nothing specific."

"Four generations of heartbreakers. Four generations of boys born into the family. Three generations of philandering men and bitter women."

"You and your brothers are the fourth generation?"

"Yeah. We saw what our uncles did and how our father treated our mother. He was out with women several times a week. Earl Haynes believed everything he did was fine as long as he actually slept in his bed. Everyone in town knew about his affairs, including my mother."

She sucked in a breath. "You and your brothers knew, too?"

He nodded.

"How awful." She shook her head. "I don't understand how someone could act like that."

"It was easy."

"What do you mean?"

''The men in my family have a natural ability to attract women.''

She raised her chin slightly. ''I hadn't noticed.''

''Gee, thanks.''

She looked startled, then laughed. ''Oh, I didn't mean that the way it sounded. What I meant was—'' She paused.

He waited, wondering what she was going to say. Would she claim to be completely unaffected by him, and if she did, would he believe her? He knew all the tricks, but he didn't use them anymore. But he'd caught Holly staring at him a couple of times. She might not be swooning, but he doubted she was immune.

Finally she flipped her hair off her shoulder and smiled. ''What was the question?''

''I'll give you a break,'' he said. ''You don't have to answer it.''

''What happened with your parents?''

''They're divorced. My dad's living in Florida with wife number five. I only met numbers two and three, but if she's anything like them, she's about twenty-five with an IQ smaller than her waist. Dad was never much into substance.''

''And your mother?''

Jordan didn't want to think about that. ''She left when I was in high school. No one knows where she is.''

Despite his best efforts, the day came back to him. It had been an afternoon in the spring. Sunny, warm, perfect. He had been there, although neither parent had known. He'd seen everything. He knew the truth.

He shook his head, and memories were banished to a dark place he preferred not to explore.

Holly leaned forward and touched the back of his hand. ''I'm sorry,'' she said. ''I didn't mean to bring up painful memories.''

She was the nurse again. Comforting and impersonal. For reasons he didn't understand, he wanted more. He turned his hand so her fingers grazed his palm. Instantly sparks arced between them. She stiffened. His blood heated. Before she could pull away, he captured her palm in his.

Her eyes widened, and she swallowed. "I, ah, it's really late. I should probably go."

"Thanks for dinner," he said. "It was great." He brushed his thumb against the back of her hand. Her skin was soft and warm.

She rose, but before she could pull away, he gave a quick tug. She resisted for a moment, then settled on the edge of the bed. Her long hair swung around her shoulders, shielding then exposing her face.

He turned his hand slightly and rubbed his thumb against the inside of her wrist. Her pulse was rapid. Her lips parted, and he wondered if she was having trouble breathing. His gaze dipped lower, to her full breasts. He wanted her.

Color rose to her cheeks, blending with the freckles. Her pupils dilated. He inhaled the sweet essence of her body. It would be easy to pull her close. Easy to draw her into his arms and kiss her until she forgot where and who she was. He might hate that part of him, but like his brothers, he was every inch a Haynes. He knew how to seduce a woman.

But not Holly, he thought as he gave her hand one last squeeze before releasing her. Not because he didn't like her, but because he did. And because he wanted her to come back again.

She stared dreamily at him, swaying as if propelled by a secret breeze. Then consciousness returned, and she stiffened.

"I should head home," she said again.

''I'll see you tomorrow.''

She smiled, then was gone.

After the sound of her car disappearing down the driveway had faded, Jordan stared at the ceiling. Something had happened tonight. Something he didn't want to think about.

Somehow he and Holly had connected. He didn't tell many people about his past, and he suspected she felt the same way. But they'd both shared. He wasn't sure what that meant, but he knew it was dangerous. So was his thinking that she was special and sweet.

He shifted under the sheet, and a tuft of cat hair floated to the floor. Too sweet for that damn cat, he thought. And too trusting to be staying alone in the business district at night. Glenwood might not be a hotbed of crime, but bad things had happened here. He would call the sheriff's station and make sure they patrolled the area.

Before he could get up and walk to the phone, Louise returned. As she did every night, she came in and checked on him.

''Holly already gone?'' she asked as she leaned against the door frame. She brushed her blond bangs out of her eyes.

''About ten minutes ago.''

Louise started to leave.

''Wait,'' he said. ''Holly asked you if she could use the shower.''

''Is that a problem?''

''No. I didn't know she was living in her store. I don't think it's safe.''

Louise folded her arms over her chest. ''I'm sure if she had somewhere else to go, she would.''

''She said she couldn't afford an apartment.''

Louise reached for her right earring and toyed with the small cup and saucer. ''I know what you're thinking Jordan. Your heart is in the right place, but Holly isn't going to accept money from you. Probably not even a loan.''

"I figured that.''

She gave him a tentative smile. "It was nice of you to be concerned.''

He looked away from the older woman. His instinct was to say something rude. The problem was he was warming to her. It didn't matter how much trouble he was, Louise still took care of him. He knew it was about his family and not about him, but that didn't change much. He was torn between feeling guilty for acting like a complete bastard and anger for what she'd done.

When he reminded himself it was a long time ago, a voice in his head said if it hadn't been for her, everything might have been different. He remembered the lies and the secrets, then he got mad and it was easy not to be polite.

Life was hell sometimes.

"You think she'd let me pay her for keeping me company in the evening?'' he asked.

"Lord knows I take money for putting up with you, but Holly seems to like you. No accounting for taste.''

He turned away so Louise wouldn't see his smile. He liked Holly, too.

"I'll figure out something," he said. "She can't stay there indefinitely. In the meantime would you bring me the portable phone? I want to call the sheriff's office and ask them to patrol that part of town at night.''

Louise slowly shook her head. "Mostly you're a pain in the butt, Jordan, but sometimes you can be a real nice guy.''

"Don't let it get out.''

She grinned. "Who would believe me?''

Chapter Five

When Holly arrived the next day, Louise was already gone. The housekeeper had left a note on the front door explaining she was baby-sitting for one of the "friendly" Haynes brothers and for Holly to come on in and make herself comfortable.

Holly tested the front door and found it open, then she stepped inside. The house was silent, and there weren't any smells of cooking. After letting Mistletoe out of her basket, Holly walked into the kitchen, where she found another note telling her that Louise had prepared a casserole for dinner. It was in the refrigerator and would require forty-five minutes at three hundred and fifty degrees to heat. There was also a salad and a loaf of French bread.

"I could get used to this," Holly said softly, and smiled. Mistletoe strolled into the kitchen and wrapped herself around Holly's legs.

"She even left you some chicken."

Mistletoe purred.

"You like Louise, don't you?" Holly said, bending over and stroking her cat. Mistletoe raised her head to have it scratched between her ears. Her purr rumbled louder.

"I like her, too," Holly said. "And I like Jordan." She crouched down and rubbed under Mistletoe's chin.

"I have a confession," she continued. "I feel badly that Jordan got hurt saving your life, but I'm not completely sorry that he's having to rest for a while, if that makes sense."

Mistletoe looked at her with bright green, knowing eyes.

"I like coming here to visit him," Holly whispered.

Mistletoe's gaze never wavered. She seemed to figure out the topic of conversation, because her eyes narrowed and she gave a short, sharp *pftt* before walking off.

Holly followed her into the hallway, then made her way through the library. At the door to the study, she paused.

Jordan sat up in his hospital bed. Today he wore a cobalt blue T-shirt. While she missed his bare chest, the man sure knew how to fill out clothes. The shoulders were pulled tight, and the much-washed fabric molded itself against his chest.

Dark hair hung over his forehead, and his brow was furrowed in concentration. As always he took her breath away. Her legs began to tremble, and she wondered if she would be able to get out a coherent thought. After so many days she would have thought she would get over her attraction or befuddlement, but she hadn't. Briefly she wondered if it would always be like this.

She smiled. Always. As if they were going to continue to see each other. No doubt as soon as he was up and around, Jordan would be delighted to see the last of her. He only bothered with her because he was bored by spending so much time in his own company. Once he could resume his life, he wouldn't have time for a slightly over-weight, shy, twenty-eight-year-old virgin.

She raised her hand and knocked on the door frame. Jordan looked up.

"I've been waiting for you," he said, deepening his voice until it sounded like thick dark chocolate blending with rich cream.

"I was delayed at the store. A couple of women came in wanting to buy wreaths. I have so many to choose from, they had trouble making up their minds. In the end they bought six."

Jordan set down the papers he'd been studying. "Far be it from me to interfere with your business." He motioned to the chair next to him. "Have a seat. I want to talk to you about something."

She settled down next to him, and he handed her an old photograph. She studied it for several seconds before recognizing the structure in the picture.

"This is your house," she said.

"Yeah. Right after it was completed. Check out the old cars in front."

Although the mansions in Glenwood had been constructed in the Victorian style, most of them had been built around the turn of the century or a few years later. They'd been the first in the area to have complete indoor plumbing and that newfangled invention: electric lights.

Holly noted the beautiful lines of the house, then realized the just-planted saplings all around the yard had grown to be the majestic oaks and pines she'd parked under today.

"Can I make it look like it used to?" Jordan asked.

"Sure. With enough time and money, anything is possible. Some original fixtures, switches and that sort of thing might be hard to find, but practically it's often better to use reproductions. If the structure is sound, you can do anything. I assume you had that checked before you bought the place.''

He nodded.

''Then the rest of it isn't that bad.''

She stared at the photo and wondered what it would be like to own something as wonderful as this house. Maybe Jordan would let her help him with some of the work. She would be thrilled to give him the benefit of her experience.

She held the picture, but instead of seeing the image, she saw Jordan laughing. Her mouth curved up in response. He was so good-looking he would be dangerous to be around for any length of time. But she would try to muddle through.

A part of her wondered why he was being so nice to her. She knew some of it was because she was keeping him company. Foolishly she wanted him to act that way because he liked her.

What a silly dream, she told herself, and knew it came from her loneliness. While her mother had been ill, especially the last couple of years before her death, Holly hadn't had time to make and keep friends. If she wasn't working to pay the bills, she was home caring for her mother.

After her mother's death, she'd been too numb to think about anything but surviving. Since moving to Glenwood, she'd finally been able to acknowledge the emptiness she carried around inside. However, she hadn't had a chance to do anything about it. Being with Jordan was both perfect pleasure and penetrating pain. He made her laugh and feel as if she finally fit in somewhere. He also pointed out the silence of her days and coldness of her nights. He made her want things she'd never had. He made her dream again.

While she didn't mind the dreaming, sometimes she

found the process uncomfortable. Since meeting him, he had been the focal point of her dreams. Silly and pointless, she reminded herself. Jordan Haynes was—

A large hand moved up and down in front of her face. "Holly, are you still in there?"

She blinked several times and stared at him. "What?"

"I'm talking and talking, but you're a million miles away."

She laughed to cover up her rush of embarrassment. Thank goodness he couldn't know what she was thinking.

"Sorry. This photograph set me off." She handed it to him, then folded her hands in her lap. "You have my complete attention. What were you saying?"

"I have a proposition for you."

"P-proposition?" Her mind went blank for a split second. Her body filled with that mysterious heat Jordan was forever setting off in her.

She was reasonably sure she was attracted to him. Her body was always tingling, burning, humming and shaking when they were together. But she didn't know what any of that meant. Was it normal? Would she get over it? Was it specifically about him, or would it have happened if she spent time with any good-looking man?

If only she had more experience with the male gender. If only she could know what to do.

He picked up a couple of photographs showing the interior of the house as it had been seventy years earlier. "I've wanted to start work, but I haven't had the time. And now with this—" he motioned to his hospital bed "—it's going to be a while until I can get going."

Holly bit her lower lip. She wasn't sure where he was going with this. Did he want her to offer to help? She would be happy to.

"That's where you come in," he said, and gave her a

winning smile. She was relieved that she was sitting down. If she'd been standing, she would have been concerned her knees would give out.

"I want to hire you," he said.

"Really?"

He nodded.

"I've never done anything like that before," she said slowly. "Although I don't know why I couldn't." She thought for a moment. "I would love to work on the house. It's wonderful. Just the dining room alone, with those high ceilings and the beautiful chair-rail molding. I do have the store, though. That would be my first priority."

"No problem. The store's closed Sunday and Monday, right?"

"Yes."

"What about working Monday and two evenings?"

Holly twisted her fingers together and hoped she wasn't grinning too broadly. Jordan didn't want to get rid of her. He wanted to see her again. So what if it was just about restoring the house? He would still be here, and they could talk. Maybe—

"I'd like to pay you with cash, and room and board."

Her head snapped up, and she stared at him. "What?"

He leaned back against the bed and met her gaze. "You're surprised."

"I don't know what to say." She didn't know what to feel, either. Room and board? He expected her to live here? With him?

Then she remembered what had happened the previous day. She'd admitted she was living in the store and had used his shower. He thought she was homeless and destitute.

"I don't need your charity," she said, and rose to her feet.

He grabbed her hand before she could leave the room. "It's not charity," he said, tugging her close until she was standing next to the bed. "Please don't be angry."

His dark eyes widened slightly. She tried to read what he was thinking. She didn't think she saw pity, but how would she know?

When he pulled on her hand again, she had no choice but to sink onto the mattress beside him. Her breathing increased slightly as she noticed he continued to hold her fingers in his. This wasn't a medicinal touch. This was…well, she wasn't sure what it was. Her heart pounded rapidly, thudding against her ribs. She was having trouble thinking.

"The house needs work," he said quietly. "You're the town expert."

"I'm sure there are other people just as qualified as me."

"None that I know."

"This is all an elaborate ploy," she told him. "You're offering me a place to stay because you feel sorry for me."

His thumb stroked her palm, disturbing the last few remaining connections in her brain. She stared at him, at the square shape of his jaw and his firm mouth. Faint stubble darkened his cheeks. She was close enough to see the laugh lines around his eyes and the slight bump on the bridge of his nose.

His skin was tanned, different from her paleness. Everything about him was different. The way he talked, his scent, the shape of his body. The differences both frightened and intrigued her.

"I'm offering you a place to stay for two reasons. First I like your company. Second I don't think it's safe for you to live at your shop. The business district is deserted at night. If something were to happen, you would be in that part of town alone.''

But she barely heard what he was saying. He liked her company. Wasn't that the same as liking her?

The offer was tempting. Not just because of Jordan, although he was the biggest temptation of all, but also because she missed living in a real home. She could take a shower every day and cook in a kitchen with more than a hot plate. She could sleep in a regular bed and not in a sleeping bag on an uncomfortable antique sofa.

''Say yes,'' he commanded.

She pulled her hand free of his fingers so she could think. There were merits to his plan. ''Mistletoe would have to come with me. I couldn't leave her in the store.''

Despite the animal's sweet nature, the Persian and Jordan didn't get along. Holly had tried explaining that Jordan had saved Mistletoe's life, but the cat remained unimpressed.

Jordan exhaled deeply. ''I figured that. Mistletoe can stay here, too.''

''She really is grateful to you,'' Holly said.

''Oh, yeah, I can tell. So what's it going to be? Are you going to help me out here or callously abandon me?''

He made it sound as if she would be doing *him* a favor when it was really the other way around. She was tempted. Very tempted. She'd never lived with a man before and would probably never again live with one like Jordan. Should she just take the opportunity and be grateful?

''Louise will still be here,'' he said.

''That's nice. I like Louise.''

He ignored that. ''I meant, so you wouldn't have to worry. She'll be here to act as chaperon.''

Holly stared at him. He thought she was worried he

might try something? Before she could stop herself, she laughed.

He didn't share her amusement. "I think I've just been insulted," he muttered.

"No," she said quickly to reassure him. "I wasn't laughing at you. While I appreciate your concern, I wasn't worried that—" Her throat closed. "Well, that you would, you know." He still looked confused and vaguely put out. She drew in a deep breath. "I know you would never be interested in someone like me."

"Why not?"

She opened her mouth, but couldn't find any words. Why not? It was so obvious. Because he was Jordan Haynes and she was just a silly woman who didn't know diddly about men. "Because, well, I don't know much about men, but there must be a hundred reasons."

"Name one."

She could have named ten, but they were all too embarrassing. She wasn't pretty enough, she wasn't skinny enough, she wasn't anything enough.

His gaze narrowed and seemed to focus on her face. "You're right about one thing, Holly. You don't know anything about men."

He reached for her hand. She let him take it, not expecting him to tug her forward. She found herself falling toward him. She put out her right hand to keep herself from landing on his chest. She was leaning toward him, embarrassingly close to his face. His eyes darkened to the color of the night sky. His sweet breath fanned her face.

Deep inside, that unexplainable heat flared to life. She told herself to run away, but she couldn't move. Something was going to happen; she could sense it. And no matter what it was, she wanted to experience it fully.

She expected a quick, witty retort or maybe a hug, but

she didn't expect him to kiss her. In that heart-stopping moment, when he moved closer and his attention focused on her mouth, she realized his intentions. And then it was too late.

His lips brushed against hers. She jerked awkwardly, and he wrapped his free arm around her back, drawing her closer. She sat stiffly, one hand captured in his, the other braced on the bed.

Jordan lifted his head slightly and smiled. "Relax. This isn't going to hurt." Then he raised the bed until they were eye to eye. He released her hand and put both arms around her. Not having anything else to do, her hands fluttered nervously.

"Put them on my shoulders," he murmured, and it was the last thing he said for a long time.

As she followed his instructions and rested the tips of her fingers on his broad shoulders, his mouth once again brushed hers. Holly had been kissed once, years before. It had been the chaste, innocent kiss of inexperienced teenagers. It had not prepared her for Jordan.

He claimed her mouth. His lips moved back and forth, exploring her lips, discovering every millimeter of skin. She was too stunned to respond. She could feel the warmth of him radiating toward her like a heater. Through the tips of her fingers, she sensed his strength. He drew her closer, and powerful muscles shifted.

One of his hands pressed against her spine between her shoulder blades. He kneaded her slightly. Perhaps the action was meant to relax her, but she was too overwhelmed by sensation. Her mind flitted from place to place, receiving all the sensory input and trying to sort it out. His other hand cupped her hip. The intimacy embarrassed her. She felt awkward, all large curves and stiff muscles. She couldn't flow with the moment.

He moved his mouth away from her lips and planted a kiss by her chin. An electric jolt rippled through her. Another kiss caressed her jawline. He slipped toward her ear, ending up by her neck. Sizzling impulse leapt just under her skin, and she fought against the need to sag against him. Holding herself stiff and straight took so much energy.

Then Jordan licked the sensitive skin just under her ear. Heat exploded inside her. The unfamiliar fire whipped through her, fanned by needs she didn't understand. Her breasts ached as if they'd swollen. For the first time in her life, she could actually feel the inside of her soft cotton bra pressing against her nipples. It was uncomfortable.

Between her legs the first flicker of awareness sparked to life. A heaviness filled her, and she pressed her thighs tightly together to hold all the feelings inside.

He returned his attention to her mouth again. This time she kissed him back. She moved her lips against his. Oddly enough it was getting more difficult to breathe. She relaxed her fingers and held on to his shoulders. The hand on her back began to stroke up and down, while the one on her hip squeezed and kneaded.

Then he did the most amazing thing. He touched her lower lip with his tongue. Her breath caught in her throat, and all her attention focused on that tiny damp spot on her sensitized skin.

She didn't know what to do. She'd read about that kind of kissing in books, of course. She knew that other people did it. But she'd never imagined she would have the chance to experience it herself. There was something faintly wicked about the thought. Delightfully wicked.

When he stroked her a third time, she knew he wanted her to open her mouth. She wanted it, but it seemed too bold and flagrant. As if she were begging him to kiss her.

Confusion settled on her like a blanket. She didn't know what to do. She couldn't think.

"You're thinking too much," Jordan murmured.

She jerked back in shock and stared at him. "How can you read my mind?"

He opened his eyes, exposing dilated pupils and a hungry expression. "I don't have to. Your body gives you away. You're too scared to relax. It's just a kiss, Holly. It can't be your first one." He smiled at the thought.

"Of course not," she said, reminding herself technically it wasn't a lie. There *had* been that kiss when she was fifteen. Even if it hadn't been anything like this, it still counted.

He cupped her face in his hands. "You're lovely," he said, then slid his fingers into her hair. She wore it in a loose French braid, and he wove through the strands, massaging her scalp and making her want to moan with pleasure.

"I'm not at all lovely," she said. "I'm—"

She never got to finish her sentence. He swooped down and kissed her. Before she could press her lips primly together, he'd slipped inside.

At the first touch of his tongue on the inside of her lower lip, her body froze. As he brushed the tip of her tongue with his, her heart stopped. She'd expected to like kissing him; she hadn't expected to be moved to another dimension.

He circled her, stroked her, teased her. Sensations filled her being. The feel of him, the textures, the sweet taste, the heat, the closeness. One hand continued to stroke her hair and scalp. The other dropped back to her hip. But this time, instead of staying still, it slipped around and cupped her behind.

There was too much to think about, too much to experience. She would perish from sensory overload. She would perish if he ever stopped.

He continued to kiss her, so she continued to live. Gradually he withdrew his tongue. She waited for him to return. When he did, it was just to tease, then escape. They played that game several times before she realized he wanted her to follow him.

The concept should have overwhelmed her. Instead, she found herself eager for the experience. This was her first adult kiss, and she was determined to enjoy every minute of it.

She did to him as he'd done to her. She slipped into his mouth, pausing to taste his bottom lip. He felt unfamiliar but exciting. She wanted more. She continued forward and touched his tongue with hers. They began a sensual dance that made her skin burn and her blood heat.

Before, her mind had raced as she tried to figure out what she should be focusing on. Now she couldn't think at all. She could only drift along on a current of need and excitement.

So this was passion, she thought as he drew her closer and her breasts flattened against the hard plane of his chest. This was desire. This was sex.

Jordan moaned low in his throat. She wondered if everything felt as good to him as it did to her. He must have kissed hundreds of women. She probably didn't measure up at all. But she couldn't find it in herself to care. All she wanted was for the moment to go on forever.

But eventually it had to stop. Jordan broke away, then rested his forehead against hers and stared into her eyes. They were both breathing heavily.

He gave her a crooked smile, then brushed a strand of hair from her face. "Amazing," he murmured, his voice thick and husky.

"You think so?" she asked, hoping he wasn't just being kind. The kiss had been a miracle for her, but she didn't have anything to compare it to.

"I know it was." Some of the light faded from his eyes. "I'm sorry, Holly. I shouldn't have done that."

Sorry? Because it was so hideous? She straightened and tried to pull away. His left arm was still around her, and he didn't release her.

"Wait a minute," he said. "I'm not sorry I kissed you, I'm sorry that it might have scared you away. I want you to come stay here. If you agree, I don't want you worried that I'm going to be attacking you. I can control myself."

She blinked several times, but none of it made sense. "You didn't scare me," she said finally. "I know you wouldn't, well, you know, do anything bad." She could feel the heat creeping up her cheeks, and she ducked her head. "I trust you."

Damn. Jordan stared at Holly and didn't know if he should be flattered or take off in the opposite direction. She trusted him. Great. Right now he was hard and hot from wanting her, and he didn't feel like being noble. But he would be because she was innocent. It was unlikely that Holly was actually a virgin, but she was the next-closest thing. He hadn't been sure before, but he was now. Her kiss had been tentative. At least at first.

Just thinking about her shy foray into his mouth made him want to bed her right here. If he'd had the strength, he might have hauled her next to him. But he was battered and sore, so she was going to escape unscathed. Just as well for both of them. He liked Holly. He didn't want to screw up her life. Or worse, destroy it. And that's what would happen. He knew the dangers of getting involved. He knew the price everyone paid. He didn't want that for her, and he wouldn't risk it again for himself.

He released her, and she half turned away from him. Her spine was straight, and her hands rested neatly in her lap. But he knew she was still aroused. He could see it in the outline of her nipples through her bra and blouse, and hear it in her still-rapid breathing. She'd wanted him. The thought both frustrated and aroused him.

"You never agreed to stay," he said.

She glanced at him. Her blue eyes darkened with confusion. "Jordan, I—"

The front door opened, and the sound of familiar voices filled the house.

"Where do you think he's keeping himself?" a man asked.

"In the study," a woman answered. "He didn't want to deal with the stairs."

Holly stood up. "Who are those people?"

"My family. At least part of them." He leaned back and grinned. "This will teach you to keep the front door locked."

She looked around, as if searching for an escape. It was too late. Kyle Haynes, Jordan's younger brother, walked in. He had that damn cat in his arms.

Kyle glanced from Jordan to Holly and back. He raised his eyebrows and grinned. "In here, guys. I found something very interesting."

Chapter Six

Holly stared at the man in front of her. He looked a lot like Jordan, but there were subtle differences. The stranger had similar features, and he was nearly as good-looking, but his smile was all wrong. Jordan's made her feel as if she were on a roller coaster, while this man's didn't make her feel anything.

"You might as well take a seat," Jordan told her. "They're going to be here for a while."

"They're staying? Then I should leave."

"No. Don't do that. You're going to have to meet them eventually." If you stay here. That was the unspoken part of the sentence.

Her head was spinning. Too much had happened too quickly. His offer, their kiss.

The kiss. The kiss that had filled her body with an incredible need she still didn't understand. Jordan had changed her with just his touch. It was as if he'd disassembled her being, then put her back together, but with everything in a slightly different place. She felt confused and unable to deal with what was happening.

"Holly," he said quietly, "come here for a second." He patted the side of the bed.

She moved closer but didn't sit down. She could hear more voices in the hallway. How many of them were there and what were they going to say when they found her in Jordan's bedroom? She couldn't even rely on the truth to see her through. They *had* been doing something. Something very intimate. What if their visitors could tell?

She took a step back and bumped into the nightstand. As she turned to steady the lamp, Jordan grabbed her hand and tugged her until she was right next to his bed.

"Your fingers are freezing," he murmured.

"I know. I'm terrified."

"Picture them in their underwear if it helps."

She glanced at the stranger who was still petting Mistletoe. Her cat was vibrating in ecstasy, rubbing her head against the man's chest and demanding more attention.

Jordan's fingers tightened on hers. "Forget about picturing anyone in his underwear. It was a bad idea."

She looked down at Jordan. He shrugged as if to say it didn't matter, then he gave her a wink. She tried to relax.

"You going to introduce me?" the man holding her cat asked.

Jordan grinned. "Maybe I don't want to."

"I can see why."

The man glanced at her, and Holly had to fight embarrassment.

"I might as well get it over with," Jordan said. "Holly, this is my younger brother, Kyle. He's married to Sandy, who is too smart to have connected up with someone like him, but there's no accounting for taste."

"Hey, wait a minute," Kyle said, and moved farther into the room. He put Mistletoe on the bed. Instantly the cat began spitting. Kyle grinned. "I see the lady doesn't care for you, Jordan. Can't say that I blame her. What with you being the homely brother and all."

Holly was stunned. Kyle had called Jordan homely? Was he crazy?

Jordan ignored the insult. "The cat knows you're the baby, so she's practicing with you until she has her own."

Kyle picked up the cat again, and Mistletoe snuggled in his arms. Holly sank into the chair next to the bed.

"I told you she was friendly," she said, pointing at the purring feline. Mistletoe seemed like the safest topic of conversation.

"Yeah, right," Jordan muttered as the bedroom door pushed open more.

Two women and one more man entered the converted study. They stared from Jordan to Holly and back. The man glanced at Kyle. "Where'd you get the cat?"

"She's mine," Holly said as she stared at him. He looked just like Jordan. Oh, not exactly. The shape of the mouth was different. They weren't twins, but they were obviously brothers, as was Kyle. Tall, dark and handsome. Apparently it was a Haynes cliché. She could have picked any of the three out of a crowd.

Then she realized everyone's attention had focused on her. She swallowed and wondered if they would think her rude if she ran out of the room screaming.

"This is Holly Garrett," Jordan said, giving her fingers a slight squeeze. "She's been in town about six months. She owns that antique store, A Victorian Parlor. She's an expert at restoration and is going to help me with the house."

Everyone started talking at once.

"I hate the wallpaper in the upstairs hall," the woman with long brown hair said. "It's too modern. Do you have sample books at your store?"

"The exterior of our house needs painting," the second woman said. "I just can't decide on the color. I want it to be authentic. Do you have any suggestions?"

The man who had come in last glanced at his brother holding the cat. "You know this is going to mean more work for us."

"I know."

Holly shrank in her chair, glancing from face to face, not sure which question to answer first. She leaned toward Jordan. "Who are these people, and what do they want from me?"

"It's perfectly safe," he told her. "I know we're a little overwhelming at first, but you'll grow to like us."

Holly wasn't so sure.

Jordan held up his free hand. "Let's not scare Holly off in the first few minutes."

There was a moment of silence.

"You're right, Jordan." The woman with long hair stepped forward. She held out her hand to Holly. "I'm Elizabeth. I know this family is terrifying at the beginning. I had it easy. I was the first of the brides. Not counting the failed marriages." She grinned. "The Haynes brothers are starting to get this relationship thing right."

"Oh?" Holly licked her lips and searched the other woman's face, trying to memorize her features. She hadn't expected to get involved with Jordan's family, but if she was going to be living here, she might have contact with them. Especially at this time of year. "You're Elizabeth."

Elizabeth flicked her long brown hair over her shoulders. "I'm married to Travis." She linked her arm through the crook of her husband's elbow. "He's the second of the four brothers. This is Sandy."

Sandy waved. "I'm married to Kyle, who has obviously made a friend for life." She motioned to Mistletoe still purring in Kyle's arms.

"The wives are easy to separate," Elizabeth said. "I have brown eyes, Sandy has green. Jill is a tiny redhead."

"And Rebecca is tall with long dark hair. She's also really skinny," Sandy said, then sighed. "If she wasn't so nice, I could hate her."

"But I thought there were only four brothers," Holly said, confused. She was just starting to keep everyone straight, but obviously she had it wrong.

Elizabeth plopped on the edge of the bed and patted Jordan's knee. "There are. Travis, Kyle, Craig, whom you haven't met yet, and Jordan."

"Then who is Rebecca married to?"

"Austin," they all said at once.

Jordan brought her hand to his mouth and kissed the back. "You'll figure it out," he promised.

She wasn't so sure. Especially not now, with her arm trembling uncontrollably and her heart pounding with the realization that everyone in the room had seen his kind gesture.

Elizabeth tugged at the sleeve of her sweater. Everyone was dressed casually in jeans topped by sweatshirts for the men and sweaters for the women. It was cozy in the house, but the evening temperature would dip to forty degrees.

"Austin is a friend of the family," Elizabeth said. "Not a brother by birth, but he's been unofficially adopted."

Sandy settled on Jordan's other side and grinned. "Interestingly Austin and Jordan are the most alike. They brood."

"You don't brood," Holly said without thinking.

Jordan smiled. "I like this girl."

Elizabeth eyed him speculatively. "It's been a long time since you've brought anyone home."

"Oh, I'm just a friend," Holly said quickly. Attention focused on her. She cleared her throat. "Jordan isn't interested in… I'm not… We're friends. Really."

Knowing looks were exchanged. Holly realized that she and Jordan were still holding hands. She tried to pull free, but he wouldn't let her. She crossed her legs and attempted to act casual.

"How long have you known Jordan?" Sandy asked.

"Yeah," Kyle said, leaning against the wall. He was still stroking Mistletoe. "Interested minds want to know."

"A couple of weeks," Holly said, stretching the truth a little.

Elizabeth leaned close. "So what do you think of our James Dean?"

"Excuse me?"

Sandy chuckled. "Oh, Jordan's the mysterious brother. Didn't you know?"

Holly shook her head.

"Craig is the oldest," Elizabeth said. "So he's responsible and a little uptight, but Jill is curing him of that."

"And fast," Sandy added.

"I hate this part," Travis interjected. He leaned against the doorjamb and folded his arms over his chest.

"Me, too," Kyle said.

The women ignored them.

"Travis is next. He's the ladies' man." Elizabeth glanced at her husband. "He does a fine job, too, but now it's just for an audience of one."

For a moment they stared at each other. The love between them was as tangible as the floors. It filled the room and made Holly feel as if she were spying on something intimate.

"Next comes Jordan," Sandy said, breaking the spell. "He's the loner."

"Am not," Jordan said mildly.

"Then why are you always on the outside looking in?"

"I'm not. It's a matter of perception."

"Oh, sure. We all believe that." Sandy brushed her bangs out of her eyes and smiled. "Finally we have Kyle. He's the baby and the charmer. My prince who came to rescue me."

"You sure resisted," her husband muttered.

"Not anymore."

Holly shook her head. There was too much to take in. Names, relationships, faces, histories. She would never get it right.

Elizabeth stood up. "I'm going to make coffee."

"I'll help," Sandy said.

The two women started from the room. The men watched them go. Elizabeth came back and physically tugged Travis and Kyle after her.

"Give them a minute alone," she said under her breath, but Holly caught the words. Then everyone was gone.

"You okay?" Jordan asked.

She shook her head. "How do you keep them straight?"

"It's easy for me. I grew up with my brothers, so I'm used to them. I was about ten or twelve when I met Austin. As for the wives, they came along one at a time. I'm sorry you're going to have to meet everyone at once."

She turned in her chair and faced him. "I don't understand. If you're all so close, why aren't you staying with one of them instead of here alone?"

He grimaced. "They argued over who was going to take

me in, but I would rather be in my house. It's the holidays. I didn't want to be in the way.''

''They love you very much,'' Holly said.

''I know. I love them.''

''That must be nice. My mom loved me a lot, but there was only her. I used to wish for brothers and sisters.'' Especially at Christmas. It was the time she most disliked being an only child.

''You can borrow mine,'' he said. ''Then you never have to worry about being alone again.''

The idea tempted her. She studied his dark eyes. ''Is that the best part of a large family?''

''Sure. Plus I know they're here for me. I can depend on them.''

She studied their joined hands. His fingers were long and tanned. Sometimes he made her feel small and delicate, a miracle of sorts. She wondered what it would be like to depend on someone. She'd never been comfortable with the concept. She didn't depend on anyone. Life had taught her it wasn't safe.

''I envy you that,'' she said.

They shared a smile, then heard noise in the hallway.

''Ready for the next assault?'' he asked.

She nodded.

He squeezed her fingers. ''I'll be right here,'' he promised.

For that moment she believed him.

''Hey, gorgeous. Want to run off to the Bahamas?''

Holly glanced up and stared at the man in front of her. Her brain clicked slowly as she assembled the individual features in her mind. Tall, dark hair, good-looking. Haynes brother. One she'd met. Which one? The man grinned, and she had her answer.

"Hi, Kyle. What are you doing here?"

He unzipped his leather jacket, exposing the shirt of his khaki sheriff's uniform and leaned against the counter. "Was that a no?"

"To what?"

He looked hurt. "My illicit offer to run away."

She laughed. "What would Sandy say?"

"Oh, we'd have to bring her with us. Otherwise, she'd get really mad."

"As tempting as that sounds, I'm going to have to pass."

He winked. "Let me know if you change your mind." He glanced around the store. "Great place. Do me a favor. If you see Sandy coming, close up shop. I don't mind spending the money, but I know she's going to talk me into doing work."

Holly laughed. "You could always hire someone."

"Jordan's got the best help already. Where does that leave the rest of us?"

It took her a moment to figure out what he was saying. "Oh, well, I won't be working on his house too long." She felt her smile freeze on her face. Did he know that she was going to be living with Jordan? Well, not exactly living with him. They would be in the same house but not living *together*.

Kyle glanced at his watch. "You close at five, right?"

She nodded. There weren't any customers in the store, so there was no point in staying open late.

"Are you packed?" he asked.

"P-packed?" She had the answer to her question.

"That's why I'm here. Jordan asked me to help you move your things." He glanced down. "There you are, sweet girl. I'd wondered where you'd run off to." He bent over and picked up Mistletoe. "Jordan said you were a miserable excuse for a cat, but you're just picky about who you like, aren't you? You have excellent taste.'' As he spoke, he stroked the cat's gray ears and under her chin. She purred her pleasure.

''It's really not fair,'' Holly said, watching the two of them. ''Jordan saved her life, but she doesn't care.''

''It's a personality thing. My brother doesn't have any.''

Holly bristled. ''He does, too. Jordan is very nice. Charming, funny, sweet…'' Her voice trailed off when she realized Kyle was staring at her.

He raised his eyebrow, then spoke to Mistletoe. ''We think Holly likes Jordan, don't we?''

Mistletoe declined to comment.

''You tricked me,'' Holly muttered, wondering if he thought she was a fool.

''Just doing a background check,'' Kyle said, his voice kind. ''Jordan's been out of the mainstream for a while. We were all surprised to hear about you.''

''I'm not… We're just…friends.''

He set Mistletoe on the counter, then leaned close. ''It's okay, Holly. You don't have to explain anything to me. And for what it's worth, Jordan likes you, too. Now, go pack your things.''

It only took her about fifteen minutes to gather her few belongings together. Kyle carried them to her car, then put Mistletoe in her basket. He set the cat carefully on the front seat.

''I'll follow you over to Jordan's and help you unload.''

''You don't have to do that,'' she protested.

''I want to.'' He closed the passenger door.

Holly started the engine. Confusion clouded her mind, and she drove automatically.

Kyle had said that Jordan liked her. Was it true? Did he? And if he did, what did it mean? Her stomach tightened with nerves. Oh, my, if he liked her, she couldn't live with him. But she wanted him to like her—didn't she?

"Now what?" she asked aloud.

It didn't matter. So what if they liked each other? They were friends, nothing more. They certainly weren't going to have a relationship. Jordan wouldn't want a woman like her. He would want someone sophisticated and experienced. Besides, she didn't want a relationship, either. People had always let her down. An emotional commitment would require trust, and she wasn't ready for that. She might never be ready.

But he'd kissed her.

That kiss. She couldn't forget it. Last night it had haunted her dreams, awakening her time and again. She'd lain in bed listening to her heart pounding, feeling strange heat in her body, fighting a restlessness she didn't understand.

That kiss had been the most amazing thing she'd ever experienced. However, she didn't have a whole lot of experience. This was the nineties. People kissed all the time. Jordan had probably forgotten that it had happened. She would be foolish to think it made any difference.

By the time she arrived at Jordan's house, she'd nearly convinced herself that was true.

Louise met them at the door. "Jordan's asleep," she said, then pressed her finger to her lips. "He spiked another fever today. He's been grouchy as a grizzly, so I'll thank you to be quiet. The longer he sleeps, the better for me."

She looked at Holly. "I can't tell you how happy I am that you're going to be here. I'll still take care of him, but I'm sure he'll be in a better mood with you around. Your bedroom is through here."

She led the way up the stairs. The third door on the left

was open. Holly stepped inside and gave a start of surprise. The room was beautiful.

Original wallpaper—a pattern of cream background covered with pale blue roses—gave the room a cozy feel. A nineteenth-century four-poster bed stood in the center of the room. The dresser matched. There was a tall wardrobe instead of a closet, and several throw rugs on the hardwood floor. A small table and two chairs provided a conversation area in front of a window.

"It's stunning," she said softly.

"I thought you'd like this better than one of the remodeled bedrooms."

Kyle entered and set her suitcases on the bed. "You really want to sleep with all this old stuff?" he asked.

Louise slapped his arm. "You've always had more charm than sense."

"That's why you love me." He leaned down and kissed Louise's cheek.

She made a *humph* noise in her throat. "Get on back to your family."

Kyle walked over to Holly and gave her a quick hug. "Call me if you need anything."

He left the room.

Holly stared after him, amazed that she'd been accepted as easily as that.

"The bathroom is new," Louise said, pointing to a door on the left side of the room. She crossed to the bed and opened the basket. Mistletoe stuck her head out. "I'll bet you're hungry."

The cat meowed.

"I thought so." Louise patted her head, then started for the door. "You go ahead and unpack. I'll feed Mistletoe, then come up and check on you."

"Thanks."

Holly hung the clothes she wore at the store in the wardrobe. She was still surprised by everything that had happened. Jordan's family was accepting her as if they'd known her for years. She wasn't sure why. Were they like this with everyone? She knew three of the brothers worked in law enforcement. She would have expected them to be suspicious of strangers.

Louise returned with a tray. She set it on the table. "Hot cocoa and cookies. A little snack to tide you over until Jordan wakes up."

"How's he doing?"

Louise shrugged. "His fever seems better, and he's sleeping. It's his own fault. He's been doing too much. His body needs rest."

Holly nibbled on her bottom lip. Was the fever her fault? Yesterday she and Jordan had shared a passionate kiss. Could that have been too much for him?

"Have a seat," Louise said as she took one chair. She was wearing a fire-engine red jumpsuit unbuttoned low enough to show off impressive cleavage. Her earrings were a cascade of crystal and red beads that hung nearly to her shoulders. Makeup accentuated her blue eyes.

Holly sank into the chair and took the offered mug of cocoa. "I'm so confused," she said.

"About?"

"Everything. Jordan's family is being nice to me."

"So?"

"They don't know me. I could be a horrible person."

Louise laughed. "Not if you lived another five hundred years." Her smile faded. "You remember the story of the Three Musketeers?"

Holly nodded.

"That's the Haynes boys. All for one and one for all. They look out for each other. If one of them likes someone, that person is drawn into the family. That's what happened to Austin, and to me.''

''How long have you known the family?''

Louise took a sip of her cocoa. ''I knew the boys' father. Earl Haynes was the sheriff when I was growing up. He was as good-looking as his sons. They're good men, but Earl had the devil in him. He liked ladies, and they had a hard time resisting him.''

She was silent, remembering a past Holly didn't share. For a moment Holly wondered if Louise had a connection to Earl Haynes, but realized that was unlikely. Someone would have said something about it.

Louise shook herself, as if tossing off memories. ''Anyway, once they got word that Jordan invited you to stay here, they took that to mean you were being accepted. Now you're part of the family.''

''That's impossible. They don't know me.''

Louise looked at her a long time. Her blue eyes were sad. ''You have any family?''

''No. My mother died three years ago, and she was my last relative.''

''I understand that. I'm alone, too. Sometimes it gets damn ugly. The Haynes boys invited me into their circle, except for Jordan, of course. I don't belong, but they let me pretend. I'm grateful to them. Come Christmas, I'm going to be in a house full of children and laughter. They remember my birthday. It sure beats spending those times alone.''

Without thinking, Holly stretched out her hand. Louise took it and smiled. ''Aren't we a sorry pair,'' the housekeeper said lightly.

''I think we're very lucky. I'm glad you're my friend.''

Louise sniffed. ''Don't go getting all emotional on me,'' she said, setting her mug on the tray and standing up. ''I'll end up with my mascara under my eyes. I hate it when that happens. I'm going to go start dinner. Then I've got class with Professor Wilson.''

Holly followed her down the stairs, then detoured into Jordan's study. He was asleep with the sheet bunched up around his waist.

Dark hair narrowed as it arrowed down his belly. Where the sheet dipped dangerously low, she saw the first hint of black curls that surrounded his—

Holly jerked her attention to his face. Oh, God, he was *naked!* She'd never seen a naked man before. She had a vague idea of what they would look like down there, but no real practical experience.

Before she started to hyperventilate, she reminded herself this was a sickroom. Jordan needed her care and concern, not her adolescent interest.

There was a bowl of water on the nightstand. She dampened the washcloth Louise had left, then brushed it over Jordan's face. She could feel the heat radiating from him. She sat on the edge of the bed and continued to cool him. She ran the cloth over his chest and his arms.

The familiar ministrations were almost comforting. She'd done this countless times for her mother. The fact that Jordan was a man didn't matter. It was all about healing.

She murmured soothingly, telling him he would soon be better. The fever would break, and his strength would return. Over and over she dipped the cloth in the water, squeezed it dry, then brushed it over his chest and face. After twenty minutes he opened his eyes.

''Holly?''

''I'm right here. How do you feel?''

He squinted at her, then cleared his throat. ''Hot.''

''You've got a fever. Do you want some water?''

"Yeah."

She raised the bed slightly, then poured a glass from the pitcher. He tilted his head forward. She shifted so she could support his shoulders, then held the glass to his mouth. He sipped slowly.

When he was done, she continued to stroke him with the cloth. With her free hand she touched his face, then his arm. His eyes fluttered closed.

"That's nice," he said.

"You're trying to do too much," she told him. "You've got to concentrate on getting better."

He opened one eye. "And I was about to tell you how glad I was to see you. I take it all back."

She smiled.

"Did Kyle get you moved?"

"Yes. I'm right upstairs." She leaned closer and brushed his hair off his forehead.

His eyes opened, and he stared at her. She was close enough to kiss him. She refused to think about that. Right now he needed a nurse.

"You brought that damn cat, didn't you?"

"Of course." She moved the washcloth across his chest.

"It's good that I know you," he muttered.

"What do you mean?"

"You're the touchingest nurse I've ever met. If I wasn't so sure you were innocent, I would swear you were coming on to me."

Holly froze. In her mind's eye she saw how this must look to him. She was sitting on his bed with her hips pressing intimately against his. One hand caressed his face while the other stroked his chest. Okay, the hand on his chest held a washcloth, but that was just window dressing.

"I…" She closed her mouth and wished she could die.

"Don't stop," he said. "I like the attention. I know you

mean it impersonally, like a nurse, but my body doesn't exactly understand.'' He reached for the sheet.

Holly sprang to her feet. When all he did was draw the material up to his chest, she realized she'd overreacted. She dropped the washcloth and pressed her hand to her face. She was going to die. Absolutely die.

She turned on her heel and raced from the room.

''Holly, wait!'' Jordan called after her.

She ignored him and kept running. When she reached the cool quiet of her room, she threw herself on her bed and shut her eyes.

How could she have been so silly? Why had she made a fool of herself? It was horrible. She was never going to be able to face Jordan again.

She heard a faint meow-purr, then Mistletoe jumped on the bed and sniffed her face.

''Your mother is a fool,'' she said, pulling the soft cat down next to her. Mistletoe settled against her side.

What must Jordan be thinking about her? She so wanted to impress him. It was obvious she didn't have a clue as to how to act around men, and he was the last male she should be practicing on.

She wanted to run away and never face him again. The only problem with that plan was the reality of the situation. She had just moved into Jordan's house. This time there was no escape.

Chapter Seven

Jordan had heard Holly come into the house, but so far she hadn't come looking for him. At first he'd told himself she was busy, but after nearly an hour he knew she was avoiding him. The big question was why?

What had he done or said to offend her? He didn't remember much about the previous evening. As Louise had delighted in informing him when he'd finally awakened from a long and restless sleep, his overactivity had caused him to spike another fever. If he kept this up much longer, he was going to fry his brain.

He'd thanked the housekeeper for her concern and had privately agreed with her assessment. He had to start following the doctor's instructions, or he was never going to get well. That meant staying off his feet most of the time. Which he planned to do, just as soon as he found out what was wrong with Holly.

Moving slowly, he peeled back the sheet and swung his

feet to the floor. There was a pair of jeans tossed casually over the nightstand. He grabbed them and tugged them on. He considered a shirt, but didn't think he had the strength. Besides, Holly had seen him bare chested before and hadn't seemed to notice. He doubted she was going to start now.

He braced himself on the bed and nightstand, then pushed to his feet. The muscles in his legs trembled but didn't give way. After a couple of minutes he felt strong enough to start walking.

Louise had left nearly an hour before. He'd heard her car pull out right after Holly had arrived. The house was huge, and Holly could be anywhere. Once in the hallway, he stopped and listened, then followed the faint scraping sound coming from the dining room.

He grabbed the railing and climbed the three stairs to that level, then rounded the corner. The large crystal chandelier's light filled the room. A radio sat in one corner of the bare floor. Strains of classical music drifted toward him. Holly had pushed a drop cloth close to one wall. A piece of plywood resting on two sawhorses gave her a large work space. There were bottles and brushes, a few cans and a spatula. He took all that in quickly before turning his attention to her.

She stood with her back to him, carefully peeling off strips of wallpaper. She wore jeans that hugged the curves of her hips, rear end and thighs. For a moment he couldn't think about anything but holding her against him. He wanted to trace the curves, cup her softness, touch her, taste her, be with her, in her.

Although he hadn't dated in a while, when he had, he hadn't favored one particular type of woman. He found all their bodies attractive, all their differences intriguing. But looking at Holly, he felt a stirring deep inside, as if she aroused him on a more primal level. He wasn't sure why. She wasn't fashion-model thin, but in his mind that was the best part. He tried not to think about how she would feel on top of him, her breasts spilling into his hands, her legs brushing against his.

He swallowed hard and ignored the pressure between his legs. Holly raised her hand to test the seam of the wallpaper farther up the wall. Her sweatshirt rose a couple of inches, exposing pale white skin and the curve of her waist. He swore silently. If she could destroy his self-control without even trying, he didn't want to know what she could accomplish when she put her mind to it. Heaven help them both.

"Hi," he said.

She spun toward him. The spatula went clattering to the floor, and she covered her cheeks with her hands. Her blue eyes widened. "I didn't hear you," she said breathlessly.

"Sorry. I didn't mean to scare you." He motioned to the wall. "What are you doing here?"

She turned her attention to the wall, staring at it blankly as if she had no idea what it meant. In the few moments before she spoke, Jordan studied her profile.

She had a small nose and full lips. Freckles dotted her cheeks and nose. Her thick hair had been pulled back into a ponytail that hung to the middle of her back. He did his best not to notice the thrust of her breasts. He didn't want to be in more trouble than he was. Life would be a lot easier if he could remember what he'd said or done to upset her.

"This is the dining room," she said at last. "I'm working on the wallpaper. I use these chemicals instead of a steamer because I don't know what's underneath. They didn't use the same kind of building materials seventy years ago. I brought home some wallpaper books for you to look at. There are two ways to go. There are reprints of original wallpaper or Victorian-inspired prints.''

She gave him a quick look, then returned her attention to the wall. ''I think you'd be happier with a Victorian-inspired print. The reproductions are often too busy for contemporary tastes. Also, you've got a chair rail running around the room.'' She touched the molding about three feet off the ground. ''You could paint under the chair rail, then use paper above it. That's not how many of the Victorians did things, but it looks nice. I'm not sure how authentic you want the rooms. For most people it's a compromise between the flavor of the period and what they can actually live with.''

She paused to take a breath. He realized she was babbling, and hoped that was a good sign. She seemed more nervous than angry. He moved closer, then leaned against the doorjamb to steady himself.

''I don't want to talk about the dining room,'' he said. ''I want to talk about why you're avoiding me.''

She gasped softly and ducked her head. He could see the color climbing her cheeks. ''You know why.''

At least she'd admitted it. That was something. ''Holly, I don't—''

She cut him off with a wave of her hand. ''I understand.''

''No, you don't.''

''I do. It's silly, really. My only excuse is that while my mother was ill, I took care of her. One of the nurses told me once that chronically ill people don't have much human contact. Oh, they're bathed and fed, but no one touches them just because. They need that contact. It keeps them connected and feeling alive. I did that for years. I guess it's a habit.''

She turned her attention from the wall to him. Her mouth twisted. "Pretty stupid, huh, but I swear it's the truth."

"I appreciate your honesty, but I don't know what the hell you're talking about. What exactly are you apologizing for?"

Her mouth opened and closed a couple of times before she got the words out. "You want me to *say it?*"

"If it's not too much trouble." At her look of incredulity, he shrugged. "I had a fever last night. I don't remember what happened."

"You don't remember?" Her voice rose in volume and pitch. She spun on her heel and began to pace the room. "He doesn't remember. I don't sleep the whole night, and he doesn't remember. Great. Just perfect. I knew it. I'm not ready to be out in the world. This proves it. I should have become a nun."

When she passed in front of him, he grabbed her arm and held her in place. "Would you please tell me what you're talking about?"

She drew in a deep breath. "You had a fever. I was trying to cool you off."

"So?"

"I was…touching you."

Where? For how long? Had she liked it? He was sure he had. His blood heated on cue and headed south. He released her arm, but she didn't move away. "And?"

"And, that's it. I used a washcloth and wiped off your face and chest." Her gaze lowered to the floor.

"Wish I'd been conscious," he muttered.

"What?"

"Nothing. I appreciate the concern and the effort. So what's the problem?"

She linked her fingers together in front of her stomach,

then released them. "You were sort of asleep and then you woke up."

Now it was Jordan's turn to be embarrassed. Had he made a pass at her or worse, although he wasn't sure what would be worse. Maybe he'd flashed her.

"And," he prompted.

"And, well, you said I was the touchingest nurse you'd ever been around."

"And?"

"What do you mean 'and?' Isn't that enough? You said if you didn't know better, you would think I was making a pass at you."

He searched his brain for some other meaning to her words. "I don't think I understand."

"I was *touching* you," she shrieked.

"What's the problem? I happen to like you touching me."

She gave a strangled moan and sank slowly to the floor. After drawing her knees to her chest, she lowered her head until he couldn't see her face. "I just want to die."

Jordan tried to crouch next to her, but it hurt too much. Awkwardly he lowered himself to the floor and braced his sore back against the wall.

"I'm really sorry," Holly murmured. "It's really all because of my mom. I was just so used to taking care of her that I—" She paused and looked at him. "I said this already, huh?"

"Yeah."

She nodded. "I just didn't want you to think…" Her voice trailed off.

"Think what?"

She shook her head as if indicating she couldn't speak. Jordan tried to understand her state of mind, but he didn't know what the big deal was. So she'd touched him. So he'd commented on the fact. It was hardly a hanging offense.

He stretched his legs out in front of him, then winced as the injured muscles protested. He placed his palm on her arm, then slid down until his hand was over hers. That seemed to give her courage.

"I didn't want you to think I was coming on to you," she said. "That never crossed my mind."

"Bummer."

"What?" She stared at him as if he'd grown a second head. "You can't be serious."

"Why not? I'd love to have you come on to me." He tugged on her hand until she relaxed enough to let him lace his fingers with hers, then he rested their joined hands on his left thigh.

She stared at him. "But I'm… But you're…" She shook her head. "You're teasing me, right?"

"Nope."

"But I'm not sexy. I don't even know how to be sexy. I'm inexperienced to the point of being stupid around men, and I'm fifteen pounds overweight."

He forced himself to keep staring at her face when what he really wanted to do was drop his gaze to her breasts. "Don't you dare lose a pound. You're perfect."

Conflicting emotions raced through her eyes. He could see she wanted to believe him but she didn't dare. Jordan frowned. Why didn't Holly know she had the ability to turn him on? Had someone hurt her that badly? Animal rage surged inside him. If a man had caused her to doubt herself, he would find him and punish him.

"Wow," she said. "That was pretty amazing."

"What?"

She shrugged. "Your family mentioned you were the brooding one in the group. I didn't believe them. You've always been so friendly. But just now you got this look on your face.''

''Sorry. I was thinking about something else.''

''I could tell.'' She stared at him. ''Do you really brood?''

''Sometimes.'' But not around Holly. When he was with her, he forgot about being on the outside looking in. With her, he belonged.

Warning lights began to flash, but he ignored them. He knew his friendship with Holly was dangerous, but he was willing to risk it. After all, it was just temporary. When she could afford her own place, she would move out and disappear from his life. So it was safe to enjoy the short time they had together.

She shifted and sat cross-legged. His knees hurt just thinking about trying that position.

''Jordan, do you really think I'm sexy?'' She shook her head. ''Sorry. I shouldn't have asked. I'm not fishing for compliments. I've just never thought of myself that way. I've never been involved with a man, so I don't know how they think.''

It took every ounce of self-control not to pull his hand free of hers. Jordan sat very still, trying to absorb what Holly had just said. She'd never been involved with a man. No way could she mean that. He'd suspected she was innocent, but not *that* innocent.

''By 'never,' you mean less than ten or something, right?'' he asked desperately.

She stared solemnly. '' 'Never' as in 'none.' I had a boyfriend when I was fifteen. That lasted for a couple of months. He even kissed me a few times, but it wasn't anything like when you and I did.'' Her voice got lower and lower. ''Then my mom was diagnosed with the cancer, and

I didn't have a lot of extra time to spend with him. He didn't understand.''

"Teenage boys are notoriously selfish," he said. "I know. I was one once." He shifted his hand so he could brush his thumb back and forth across her palm.

She smiled at him. "I tried to understand. In my head it made sense. We were both young. He wanted to have fun. There was this dance, and I was supposed to go with him. But my mom was just out of the hospital. I was scared she was going to die. I didn't want to leave her alone, so I told him I couldn't go."

He could hear the pain in her words. Jordan released her hand and draped his arm around her shoulders. At first she stiffened, then slowly she relaxed against him. Her head rested on his chest.

"He took someone else," he said quietly.

She nodded. "This girl. Colette. Can you imagine a fifteen-year-old named Colette? I blamed her because that was easier than facing the truth. After the dance he stopped calling me. We never went out again."

He rested his chin on the top of her head and ignored the heat from her hand resting on his thigh. "Who was next?"

She sniffed. "No one. That's the entire story of my love life. Pretty pathetic, huh?"

"You didn't date?"

"I tried, but not a lot of single guys came into the antique store. I went to the local junior college, but I didn't have extra time to socialize. Just when I thought it was all going to be okay, the cancer came back."

"I'm sorry," he murmured.

"Thanks. I'm fine with most of it. Mom and I never wasted time with each other. We got to say goodbye. A lot of people don't get that chance. I do regret how I grew up. I had to do it fast, and I missed out on a lot of stuff like dating.''

It was worse than he'd thought. If she'd only dated one guy when she was fifteen, then she was a virgin. He winced at the word. So much for a quick affair. He wasn't usually the type, but he would have made an exception for Holly. Now he couldn't. She was too innocent.

''You're twenty-eight?'' he asked.

''Twenty-eight and never been kissed.'' She laughed and glanced up at him. ''Well, I've been kissed, but I've never done anything else. I've never even seen a man naked.''

She squeezed her eyes shut and ducked her head. ''Oh, my, I can't believe I said that.''

Jordan was having a little trouble with it, too. He was torn between running for cover and volunteering his services. Between the subject matter of their conversation and her nearness, he could give her an eyeful. Hell of a time to develop a conscience.

''What are your plans?'' he asked. ''Find some nice guy, get married and have a couple of kids?''

''I'd like to, but I don't think it's going to happen. I haven't had great luck with relationships.''

''One relationship isn't enough to judge.''

She straightened and looked at him. ''That's a kind of luck. Relationships require trust, and I'm not very good at that.''

''You had a good one with your mom.''

She smiled. ''It's hardly the same thing, but yes, we did have fun together. When she was feeling well, she used to take me places. We got great at having a good time with no money. We went to exhibits and parks. The free day at the zoo.''

A single strand of hair slipped onto her cheek. Holly brushed it away impatiently. ''She used to take all the holidays seriously. Half the garage was filled with decorations. Not just for Christmas, but for all of them. We had painted pumpkins for Halloween, decorated flags for May Day, stuffed hearts for Valentine's. On her last Christmas she gave me Mistletoe.''

It was as if the cat heard her name. The gray, flat-faced spawn of the devil strolled into the dining room. Her belly hung low, and she walked with a rolling gait.

"Hi, sweetie," Holly cooed as she reached out to pet her cat. Mistletoe sat down to accept the attention. As she purred, she glared at Jordan.

"That cat hates me," he muttered.

"I don't know why. She's normally very friendly."

"Sure. That's why she spends the afternoon spitting at me."

"She does not."

"Sure, she does. She knows exactly when I'm nearly asleep, and she comes in and hisses. Once I'm awake, she leaves." He glared back at the cat.

"She really likes Kyle."

"That proves my point."

Holly laughed.

Mistletoe rose to her feet and gave a quick *pftt* before heading out. As she passed by Jordan's feet, she swiped out with her right front paw. He pulled back just in time to avoid being skewered.

Mistletoe raised her tail to a saucy angle and sauntered out of the room.

"She's a miserable animal. I hope she doesn't pass her personality on to her kittens."

"She's sweet," Holly protested. She stared after her cat. "But I have to admit, she doesn't like you much." She smiled at him. "So I'm even more grateful that you let me bring her with me. And thanks for letting me be here, too.

I don't want you to think I'm going to be in the way for the holiday stuff.''

"You won't be in the way. The family is huge and one more only means more fun.''

"Thanks. Work keeps me busy during the day, but nights are hard. Especially at this time of year. Okay, okay, enough emotion. I don't want to get all weird and cry or embarrass you.''

"I don't embarrass that easy.''

"I do.''

"I noticed.''

She glanced at him out of the corner of her eye. "So you're not mad at me anymore?''

"I was never mad. Just confused.'' He leaned over and kissed her forehead. He wanted to do a whole lot more, but that seemed the safest at the moment. "Friends?''

"I'd like that.'' She scrambled to her feet. "So what do you think about the wallpaper?''

As she discussed his various options, he thought about all she'd told him. She'd been alone for a long time. Even before her mother had died, Holly had been responsible for too much. He couldn't change her past, but he could give her a Christmas to remember. He vowed then to make that dream come true.

Chapter Eight

Holly glanced around her store in amazement. She and her mother had often talked about what they wanted A Victorian Parlor to be. They'd discussed the separate rooms, a formal parlor set up in the front, alcoves of decorative items, paintings, several tables with wallpaper and fabric samples. Furniture was scattered throughout the store, but the majority of it was in the huge room to the rear. As they'd planned, she'd filled the store with soft lighting and homey scents. From the moment she'd put the sign up and opened her doors, business had been good. In the past couple of weeks it had become spectacular, and she knew exactly who was responsible. Jordan.

Even on a Thursday afternoon the shop was crowded. Women clustered together in groups and cooed over the ornaments displayed on several Christmas trees. Her wreath inventory was down by half. If business kept up at this pace, she would sell out before Christmas. She was thrilled about all the sales.

In order to keep prices down, she'd bought in as high a quantity as she could afford. The purchases had drained her financial reserves to zero. When she'd worried about making a wrong decision, she'd consoled herself with the fact that the Christmas items wouldn't spoil. What she didn't sell this year, she would sell next. In fact, part of her plan had been to buy two years' worth of inventory. Instead, she was selling it all in one year.

The front door opened, and a handsome couple walked in. The man was tall, maybe six feet four, with dark hair and an earring glinting from his ear. He looked dangerous, the kind of man who was deadly to women and their hearts. The woman also had dark hair, but hers was curly and long, nearly to her waist. She was slender and dressed in a wool jumper over a long-sleeved white blouse.

Holly studied them for a moment and realized she'd seen them when she'd first visited Jordan in the hospital.

The woman caught her eye and smiled, then started in her direction. She glanced at the tag on Holly's apron.

"You must be Holly. I recognized you from Elizabeth's description," she said. "I'm Rebecca Lucas, and this is my husband, Austin."

The three of them shook hands.

"Thanks for stopping by," Holly said, then motioned around the store. "Are you looking for anything in particular, or do you want to browse?"

Rebecca glanced at her husband. "You want to run for the hills, don't you?"

Austin shifted his weight from foot to foot. "Too much girl stuff. And it smells weird in here."

Holly laughed. "Most men feel that way. If you head toward the back and through the room with the furniture, you'll find an alcove with coffee, a couple of chairs and a TV. Most of the husbands hide out there.''

"Go on," Rebecca urged. "I want to get some decorations for the house and have a chat with Holly."

Austin looked at his wife for a moment. Holly saw a flash of love so bright, it nearly brought tears to her eyes. He touched Rebecca's face. The tender gesture was at odds with his dark and dangerous appearance. Then he turned and headed for the back room.

Rebecca stared after him. "I know what you're thinking. I used to picture him as a pirate and wish he'd kidnap me and hide me on his desert island. But behind that tough exterior is a very gentle man."

"If you say so," Holly murmured, wondering how someone as innocent looking as Rebecca had tamed such a hard man. She pushed the thought from her mind. "Do you want something particular for your house?"

Rebecca tilted her head. "Elizabeth told me your wreaths were beautiful. I'd like a couple for the foyer. And maybe some ornaments for the tree."

"The wreaths are on all the walls. Everything I have is out. Do you have a particular theme? I have angel wreaths, toy wreaths, some with fruit, plain, fancy, whatever you're looking for."

Rebecca laughed. "I'm not organized enough to have a theme. I just want something pretty." She glanced around at the crowded store. "You've got plenty of other customers. Go ahead and help them while I look around."

Holly saw a couple heading for the cash register, so she excused herself. For the next half hour she rang up purchases and wrapped delicate ornaments. Then the crowd faded. Holly saw Rebecca talking to another couple. Even if they hadn't introduced themselves, she would have recognized the man as pure Haynes. He had the tall, dark good looks of all the brothers. There was a bit of gray at his temples, a few more lines, so Holly guessed he was the oldest. She was right. Craig and his petite redheaded wife, Jill, were in town for a few days.

Rebecca saw her and motioned her over. "Have you met these two?"

Holly nodded. "They introduced themselves when they first came in." She smiled at Jill. "When's the baby due?"

Jill touched her rounding belly. "May. I wish it were tomorrow. I remind myself she'll be worth it, but the waiting is hard."

"I remember how that feels," Rebecca said. "Are the boys excited about getting a sister?"

"Very," Jill said. "Danny is so thrilled he won't be the youngest anymore." She leaned against her husband, who wrapped his arm around her shoulders.

Holly ignored the flicker of envy that filled her. Holidays were the worst, she told herself. Since her mother had died, she'd really felt alone at Christmas. But soon it would be the first of the year, and everything would return to normal.

"You had the test to determine gender?" Holly asked.

Craig and his wife exchanged a glance. "Not exactly," Jill said. "It's sort of a family thing."

"There hadn't been a girl born to the Haynes family in four generations," Craig said. "I'm one of four brothers, my father is one of six and so on. We figured we couldn't have girls."

Rebecca brushed her long dark hair off her shoulder and smiled. "Then Travis married Elizabeth, and they had a girl. Everyone was stunned. Next Kyle and Sandy had a daughter. Jordan is the one who came up with the theory."

"What theory?" Holly asked.

Jill sighed. "It's very romantic. Haynes men have a

daughter when they're in love. If they're not, they just have boys.''

"So if you want to have a boy, you have to have a fight first?'' Holly asked.

Craig chuckled. "I don't think that would work. We'd still be in love. So Jill's convinced it's a girl. So far, the ultrasound is proving the theory correct. I guess we'll find out in May.''

"Not being married to one of the Haynes brothers,'' Rebecca said, ''I'm free to have a child of either gender.''

Holly wondered if the theory was true. But that didn't make sense. There were four brothers. Did that mean their father had never loved their mother? She thought about asking, then figured this wasn't the time. Maybe later she would discuss it with Jordan.

Craig and Jill had completed their shopping. Holly rang up their purchases, then wrapped everything. Craig collected the packages.

"Louise has our phone number,'' he said. "Call us if you need anything.''

Jill gave her a quick hug, then laughed when Holly bent to avoid her belly. "I know, I'm getting bigger every day. I'm so pleased Jordan's found you.''

Holly didn't know what to say. She walked to the front door and held it open. When they were gone, she turned and saw Rebecca leaning on the counter staring at her.

"Is something wrong?'' Holly asked, touching a hand to her hair and hoping she hadn't smudged her cheek.

"No. Everything is exactly right. I had wondered what it was about you that Jordan liked. Now I understand.''

Holly felt herself flush. She glanced around the store and was relieved when she realized most of the customers had left. There were a few browsing in the other rooms, but she and Rebecca were the only people up front.

"He doesn't exactly like me." Hmm, that wasn't right. "What I mean is we're just friends. I'm staying with him to help him fix the house."

Rebecca raised her eyebrows. "So you are living together. Elizabeth told me you were, but I didn't believe her. Imagine Jordan letting a woman into his house."

"But it's not like that."

"Then why are you blushing?"

"Because I—" Holly clamped her mouth shut. She was only making it worse.

Rebecca shook her head. "I'm teasing you, Holly, and I shouldn't. I was just as tongue-tied when I was first around Austin. There's something about the men they grow here. I wish I could tell you it gets better, but it doesn't. Austin still has the power to make me feel clumsy and foolish, but he's too sweet to use it. Instead, he makes me feel beautiful and loved."

The sharp jab of envy returned, this time stabbing a little deeper. Holly wouldn't mind feeling that way once in a while. But it wasn't to be. She'd chosen her path a long time ago. Love required trust, and too many people had let her down for her to ever take that leap of faith again.

She glanced out the front window and saw Craig tenderly helping his pregnant wife into the car. Concern and affection filled every gesture. She wished it could have been different for herself. She wanted too much.

"But it's not like that," Holly said as she walked to the counter. "We really are just friends." And sometimes she wasn't sure about that. So many things confused her. The way his kiss had made her feel, the passion—at least, she *thought* it was passion—that had flared between them. Her embarrassment when he'd pointed out how much she touched him while he was ill, then the gentle way he'd tried to make her feel better. She still remembered the feel of his arms around her. She didn't know what to think.

Rebecca stretched out her arm and rested her hand on top of Holly's. "I'm teasing you, and that's not fair. I know how difficult it is in the beginning. The family is overwhelming."

"But wonderful. Everyone has come in to buy things. Even you and Austin." Holly frowned. "He's really not related?"

Rebecca shook her head. "They all met when Austin and Travis were in junior high. Austin was a bully, but the Haynes family gave him a place to belong. It's what those brothers do best."

She glanced around as if checking to make sure they were alone, then lowered her voice conspiratorially. "I'll tell you a secret. They didn't grow up in a very happy home, and they learned early on to depend only on each other. They all wanted a loving wife and family, but it seemed beyond them. They tried relationships and failed. Each of them gave up, resigned to living alone. But they were wrong." Rebecca smiled. "First Travis found Elizabeth, then Kyle courted Sandy. Just last year Jill dropped into Craig's life. It's not that the Haynes brothers didn't know how to love—it's that they hadn't met the right woman."

Holly backed up a step. "I'm not the right woman."

Rebecca studied her for a moment. "Too bad, because you'll never find another man like Jordan or another family like this one. They'll take you in and love you until you never have to be afraid again."

"I'm not afraid," Holly said quickly, then wondered why she bothered to lie. Of course she was afraid. Sometimes she was afraid she would die of the loneliness.

"My mistake," Rebecca said lightly. "I thought you

might want something special with Jordan. It's fine that you don't, but do me a favor. Don't break his heart.''

''He's not interested in me that way.'' Holly glanced down at herself. The long apron she wore only emphasized her wide hips. ''I'm not his type.''

Rebecca's smile widened. ''Aren't you?''

Before Holly could say anything else, Austin came out of the back room and wanted to know if they were going to live there permanently. Rebecca laughed, then pointed to half a dozen wreaths she wanted to buy. Austin got them down, then collected the ornaments she indicated she liked.

As Holly wrote up the order, she had to clench her jaw muscles to keep her mouth from hanging open. Somewhere she'd heard a rumor that Austin and Rebecca were wealthy. They'd just bought more in a few minutes than any three other customers combined. She frowned. That wasn't true. All the Haynes family members had bought a lot.

A warm feeling stole over her. Her stay in Jordan's house was temporary, as was her connection with his relatives. Because she was part of Jordan's life, they were including her. She realized she should enjoy the time while it lasted and give back with the same generous spirit. She had much to be grateful for. It was almost Christmas, and this year she wasn't going to be alone.

Jordan dipped his brush in the can of paint, then straightened. Every muscle in his legs complained.

''I heard that,'' Holly said without looking at him. ''You're doing too much.''

''I'm fine.''

''And a liar.''

He grinned. ''Okay, that too. I'll finish this door frame, then I'll quit for the night.''

"Good. If you have a relapse, your relatives will blame me."

He glanced at her. She was sitting cross-legged on the floor. She wore tight jeans that outlined every generous curve and an old sweatshirt that had faded to a misty gray. Her long blond hair had been pulled back in a braid to protect it from the paint that splattered the front of her clothing.

She wielded a paint brush and roller with the speed and finesse of an expert. In one short week his dining room had been transformed. The floors had been in better shape than either of them had realized. Someone had coated them with wax. Once the buildup was removed, the natural beauty of the hardwood shone through. The old wallpaper was gone. The ceiling had been painted creamy white, and next week Holly would hang the new wallpaper. He had taken her suggestion and used the chair rail as a dividing line in the large room. The bottom would be painted colonial blue. Holly was doing that now. The top would be papered. It wasn't authentic, but it fit the shape and function of the room.

"I called about the furniture," Jordan said. He was in charge of painting door frames to match the ceiling and the chair rails. "It will be here in a week."

She looked at him over her shoulder. "Great. Just in time for Christmas."

The chandelier illuminated her features. She'd gotten into the habit of washing off her makeup when she came home from work. He could see the freckles sprinkled on her nose and the tops of her cheeks.

"Speaking of which," she said, "are you going to get a tree?"

"Sure. Sunday. It's the annual Haynes family Christmas-tree hunt."

Her eyebrows drew together. "How do you hunt Christmas trees? They can't run away."

"It's what we call it. Just the men and the kids. We leave women folk at home."

"Sounds odd, but okay." She ran her roller across the paint pan, then returned her attention to the wall. "I've put aside a few ornaments from the store. I'd like to contribute them to the decorating."

"I'd like that," he said. "I always chop down a big tree, then it looks sort of bare and I have to feel sorry for it."

She shifted until she was on her knees, then worked the roller back and forth, smoothing on paint evenly. "I hope you don't plan to do your own chopping."

It was making him hurt just watching her paint. "Doubtful. I'll get one of my brothers to do it."

"Speaking of them, Craig, Austin and their wives were in the store today. In the last couple of weeks half the town has been by to stock up on Christmas supplies. This is going to be my best month yet." She gave him a shy smile. "I know I have you to thank for that."

He shrugged. "I made a few phone calls. No big deal." There was a light in her eyes that made him feel uncomfortable. He hadn't done anything special.

"It is a big deal, and I appreciate the business. I'm keeping my fingers crossed that they came to the shop as a favor to you, but that they really liked what they saw so they'll come back again because they want to."

Jordan put down the paint brush and stretched.

"How are you feeling?" she asked.

"Sore but better. I'm more mobile. I was up most of yesterday, and there aren't any repercussions today. If I continue to heal, I'll be back at the fire station by the first of the year."

"Do you miss work?"

"Yeah. I like my job."

"Me, too." She smiled.

He bent down and picked up the brush he was using and returned his attention to the door frame. They worked well together. There was just the right amount of conversation, sprinkled with laughter. He didn't have to think when he was with her. He considered telling her that, but didn't think she would appreciate the news or view it as a compliment.

"It will be nice to be here for the holidays," Holly said. "Thanks for including me."

"You're no trouble at all."

Before he could say anything else, Louise walked in with a couple of sodas. "I've got to leave for my class," she said. "I brought you these."

He took the cola drink she offered him. "Thanks."

Her eyebrows arched in surprise. "You're welcome."

"You're the best," Holly said, and popped the top on her diet soda.

"I finished the salad," Louise said. "The steaks are ready to go on any time you want to cook them, and the baked potatoes are washed." She addressed her comments to Holly, but kept glancing at him.

Jordan understood her wariness. Since Holly had moved in, he'd made an effort to be polite to Louise. It was an armed truce. He needed the housekeeper to stay, because she made Holly's presence possible. Louise was their chaperon. If she left, Holly would go, too. He didn't want that. He figured he should probably be smart enough to figure out why, but he didn't want to have to think about it. He only knew that he liked having Holly around. If the price of that was civil conversation with Louise, he would gladly pay.

As much as he hated to admit it, sometimes he forgot he wasn't supposed to like Louise. The older woman was funny and great at her job. She genuinely cared about his family. He wondered how much of that came from guilt. If he let himself forget the past, he could be friends with her, but he wasn't willing to do that yet.

"Enjoy your class," he said.

Louise gave him another puzzled look, then left.

Jordan finished the door frame about the same time Holly finished the first coat of blue paint. She stood up and surveyed her work.

"It's going to be stunning," she said. "The colonial blue is just the right color." She glanced at her watch. "You hungry?"

"Starved."

"Let's go fix dinner."

He followed her into the kitchen. He liked watching the sway of her hips as she walked. The feminine motion appealed to him on a basic level. It was tough to hang back and be polite when all he really wanted to do was haul her close and have his way with her right there on the hall floor.

When they entered the kitchen, there were stacks of cookie sheets in the sink.

"Louise has started baking," Holly said as she studied the counter. She pointed to a foil-covered dish. "Samples for dessert. I can't wait."

"Louise bakes every year for Christmas. It's a tradition."

She pointed to one of the chairs by the kitchen table. He sank down and relaxed, letting the pain ease out of him. Holly worked quickly. In the past couple of weeks she'd become familiar with the kitchen.

"My Mom used to make cookies, too," she said as she

pricked the potatoes with a fork and set them on a dinner plate. "I think they were sugar cookies. You know, the kind you can decorate. I was in charge of the icing." She leaned against the tile counter and smiled. "I used to get more on my clothes and eat more than ever got on the cookies. She always did special stuff like that with me. We had a lot of fun."

A single strand of blond hair fluttered near her cheek. She brushed it away slowly. Her blue eyes were large and thoughtful, focusing on a past he could only imagine.

"What other traditions did you have?" he asked.

"She used to fill a stocking for me. I loved it. There wasn't anything expensive. Oranges, those chocolate kisses, pens for school, adhesive tape." She looked at him. "What is it about kids and sticky stuff?"

"I'm not sure, but they do love it."

"We always had a real tree. It wasn't very big, but it was beautiful, especially at night, with the lights."

"Did you ever see your father at the holidays?"

Instantly her face changed. All emotion faded, along with her color. Her mouth straightened, and she folded her arms over her chest.

"I met him once," she said. "It was about six years ago. My mother was very ill, and the expenses were enormous. I knew who he was. He has a lot of money. I thought maybe—" She swallowed. "I went to see him to ask him if he could help with the medical bills. He said no and that I shouldn't bother him again."

Hurt hovered around her like fire. He could see it burning away her self-control. He ached *for* her. "I'm sorry."

"Don't be." She shrugged. "It's no big deal. I didn't care on my behalf. I was worried about my mom. I didn't want her to know I'd gone there or that he'd turned me down."

Jordan glanced at his lap and was surprised to see his hands curled into tight fists. Consciously he relaxed. Holly's father was a first-class bastard, and he would like nothing more than to teach him the price of hurting his own daughter. Holly might claim not to feel pain, but he could see it and feel it radiating from her. She raised her chin slightly and blinked. He realized she was fighting tears.

"I suppose it's silly," she said, her voice thickening. "But he never said anything about being my father. I thought he would. I guess I wanted him to acknowledge me. But he didn't say a word."

Jordan stood up and crossed the linoleum floor. When he was in front of her, he held out his arms, inviting her to find comfort with him. He didn't touch her, somehow sensing the decision had to be hers.

She hesitated for a moment, then threw herself against him. Her hands clawed at his sweatshirt, and her face pressed against his chest. A sob shook her, then another. He held her close.

"It was so h-horrible," she said, the words muffled and broken. "I just stood there staring at him. I could s-see we even sort of looked alike. But he didn't say anything. He didn't care about her, and he d-didn't care about me. I thought fathers were supposed to love their children."

Jordan thought about his father. "They are, but not all of them do."

He cupped the back of her head and ran his other hand up and down her spine, all the while murmuring soothingly. He ached for her. It wasn't a physical pain like he had from his injuries. This was down to his soul and into the blackness. It was a hungry pain of loss and emptiness, of forgotten promises and broken dreams. The depth and intensity stunned him. Most of the time he was able to disconnect from everyone else. He was used to not feeling much at all.

When her sobs lessened, he kissed her cheek and brushed the tears from her skin. She continued to cling to him, and he continued to hold her. He knew he was supposed to be comforting her, but there was something soothing and welcoming in her warmth. He tried to ignore the way her breasts flattened against his chest and her thighs brushed his.

She sniffed a couple of times. ''I must look horrible,'' she murmured. ''I always do when I cry. My eyes get puffy, and my nose gets red.''

''I think it's cute.''

She laughed, then stepped away from him. ''Thanks, Jordan. I appreciate it.'' She cleared her throat. ''I want to go take a shower. Would you mind if we put off dinner for a half hour or so?''

''That's fine.''

She nodded, then started for the door. He called after her, ''Holly, your secret is safe with me.''

She glanced at him. ''I know. You're a good friend.'' Then she left the room.

He stared after her in equal parts of pleasure and annoyance. He was pleased that she trusted him to hold her and keep her secrets safe. After all, he was a master at keeping secrets. But he didn't like her thinking of him as a friend.

How else should she think of you? a voice in his head asked mockingly.

Jordan didn't have an answer for that. He didn't want a relationship; at least, that was the story he always told himself. He knew firsthand the dangers involved. But a flicker of need inside warned him letting Holly go wasn't going to be as easy as he'd first thought.

Chapter Nine

Holly smoothed the oversize sweater, then reached for the towel on her head. When she pulled it loose, her wet hair tumbled onto her shoulders. She stared at herself in the mirror, then shook her head.

It didn't matter that she'd spent several minutes splashing cold water on her face. She still looked puffy and red eyed. It was obvious she'd been crying.

She should have changed the subject, she told herself. She could talk about her mother and their holiday traditions, and she could talk about that ill-fated trip to visit her father, but she couldn't talk about them together. Every time she thought about what that man had said, how cruel he'd been, she got so mad and so hurt for her mother that she…

Tears burned, but this time she blinked them away. She wasn't going to cry any more. She was supposed to be here looking after Jordan, but every time she turned around, he was taking care of her.

She reached for her brush and began the slow process of untangling her hair. When that was done, she plugged in the blow dryer, then bent over at the waist and started drying her hair. The low, steady roar of the machine was soothingly familiar. She cleared her mind of unpleasant thoughts and resolved only to think about nice things for the rest of the evening.

That was easy, she thought with a smile. She would focus on Jordan. A delicious, sensual shiver went through her as she remembered what it had been like when he'd held her. She knew he'd meant it as a comforting gesture. But she'd liked the feel of his arms around her. She'd felt safe and comforted at the same time. He was strong yet gentle. Usually she didn't show a lot of herself to other people. She didn't have much experience with relationships, even friendship, and her awkwardness made her wary. But around him, she forgot to be afraid.

Very out of character, she told herself as she straightened and began to dry the front of her hair. But then several family members had told her that Jordan was a brooding loner, and she'd never seen that part of him. Maybe they were different with each other than they were with the rest of the world. Maybe the odd circumstances allowed them to let go of the barriers normally in place. She would like to believe Jordan thought of her as special, even though she knew she was fooling herself. He probably had dozens of women in his life. He wouldn't have time for her.

Then why aren't any of those women here? a voice in her head asked.

Holly didn't have an answer for that. She didn't want to think about it, either. If she allowed herself to hope, she would end up being disappointed, or worse, hurt. She didn't want to do that. Besides, there was no point in wishing for a romantic relationship when she wasn't willing to commit to one.

Something warm rubbed against her leg. She glanced down and saw Mistletoe.

"We always want what we can't have," she said, then turned the blow dryer to warm and patted the counter.

Mistletoe was huge, with her wide belly hanging low. The cat couldn't make the jump to the counter easily, so she jumped onto the toilet, then stepped across. When she stretched out by the sink, Holly petted her soft fur.

"How's my pretty girl? Are you enjoying this big house?"

Mistletoe purred. Her wide, flat face and green irises made her look wise. Her eyes closed in pleasure as Holly pointed the blow dryer at the cat's coat.

Mistletoe loved the heat of the machine. She could lie there for hours being warmed and petted. Her purr rumbled as low as the motor. Holly felt the vibrations through her fingers. She turned the dryer off after a few minutes. Mistletoe bumped her fingers with her damp nose as if asking for more.

"Wait until you have your babies," Holly said.

Mistletoe stretched, then rested her head on her front paws, as if she intended to nap on the counter.

"Fine by me," Holly said. She glanced in the mirror. Her nose was still red, but some of the puffiness had gone down around her eyes. Her hair wasn't completely dry, but that always took forever. She pulled it back into a loose ponytail and walked out of the bathroom. First she would check on Jordan, then she would finish dinner.

As she approached the study, she heard a muffled curse. When she walked in the room, Jordan was pacing shirtless.

He held his right arm close to his chest. Lines of pain stretched from his nose to his mouth.

"What's wrong?" she asked as she hurried to his side.

"I painted the baseboards. At least, I started to. Then this muscle seized up in my back." He tried to straighten his arm, then grimaced.

Holly walked behind him. She touched him by his shoulder blade and felt the large knot of muscles. "I used to massage my mother," she said. "Do you want me to try and do you?"

He turned so he was facing her. "I'm in too much pain to be done," he said, then grimaced.

She stared at him blankly. "You don't want me to rub your back?"

"Yeah, that would be great."

"Then why did you say—"

He cut her off with a shake of his head. "Joke. Bad timing. Forget it." He glanced around the room. "Where do you want me?"

"Lie down on the bed." As soon as she said the words, she started to get embarrassed. Thankfully he did as she asked without looking at her first.

She went into the bathroom by his room and found a bottle of body lotion. As she returned, she tried not to notice how he looked wearing jeans and nothing else, stretched out on clean white sheets. Her insides felt funny, as if they were being jolted by a slight electric shock. She wore socks but not shoes, and she couldn't stop her toes from curling.

He was hurt, she reminded herself. He was in pain and he needed help. This was medicinal. She wanted to heal, not indulge in some bizarre fantasy.

She approached the bed slowly. His eyes were closed,

and a dark lock of hair fell across his forehead. A twitch by his mouth was the only indication of his pain.

She sat on the edge of the bed and uncapped the lotion. After pouring some in her palm, she shifted so she was facing his back and touched her hands to his skin.

He was hotter than she'd expected. While she worked at the knotted muscles, part of her mind stood back and noted differences. Her mother's skin had been thin, her back more narrow, her muscles easily manipulated. Jordan was pure male in his prime. Lean ropes of strength challenged her trained fingers. She pressed her palms against the tightness, trying to force the lactic acid out, and with it, the pain.

She leaned toward him, using her body weight to increase the pressure. Her conscience split in two. One side was the nurse, noting the slight relaxing of tension in his body. That portion of her allowed her to straddle his narrow hips so she was able to put more pressure into her massage. The other part of her, the shy, inexperienced woman, was shrieking at what was going on. She couldn't believe she was doing this, on his bed, in his room, with nothing but a few layers of clothing between them.

As she worked, moving slowly, starting her strokes low at the small of his back and sliding up, she tried to ignore the curve of his rear pressing intimately against her. She tried to ignore the dryness of her throat and the nearly uncontrollable urge to giggle. She wanted to stand up and scream, *Look at me. I'm touching a man's bare back.* But she doubted Jordan would understand.

She rubbed the knot and found it was much smaller. Jordan groaned. "If I pay you a million dollars, will you promise to never stop?" he asked.

"Do you have a million dollars?"

"Not with me."

"Too bad. I would have promised."

She stretched up until she reached his shoulders and neck. She squeezed the muscles there.

"This is heaven," he murmured. "I haven't felt this good in weeks."

"I aim to please."

"You're doing a damn fine job." He raised his head. "You're also probably getting a cramp in your hands."

She shook out her fingers. They were a little sore. "I'm fine."

"Stop for now," he said. "You can do more later."

"Sure."

She slid off him. Now that she wasn't massaging him, the nurse inside her faded away and she was left with just the woman. Awkwardness returned, and with it a feeling of self-consciousness. She needed to get away from this bed.

But before she could leave, Jordan turned toward her and grabbed her hand. "Don't go."

It wasn't what he said; it was the way he said it. Holly stared at him. The low, throaty sound of his voice vibrated in her ears. Something about the tone or the pitch sparked an answering resonance deep in her soul. *Don't go.* He said it the way she'd always imagined men said it to women. She was immobilized. She felt as if she'd forgotten how to breathe.

A dark light flared in his eyes. Some forbidden spark that tempted her. She wasn't sure what she was being tempted for or with. Their gazes locked. She thought about looking away, but he held her in his spell. The room faded around them. There was nothing in the world but the man in front of her.

"Holly."

He spoke her name as if the sound were precious to him.

She tried to swallow, but nothing was working. It was then that she noticed he was circling her palm with his thumb. Sensations skittered up her arm, diffusing in her chest, then refocusing in her oddly sensitized breasts.

"I want to kiss you," he said, his gaze never leaving hers. "And touch you. If that frightens you, then you can go, now or later. I'm not going to make love to you, though. Not because I don't want to, but because—" He paused, then gave a rueful grin. "I couldn't handle the pressure right now. Maybe when I'm stronger."

She blinked several times, sure she couldn't have heard him correctly. He announced he was going to kiss her and touch her? Just like that? He was talking about sex? And it wasn't even seven o'clock? Was he crazy?

But curiosity and anticipation were stronger than terror. The thought of leaving was quickly pushed aside. She remembered Jordan's last kiss, and definitely wanted to repeat the experience. Most women experimented with the opposite sex while they were still in high school, or at least in college. Holly knew she was backward when it came to the man-woman thing. Even if Jordan hadn't made her blood race and her heart pound, she still would have been tempted to kiss him again.

If nothing else, she trusted him not to hurt her or do something that would make her uncomfortable.

"You're not leaving," he said. "So the idea of kissing me doesn't horrify you?"

Embarrassment forced her to look away. How long were they going to *talk* about it? Couldn't they just do it? She shook her head.

"Good."

He tugged her closer. She resisted and sat straighter.

One corner of his mouth curved up in a smile. "I'm in

a weakened condition. You're going to have to come to me.''

She stared at him uncomprehending.

''I can't sit up,'' he said.

''Oh.'' Then she got it. The muscles in his back. His pain. *''Oh!''* He needed her help. She could do that.

But when she went to lean toward him, she found she *couldn't* do that. It was too bold, too beyond her comfort level. She didn't know what to do.

''Jordan, I can't.''

''Yeah, you can. Kiss me, Holly.''

She stared into his eyes, then allowed herself to get lost in the dark depths. She leaned forward and touched her lips to his.

The hand he was still holding got caught between them, and her wrist bent back. Sharp pain shot up her arm, and she pulled back. It wasn't going to work.

''I'm just not good at this,'' she muttered, and turned away.

''Sure, you are.'' He raised the bed a little, then patted his belly. ''Straddle me like you did when you were giving me a back rub.'' He grinned. ''I'm pretty sure I can stand it.''

She eyed him doubtfully. She might not have ever seen a man naked before, but she knew where all the parts went. If she straddled him, then his…his…she-knew-what would be pressed awfully close to her private parts, and she wasn't sure that was right or even legal. Although the statement about him being able to stand it was confusing. Would it hurt him?

''Never mind,'' Jordan said suddenly. ''Bad idea. Why don't you let me get some rest?''

Now Holly was really confused. What was going on?

One minute he wanted to kiss her, the next he was dismissing her?

Then she looked at him closely and recognized the tension around his mouth. He was embarrassed. She wasn't sure by what, if it was his weakened condition or the fact that he thought she wasn't interested. It didn't matter. Holly's already soft heart melted. She grabbed his hand in both of hers.

"Don't be mad," she said quietly. "I don't mean to be shy, but this is all new to me."

He gazed at her for a minute, then relaxed perceptibly. "Yeah?"

"I swear. Tell me what to do."

His eyes narrowed. "Is this some sort of new-tech nursing technique?"

"I'm sure kissing is considered a breach of professional ethics." Her voice was prim. "I've never heard of it being prescribed for medicinal purposes."

"A guy can always hope."

He smiled and she relaxed. "Tell me what to do."

"Straddle my stomach."

Feeling as coordinated and elegant as a newborn giraffe, she did as he requested. Thank goodness her sweater was loose so he couldn't get a good look at her body. That would be too embarrassing to stand.

"Lean forward," he instructed. "Rest your forearms on the bed."

"But then my—" She glanced down at her breasts. "Then I'll be touching you with my chest."

His smile broadened. "That's the point."

"Oh. Are you sure?"

"Trust me."

She did as he requested. Their faces were inches apart. She could feel his sweet breath fanning her face. Her breasts nestled against his lean strength as if they'd spent their whole lives looking for this one spot to rest.

Holly wasn't quite as comfortable. She didn't know what to do with her hands. She felt as if her butt was sticking up in the air. To make matters worse, every inch of her was tingling and trembling, and she couldn't catch her breath.

"This would have been a whole lot easier when I was sixteen," she murmured.

"Not for me. Back then I was more interested in results than the process itself."

She didn't know what that meant, but before she could ask, he raised his head slightly and kissed her.

It was better than she remembered. His lips were firm and warm as they caressed hers. He brushed against her sensitive skin, awakening the nerve endings and reminding them why they'd been put there.

He opened his mouth. She didn't need urging to follow suit. The anticipation of those few seconds waiting for his tongue to touch hers nearly made her swoon. Suddenly she knew what to do with her hands. She cupped his face and urged him closer. She buried her fingers in his thick dark hair and tried to communicate her need.

He got the message. He invaded her mouth, touching, stroking, tasting, leaving wickedly wonderful sensations in his path. He stole her breath, made her relax against him, made her want more. She squirmed in delight when he drew her lower lip into his mouth and suckled it. The gentle tugging started a chain reaction that coiled all the way to that waiting place between her thighs. Tremors rippled through her.

This wasn't a kiss; it was a life-changing event. She felt herself being pulled under, drowning, and she didn't care. She followed his retreat, invading his mouth, assaulting him as he'd assaulted her. She felt answering shudders in his muscles.

His hands stroked down her back. One played with her hair, while the other discovered the sweet spot where her derriere curved into her legs. He touched that place over and over again. It tickled yet sent hot rivers of feeling through her legs and up her chest.

She wanted to kiss him forever. She liked the hard breadth of his body below hers. She'd been denied physical passion so long, she wasn't sure she would ever get enough.

He reached for the hem of her sweater and tugged it up. Holly broke their kiss. "What are you doing?"

"Nothing."

When the sweater was bunched around her waist, he slipped his fingers under it and began to touch her bare skin.

"You're doing something. I can feel it."

Lines deepened by the corners of his eyes as he smiled faintly. "I don't know what you're talking about."

She wasn't sure she did, either. He traced her spine up to her neck. His soft touch sucked away her strength. She couldn't even protest, not that she wanted to.

He touched her shoulders, then down her sides and over her ribs. Without planning the action, she raised herself slightly. She didn't even know what she'd done until his hands slipped under her, circling around and coming to rest on her breasts.

Large hands cupped her full curves. He didn't move, but just supported their weight against his palms. She closed her eyes and concentrated on the sensations. No man had ever touched her there. Everything was new. The whisper of embarrassment, the tingling, the way her nipples puckered and ached for more of his caress.

Then he began to stroke her. His thumbs swept across the taut peaks. She felt the jolt clear down to her toes. Her arms trembled violently, then strength faded and she collapsed against him.

He didn't give her time to have regrets. He claimed her mouth, sweeping inside, taunting her, tempting her, teasing her until all she could do was cling to him.

She didn't recognize herself anymore. She was painfully alive and aware of her body. She'd never thought about physical pleasure before, and now she couldn't think about anything else.

His hands stroked her back. She was vaguely aware of a slight tugging on her bra, but she ignored it. Jordan could do whatever he wanted. She was never going to protest again.

"Sit up," he said, then kissed her cheek and her jaw.

She did as he asked. She swayed for a moment, finding balance, then glanced down at him. His bare chest was in reach. Not sure where she gathered the courage, she placed her hand on top of his breastbone. His eyes closed slowly, and he breathed her name.

"Touch me," he said.

She wasn't sure where or how, but figured she couldn't really hurt him. She brushed her hands against the sprinkling of hair between his flat nipples. She traced the shape of his ribs and the width of his shoulders. She wondered what he would taste like, but couldn't bring herself to test his skin to find out.

After several minutes he stilled her hands. "Take off your sweater."

"Why?" she asked, her voice squeaking on the single syllable.

When he didn't answer, she swallowed hard. Okay, take off her sweater. No big deal. Hadn't she just promised herself she was going to do whatever he asked? Besides, if she took it off he might touch her breasts again, and wouldn't that be lovely?

She did as he requested and in the process realized he'd unfastened her bra. She didn't want to think about how awkward it must look as she tried to pull one piece of clothing off while attempting to keep another firmly plastered against her chest.

Finally she was able to pull her sweater over her head with one hand while the other held the bra against her breasts. She tossed the sweater on the floor.

"That, too," he said, tugging on the hook end of the undergarment.

"I can't," she said miserably.

"Why?"

She looked away. "They're too big. It's ugly. I always wanted those little perky breasts like you see in the magazine ads."

"Everything about you is beautiful."

She glared at him. "Oh yeah, right. Including the extra fifteen pounds. I'm stunning. Modeling agencies are pounding at the door to get me to work for them."

He studied her for a moment, then nodded as if he'd come to some conclusion. "Scoot up."

That she could do. She scooted a little closer.

"Close your eyes."

That request made her suspicious, but she did as he asked. Still, she didn't release her death grip on her bra. Fortunately he didn't try to take it away from her.

Instead, he placed his hands on her thighs. He stroked her from knee to hip bone. With each back-and-forth, his hands slipped closer and closer to the insides of her legs until at last his thumbs brushed over private places. She jumped.

"Keep your eyes closed," he said.

She found it difficult to breathe, but it was easy to not look. He kept his thumbs there, touching, pressing more than moving. He seemed to be looking for something. She was about to tell him there wasn't anything there when he found it.

He rubbed a tiny spot. A shudder raced through her, and goose bumps broke out on her skin. What was that? Would he do it again? He would and he did. Several times he touched that magical place, caressing her until she was weak. Then he moved away and stroked her bare arms and shoulders.

Her breasts ached. There was no other word to describe the heavy sensation that filled them. Her nipples were tight. She needed relief, but didn't know what to do. She suspected Jordan had the answer. But that would mean letting him look at her. The battle was lost the moment he traced a single finger over the outside curve of her left breast. The soft touch was so sweet, she wanted to weep. Instead, she relaxed and let him pull the bra away.

Within fifteen seconds she wondered what she'd been fussing about. After a minute she decided she'd been a stupid fool.

He touched her breasts as if they were precious and objects of worship. Long fingers caressed every curve, every inch of sensitized skin. His thumbs teased her nipples, circling the tight peaks until she could think of nothing else but having him touch her like that for always.

"If I give you a million dollars, will you promise never to stop?" she asked.

"I'll promise without the million dollars," he whispered. "Why would I want to stop?"

She opened her eyes and glanced down. His tanned fingers contrasted with her pale skin. Somehow, with him touching her, she could believe she wasn't ugly there. When his thumbs and forefingers gently pinched her nipples and she saw, as well as felt, the delicious tug, her hips arched involuntarily.

Her breathing increased, and she didn't know why. Her skin was hot; her panties felt damp. Everything confused her, but it was wonderful.

When he urged her to stretch out next to him, she didn't protest. She lowered the bed so it was flat as he used a couple of pillows to support his back. He turned on his side so he faced her. Then he did the most amazing thing. He bent his head and took one of her nipples into his mouth.

The moist heat overwhelmed her. She whispered his name, then buried her hand in his hair to hold him in place. Unbelievable heat and longing filled her.

He suckled her breast, then moved to the other side and repeated the wondrous event. She barely noticed his hands slipping under her leggings and brushing against her bare skin. It was only when one of his fingers touched that magic spot between her legs that she realized what he was doing.

But then it was too late. He'd begun to move back and forth, then around. Speech was impossible. She half expected her heart to stop beating.

"Relax," Jordan whispered, then stuck his tongue in her ear. "I'm not going to hurt you. I'm going to make you feel good."

He was. Absolutely. She tried to tell him, but she couldn't.

He nibbled on her lobe. "Do you feel the pressure building?"

She nodded. It was incredible. Every fiber, every cell, focused on his fingers and what he was doing there.

"Have you ever felt anything like this before?"

"No," she gasped.

"Good. Just go with it." A spasm jerked her body. He chuckled. "It's not going to take very long."

She wasn't sure if that was good or bad, but decided it didn't matter. He bent over her and kissed her. Their tongues danced. He drew her into his mouth and sucked. The quick spasm matched the rhythm between her legs. She thought she would die of the pleasure.

Then his hand shifted slightly. She became aware of an insistent, pleasurable pressure. She focused on it. Something she didn't understand swam just out of reach. Jordan broke the kiss, then bent over her breast. He stroked his tongue against her nipple. That was all she needed.

For a moment the world stopped, suspended on a point of pleasure so intense, she finally understood why lovers were willing to risk everything for this moment. Then time resumed, and the release crashed through her body. She gave herself up to it, riding it, feeling it, becoming one with the man at her side, knowing nothing would ever be the same again.

Jordan watched Holly's face, the flush that climbed from her chest to her cheeks, the way her lips parted as if she needed to draw in more air. At last her eyes fluttered open.

"Wow," she said reverently.

"Pretty amazing, huh?"

Her hand fluttered for a moment. "I need a new set of words to describe that."

He kissed her forehead. "I'm glad."

He was. Except for the intense, throbbing pressure in his groin, he felt great. He couldn't give Holly everything she deserved, but he had opened a door for her. He was pleased that she'd found pleasure in his arms.

He kissed her gently. "What about my dinner?"

She stirred. "Hmm, I'm hungry, too. Steak and baked potato. Give me fifteen minutes."

She sat up slowly, then stretched. Her long hair tumbled down her back. As she raised her arms, he saw her left breast and the rosy-tipped nipple. His erection flexed against the fly of his jeans, but he ignored the signal. He'd promised not to make love with her, and he intended to keep his word. Holly was innocent enough not to realize he was aroused and suffering. Better for both of them if she didn't offer to take care of him.

She stood up and reached for her bra. He had a brief view of her bare chest before she turned quickly and dressed. Surprising him, and probably herself, she bent over and gave him a quick, hot kiss before she left to start dinner.

Jordan stared after her. Holly Garrett was deadly. He could feel the danger all the way down to his soul. There was something about her that appealed to him. Was it her innocence or her sweet spirit? He wasn't sure. All he knew was she made him want things he could never have. He treated her differently than he'd ever treated another woman. In the past he'd always held back. With her, he wanted to give.

But he couldn't get involved. He knew the price love required. His parents, Travis and his first wife, Craig and Krystal. Everyone he knew and cared about had paid a high, ugly price for the privilege of love. He was going to play it safe. That's why he'd always held himself at arm's length from relationships.

So how had Holly slipped inside his barriers? Was it because they'd never officially dated? She'd just been around, and he'd grown to like her.

He drew in a breath. For the first time in his life he wanted more. He wanted to be with her, make love with her, hold her, confess his darkest secrets. For the first time he was tempted. He wanted to believe it was possible, that this time was different. But he'd learned his lesson too well for that. This time was exactly the same. If he risked getting involved, both he and Holly were going to get burned.

Chapter Ten

It was early afternoon on Sunday when Louise and Holly pulled the last cookie sheet from the oven. They'd finished decorating the sugar cookies while the batch of chocolate-chip cookies had been baking. The delicious smells filled the house. Vanilla and chocolate, sweet icing, cinnamon, all surrounded by the homey scent of fresh-brewed coffee for the expected guests.

Louise expertly transferred cooled cookies to a large plate then handed it to Holly. "Take these into the living room," she said.

"But there are three plates in there already."

Louise winked. "I know how these girls eat. The cookies will disappear. Trust me."

Holly did as she requested. Once in the living room, she rearranged the plates of treats, then glanced around at the open area. Jordan's contribution to furniture had been a single sofa and a rather ratty-looking recliner. The dimensions of the room were substantial. In honor of the events of the day, Holly had loaned a few antique sofas, some tables and floor lamps. Nothing matched, but at least everyone would have a place to sit.

She stared at the plain white walls and thought about how beautiful the house could be. They'd finished the dining room yesterday. Kyle and Travis had come over to help move in the furniture Jordan had ordered. With some time and effort the rest of the house would be just as lovely. She wanted to be a part of the project.

As she ran her fingers along the stiff back of a Victorian-influenced blue settee, she imagined the house filled with laughter. She'd been happy here. Others could be, too. She wondered what it would be like to live here permanently, to know she was going to raise a family here. She'd thought about having children, of course, had wanted to, but didn't think it was likely. She wasn't sure she was prepared to be a single parent. The thought of raising a child on her own terrified her, and she admired those who were able to keep it all together without someone else to depend upon.

She'd thought of family, but she'd shied away from marriage. She knew she would never trust anyone enough to be able to commit to forever.

She heard voices in the kitchen. Louise's higher pitch followed by Jordan's low rumble. Her heart began to beat faster. Funny, after all they'd been through, working on the house every day, talking about nearly every aspect of their lives, he still had the power to make her knees weak.

A restlessness swept over her, propelling her to walk faster through the room. Energy she didn't understand filled her, spilling out, making her want something, if only she could figure out what that something was.

Jordan?

The thought came unbidden, but once it arrived, she couldn't let it go.

Heat coiled low in her belly as she remembered how he'd touched her and what wonderful pleasure he'd brought her. There hadn't been a repeat of that incredible time together, but the aftereffects lingered.

He touched her more now. He stole kisses in the hallway. She'd even kissed him once, although the thought of it still brought a flush to her cheeks. If asked, she wouldn't be able to define their relationship. They weren't dating or lovers. They seemed to be more than friends, although she wasn't sure. Most frightening of all, she was starting to sense she might be able to trust Jordan. If she did, if she allowed herself to fall for him, that would ruin everything. No matter how nice he was to her, in her heart she knew she wasn't his type. When he was healed and able to get on with his life, he would go back to the kind of women he was used to.

The sound of cars in the driveway broke through her musings. She walked to the front window and stared out. A gleaming Mercedes pulled up first, followed by a minivan and two sport-utility vehicles. One had a small open trailer hitched to the back bumper.

Adults and children spilled out onto the driveway. Holly stared in amazement. She'd met most of the adults of the family, but not many of the children. It was one thing to know intellectually that Craig had three boys and Sandy and Kyle had four children, counting the baby. It was quite another to see all of them running around.

She watched as the adults called to each other and laughed. The women hugged, and the men shook hands. It was as if they hadn't seen each other in months instead of just a few days. Holly fought a tightness in her throat. She envied Jordan his beautiful Victorian house, but even more than that, she envied him his close, loving family. While she appreciated that they drew her in and made her feel welcome, she wished she was there because she belonged instead of on a temporary basis by virtue of living in Jordan's house.

She wondered if Louise fought these feelings. She and the housekeeper had talked about their solitary lives. The Haynes family offered a refuge.

"Are they here?" Jordan asked as he walked into the room. He moved easily with a natural elegance that only added to the temptation he already provided. Late last week he'd started physical therapy, and the exercises and treatments seemed to be easing his pain.

"They just pulled up." She looked at him, then at the jacket he was holding. "Are you going to be all right?"

"I swear I won't cut down a single tree." He made an X over his heart. "My brothers will take care of that." He moved next to her and tugged on her long braid. "Don't worry, I'll be fine. I'll see you later this afternoon."

He started for the front door. Out of nowhere Mistletoe materialized and sauntered in front of him. He had to side-step suddenly to avoid tripping on her. Jordan swore under his breath. Mistletoe gave him a long, unblinking stare, then turned away and began washing her face.

"Mistletoe, that's rude," Holly said. The cat ignored her.

Jordan opened the front door and moved out onto the porch. Holly followed. She watched as he walked down the steps and greeted his family. His sisters-in-law fussed over him, while his brothers teased him about being a slacker. Holly smiled and knew even though it was temporary, she was going to enjoy every minute she had with this family.

Elizabeth, Rebecca, Jill and Sandy started up the stairs

toward the house. As they did, Louise came out onto the porch and shrugged into her coat.

"Everything is set up," the housekeeper said. "The coffee is in a carafe, and I've started a second pot. You know where everything else is."

Holly stared at her disbelievingly. "You're not leaving."

"Sure. I always go with the guys. Someone has to be around to keep track of the little ones. Take the girls to the bathroom, that sort of thing."

Holly glanced from Louise to the four women she didn't really know. "But I can't be the hostess." It wasn't right. Besides, she was terrified.

"You'll be fine." Louise gave her a wink. "If there's a lull in conversation, ask them how they met their husbands. That will keep them talking for hours."

With that, she walked down the stairs and approached the minivan. Holly looked at the four women now standing in front of her. "Hi," she said awkwardly, and stepped back to let them in.

Elizabeth led the way. She paused and gave Holly a hug. "Thanks for having us."

"My pleasure," Holly muttered, not wanting to say it hadn't been her idea to entertain these women alone. She'd thought Louise was going to be here. Whatever were they going to say to each other?

They all walked into the living room and found seats. Holly busied herself taking coats and bringing in the coffee. How long would the men and children be gone? Two hours? Three? It was only one in the afternoon. What if they were gone until dark? How would she survive? She couldn't think of a single thing to talk about.

When there was nothing else to keep her in the kitchen, she reluctantly made her way toward the living room. The four women there were chatting easily, as if they'd known each other for years. They had, Holly reminded herself.

She hovered by the entrance to the living room until Elizabeth saw her and patted the sofa where she was sitting. "Come sit with me," she said.

Holly crossed the room and perched on the edge of the seat. She forced her lips into a smile, hoping it looked more natural than it felt.

Jill, her pregnant belly rounding the front of her flannel maternity top, reclined on a chaise by the fireplace. Rebecca and Sandy shared a sofa across from the one Elizabeth and Holly sat in. Holly felt everyone staring at her.

"I've got it," Rebecca said as she snapped her fingers. "I know what's different. You're blond."

Holly touched her head self-consciously. "I know."

"None of us are. The Haynes brothers generally prefer brunettes."

"Excuse me?" Jill said, pointing to her own red hair. "That's not completely true."

Elizabeth laughed. "Craig always has been his own man." She nodded slowly. "You're right, Rebecca. Holly is our first blonde."

Holly held up her hands. "We're just friends. Jordan and I don't date."

Knowing looks were exchanged. Holly felt herself flush.

"Sandy, throw me a pillow, please," Jill said. She grabbed the pillow as it flew toward her, then tucked it under her back. "Everything hurts. Little people like me aren't supposed to puff up this much. It's fine for you tall types."

Rebecca tossed her long, dark, curly hair over her shoulder. "Jill is our poor little troll."

"I'm not a troll, I'm short. Something people like you can't appreciate. Do you know what it's like to never be able to reach the top shelf at the grocery store? I have to stand there waiting until a tall person walks down the aisle. It's humiliating.''

Sandy leaned back against the sofa and sighed. ''I can't believe you've already got Craig's three boys and you're going to have another child.''

Rebecca, Elizabeth and Jill stared at her, then laughed.

''You had three kids, then had a fourth with Kyle,'' Elizabeth said.

Sandy nodded slowly. ''I know. I can't believe Jill was as foolish as I was. Four children. Do you know how much laundry that is?''

''I refuse to think about it. Anyway, Louise will come to help.'' Jill touched her belly. ''I know it's going to be a lot of work, but it will be worth it.''

Rebecca leaned forward and grabbed a plate of cookies. She took two, then passed it on to Sandy. ''You don't regret the baby for a minute,'' she said.

''You're right,'' Sandy said. ''Although four is a handful. That's why this afternoon is so wonderful. In fact—'' she glanced at Holly ''—you might never get rid of me.''

''At first I thought the men taking their children to get Christmas trees and not taking the wives was a bad idea,'' Jill said. ''I thought I might feel left out.''

''Don't,'' Elizabeth told her. ''It's cold out. The children constantly have to go to the bathroom, although not at the same time. They argue, they whine, they can't agree on the tree they want. Oh, and the men will come home with huge monstrosities that won't even begin to fit in the house.'' She took the plate from Sandy and picked out a couple of cookies, then handed it to Holly. ''It's much better to stay in here and be warm. We have witty conversation, no husbands, no children. Gee, Holly, Sandy's right. None of us will want to leave.''

"You're welcome to stay as long as you like."

Elizabeth winked. "Oh, sure. We believe that."

Sandy started to prop her feet up on the coffee table, then froze and looked at Holly. "Is this a valuable antique?"

"No, it's Jordan's."

"Whew! Okay then, let's trash the place."

Everyone laughed. Holly joined in and felt some of her tension ease away. These women were nice to her, and she appreciated that. She enjoyed their company. By the end of the day she would probably be able to figure out who was married to whom. Except for Rebecca, who wore a dark wool jumper over a cream turtleneck, they were dressed in jeans and sweatshirts. No one had on a lot of makeup or expensive jewelry. They were friends, and they obviously welcomed Holly into their circle. She wished she could tell them how much that meant.

Elizabeth looked at Jill. "How are you feeling?"

"Tired, even though I've been sleeping well."

"It gets worse."

Jill grimaced. "I sort of figured that. When are you going to have another one?"

Elizabeth poured herself a cup of coffee. "We've been talking about it. Little Jessica is nearly two. If we're going to do it, now's the time. I want another baby. Of course, that would mean three girls." She shook her head. "You know what they say."

Holly stared at her. "About having girls?"

Elizabeth nodded. "With boys you just have to worry about one—" she pointed to her lap "—you know. But with girls you have to worry about all of them."

Laughter exploded in the room. When they had quieted, Jill said, "I think you should have another baby."

"We're thinking about it, too," Rebecca said. "Of

course, not being married to an official Haynes brother, I have the option of either a boy or a girl.''

Jill glanced at Holly. ''How long have you known Jordan?''

Holly cleared her throat. She reached for her coffee, then changed her mind. Better to not have something to spill. ''A few weeks. After my apartment was destroyed in that last big storm, he offered to let me live here for a while. I'm helping him restore the house in return for room and board.''

Jill stared at her. ''You're *living* with him?''

Holly felt color flare on her cheeks. ''No,'' she said quickly, then realized she was.

''They're not living together,'' Rebecca said.

''What would you call it?'' Jill asked.

''Louise is here,'' Elizabeth said. ''I'm sure everything is very circumspect.''

For the second time in ten minutes, laughter broke out in the room. ''A Haynes brother behaving himself,'' Sandy said. ''Oh, that's new.'' Her smile faded. ''I suppose out of all of them, Jordan is the most likely to be a gentleman.''

''The first time I met Travis, he picked me up and carried me,'' Elizabeth said. ''It was very romantic.''

''Fine for you,'' Sandy grumbled. ''The first time I met Kyle after I moved back here, he came riding up on his motorcycle, all tanned and muscled. I couldn't even speak. There I was, a grown woman with three children, and I couldn't form entire sentences. I didn't know whether to throw myself at him or run away screaming.''

''I was naked,'' Jill said brightly. Everyone turned to stare at her. ''Okay, maybe not naked, but I was just wearing a skimpy little robe. I thought it covered me just fine.

Craig later told me it didn't. He spent our whole first conversation in a very uncomfortable state."

Elizabeth raised her eyebrows. "I believe Rebecca has
the best story of all."

"It's silly," Rebecca said, and nibbled on a cookie.

Jill brushed her short red hair off her forehead. "I don't
think I ever heard this story. What happened?"

Rebecca waved her hand. "Nothing."

"Not nothing." Elizabeth picked up her coffee and gestured with the cup. "Rebecca had a crush on Austin. It
was very tragic. She couldn't even be in the same room
with him without knocking something over or spilling. So
one day she went to see him."

Rebecca drew in a deep breath. "If the story has to be
told, I'll tell it. Although I don't know what purpose it
serves."

"Entertainment," Elizabeth said.

"I went to see him at his house. It was raining, and my
car got stuck. When the storm got worse, he lost his phone,
so we couldn't call for a tow truck." She folded her hands
primly in her lap. "There. Are you happy?"

Elizabeth grinned. Her brown eyes danced with amusement. "That's not the whole story. Tell us the good part."

"I had to spend the night."

"And?"

Rebecca rolled her eyes. "We made mad, passionate
love. All right? Can we drop this now?"

Holly was surprised. "The first night you went over to
his house?"

"It was an accident."

Jill sat up. "Honey, there are no accidents."

Rebecca smiled. "You're right. I seduced him. Although
he denies it. He says he was the one doing the seducing."

"They all do," Sandy said. "It's better to let them think

that. At least they've all grown up. You should have been here in high school. They were dangerous heartbreakers then. No female was safe.''

''Did your heart get broken?'' Holly asked.

''Not really. Jordan and I went out for a while, but we didn't have chemistry, so we ended up being friends. Good thing for all of us. It would have been so awkward to face him as my brother-in-law if we'd gone at it hot and heavy in the back of his car.''

At first Holly didn't recognize the tight feeling inside her belly. Then she realized it was annoyance. She didn't want any of these women to have a past with Jordan. It was illogical and unfair, but it was how she felt.

Then Sandy's smile faded. ''All teasing aside, I think we're very lucky women. The Haynes brothers, including Austin, are about the best men I've ever met.''

''You're right,'' Elizabeth said. ''I never thought I'd be willing to risk caring about anyone again. Travis taught me differently.''

''I agree,'' Jill said, then sniffed. ''But can we please not talk about this. I'm pregnant, and it doesn't take very much to make me cry.''

Sandy leaned over the sofa and took her hand. ''Don't cry. We'll tell funny stories instead.''

Holly reached for the carafe of coffee. It was empty. ''I'll go get some more,'' she said, and stood up.

''I'll help,'' Rebecca said, and followed her.

When they were in the kitchen, Rebecca shut the door. ''I don't mean to intrude. I just wanted to make sure that you're all right. This is new to you, and sometimes the teasing can be a little overwhelming. For what it's worth, if we didn't like you, we wouldn't be telling these wild stories.''

Holly felt her eyes tear, and she didn't have the excuse

of being pregnant. "Thank you for that. All this is very different for me, but I like having everyone here. You're all so nice and you barely know me."

Rebecca touched her arm lightly. "We heard good things about you. Jordan has talked to his brothers and to Austin. Word gets out. Jordan mentioned your mom died a couple of years ago and you're all alone. We're happy to share our holidays with you."

"Thanks."

Rebecca leaned against the counter. "Austin and Jordan are a lot alike. They're both loners."

"I don't understand. Everyone says that to me, but Jordan's not a loner. He's friendly and open. He's got a great sense of humor. Sometimes I feel as if you're talking about someone else."

Rebecca's delicate eyebrows rose slightly. "Interesting. You're seeing a side of him he keeps hidden from most people. I wonder what that means."

"Nothing," Holly said quickly.

"You know what they say about people who protest too much."

"We're just friends." She ignored the image of the evening she'd spent in his bed. Nothing had happened, she reminded herself. They had both been fully dressed. Well, she didn't have her shirt and bra on, but aside from that…

He'd touched her, though. Touched her in the most intimate way a man can touch a woman. And he'd made her feel wonderful things. He'd shown her the possibilities.

"Why isn't Jordan married?" Holly asked.

Rebecca reached for the pot of brewed coffee and began to pour it into the carafe. "Probably because he doesn't date."

"How could he not? He's so good-looking and fun. There must be women crawling all over him."

"Maybe, but he manages to ignore most of them." Rebecca looked at her. "You're the first woman I've seen him with since I moved to Glenwood, and that's been nearly four years."

Holly couldn't take in that thought. It didn't make sense.

"Jordan holds a lot of himself inside. He doesn't open up easily or share what he's thinking."

"I agree with that," Holly said. Jordan rarely talked about personal things. She didn't have a clue as to what he was thinking about her, or their situation.

"The Haynes brothers don't make it easy," Rebecca continued, "but they're worth the trouble. Just one warning. Once you fall in love, there's no getting over it."

Holly took a step back. "You don't have to worry about me. I'm not going to fall in love with Jordan. I know I'm not his type."

Rebecca picked up the full carafe. "Of course you're his type. But that's not what's at issue. As for not falling in love, we don't always get a choice. I'll go ahead and take this back to the living room."

Holly stayed in the kitchen for a few more minutes. Love? The concept startled her. She'd never thought of her feelings in that context. She didn't love Jordan. She barely knew the man. But the word had a nice ring to it. Love. She would like to love someone and have him love her back. But that required trust, and she'd been let down too many times.

She shook her head. Everything was too confusing. This time last month she'd been living a solitary, albeit happy, life. It had been just her and Mistletoe. Her business had been growing steadily, and she was content. Now her life was upside down. Still, she wouldn't trade it away for anything. Looking at the world from a new point of view showed her things she'd never seen before.

She glanced at the clock and saw it was nearly two-thirty. Then she hurried back to the living room. She hoped the men and children didn't return too quickly. She wanted to spend some time with her new friends.

The crowd returned a little after seven. They'd called at five to say they were stopping for dinner. The ''hunt'' had been successful, but everyone was hungry. The women had ordered pizza and continued the fun until the cars had pulled up in front of the house.

They grabbed coats and walked onto the porch. Holly saw the small trailer was now filled with several cut trees. Children circled the cars, calling out for their fathers to make sure they put each tree on the correct car.

Jordan headed for the stairs. Holly could see he was limping.

''Are you all right?'' she asked as she hurried to the edge of the porch.

He looked up. The light by the door illuminated his face. There were shadows under his eyes and lines of strain around his mouth. ''I'm tired,'' he said.

''You're hurting.'' She tucked her arm under his and helped him inside. He collapsed on one of the sofas.

When she would have settled next to him, he waved her away. ''Go be social,'' he said. ''I'll be fine here. Oh, and make sure Kyle brings in the tree.''

Holly hesitated, not wanting to leave him alone but knowing she should see everyone off. Reluctantly she returned to the porch. Elizabeth pulled her to one side.

''I have a favor to ask,'' the woman said. ''May I bring over several presents? They're for the children. I'm afraid they're going to find them. I know it will be okay with Jordan, but I don't want him to be responsible for them.

Men don't remember things like bringing presents back in time for Christmas morning.''

"Sure," Holly said. "There are plenty of closets here. Do you want me to wrap them?"

"They're already wrapped. But thanks for the offer." Elizabeth squeezed her hand. "I know there isn't a romance between you and Jordan. Speaking for all the Haynes wives, I wanted to tell you, we would love it if you two got together. You're good for him, and I think he's good for you, too." Elizabeth's brown eyes danced. "If he's anything like his brother, I promise you won't be disappointed when the lights go out."

Holly already suspected that. "You've all been so nice to me. I don't know how to thank you."

"You don't have to."

Impulsively Holly gave her a hug.

"Hey, if there's hugging going on, I want to be included," Kyle said as he carried one end of a huge fir tree up toward the open front door.

"Talk to your wife," Elizabeth said.

Travis came up the stairs, holding the thick end of the tree. "Wife," he said.

Elizabeth laughed.

Holly led the way inside. Austin followed behind with a tree stand. In about ten minutes the tree was up in the living room's bay window. Five minutes after that the appropriate trees had been tied onto car roofs and everyone had left.

Holly checked on Jordan. He pulled himself to his feet and grimaced. "I'm tired," he said. "Would you mind if we decorated the tree tomorrow?"

"Not at all. I'm worried about you."

He gave her a half smile. "I'll be fine. I just need to rest."

The front door opened, and Louise stepped inside. "What a day," she said. "Those little ones about ran me into the ground."

Jordan's jaw tightened. Had something happened to upset him?

"I have a few ornaments I brought from the store," Holly said. "I want to bring them down before I forget." She waved at Louise and headed for the stairs.

"The tree looks nice in here," Louise said.

Jordan grunted.

Holly started up the stairs. Some premonition made her slow her step. Something was going to happen. She could feel it.

"Do you want me to hang the lights tonight?" Louise asked, her voice slightly muffled as she walked into the living room.

"No," Jordan roared. "Haven't you done enough today? Just stay the hell out of my life."

Chapter Eleven

As soon as he said the words, Jordan wanted to call them back. It would be a big mistake to get into this now. They were both tired, and nothing would be accomplished.

But watching Louise with his nieces and nephews had been more than he could stand. She'd held the little ones, played with the older ones. All the kids adored her. He hated knowing she'd wormed her way into his family under false pretenses.

Louise tossed her coat over a chair by the entrance to the living room, then she walked toward him. Her cheeks were flushed, her blue eyes bright with anger. In her purple slacks and fuchsia shirt, she didn't look like anyone's idea of a dangerous person, but he knew the truth...and her secrets.

She came to a stop about three feet in front of him. After planting her hands on her hips, she glared at him. ''I've had it with you, Jordan. I've been here nearly a month.

I'm tired of the rude comments, the innuendos and hostile looks. Your attitude stinks. If you've got something to say, then be man enough to say it.''

He stared at her for a long time. ''You don't want to hear this,'' he said at last, his voice low.

''Try me. Or are you only good at being a bully?''

The taunt did what it was supposed to. The heat of his anger increased. He made one last effort to maintain self-control, then let it go. ''I don't like you, Louise. I haven't for a long time.''

''Why?'' she asked, her confusion obviously genuine. ''What did I ever do to you?''

''You destroyed my family.''

She stared at him as if he were crazy. ''I don't know what you're talking about.''

He focused his attention on her face. He wanted to see her admit the truth. ''I know about your affair with my father.''

His expectations were fulfilled. Louise paled to the color of chalk, then sank onto the sofa behind her.

''Oh, Lord,'' she murmured. ''After all these years.'' She raised her head and looked at him. ''How did you find out?''

''That's not important. The point is I know what you did.''

She tried to smile, but her lips were trembling too much. ''What I did? You make it sound like I planned the affair. I didn't. I was just seventeen. Still in high school.'' She turned away. ''A virgin.''

He saw the flush of color on her cheeks. Jordan steeled himself against any hint of softer emotion. After what she'd done, she deserved to suffer.

She drew in a deep breath. ''He came to the high school and talked about drunk driving. I was sitting in the front row. Your father was older, of course, but a handsome, charming man. He smiled at me and—''

"Spare me the details."

Her spine straightened. "All right. Have it your way. I was seventeen, and Earl Haynes seduced me. There, I confess my crime. Are you happy? What I did was wrong, I admit that. I knew he was married." She was silent for several seconds. "I'm not proud of what I did. My only defense is that I was naive."

"He had a wife and four sons. Did you ever think about what your so-called innocent affair would mean to us?"

She flinched.

Jordan fought to keep his anger flowing. He didn't want to feel anything for the woman in front of him. Not compassion or empathy.

"He said no one would ever know."

"There's an excuse."

"I'm not excusing, I'm explaining. I was so young."

He folded his arms over his chest. "That's it, then? You were young? Don't you want to declare undying love for my father?"

Her blue eyes darkened with regret. "I didn't love him, Jordan. I don't know if that makes it worse or better, but it's the truth. You can say whatever you want, but none of it will be more ugly than what I've already said to myself." She drew in a deep breath. "It was twenty-nine years ago. Maybe it's time to let it go."

"You'd like that, wouldn't you?" he said. "But there's so much more to the story."

For the first time she looked frightened. "What do you mean?"

"I told you I knew everything. I know that you left town nearly thirty years ago. I know you were pregnant and that you had a child."

Louise's eyes fluttered closed. He suspected if she hadn't been sitting, she would have swooned. As it was, she swayed on the sofa.

"No," she murmured. "No. Not now. Not after all this time." She covered her face with her hands.

"What happened to the child?"

"Adoption."

He'd expected as much. Even so, the single word shocked him. There was another Haynes in the world. A half sibling he didn't know.

He glanced at Louise. Her shoulders shook, and she rocked back and forth, but she was silent in her pain. Jordan found he had to turn away.

He'd expected to enjoy this conversation. He'd rehearsed it a thousand times in his mind. Louise had always been broken and crying, begging forgiveness. But he didn't feel any satisfaction. Lives had been destroyed, and it was too late to bring back the past.

"I've been punished enough," she said. "You have no right to discuss this with me. What happened between your father and me was a mistake, but no one ever knew. I'm not responsible for the destruction of your family. Earl Haynes did that all on his own."

He turned back toward her. There were tears on her cheeks, and for the first time she looked every day of her forty-six years. "That's where you're wrong. Seventeen years ago you came back to Glenwood, and my father got in touch with you."

Her mouth opened. "No," she breathed.

"Yes."

"No. I mean, Earl contacted me, but I wouldn't have anything to do with him. I was older. I'd learned from my mistakes. Jordan, I swear, I refused to even talk to him. I wasn't interested in having a relationship. He was married, and even if he hadn't been, I would never have trusted him.''

"Too bad you didn't make that clear.''

"What?''

"You should have told him you wouldn't be interested even if he were single.''

"I did.''

"He didn't believe you.''

She frowned. "What are you talking about?''

This time Jordan didn't have to search for the anger and pain. It swelled up inside him, fueled by ugly wounds left over from a childhood fraught with hurt.

"My father was convinced you would want him if he wasn't married. Because of you, he asked my mother for a divorce.''

"That's crazy.''

Jordan curled his hands into fists. "After twenty-five years of screwing everything in a skirt in a fifty-mile ra-dius, after twenty-five years of being a complete bastard to my mother and beating the crap out of his kids, my father wanted a divorce. So he would be with *you*.''

Louise stared at him wide-eyed. "I don't believe you.''

"You damn well better. I was there. I heard every-thing.''

She shook her head. He didn't know if she still didn't believe him or if she didn't want him to continue. He didn't care which; he was determined to finish his story.

"After he asked for the divorce, he left. My mother stood in the kitchen, her home for the last twenty-five years, and she started to laugh.'' He shuddered. "I still remember the sound,'' he added softly.

It had been horrible. He'd been sixteen, just old enough to believe he couldn't cry anymore or ask for comfort.

"Jordan, I—''

He cut her off. "She left. She packed her bags that afternoon and left. I begged her not to go, but she wouldn't listen. She said we were all old enough to take care of ourselves, then she was gone." He glared at the woman sitting on the sofa. "She never contacted us again. Not a phone call or even a letter."

"I'm sorry," Louise said as a tear rolled down her cheek. "I'm so sorry. I never meant to hurt any of you."

"That's not good enough."

He walked over to the fireplace and stared at the unlit logs. He was filled with conflicting emotions. In a small corner of his mind, he felt compassion for Louise. She *had* been young, and she'd gotten in over her head.

She should have known better, he reminded himself. If she hadn't slept with a married man, none of this would have happened. He poked and prodded his anger until it flared back to life.

So many lives ruined. Hers, his mother's, his brothers'. "What happened to the child?" he asked.

"I don't know. I never saw her again."

Jordan froze. For one intensely agonizing second every cell in his body screamed in pain. Then he sucked in a breath, and the moment passed. But it left him weak and shaking.

"Her? You had a girl?"

"Yes. Why is that surprising? Oh, Lord. You can't really believe that family curse, can you?"

The Haynes curse. No female child had been born in four generations. Until Travis had fallen in love with Elizabeth. Until Kyle had fallen in love with Sandy. Haynes men who love their wives have girls. Haynes men who love the one they're with have girl children. Louise had a girl.

The son of a bitch had loved her. Really loved her. He'd

never loved his wife. Jordan doubted his father had cared about his sons, either.

His chest tightened, and it was hard to breathe. He turned on his heel and left the room. Once in the foyer, he didn't know where to go, so he stepped outside, onto the porch.

The night air nipped at his skin, but he didn't care about the cold. At last he could draw in a breath. He exhaled a steamy cloud of air. The front door closed, and he heard Louise's footsteps on the wooden floor.

"I'll pack my bags and be out of here by morning," she said.

He wanted her gone but it wasn't an option. "No. You can't go. I've kept this secret for seventeen years. If you go, I'll have to explain. I'm not going to ruin everyone's holiday by confessing all now. Besides, if you left, Holly wouldn't be comfortable staying here with me alone. I want her to have one good Christmas. I want you to stay until after the first of the year."

"Fine."

He couldn't tell her emotional state from that single word, but he didn't care what she was thinking. Even though having a daughter wasn't her fault, he blamed her for that final insult.

He heard the front door open, then Louise spoke. "I was only seventeen," she said. "I made a mistake. I didn't know what I was doing."

"You knew enough to destroy my family."

She sucked in a breath. "You're never going to forgive me, are you?"

"No."

"As quickly as that? You don't even have to think about it?"

He didn't answer.

After a moment she said, ''It must be nice to always be right. You obviously get a lot of satisfaction from that. I've been wrong lots of times, but then you already know that. Tell me something. What's it like never to make a mistake? What is it like to know there isn't one single thing you're ashamed of?''

Louise didn't wait for an answer. Instead she went into the house and closed the door behind her.

Jordan stood alone in the cold. Somewhere out there was his half sister. He didn't know anything about her, and she didn't know anything about him. She didn't know that she was a Haynes, and that was a lucky break for her.

He tried to imagine what she would look like. She must be—he did some quick calculations—twenty-eight. Only a couple years younger than Kyle. They had a little sister. He hoped she'd had a better life growing up than the Haynes brothers. He hoped there had been parents who had cared about her.

He held on to the porch railing and wondered what he was supposed to do now. After the New Year, Louise would leave. She probably expected him to tell his brothers all he knew, but he wouldn't. It was her secret to keep or give away. He didn't care what she did as long as she got the hell out of his life.

Holly stared into the darkness, but sleep would not come. She glanced at the clock. It was after midnight. Finally she gave up and threw back the covers.

The corner of the blanket hit Mistletoe's butt, and the cat murmured a sleepy protest. Holly petted her in apology, then pulled on her robe and slippers. If she couldn't sleep, maybe some milk or an hour of pacing would help.

She crossed the room and opened the door, then stepped into the hallway. The house was silent, a contrast to the noisy thoughts swirling through her brain. It had been wrong of her to listen to Jordan's conversation with Louise, but she hadn't been able to help herself. She'd been heading upstairs when Jordan had told Louise to stay the hell out of his life. Holly had climbed to the top of the stairs, then sunk down on the landing and eavesdropped. She'd heard everything, except whatever they'd said when they went outside.

She didn't know what to think. At last Jordan's anger made sense. He'd been sixteen when he'd found out the housekeeper had had an affair with his father, and that the affair had led to the birth of a child.

A baby. Holly pulled her robe tightly around her and hugged her arms to her chest. Fierce longing filled her. It was probably the result of the afternoon spent with Jordan's sisters-in-law, all of whom had children.

When Holly reached the bottom of the stairs, she saw a light coming from the study where Jordan slept. She hesitated, not wanting to intrude but wondering if he was in pain from his strenuous day.

She crossed through the library, then stopped at the open door to the study. Jordan was sitting up in bed. He was holding a book but staring off into space rather than at the pages. He didn't notice her at first, and she took the opportunity to study him.

He wore sweats, and the loose-fitting clothing merely hinted at the strength concealed beneath the soft fabric. Lines of tension straightened his mouth. Undiluted pain filled his eyes.

"Jordan?"

He glanced up at her. Instantly his expression shuttered. A second before, she'd been able to read his soul; now she didn't even know what he was thinking. She recalled Rebecca's claims that Jordan was a loner, always on the outside looking in. For the first time she believed that might be true.

"You're up late," he said, putting the book on the bed.

"I couldn't sleep." She stuffed her hands into the pockets of her robe. "I wanted to make sure you were okay."

He turned his dark stare on her. "Why wouldn't I be?"

He was a cool stranger, and that frightened her. "You were gone a long time today, and I was concerned you might have overdone things physically. Are you in pain?"

He closed his eyes briefly. "No."

She wondered if she should leave or risk staying. The cowardly part of her said running wasn't a bad idea, but her compassionate nature won out. She settled on the overstuffed chair next to the bed.

There wasn't an easy way to say it, so she just blurted it out. "I was standing on the stairs. I heard everything."

He opened his eyes, but he didn't look at her. Instead, he stared at a place behind her left shoulder. Not a single twitch of a muscle gave his thoughts away.

"Jordan?"

"It doesn't matter," he said. "It was a long time ago."

"Of course it matters. There are so many unresolved issues. I'm sorry you had to carry this around for so long. It must have been hard for you."

He didn't respond.

She drew in a slow breath. "You know, it's not all Louise's fault."

He grimaced. "Being female, you *would* take her side."

"That has nothing to do with anything."

"If it's not her fault, then whose fault is it?"

"Louise deserves some of the blame, just not all of it."

"How convenient of you to take care of assigning blame," he said sarcastically. "Why don't you divide it all up, then let me know how much is mine, how much hers and how much belongs to everyone else? After all, you're such an expert on relationships.''

His words pelted her like sharp stones. She felt the individual blows, even though she would bear no physical scars. This Jordan was hard and ugly. She didn't like him or trust him. But she still cared about him, so she stayed in her seat.

As if he read her mind, he looked at her and gave her a weak smile. ''Sorry. I don't mean to be such a bastard. There's a lot going on, and it's tough to talk about. You can't understand this situation, Holly. You're too innocent.''

''As innocent as Louise was when this first happened to her?''

The smile faded. ''One point for your side.''

She felt his pain and tried to ignore her own. ''Jordan, this isn't about points, or winning and losing. It's about life. You've got to come to grips with this. Not for Louise, but for yourself.''

''You don't know what the hell you're talking about. If she'd just slept with the old man, I could have understood that. He was a first-class bastard, and he would have enjoyed seducing schoolgirls. I doubt Louise was the first or the last. But that's not all she did. She should have just stayed away. Instead, she had to come back. She returned to town and destroyed my family.''

His rage was a tangible creature, living and breathing in the room with them. Holly gathered her courage. ''It sounds to me like your family was destroyed long before Louise came back to town.''

''We had problems. Everyone does. But if she hadn't come back, my mother wouldn't have left. Now Louise is here, in everybody's lives. I hate that. Every time I turn around, she's at another family function.''

"She's not hurting anyone. She takes good care of the family. What's wrong with that?"

"She's playing us for fools."

"No." Holly leaned forward and clasped her hands together. "She cares about everyone in the family, even you. She loves the children."

"Love." Jordan laughed harshly. "It will be the death of us."

A coldness swept over her. "What do you mean?"

"This love you're so proud of only destroys. If you'd asked my father, he would have said he loved his sons. The beatings were just to keep them on the right track. He loved his wife. So what if he fooled around? He slept in his own bed every night. That made things okay. His father and uncles, his brothers, even his grandfather had done the same thing before him."

He paused for a moment and leaned back against the hospital bed. "You want to hear about love? Craig loved his first wife, Krystal. She was an alley cat, but he didn't know for years. She was just like our father. She came on to each of his brothers. It scared us, and we never told him. Krystal claimed she loved Craig. Supposedly she loved her boys, although she managed to leave them and never once visit them after the divorce. Love destroys everything it touches."

Holly didn't know what to say to him. Her first instinct was to tell him he was wrong. Love didn't hurt. But it had hurt people in her life. Her mother had loved her father, and he'd let her down. Even when she was dying, he couldn't be bothered to help.

Holly knew love sometimes did hurt. Like when her mother had died. But there were good sides to love. She'd had wonderful times with her mother.

"Sometimes love is worth the risk of hurting," she said.

"You really believe that?"

"Yes," she said. "What about your family? You care about them."

"One exception in a long, ugly list of rules."

She studied his face. He was tired. She could see that in the shadows under his eyes. She wished she could make him feel better. "We're quite a pair," she said. "You believe love hurts, and I'm afraid to trust anyone."

Like love, trust was a risky business, but when it worked, it was worth the potential for heartbreak. Did she believe it enough to convince him of that?

"I wish I had the right words to make you feel better," she said miserably.

"That's not your job. I'll be fine."

She thought about the sixteen-year-old boy who had learned ugly family secrets. He'd said he'd kept them to himself, and she believed him. He'd carried this burden for a long time. She didn't agree with his need to blame Louise, but she understood where the impulse came from.

"You're exhausted," he said. "Go to bed. I'll be fine."

She shook her head. "In a minute." She rose, then perched on the edge of his mattress. "I'm sorry," she whispered.

"You have nothing to be sorry about."

She didn't tell him she was sorry for him. He wouldn't want her pity or her understanding. Instead, she told him without words. She leaned forward and rested her head in the crook of his neck, then wrapped her arms around him.

He didn't respond in any way. She continued to hold on to him, willing him to accept her comfort. Bits of the evening's conversation filled her mind. He'd carried dark secrets for too long. She wanted to help him, but he wouldn't let her.

Her eyes burned, and she tried to force back the tears.

One escaped. Before she could brush it away, it fell on his neck.

Jordan grabbed her arms and set her away from him. He studied her face, then reached up and touched a tear. "I'm not worth even one of these," he said gruffly.

"You're wrong. You're worth so much more."

He muttered a curse, then hauled her against him. She settled against his strength and held him tight. How alone he must be, this man who refused to believe in love. How alone she was, a woman who refused to trust. Would they ever be able to take that leap of faith, or were they destined to spend their lives searching for the one thing they feared to claim?

Holly knew she didn't want that to be her destiny. She wanted more out of life. But she was afraid.

Another time she would wrestle with the demons that kept her alone. Another time she would search her heart and try to find the key to escape her solitary world. For tonight it was enough to hold and be held in Jordan's comforting arms.

Chapter Twelve

When Holly came down to breakfast the next morning, she found Louise already up and making coffee. If she hadn't known what had happened the previous night, she might not have noticed the slightly puffy eyes and shadows from sleeplessness, but she still would have known something was wrong. It took her a moment to figure out why, then she realized it was Louise's clothes.

Instead of her normally, bright, barely matching colors, Louise wore black jeans and a plain white long-sleeved shirt. Also missing were her frequently zany earrings. Plain gold studs gleamed in each earlobe.

Before Holly could say anything, she heard Jordan behind her. She turned and gave him a tentative smile. He didn't respond, but as he walked past her, he squeezed her hand.

She'd spent most of last night in his bed. They'd held each other silently. Finally, when his breathing had slowed and she'd known he'd fallen asleep, she'd made her way upstairs to her room. She hadn't been able to sleep much, instead replaying the events of the previous evening over and over in her head. Mistletoe had cuddled close, and the cat's warmth and gentle purring had been a great source of comfort as she'd wrestled with all that she'd learned.

Questions of right and wrong, who had hurt whom and why had dominated her thoughts. At last she understood why Jordan was always angry with Louise. She wished there was an easy solution for everyone, but there wasn't. She felt badly for both him and for the housekeeper.

Jordan stepped into the kitchen. Louise didn't turn around, but her shoulders stiffened.

"The coffee's not ready," she said. "It'll be a few minutes. I'll bring you a cup." The housekeeper's hands shook as she measured out the coffee grounds.

Jordan stared at her for a moment. Holly watched him. Emotions flashed through his eyes. She recognized compassion and a flicker of regret, but anything else disappeared before it could be identified. He paused in the kitchen, then turned and left.

Louise filled the pot with water. "Talk about tension," she said, then tried to smile. The corners of her mouth trembled.

"I'm sorry," Holly said, then crossed to the other woman.

Louise blinked several times. "He told you."

It wasn't a question. "No. I overheard. I didn't mean to, but…" Her voice trailed off.

Louise's blue eyes filled with tears. "Everything is going to come out eventually. I suppose you think I'm a horrible person."

"The thought never crossed my mind." Impulsively

Holly reached toward her and gave her a hug. Louise hugged her back, then quickly straightened.

"All this emotion before I've even had my morning coffee. I'm not sure my old heart can stand it."

Louise turned back to the coffeepot and flipped on the switch. Then she settled at the small kitchen table by the window.

It was a cool, crisp winter day. The clear sky provided a perfect backdrop for the bright sunlight. Holly took the seat next to her.

"Everything he said is true," Louise said, resting her hands on the table. "I knew it was wrong to fall in love with Earl Haynes, so I'm not sure why I did it." She shrugged. "There are the usual excuses. I didn't feel that anyone cared about me, and Earl made me feel special. Pretty, even. I never meant to hurt anyone."

A tear trickled from the corner of her eye. She wiped it away impatiently. "I was a fool."

"You were very young." Holly leaned toward her. "I don't understand everything that happened. I agree that you made a mistake, but you were only seventeen years old. He was an adult. He should have known better."

"Maybe."

"Not maybe. He was a mature man with a wife and four children. He took advantage of you."

Louise sniffed. "You sound so sure of everything."

"I am. He was the sheriff in town, too. He used his position and authority to his advantage. You never had a chance, Louise. Stop blaming yourself."

"It's hard to let go of the guilt," the older woman admitted. "I've carried this secret around for so long. I probably should have realized why Jordan didn't like me, but I never thought he knew." She shook her head. "Now everything makes sense. He blames me for destroying his family." She looked at Holly. "I swear I wouldn't have come back to town all those years later if I'd thought it was going to make trouble. I had no idea what Earl was going to do."

"That's not your fault, either," Holly said.

"Maybe not, but Jordan won't forgive me. Having the baby was bad enough, but forcing his mother to leave is so much worse."

Holly hated how Louise was taking all the blame on herself. Maybe because she was new to the situation, she could see more clearly. There were misunderstandings on both sides.

"Jordan's mother didn't leave because of you," she said. "She left because her husband asked for a divorce."

"To marry me."

"But you didn't want him to get a divorce. You didn't want to have anything to do with him. It's not your fault."

Louise drew in a deep breath. "In my head I know what you're saying makes sense. In my heart that's a different matter. I feel so guilty. It's not all about the Haynes family, either. Some of it is about my little girl. I think about her all the time. I want her to be happy and s-safe." Her voice broke, and she had to turn away to hide her emotions.

Holly tried to imagine what it must be like to have to give a child up for adoption. She couldn't think of anything more tragic.

"Did you get to see her when she was born?"

"Just for a minute." This time Louise managed a full smile. "She looked just like a Haynes. Big eyes, lots of dark hair. She was so pretty. And then they took her away."

"You've never tried to get in touch with her?"

"No." The tears returned. Louise brushed them away. "What would I say to her?"

"How about the truth? You were young and frightened, and giving her to a loving couple seemed to be the best thing to do."

"That sounds so nice. The truth is not seeing her is my punishment for what I did. I don't deserve to have her in my life."

Her friend's pain cut through Holly, too. She knew what that kind of emptiness and longing felt like. She understood about being alone.

"It's too bad your daughter has to be punished, too," she said softly. "Look at all she's missing. A wonderful mother and four half brothers. Have you considered the fact that she might *want* to be in your life?"

Louise stared at her. "I hadn't thought of it that way. But what if she likes her world the way it is?"

"What if she doesn't? The worst that will happen is that she won't want to see you. I know it's scary and a risk, but what if she's been waiting her whole life for you?"

"What if?" Louise echoed softly.

This year the family had chosen to go caroling on Travis's street. They bundled up against the cold, passed out sheet music and flashlights, then started down the block.

"We have to rotate where we sing," Jordan explained to Holly. "We're really bad, so we give the neighbors a break by not coming back for a couple of years."

She leaned against him and grinned. "I don't believe that."

"Most of the Haynes family is tone-deaf. Trust me, it's awful."

It had been nearly a week since Jordan's confrontation with Louise. Christmas was in three days. A sort of armed truce had settled over the house. Louise avoided him whenever possible, and he avoided her. He'd heard the house-keeper talking with Holly several times. Snatches of conversation had carried to him. He knew they were talking about the past and the child Louise had given up for adoption.

A girl. A Haynes daughter. Once again the rage filled him as he remembered his father had cared for Louise as he had never cared for his wife and family.

It wasn't fair, but then so little in life was.

They came to a stop in front of the first home. The porch light was on, and there was a lit plastic Santa on the front lawn. The Haynes family was loud and filled with laughter as they prepared to share their Christmas spirit. The smaller children were already asleep, and had been left behind with Louise to watch over them. The older ones were more interested in playing than singing.

Someone called out the name of the first song. There was a brief moment of shuffling as everyone found the right page, followed by a single note from a pitch pipe. As if that would help.

"'Hark, the herald angels sing.'"

The words were clear, but the key was wrong and the voices didn't blend at all. The neighbors came out onto the porch and tried to act pleased, but they were obviously pained by the discord.

Holly actually had a very nice voice. She sang softly, but he could hear the clear tones and perfect melody. Maybe there was hope.

Kyle heard, too. "This one can sing," he said, and grabbed her arm. "Come up front where they can hear you. Maybe they won't throw things at us."

Holly gave Jordan a quick glance. "It's okay," he told her. "You do sound better than the rest of us."

She wore a thick blue sweater that matched the color of

her eyes. The cold night air brought out the pink in her cheeks. In the light of the overhead lamp he saw her smile, and something deep inside him responded.

He liked her. The knowledge should have scared him into bolting, but all he could do was stand there and be grateful for her presence. Everything about her was wrong for him. Her decency, her innocence, her trust. But until the holidays were over, he was going to enjoy every stolen minute with her. When their time together was over, he would retreat to the darkness of his world and survive there.

His longing for her was about more than sex, he thought as she turned and went with Kyle to the front of the group. Even as the thought passed through his mind, his gaze dropped to her round hips and generous behind. He adored her lush feminine form. He knew that she agonized about an extra couple of pounds, but he didn't want her to change. He'd spent hours reliving the evening when he'd pleasured her. He could still see, taste and feel her full breasts. He wanted to feast on them forever.

But more than wanting a physical relationship, he enjoyed his time just being with Holly. He liked talking with her and working with her. He liked the care she took as she completed a task on his house. He liked her views of the world and her unflagging enthusiasm. Despite the blows the world had delivered, she still believed everything could work out for the best.

They began a second song. Jordan dropped behind Austin and Rebecca, who were absorbed only in each other. Lindsay, Sandy's oldest from a previous marriage, had brought a girlfriend with her, and they were doing more giggling than singing. Neither teenager noticed as he slipped behind them to the rear of the group.

Jordan cast a longing glance at the house to their left. Travis's house. Would anyone notice if he went back?

Before he could decide, Elizabeth moved next to him and slipped her arm through his.

"I thought Holly had cured you of this," she said, glancing up at him.

"Of what?"

"For a while you were actually like the rest of us. Smiling, participating in conversations. Once again you're brooding. Want to talk about it?"

He shrugged. He didn't have anything to say to her. He wasn't prepared to expose Louise's secret, and he didn't want to discuss their argument.

"Is it a guy thing?" Elizabeth asked.

"It's a family thing."

She stared at him for a long time. He realized she was a part of the Haynes family. He dropped a kiss on the top of her head. "Sorry. I didn't mean that the way it came out."

Her brown eyes saw more than they should. She continued to study him, then she nodded and disappeared into the crowd. A couple of minutes later Travis walked over to him.

"Elizabeth sent me to talk to you," Travis said. "What's going on?"

Jordan didn't want to talk about it, but the look on his brother's face told him he wasn't getting a choice. He shifted on the walkway and pulled his coat closer against the evening chill.

"I've been thinking a lot about Dad," he said, which was, in a way, the truth.

Travis grimaced. "Why bother? I'm glad the old man lives on the other side of the country. I wouldn't send him a Christmas card if Elizabeth didn't make me. You want to get in touch with him?''

''No,'' Jordan said shortly.

''I didn't think so. He's a bastard down to his bones.'' Travis's expression hardened. ''I'll never forgive him for what he did to all of us.''

Craig was standing nearby and overheard the conversation. As the group moved on to the next house, he dropped back to join them.

Travis spoke. ''You ever call Dad?''

''Why would I?'' Craig asked. ''I don't have anything to say to him. Nothing I've done has ever been good enough for him. I quit caring about him and his opinion a long time ago.'' Bitterness darkened his voice.

Jordan stared at his oldest brother. He'd never thought about what Craig must have gone through because he was the firstborn. He had endured the brunt of Earl Haynes's rage. Jordan remembered Craig had often taken the blame for things he hadn't done. When Travis had asked why, Craig had said he was bigger, so the beatings didn't hurt him as much. With the hindsight of an adult, Jordan knew Craig had just been looking out for his brothers.

Around them another song began. The words of peace and hope contrasted with the mood of the conversation. They paused to listen.

''You guys okay?'' Elizabeth asked when the song ended.

Travis looked at her. ''We're fine.'' But he stayed on the sidewalk with his brothers. By now Kyle and Austin had joined them. Only the women and children walked up to the next house. In the back of his mind Jordan noticed that the group sounded slightly more in key.

''I blame the old man for a lot,'' Travis said. ''I never knew how to be a husband or a father.''

"None of us did," Craig said. "I knew I was supposed to be the leader, but I never knew what I was doing. Obviously, or I wouldn't have married Krystal."

"I nearly lost Sandy because of him," Kyle said. The night air was cold, and he pulled his leather jacket closer. "I was afraid I wasn't good enough for her and her kids."

"I nearly lost Elizabeth," Travis said.

"We all made mistakes," Craig said. "Everybody does, but I know we would have done better without him and his brothers around."

"I remember not wanting to be like them," Travis said. He shoved his hands into his coat pockets.

They nodded. Jordan had made that vow, too. He didn't want to be like his father or uncles, using women, then tossing them aside. He'd wanted more. Then he'd learned how much it hurt to love someone, and he'd decided to avoid relationships altogether.

Austin cleared his throat. "For a while I thought you guys were lucky. You still had a family. Folks who cared about you. Then I figured out sometimes it was better to be alone."

"We've come a long way," Craig said, and slapped Kyle on the back. "Even you, baby brother."

"Gee, thanks."

Craig was right. They had grown and changed. None of them had turned out like their father. Jordan wondered what his brothers would say if he told them the truth about the past. No one had ever figured out why their mother had left. At first he hadn't said anything because he was too stunned. In his heart he'd hoped she would come back. He'd hated Louise and the tragedy she'd brought to their lives. Then he hadn't mentioned the truth because he'd been afraid.

In his young, sixteen-year-old mind he'd worried that if

he brought everything out in the open, Earl would marry Louise. Jordan couldn't bear the thought of her being his stepmother and a part of the family.

Conversation flowed around him. He was caught up in a dilemma. He believed Louise's affair was her secret to keep, but what about the child? Should he tell his brothers they had a half sister? She was grown up now and living her life somewhere. Did they have the right to get in touch with her? Did she want her life disrupted, or would she welcome the addition of four half brothers?

It wasn't until Holly rested her fingers on his arm that he realized that the caroling party had broken up.

"Are you feeling all right?" she asked, then touched his face. She was in her nurse mode, fussing over him.

"I'm fine." He captured her hand and brought it to his mouth, where he kissed her palm.

He heard her breath catch in her throat. "You're thinking about Louise," she said, and there was only a slight tremor in her voice.

"A little," he admitted. He put his arm around her and headed back to Travis's house.

"You haven't told them, have you?"

He shrugged. "I don't know what to say."

She snuggled close. "You're a very complex man, Jordan Haynes. On the one hand you're angry and resentful toward Louise for all that happened, but on the other hand you won't expose her secret. What does that say about you?"

"That I'm a fool."

"I prefer to think of you as a gentle soul."

"Thanks. That's what every guy likes to hear."

She laughed softly, then sighed. "Are you going to tell them about the baby?"

"I don't know. It was a long time ago. Wherever she

is, she's not a baby anymore, she's a woman. Would she want to be a part of this?" What he didn't say was that he *did* want to find his half sister. The reason he held back was Louise. By admitting the truth, he would be giving Louise a permanent place in the family. He still blamed her for everything that had happened. He didn't want to reward that by welcoming her as one of them.

"I always wanted a sister," Holly said. "You're lucky to have such a close family."

"You wouldn't say that if you'd met my father."

"I heard a little about him from Louise and from what you've told me. He sounds difficult."

"That's a nice way of putting it." He thought about the past. "If I'd figured the truth out sooner, about my father and Louise, I mean—"

"What would you have done? You were too young to have made any changes."

"You're probably right." They paused by the front steps of Travis's Victorian home. Everyone else had gone inside.

Holly stood on the first step so they were nearly at eye level. She placed her hands on his shoulders. "So you admit you were young and didn't know what to do?"

"Sure, if it makes you happy."

Her gaze locked on to his. "Louise was young, too."

Jordan tried to turn away and she tightened her hold on him. He could have broken away easily, but he didn't want to hurt her feelings.

"It's not going to work, Holly."

"Why not? It's true. She was seventeen years old. She made a mistake. You've just admitted you could have made mistakes, too. Why does it have to be all her fault? Your father was the adult. If anyone deserves blame, it's him."

He didn't want to argue about this, and he didn't want to listen to her words. "What's your point?"

"I'm saying that it might be easier to blame Louise than to blame your father, but that doesn't change the truth."

He stared at her a long time. He didn't want to believe what she was saying, but he wasn't sure he could continue to ignore it.

She studied him, her pretty face solemn. Then she smiled and took his hand. "Come inside where it's warm," she said, tugging him along with her.

As her words sank in and he took a step closer, he had a flash of longing so intense, it took his breath away. He knew she was talking about going into the house and out of the cold, but for that single heartbeat he wanted her to be talking about more. He wanted her to be inviting him into her heart.

Chapter Thirteen

They arrived home close to midnight. Holly knew she should be tired. She'd been up most of the previous night talking with Jordan, then had put in a full day at the store. Customers had been waiting when she'd first opened the doors, and she'd had to stay late to take care of everyone's requests. It seemed many people had saved their Christmas shopping for the last minute.

Instead of exhaustion, however, she felt a strange restlessness. The caroling had been great fun. The more time she spent with Jordan's family, the more she adored them. He was lucky to have so many people to care about him. For the first time in years she understood the meaning of security. Although it was only a temporary situation, she trusted Jordan to look out for her. She hadn't trusted anyone in so long. The sensation was unfamiliar, but she was willing to risk getting used to it.

Jordan held the door open for her, then stepped into the house behind her. He flipped on the lights in the foyer.

"It's so quiet," she whispered, then giggled. "I guess I can talk in a normal voice. There's no one here to wake up."

"Except the damn cat."

He took her coat and hung it up in the hall closet. Holly looked in the living room, but didn't see a sign of Mistletoe. She frowned. Her cat didn't like Jordan, but she always came out to spit at him. Mistletoe also came to greet Holly and get her cuddling.

"Mistletoe?" she called.

Jordan glanced at her. "What's the problem?"

"She's usually waiting for us by the door." A seed of worry planted low in her belly. "I hope she didn't get out."

"Unlikely. You saw her right before we left, right?"

Holly nodded.

"I was the last one out, and I know I closed the door. I had to unlock it to get back in. Louise was baby-sitting the children all evening, so she wasn't here to accidentally let Mistletoe out. She's probably sleeping upstairs."

"You're right. She's been a little tired lately. Maybe she didn't hear us come in." Holly started for the stairs.

"I'll check the downstairs," Jordan said.

"Thanks."

She sighed softly. She knew he didn't care much for her cat. And she couldn't really blame him, given that Mistletoe had taken an instant dislike to Jordan.

The old house was silent. Holly went from room to room switching on lights. Some of the second-story bedrooms had furniture, but most were bare.

Louise had a room right by the stairs. The housekeeper had fallen asleep in Travis and Elizabeth's guest room, and they'd left her there. Travis had promised to bring her back in the morning. Now Holly got on her knees and checked under the four-poster bed. Nothing. She checked the closet and even the small space behind the dresser.

"Mistletoe? Where are you?" she called as she entered the hallway.

She was halfway to her room when she heard Jordan's voice from the first floor.

"I found her," he said. "In my room."

She headed toward him. He was waiting for her at the bottom of the stairs. There was an odd light in his eyes and a half smile tugging at the corners of his mouth.

"What is it?" she asked.

He took her hand. "Congratulations. You're a grand-mother."

"Mistletoe gave birth? Is she okay?"

"She looks great. There are four kittens."

Elation followed on the heels of relief. She quickened her step. "I thought she was acting a little odd these last couple of days. I should have realized."

They entered Jordan's makeshift room. The closet door was open. Clothes had been pulled off hangers to create a nest. Mistletoe lay in the center, curled protectively around four tiny kittens.

Three were gray like their mother, and one was black. Mistletoe blinked sleepily, then gave a throaty purr.

Holly crouched down next to her and stroked her head. "What a clever girl you are. Four wonderful babies." She petted her cat but didn't disturb the kittens. They were so tiny, with thin, slick fur.

"Are you hungry?" Holly asked, then glanced at Jordan. "Do you think we should move her food in here along with her litter box? Then she wouldn't have to go so far."

"Sure." He rose to his feet and left.

While he was gone, Holly continued to speak softly to her cat. Mistletoe savored the attention, as if she knew she'd done a wonderful thing.

"She's not even spitting at you," Holly said when he returned with the cat's food and water.

"Oh, I think she got back at me already tonight." He pointed to the makeshift bed.

For the first time Holly realized Mistletoe had given birth on a pile of Jordan's clothes. On top was his favorite sweater.

"Oh, no." She covered her mouth with her hand and stared at him. "Jordan, I'm so sorry."

"It's not your fault."

She dropped her hand to her side. "You're not mad?"

"It's just some clothes, Holly. If they can't be cleaned, then they can be replaced."

"But Mistletoe has been so mean to you, and it's her fault you were injured in the first place."

He touched her arm. "It's okay. I swear."

She looked into his dark eyes, then studied the shape of his mouth. Her own father hadn't been willing to help her mother when she was dying. Through her life many people had let her down. But this man had opened his home to her, introduced her to his family and generally made her feel as if she finally belonged somewhere.

Deep in her heart, in a place that had been empty and cold for so long, a tiny flicker of hope burned brightly. She didn't understand the tingling she felt when Jordan was near or the pleasure she took in his company or the way his kisses and touches had made her feel. She didn't understand anything. She only knew that he was the most wonderful man she'd ever met in her life, and she would have done anything for him.

Jordan reached past her. Mistletoe eyed him mistrustfully, then sniffed his fingers. When she was done, he gently stroked the top of her head. The cat didn't purr, but she didn't pull away, either. After a couple of minutes he rose to his feet.

"Maybe we should let them be," he said, holding out his hand.

She took it and he pulled her up. "You're right. I'm sure she needs to rest."

As they walked through the library, he continued to hold her hand. Holly thought about pointing out the fact, but she liked the feel of him so close to her. When they reached the living room, he paused in front of the fireplace.

"Maybe we should celebrate," he said. "I've got some champagne in the refrigerator."

The only light came from the Christmas tree. She could see the planes of his face, the shape of his body, but the rest of the room disappeared into shadow. They were alone in the house, and she felt as if they were in fact alone in the world. Her stomach tightened nervously.

"I'd like that," she said, and sank down on the thick carpet.

Jordan moved to the fireplace, where he touched a match to the kindling and logs stacked there. The dry tinder caught instantly. By the time he returned with two half-full glasses, the scent of wood smoke mingled with the piney fragrance of the tree.

He detoured around the back of the sofa and hit a button on the CD player. After a couple of seconds she heard the opening bars to a familiar Christmas carol. He settled on the floor next to her and held out one of the glasses.

As she took it, she noticed her fingers trembled. She could barely touch her glass to his when he proposed a toast. Her throat was tight, her skin both hot and cold, her gaze unable to hold his. The urge to bolt for safety battled with the need to stay and be close to him.

She glanced at the tall tree they had decorated last week, then at the fire. Anywhere but at the handsome man sitting next to her.

"You're so beautiful," he murmured.

She rolled her eyes. "Yeah, right." She shifted until she was sitting cross-legged, then set her champagne on a nearby coffee table.

Jordan frowned. "You don't think you're attractive?"

The question confused her. "I don't think I have to wear a paper bag over my head, if that's what you're asking. But beautiful?" She shook her head. "I'm not like those actresses on television—skinny and sophisticated with perfect makeup."

"I wouldn't think you were beautiful if you were like them." He set his champagne next to hers, then leaned closer. He fingered a strand of her hair. "Soft. Just like I thought it would be." He cupped the back of her head and held her still. "Amazing."

She blinked. He was kidding, right? Or she was dreaming. She wasn't really having this conversation with him. Jordan Haynes, single hunk, didn't really think she was attractive, did he?

"But I have to lose fifteen pounds," she blurted out, then felt herself flush with embarrassment. "I don't have skinny thighs."

He pressed his lips against the side of her neck. "I don't want skinny thighs. You're perfect the way you are."

"But everything is too big." His lips were making her skin tingle, and she was having trouble forming words.

He moved to her earlobe and nibbled on the sensitive skin. "Trust me, Holly. You're built to drive men wild."

She jerked her head back and stared at him. "You're kidding, right?"

But he wasn't smiling. His eyes were dark, his expression intense. If she hadn't known him so well, he might have frightened her.

"Jordan?"

"Trust me. Men want you."

He might well have been speaking Russian. "Even you?" she asked without thinking, then could have cheerfully died. Right there on the rug. Instant death. She wouldn't have complained at all.

Unfortunately she continued to live. "Sorry," she mumbled. "Stupid question. I'll just head up to my room and bury my head under the pillows."

But before she could stand, he had his arms around her and was lowering her onto the rug. The fire in his eyes burned hotter and brighter than the one in the hearth.

"Especially me," he said, his voice thick with an emotion she couldn't identify. Then he kissed her.

This time she was prepared for the sensations he evoked. At the first brush of his mouth, her body filled with heat. By the time he got around to testing the seam of her mouth with his lips, she was already weak with longing.

She wrapped her arms around him and pulled him close. He was hard muscle and angles to her curves. His long legs brushed against hers.

He tasted her, explored her mouth, teased her until she couldn't catch her breath. She laced her fingers through his hair, feeling the silky strands. With her other hand she traced a line down his spine. She could feel the heat of him through his shirt.

Unexpectedly Jordan pulled away. He rolled onto his back and covered his eyes with his forearm. "Damn, this is going to hurt."

Holly stared at him. "What's wrong? I thought your back was doing better. Did you overdo it at physical therapy today?"

He gave a weak laugh. "My back is great," he said. "I don't feel a thing…there."

Then what was hurting? "I don't understand."

"Do you remember the last time we did this?" He dropped his hand to his chest.

She nodded slowly. She remembered every detail of the magic she'd felt in his arms. Some nights she couldn't sleep because she was remembering. Her body got hot, and she felt an odd restlessness.

"When a man wants to make love, his body changes."

She knew enough about the process to have figured that part out, but she didn't say anything. She also didn't dare lower her gaze from his face. Was he…like that? Would she be able to tell?

Jordan sat up and rubbed his hand over his face. "Arousal brings a certain amount of pleasure, which later turns to pain if it's not followed by release. Last time—"

She shot into a sitting position as if she'd been jolted with electricity. Humiliation flooded her. Last time he'd touched her and made her feel those wonderful things, but he'd done nothing for himself.

"I'm sorry," she said softly. "You must think I'm a thoughtless, selfish…" Her voice trailed off. She didn't have any words. She'd been a jerk. Or worse.

"Just innocent," he told her. "You didn't know."

"You should have told me. I would have done, well, *something!*"

"I'm intrigued to imagine what."

She risked glancing at him and saw that he was teasing her. Then his smile faded.

"Holly, you've never seen a man naked. You can't be

expected to understand the workings of male anatomy or the details involved in making love.''

He had a point. ''What if I want to?'' she asked without thinking. She flinched in anticipation of his rejection, but didn't take the words back.

''See me naked or make love?''

She glanced at him out of the corner of her eye. She couldn't tell what he was thinking, but he didn't look mad. ''B-both.''

The silence made her nervous. Oh, there were Christmas carols in the background, and the snapping of the logs on the fire, but Jordan didn't speak. Of course he wouldn't want her. She wasn't like his other women. She wasn't attractive enough or experienced. He wouldn't want to bother with her.

''I'm sorry,'' she said, and started to stand up. ''My mistake.'' She had to get out of here before she started to cry.

He grabbed her hand and held her fast. ''Don't go,'' he said. ''Please.'' He gave her a half smile. ''I want to make love with you, Holly. I'm stunned that you would pick me to be your first. Stunned and honored.''

''Yeah?'' She wanted to believe him.

He kissed her gently. ''Yeah.''

They stared at each other for a moment. She swallowed nervously. ''What do you want me to do?''

''Just sit there. I'll be right back.''

He headed for the stairs and took them two at a time. At least he wasn't acting as if this was going to be hideous. A small but comforting thought. She pressed a hand against her now-fluttering tummy and wondered if she was making a mistake.

She laughed softly. No. She'd chosen wisely. Jordan was tender and considerate. He would make her first time wonderful. With him, she wouldn't mind being awkward and asking questions. He had a way of easing her discomfort, even when she was embarrassed.

He returned with a thick quilt and a small box. She got up and helped him spread the quilt in front of the Christmas tree. Then she shifted her weight from foot to foot. "Are you sure it's okay to do it here?"

He kissed her forehead. "We can do it anywhere you like. I thought this would be romantic."

She glanced around at the tree and the flickering fire. It *was* romantic. "Okay."

He set the box next to the champagne glasses. "I'll take care of protection."

"P-protection?" She took a step back. Oh my gosh. They were going to have sex. Sex as in they needed protection. She stared at the box as if it contained live snakes.

"Holly, are you all right?"

"Ah, fine."

He stood in front of her and took both her hands in his. His dark gaze met hers. "I know this is strange and you're scared. I wish I had the right words, but I don't. I'm just as scared as you are."

Somehow that was comforting. "But you've done this before."

"Not with you."

Interesting logic. She liked it. "I'm afraid I'm going to say or do something stupid."

"I'll promise not to laugh if you will."

"Why would I laugh?"

He smiled. "Sex is pretty silly. Have a seat." He settled next to her, then reached for the box. "These are condoms. Have you seen one before?"

She shook her head.

He opened the box and dumped the contents onto the

quilt. Before she could pick one up, he was undoing the box and smoothing it flat. She glanced down and was stunned to see detailed instructions along with some odd-looking illustrations.

"They tell you how to use them?" she asked, her voice rising into a shriek.

"How else would you learn?"

"I thought guys just sort of knew."

"Sorry. At the beginning we're just as nervous and ignorant as everyone else."

She scanned the instructions. Involuntarily her gaze dropped to Jordan's lap. He was wearing jeans, and she couldn't tell if he was "erect" as they mentioned in step one. If she couldn't even tell that, how on earth was she going to figure anything else out?

Before she could panic even more, he reached for one of the packages and ripped it open.

"W-what are you doing?" she asked, terrified the next step was undoing his pants and pulling "it" out.

"Trying to show you it's not scary." He handed her the open package. "Take it out."

She assumed he meant "it" as in the condom and not "it" as in, well, his "it." She cleared her throat, then dumped the contents onto her palm.

The condom was flat and round, sort of an ivory color. She inhaled the faint odor of latex.

"You can unroll it," he said.

She held it between her thumbs and forefingers, then did as he suggested. When it was completely unrolled, she stared at it. The condom hung limply from her fingers.

"Somehow I was expecting more," she said.

"Still scared?" he asked.

She wiggled it slightly. "Not of this."

"Good." He rose to his feet. "I'm going to get more champagne. I'll be right back."

Holly stared at the condom. It looked like a weird little balloon. An idea formed in the back of her mind. She tried to ignore it, but once there, the idea demanded attention. She glanced toward the kitchen, but didn't see Jordan. After taking a deep breath, she cupped the open end of the condom, then brought it to her mouth.

It blew up perfectly. With three deep breaths she had it nearly as big as a loaf of bread. Behind her glass clinked against the wood table. Jordan had returned.

He crouched in front of her, took the blown-up condom from her now-shaking fingers and grinned. "Ah, I'm afraid I'm not going to meet your expectations."

"Oh, no." She buried her face in her hands and heard a whistle of air as he deflated the protection.

"My brothers and I found out they also make great water balloons."

She risked a quick glance through her parted fingers. He was sitting next to her on the quilt. Firelight made his dark hair shine. His face was in shadows, but she could see the hint of a smile tugging at his lips.

When he saw her looking at him, the smile faded. "I want to make love with you," he said slowly. "But I'm not going to rush you. I want your first time to be perfect."

She didn't care about perfection. She only wanted to be with him. "Tell me what to do."

"Trust me."

"I do."

Chapter Fourteen

Jordan touched her face, then trailed his fingers down to her shoulders. Holly remembered the last time he had stroked her and the feelings he'd evoked. Could she do the same to him?

She frowned. "Would you like me to touch you? I mean would you enjoy it?"

"'Enjoy' isn't the word I'd use." He must have caught her confusion. He smiled. "I was thinking more of ecstasy."

She wasn't sure she could do ecstasy, but she was willing to try. She shifted until she was kneeling in front of him, then leaned forward. He didn't move as she got closer. Instead of touching his mouth with hers, she pressed her lips against his neck, in that sensitive spot just below his left ear.

His warm skin appealed to her. After several chaste kisses she risked touching him with her tongue. He tasted of himself, a combination of masculinity and temptation. A faint tremor rippled through him.

She continued her exploration, tracing the curve of his ear, then trailing a damp path to his mouth. As she kissed him, he held her arms and lowered them both to the quilt.

Bodies touched, tongues stroked, breath mingled. Their slow dance of arousal left her weak and shaking, but she didn't want to stop. She figured that she'd gotten lucky with Jordan. He was a kind, gentle man who made her heart beat faster and her thighs tremble. For some reason he liked her, even wanted her. Men like him weren't usually interested in women like her, and she didn't understand what combination of circumstances had allowed him to find her appealing. Whatever it was, she was grateful. She wanted her first time to be with him because she knew he would make it wonderful. She didn't even mind being afraid.

She lay half on top of him. He shifted her so one of her legs slid between his. She braced one arm on the floor. Her free hand rested on his chest. As he tilted his head and explored her mouth, she wondered if it was all right to touch him as he'd touched her.

Tentatively, almost hoping he wouldn't notice, she spread her fingers and began moving across his chest. He moaned low in his throat. He'd laced his fingers in her hair, and now he urged her closer. The rate of his breathing increased, as did hers.

"Unbutton my shirt," he whispered, then drew her lower lip into his mouth. The sucking sensation forced all conscious thought from her mind, and it was several seconds before she could respond to his request.

Unbutton his shirt. Easy enough, she thought, reminding herself she'd unbuttoned her own shirt countless times. Surely this couldn't be harder. Could it?

She slid her hand to the center of his chest, then followed the line to the slight V below his collar. The first button came undone easily. As did the second. Then she noticed the combination of hot skin and soft, crinkly hair brushing against her knuckles. How was she supposed to concentrate while that was going on? When combined with the delicious things Jordan was doing to her lips and tongue, she didn't have a prayer.

She broke the kiss, then pushed herself into a sitting position. "I want to see what I'm doing," she said.

He raised his arms and tucked his hands behind his head. "Be my guest."

It was both easier and harder to work this way. Although she wasn't distracted by his magical touch, she was aware of him watching her. She forced herself to ignore his dark gaze and instead pay attention to his shirt.

The rest of the buttons opened easily. She worked quickly until she reached the waistband of his jeans. Now what?

"Pull out the shirt," he said helpfully.

She could do that. She tugged until the fabric came free. The cotton was warm from his body, and wrinkled. She unfastened the last three buttons, then drew the center of his shirt apart.

His chest was bare to her gaze. She stared at him. She'd seen men's chests on television and in magazines. She'd even seen Jordan's, but this time she was responsible for baring his skin to her gaze.

She could feel the heat of him, inhale his scent. He was alive and real and right in front of her. Tentatively, half-afraid he would protest, she placed her hand on his flat belly.

His muscles rippled under her touch. She glanced at him,

but his face gave nothing away. His eyes were closed as if he were completely focused on what she was doing.

She moved her hand up slowly, delighting in the way his chest hair felt against her palm. When she reached his collarbone, she brushed the shirt off his shoulders. He half sat up and shrugged out of the garment, then sank back onto the quilt.

Now his eyes were open. He placed his hands on her hips. "Straddle me," he said.

She shifted over him, but this time when she came down, she wasn't on his belly. She could feel his hips between her thighs and something else. Something hard and long. Something that made her insides feel funny and that place between her legs tighten.

He held out his hands. She laced her fingers with his. Slowly he began to draw her closer. She had to lean toward him, then allow him to lower her to his chest. The action required cooperation and trust.

He met her halfway, touching her mouth with his. They kissed. She felt herself slipping into a world she didn't understand. A world of sensation and desire. She wanted and needed, but the specifics required eluded her. Her body strained toward the release he'd offered her once before. She wanted to feel his hands on her, his mouth touching her breasts.

She broke the kiss and lowered her head until she could kiss his chest. She tasted him there, then trailed through the dark hair to his belly button. She nipped his skin, delighting in his involuntary reactions. He groaned when she suckled his flat nipples. He sighed when she ran her hands from his shoulders to the waistband of his jeans. He gave a half laugh, half strangled moan when she kissed the sweet spot under his ear.

Still straddling him, she leaned close and whispered, "I want to see you."

His hands moved to his belt. As she moved off him, he unbuttoned his jeans. When he sat up, he removed his boots and socks, then put his hands on the waistband.

"You sure?" he asked.

She nodded. Somehow still being fully dressed made her feel safer.

He pushed off the rest of his clothing, then lay back down.

Holly stared intently at his feet. Her courage had momentarily deserted her.

"Scared?" he asked.

"Uh-huh. But you have nice feet."

"Thanks. Check out the knees. They aren't too bad, either."

Knees? Well, okay, that would be safe.

"Give me your hand," he said.

"What? Are you crazy? You want me to touch it?"

Involuntarily her gaze shifted to his face. Now she was in the same trouble, but only from the other end.

"Are all virgins this much work?" he asked, his voice teasing.

"Gosh, I really hope so. I'd hate to be the only one."

She was sitting next to him, her hip pressed against his. It would be so simple to just look down, but she couldn't.

"Give me your hand," he said again.

She drew in a deep breath and did as he requested.

"Now close your eyes."

That was harder, but slowly she lowered her lids.

Surprisingly the darkness comforted her. What she couldn't see couldn't hurt her. Not perfect logic, but it worked for the situation.

He drew her hand across his belly. She felt his skin and

the crisp hairs. Then her hand bumped into something else. Something so soft it made her think of velvet and satin blended together.

She relaxed her fingers and let him guide her. She found herself holding him. He was long and hard, a steel sheath encased in whisper-smooth skin. From top to bottom she let her fingers discover him.

At last she opened her eyes and stared at him. Her pale fingers gripped him confidently, as if she'd done this a hundred times before. Okay, maybe not a hundred, but at least ten. She touched the thick hair protecting his maleness, then slipped lower to the soft, tender sacs between his legs.

The contrast of shapes and textures amazed her. He was so different from herself. Male to her female. She studied his long, lean legs, then brushed the tops of his thighs.

"This is nice," she said, amazed that it was.

"I'm glad you approve."

She continued touching him, then moved her hand up and down in the motion he'd shown her. "Do you like this?"

A muscle tightened in his jaw. "Oh, yeah."

She glanced from him to the deflated condom resting on the rug by the leg of the coffee table. "It's good that those things stretch. Otherwise, it would never fit."

He gave a strangled laugh, then grabbed her shoulders and lowered her to the floor. "Enough," he said. "You're driving me crazy."

"What did I do wrong?" she asked, suddenly panicked. "Did I hurt you?"

"Nothing's wrong," he said, looming over her. The fire burned bright in his eyes. "Everything is right, Holly. That's part of the problem. When you're touching me, I start to lose control."

"And that's bad?"

He smiled slowly. "That's very good."

"Then why—"

He cut off her words with a kiss. His tongue plunged inside and circled her own. He tasted her thoroughly.

She reveled in the feel of him on top of her. When he reached for the hem of her sweater, she helped him pull it over her head. The last time he'd done that, she had been shy, afraid to show herself to him. Now she wanted him to touch her bare skin and take her to that place she'd been before.

Her bra followed her sweater onto the growing pile of clothing. Jordan cupped her full breasts, stroking them gently, teasing her nipples into tautness, then drawing the tight points into his mouth. His fingers traced patterns on her ribs before reaching for the snap on her jeans. She didn't want him to stop kissing her breasts, but she did want his hands between her legs, so she raised her hips enough to push off the rest of her clothing.

And then she was naked before him. For a moment she worried about those extra pounds and the fact that no man had ever seen her completely bare. Then he ran his hands from her ankles to her thighs, and she didn't care about anything but being with him.

His mouth settled on her breast. She held his head in her hands and urged him to suckle deeper. His bare legs brushed against hers. His hair tickled. She felt his hardness pressing into her hip, and wondered what it would feel like when he entered her. Would it hurt? Would it feel wonderful?

Then his fingers slipped between her thighs, and she forgot to worry about anything. The tension she remembered from the last time they'd done this returned, only faster. Her muscles tightened as her whole body prepared itself for release.

Then his fingers were gone, and his mouth moved away from her breasts. She wanted to sob in protest. Why was he stopping? But he didn't stop completely. He trailed kisses down her ribs to the slight mound of her belly. He paused long enough to dip into her belly button and make her squirm.

Had she known what he was going to do, she would have tried to stop him. Had she known how good it was going to feel, she would have begged him to do it sooner.

He kissed her lower and lower on her belly, then moved down to kiss her thighs. When she would have closed her legs against him, he nudged to keep her knees apart. Fighting embarrassment and embracing the hopeful belief that anything this wonderful couldn't possibly be bad, she did as he requested.

Then he kissed her there. A slow kiss, tasting her, teasing her, making her want to scream and faint and beg him to never, ever stop.

Tension returned and with it the promise of a release beyond anything she'd ever imagined. In just a few minutes she was panting and ready, poised yet caught in pleasure too wonderful to end.

The intimacy of the act delighted her. That he would want to touch her that way, there. She felt her body begin to collect itself. Pleasure spiraled, circling higher and higher as the pitch increased.

He flicked his tongue faster, and she was his. Drawn up and out, ripped apart, then put back together. Disassembled with every beat of her heart, assembled by the touch of his tongue.

When her body stopped shaking, she found herself in

his arms. He held her close and brushed the hair from her face.

"Jordan?" Her voice shook.

He smiled gently. "How was it?"

She laughed. "I know you don't have to ask. I vaguely recall mumbling something, and I'm sure you heard."

"You weren't mumbling, you were screaming." The twinkle in his eyes told her he was teasing.

"I'm not the screaming type."

"I could change that."

She sighed. "I think you could." Something flexed against her hip. She wiggled closer. "Now, please."

He looked into her face as if trying to judge her true feelings on the subject, then he pushed up and reached for one of the condoms.

She'd been afraid that watching him put it on would be awkward, but instead she found herself fighting tears. His willingness to protect her, his genuine concern, touched her down to her heart. Emotions filled her chest. She didn't want to identify them now. Later, when she was alone, she would figure out what they meant.

He knelt between her legs. Their gazes locked. This was a moment of no return. Once the act had been completed, she would no longer be a virgin.

"Yes," she said.

He pressed into her. At first she felt a slight pressure. He was large and she was untried, so her body had to stretch to accommodate him.

He leaned forward and kissed her right breast. The slow tug as he drew her nipple into his mouth sparked an answering response deep inside. He suckled again, then pushed in.

The brief pain surprised her. She stiffened and he stopped.

"It's okay," she said. "I guess now you know I wasn't kidding about being a virgin."

"Holly, I—"

"No." She flexed her hips, urging him in deeper. "I want this. I want you."

With one steady thrust he buried himself in her. When she had adjusted to his width and length, he withdrew and plunged inside again. She closed her eyes and found herself caught up in the rhythm of their erotic dance. The low stirring became tension, followed quickly by the urge to press on to a release.

She arched toward him. He moved in and out of her more quickly, then reached a hand between them and touched her most sensitive place.

His fingers brought her to the edge, then she found herself calling his name. Once again she was caught up in the spiraling magic. This time he followed her, straining against her, his muscles hard, his face a mask of intense pleasure. Together they completed the ancient dance of male and female, afterward settling into the safety and warmth of each other's arms.

When Jordan rolled over and opened his eyes, the room was dark. His internal clock told him dawn was still a couple of hours away. At first he didn't recognize the shadowy shapes in the room, then Holly shifted, cuddling against him, and he remembered everything.

They'd made love. He smiled slowly and reached out to stroke her smooth skin. Her heat warmed him to his soul.

After exhausting themselves in front of the Christmas tree, they'd come upstairs to her room. Not only was her bed bigger, but neither of them wanted to disturb Mistletoe, who was in Jordan's closet.

Once in bed, Holly had gotten shy, wanting to put on a

nightgown instead of sleeping naked. When words hadn't worked to persuade her, he'd tried kisses. He wasn't sure who had persuaded whom, because they'd ended up making love again, slowly, erotically.

He could still see her body beneath his, feel her passion and taste her sweet skin. She'd been all he'd imagined her to be, and more. He'd wanted to take her again and again, but sleep had claimed them before he could act on his fantasy.

Now, listening to the steady rhythm of her breathing and fingering the silky hair he admired, he wondered how he'd gotten so damn lucky. He'd never met a woman like Holly, and he doubted he would again. She was honest and open, loving, generous, pretty and sexy enough to make him hard in less than five seconds. In short, she was perfect, and that scared him to death.

He slipped out of bed and made his way down the stairs. Once in his makeshift bedroom, he flipped on the lamp by the bed, then checked on Mistletoe. She was curled up on his sweater, dozing. He reached above her and collected his robe, then put it on. After tying the belt, he crouched in front of the cat. Mistletoe glared at him, then spit softly.

"I'm not impressed," he murmured.

Mistletoe stood up. Her babies made soft mewing sounds, then settled back to sleep. After stretching, Mistletoe stepped out of the closet and wound her way around Jordan's legs. When he reached down to pet her, she hissed at him, then bumped her head against his hand as if asking to be scratched there.

"Make up your mind," he told her.

She ignored him and continued to growl and hiss between bouts of purring. Then she ate some food and drank a little water.

Jordan moved to the bed and stretched out on top of the

blankets. Mistletoe followed, then climbed on his chest and stood there. They were practically nose to nose, and he could smell the cat food on her breath. She flattened her gray ears, then began to knead. Sharp claws dug in through the terry-cloth robe. He winced with each press of her paw. She seemed to delight in causing him discomfort, because she kneaded deeper, then sank down on top of him and breathed in his face.

He reached up and scratched under her chin. Mistletoe arched her head. When he stopped, she licked his fingers, then nibbled as if warning him to continue or suffer the consequences. He continued.

As he stroked her soft fur, he found himself thinking about Holly and their night together.

She'd been a virgin. He'd known that fact; they'd even discussed it. But knowing it and actually being the first man to make love to her were two different things. He'd felt the tightness, the protective barrier that, once broken, could not be repaired. The act of making love with her had been different from making love with anyone else.

In a primitive male way, he felt a connection and sense of responsibility. She'd marked him with her innocence, and he'd claimed her with his seed. If he were a different kind of man, he would want to hold on to her forever.

If he were a different kind of man, she would be safe with him.

But he wasn't different. He was stuck in a world where he could not escape the truth. Because he respected her and cared about her, he would not try to destroy her by loving her. As he stroked Mistletoe and listened to her purring, he swore he would treat Holly right. He wouldn't betray her or let her down. Others had done that before him, but he was going to be different. He was going to give her the best gift of all. He wasn't going to hurt her. If the price of that was not loving her, then so be it.

Holly woke to the smell of coffee. She opened her eyes and saw sunlight streaming into her bedroom. Despite the familiar furniture, something was different. She blinked as she tried to figure it out. Then she remembered last night. In the same instant she realized she was naked beneath the covers and that Jordan was entering the room.

She stared at him and felt her heartbeat increase. His hair was tousled, his face unshaven. He wore a white terry-cloth robe loosely knotted around his waist. Bare legs led to bare feet. He was gorgeous and smiling at her.

"I brought you breakfast," he said, holding out a tray. "Are you hungry?"

"Starved." After pushing her hair out of her eyes, she started to sit up. The sheet chose not to cooperate, and there was a quick tug-of-war as she tried to get into a sitting position without flashing Jordan.

He set the tray over her lap, then leaned toward her. "You don't have to work so hard to cover up. I've seen it all, and it's lovely."

Before she could recover enough to speak, he settled on the bed next to her and poured them both a cup of coffee. There was also toast and fruit.

"I checked on Mistletoe," he said. "She ate breakfast, and the kittens seem fine. They don't have their eyes open, though."

"That takes a little while," Holly commented automatically, not able to believe they were practically naked, eating breakfast in bed after making love. As if this were *normal*. She wanted to shriek. It wasn't normal, at least not in her world. Normal was living alone and being lonely, not passion in front of a Christmas tree and a man who threatened to steal her heart.

"How do you feel?" he asked.

She took a quick sip of coffee and nearly burned her tongue. "Fine," she said, her voice a high-pitched squeak.

"No repercussions?"

"Like what?"

He smiled. "Are you sore?"

Sore? "From what?"

He reached toward her and pulled at the sheet until the top of her breast was exposed. Then he touched the curve. Nerve endings caught on fire and burned all the way down to her feminine center.

"Making love. Different muscles get used. You were very tight when I was inside you. Are you tender today?"

Oh, my. Heat flared on her cheeks. He wanted to talk about it? About doing that? About making love?

She swallowed, then set her coffee on the tray. "I feel fine."

"Let me know if that changes."

She wanted to ask what he would do about it if she was sore, but then she wasn't sure she wanted to know.

He leaned forward and kissed the top of her breast, then her neck, then the sensitive skin below her ear. "You're feeling a little awkward," he said, making the sentence a statement, not a question. "I'm going to leave you to shower and dress in private. But you owe me one."

"A shower? There are four more bathrooms in this house."

He stood up. "But you're going to be in this one."

Men and women showering together? Was that even legal? Her confusion must have shown on her face, because he was laughing as he left the room.

Holly moved the tray and got out of bed. Now that Jordan had mentioned it, she was sore. Her thigh muscles ached as if they'd been stretched a couple of inches too far, and the place between her legs was a little raw. She wanted a long, hot shower. Things would be clearer when she was done.

But as Holly wiped away the steam and stared at her reflection in the mirror, things weren't better. If anything, they were more confusing.

She tucked the towel around her body and wondered if making love had really changed her. This time yesterday she hadn't known about the intimacy that joined a man and a woman. While she didn't regret what she'd done, she was beginning to realize that there was a lot more to sex than just the act itself.

She reached for a wide-tooth comb and began drawing it through her wet hair.

"I'm all grown-up," she murmured. She had a business that was more successful than she had imagined, and she was taking care of herself. She was smart, capable and she'd finally joined the mainstream. She had a lover. All she needed was a beeper or a cellular phone.

Holly sank down on the edge of the tub and sighed. On the outside she might be just like everyone else, but on the inside she was different. She'd always been a little out of step. Having a lover wasn't her style. She could say and do all she wanted, but in her heart she was an old-fashioned woman.

She wanted to love the man she gave her body to, and Jordan didn't love her. Worse, he believed that love caused pain. In his mind it created more problems than it solved. So where did that leave her?

There was nothing to be solved right now, Holly decided. She finished with her hair, then dressed and headed downstairs. Jordan was in the living room, sitting on the sofa in front of the Christmas tree. The quilt was gone, as were the fire and the empty bottle of champagne. Even so, her gaze was drawn to the place where they had made love.

She remembered the beautiful lights on the tree and the scent of the fire. She remembered Jordan touching her with his hands and his mouth, loving her until the world disappeared and they were alone in the universe.

He stood up as she entered the room. He'd showered, too, and his dark hair was brushed away from his face. A worn sweatshirt hugged his shoulders, and faded jeans clung to his thighs with the familiarity of an old lover. She'd seen him dressed that way countless times before. It didn't matter. Once their gazes met, her heart rate increased and her legs started to tremble.

He stepped toward her and pulled her into his embrace. His arms were strong and sure. She felt comfortable next to him. As his mouth brushed hers, she parted for him. Her body began to heat in anticipation.

He cupped her behind and pulled her hips toward him. Something hard pressed into her belly. Now she knew what his arousal meant. He wanted to make love, and she did, too.

She broke their kiss. "Jordan, I—"

He silenced her by placing a finger on her lips. "This is all going too fast for you."

She stared at him. "How did you know?"

He touched her face, then reached down and took her hand. "I can see it in your eyes. You're confused and afraid. Last night was great, but reality is difficult to deal with. You've got to be at the shop in—" he glanced at his watch "—an hour. You've got other things to do. I'm a complication you don't need."

Her eyes burned, and it took her a second to figure out she was fighting tears. "I'm sorry," she whispered.

He hugged her. "Don't cry, Holly. Please don't be upset. I understand. You need time to think about everything that happened."

"I know." She rested her forehead on his shoulder. "I'm not crying because I'm upset, I'm crying because you're being so nice."

"I thought being nice was a good thing."

"It is." She raised her head and smiled at him. "Thank you."

"You're welcome." His eyes darkened. "I do have one request."

"Which is?"

"Don't leave me until after the holidays."

She thought about what he was asking. The store was doing so well, she had the money to get another apartment. But the thought of leaving hadn't occurred to her.

"I'll stay," she said. "To be perfectly honest, the thought of leaving never crossed my mind."

"Good." He winked. "Let's try breakfast again. This time in the kitchen."

"Sounds great."

He headed that way. Holly started after him, then stopped in her tracks. Why *wasn't* she thinking of leaving? There was no future for her here, and even if there was, she didn't want a future with Jordan or any man. She didn't trust people.

But she did trust Jordan. She cared about him and enjoyed being with him. She wasn't sure how or when it had happened, but she'd come to trust him…and care about him.

She wasn't sure when she'd started to trust him and let him inside. Maybe that first day when he'd gone back into her apartment and saved Mistletoe. Maybe the first time he'd kissed her. Jordan Haynes was everything she'd ever wanted in a man. How was she supposed to resist him?

She loved him. With all her heart.

She closed her eyes as emotions overwhelmed her. She loved Jordan. Loved him, loved a man who was terrified of love. She must never let him know. She would have to be strong. She could continue to be his friend, and he would never know the truth.

An odd combination of joy and sadness filled her. She was finally ready to trust someone enough to fall in love, and he wasn't going to want her. In his own way Jordan was letting her down just like everyone else, but that didn't make her love him less. She couldn't help her feelings. It wasn't fair, but she didn't want to take her heart back. Jordan would have it forever, whether he wanted it or not.

Chapter Fifteen

Nine-year-old Mandy shrieked in delight when she unwrapped the huge box. The Victorian dollhouse had been built by hand from a kit, then painstakingly painted and decorated. Her big eyes got bigger, then filled with tears. She leapt to her feet, ran to the sofa where her parents sat and threw herself at Travis and Elizabeth.

Jordan watched his brother hug her close.

"I'm glad you like it," Travis said, his voice thick with emotion. "All your uncles worked on it with me."

Mandy sniffed, then faced the rest of the adults. "Thank you so much. It's the best dollhouse I've ever seen."

Holly shifted on the floor where she was sitting and glanced up at him. "When did you guys build it?" she asked.

"At the end of summer." He grinned, remembering the complicated directions and short tempers. "We used to build model airplanes together, but that was a long time ago.''

She raised her eyebrows and smiled. ''Did some of you forget how to play well with others?''

''I think so. But it was fun.'' He leaned toward her and lowered his voice. ''With everyone having girls, we figured we'd better learn how to build dollhouses, or we were going to be in a lot of trouble.''

She glanced around the room. Jordan followed her gaze. Most of the children had already gone outside to play with new toys, bikes and in-line skates. Torn pieces of wrapping paper littered the floor. There were piles of bows, empty boxes and discarded directions everywhere he looked.

Did Holly see the mess, or did she see the happiness in the room? Jordan touched the top of her head, earning himself a quick smile. He knew what she saw. She had a gentle heart and a sweet spirit. She would see the good in the situation.

Travis carried the dollhouse up to the playroom. Mandy ran and got her cousin Nichole, who was her age, and both girls went upstairs with their new dolls. When Travis returned, he settled next to his wife and sighed.

''So what did *I* get for Christmas? I know I was good all year.''

''How do you figure that?'' Elizabeth asked.

He grinned. ''You kept telling me.''

She swatted his arm. Everyone laughed.

''I've been good, too,'' Kyle said. ''So what has Santa brought me?''

''Wallpaper for the dining room,'' Sandy told him, then grinned when he groaned.

Jordan saw Holly smile at the conversation. Although she had been a little shy at first, she seemed to enjoy spending time with his family. He liked watching her interact with them. His brothers were protective and caring, and his sisters-in-law had claimed her as one of their own. He'd seen her whispering with the other women. They all had secrets, and he hoped she was comfortable enough to share hers. A part of him was curious as to what the females were always talking about, but then he figured he was probably better off not knowing.

Sandy said something, and Holly responded. As she spoke, she rested her head against his knee. He leaned back in the sofa and enjoyed her closeness.

He wanted her. Making love hadn't decreased his attraction. Instead, he could now picture her naked and beneath him. He knew what she felt like when he was inside her, and he wanted to be with her again. But he understood her caution. Relationships were new to her, and she didn't want to mess up.

Hell, he was hardly an expert at relationships, either, he reminded himself. He'd never had one that worked. In his heart he still believed that love was destructive. It would be safer for everyone if they just stayed friends. Friendship he understood and trusted.

The only problem was he didn't know if he and Holly *were* going to stay friends. She filled his life with joy. Even more, she filled the empty hole in his soul. He'd only known her a short time, yet he couldn't imagine his world without her. That would be trouble for both of them. He didn't want to hurt her; he didn't want to be hurt himself.

So where did that leave them? He had no answer to the question. He would simply have to take each day as it arrived and hope for the best. For today Holly was with him, and that was enough.

"Oh, my. These can't be for me," Holly said, drawing him back into the conversation.

He glanced up and saw Elizabeth and Sandy passing out presents. There were several boxes stacked in front of Holly.

She looked up at him. "Jordan?"

He shrugged. "Don't ask me. I'm always the last to know."

She counted. "Fourteen boxes? This is crazy."

Elizabeth paused by her and touched her hand. "It's not crazy. They're gifts. We all wanted to get you something."

"But I can't accept. It's too much."

"You don't even know what it is yet," Craig said, and pointed. "At least open a couple so we can all see." He glanced at his wife. "I bet you already know what it is."

"Of course," Jill said, then rested her hand on her belly. "The women always know everything."

"Don't you hate that?" Craig said.

"Yeah," Travis grumbled. "We need to think up some secrets to keep from them."

Elizabeth kissed him briefly on the mouth. "It would never happen, but it's sweet of you to want to try." She returned her attention to Holly. "Please open one of the boxes. If you really don't want the gift, you can tell us then."

Jordan understood Holly's confusion. She hadn't known everyone was going to get her a gift. He hadn't known, either, or he would have warned her. She'd baked cookies and passed them out, but he knew she wouldn't think that was equitable.

He leaned forward and put his hand on her shoulder. "They're trying to be nice. It means they like you."

She nodded, then reached for one of the packages. When

it was unwrapped, she opened the plain brown box and removed a white china cup and saucer. The old-fashioned design reminded him of some of the dishes he'd seen in catalogs she'd brought home from the store.

Sandy pointed. "We know you lost everything when your apartment was wrecked," she said. "So we got together and bought you new china. Each box is a place setting, and the other two are the completer set and some serving pieces. Please say you like them."

"They're beautiful," Holly said, sounding a little shell-shocked. She held the cup up to him.

He took it and touched the soft, cool piece. He could see this cup in Holly's capable hands. His mind filled with the image of her in bed, dressed in satin and lace, sipping her morning coffee. Even more terrifying, he could see himself there, too.

Longing twisted his gut until he couldn't think about anything else. He wanted her. He needed her. If only there was a safe way to keep her in his life.

"Just be polite and say thank you," he told her. "You'll make my family happy, and you'll get some plates out of it, too. Not a bad deal."

Elizabeth drew her eyebrows together. "We were trying to help. I hope you understand."

Holly nodded. "You're all so wonderful. Thank you. I love my gift." She leaned over and hugged Elizabeth.

"I think it's great," Kyle said, "but twelve place settings seems like a lot for one person. Of course, if she marries—"

He stopped talking suddenly as Sandy jabbed him in the ribs.

"What'd I say?"

Jill and Elizabeth started talking at once. Craig and

Travis exchanged knowing looks. Holly blushed. Jordan knew Kyle had simply voiced what everyone else was thinking. It was obvious something was going on between Holly and himself, and they wanted to know what.

Sandy and Elizabeth got busy passing out the rest of the presents. Jordan's brothers had given him some tools for his new garage. Kyle was disgusted to find out he really was getting wallpaper, then his good humor returned when he opened a box containing tickets for a Caribbean cruise.

Sandy placed a large, flat package in front of Jordan. He looked at the tag. It was from Holly. She scooted over on the carpet to give him room to open it. He tore away the paper and exposed a stunning Impressionist painting.

"Holly, you can't give me this."

She shrugged. "It's not by anyone really famous, so don't get too excited."

She'd mentioned a find of lesser-known artists at an estate sale about six months ago. She'd sold most of the paintings, but had admitted to keeping a couple of favorites for herself.

Her blue eyes were dark with a warm and welcoming emotion. "I wanted to give you something special," she said softly so the others couldn't hear. A smile tugged at the corner of her mouth. "Just be polite and say thank you. Isn't that what you told me?"

"Thank you," he said.

"I thought it would look nice in the dining room."

He grinned. "That's the only room that's finished, so I suppose it makes sense."

There was a second box wrapped in gaudy red-and-silver paper. The gift tag had a paw print on it. "It's from Mistletoe," she told him.

"I figured that." He shook the box. "What do you think

she put inside? Something that explodes, or at the very least smells bad?''

''Jordan, Mistletoe is a wonderful cat. I'm not sure why she hasn't taken to you, but as she likes everyone else, maybe this is your problem and not hers.''

He grinned. ''Great. I've been judged and found wanting by a cat.''

He tore the paper. When he opened the oversize shirt box, he found a thick pullover sweater in black, gray and midnight blue.

''Mistletoe is sorry she used your favorite sweater for a bed,'' Holly said.

''No, she's not.''

One corner of Holly's mouth curved up. ''Even if she isn't, I am.''

Around them the other adults were opening packages. Happy comments were exchanged, along with hugs and kisses. If a few of the embraces went on a little long, it only added to the festivity of the morning.

Jordan wanted to haul Holly into his arms and show her exactly how happy she made him. Instead, he forced himself to give her a quick kiss on the forehead. Even as he reminded himself he respected her need to come to terms with their odd relationship, he wanted to claim her as his. He wanted everyone to know that they were lovers and that he cared about her. He wanted her to be comfortable touching him in public.

''Oh, look what I just found under the tree,'' Elizabeth said, and handed Holly a small, square, jewelry-size box. His sister-in-law raised her eyebrows. ''I've always been curious about your taste, Jordan. Guess I finally get to see what it's like.''

''Guess so,'' he said mildly, but his heart started pounding hard against his ribs.

He'd wanted to get Holly something special. Something that would remind her of him without being threatening. His condition hadn't helped matters. For a while he'd been afraid he wouldn't be able to get out and around in time. But the physical therapy had done wonders, and he'd been able to find exactly what he wanted.

Holly stared at the small gold-wrapped package. ''You shouldn't have.''

''How do you know? You haven't looked at it yet.''

She nodded, then fumbled with the wrapping. The black velvet box opened silently, exposing pearl earrings surrounded by a circle of diamonds. Holly stared at the jewelry, but didn't say a word.

Jordan found himself in the unfamiliar situation of feeling unsure of a gift. ''The diamonds are earring jackets,'' he said quickly. ''You can wear them with other things, and you can wear the pearls alone.'' He paused, then added lamely, ''I thought they would look nice with your long dresses and fancy blouses for work.''

Holly raised her head and stared at him. Light reflected off the moisture in her eyes. ''They're so beautiful. You spent far too much money.''

''He can afford it,'' Kyle said from across the room.

Jordan glanced around and saw they were the center of attention.

''That's right,'' Craig added. ''The last dividend check was impressive.''

Holly frowned. ''What are they talking about?''

Jordan leaned back on the sofa and grinned. ''Didn't I tell you? When Austin was starting his company, my brothers and I threw in with him. None of us had much money, but we gave him all of it. We now own a chunk of his very successful firm. In addition to being heartbreaking charmers, the Haynes brothers are well-off.''

''I guess that explains the Victorian mansions. I wondered how you did that on a fire fighter's salary.''

''Now you know.''

She stared at the earrings, then unfastened them and tried to put them in her ears. Her hands were shaking. When the task was accomplished, she sat up on her knees, then leaned forward and kissed him on the mouth.

It wasn't a passionate kiss. Even as she brushed her lips against his, color flared on her cheeks. But for Holly it was a bold, public move.

Before she could pull away, he touched her cheek and smiled at her. Her warm and welcome expression made him want…something. He couldn't explain it or define it. The need grew, pressing against his heart. If he had to put words to it, the closest he could come was that he wanted what his brothers had. Not the love. That still terrified him. But the secure relationship with someone who cared.

When all the presents had been opened, Elizabeth assigned tasks. Holly was in charge of piling up the gifts so there was room to walk around, while Jordan was sent to help in the kitchen. He was supposed to be fixing coffee, but instead, he found himself remembering Christmases past.

In the recent past he'd been the odd man out. Even before his brothers were married, they usually each brought a woman around during the holidays. He never had. Somehow sharing that part of his life had been too personal. He hadn't wanted to deal with a stranger. Better to be alone than with the wrong person.

''What do you look so serious about?'' Elizabeth asked.

He glanced up and saw her leaning against the door frame. He shrugged. "Other holidays. This one is better."

She moved toward him. Elizabeth had a heart-shaped face and wide eyes. When she'd married Travis, she'd made his brothers her responsibility, too. Once she was part of the family, birthdays were remembered and celebrated, and family dinners became a part of everyone's lives.

She planted her hands on her hips and glared at him. "I swear, if I could have just one wish, it would be to spend five minutes alone with Earl Haynes."

"My father? Why?"

"That...that *bastard* doesn't deserve to live. He hurt you four so much. I want him punished for his crimes, and I want to be there to watch."

Her fierceness startled him. Although he hadn't been thinking about his childhood, Elizabeth's words brought it back to him. His father leaving to be with another woman. His mother crying softly in her room. The four Haynes brothers not sure what they were supposed to feel, only knowing that all the toys in the world couldn't make their home an easier place to live.

"That was a long time ago," he said.

"Maybe, but you're all still suffering because of it. You think I don't see what he did to you? All of you? Sometimes Travis can't sleep because of the memories. He's a wonderful man, yet he was terrified he didn't know how to be a good husband and father." She drew in a deep breath, then smiled. "I do love to go on, don't I?"

"You can be a little intense."

"That's because I care." She stepped closer and placed her hand on his arm. "Jordan, you've got to deal with the past. Your chance at a happy present is going to slip away if you don't get a grip on this."

He moved back. "I don't know what you're talking about."

"Yes, you do. I wish there was a way to erase everything and start over, but there isn't. Your parents—" She shrugged. "I don't agree with what your mother did, but I almost understand it. After all that time, she just snapped. Still, I wish she'd stayed in contact with the four of you."

Jordan thought about what had really happened that last day. "I don't blame her, I blame the other women. They could have said no to my father."

Elizabeth stared at him oddly. "Of course they are at fault, but they aren't the only ones. They said yes, but Earl was the one doing the asking. He spent his whole life trying to seduce anything in a skirt. Maybe it's easier to blame the women, but the real culprit is your father."

She crossed the short distance between them. "I know what you're thinking, Jordan, but it's not like that. You don't have to be like him. You are your own man." She smiled. "If I wasn't so happily married, I might just make a play for you myself. Except I'd be too late." She hugged him. "Holly is very special. Don't let her get away. If you do, you'll regret it for the rest of your life."

She left the kitchen, and he was alone. As he made coffee, he thought about what his sister-in-law had said. That it was easier to blame the women than to blame his father. She was right. He did blame Louise. He blamed her for everything. Yet how much of it was really her fault? What about his father's part in the events? And his mother? In that, he agreed with Elizabeth. He understood his mother's need to leave Earl, but he resented her walking away from him without once looking back.

The Haynes family was in a hell of a mess. He shook his head. That wasn't true. His brothers had figured out how to fix things. He was the only one still fighting the past. Maybe it was time to let it go.

Holly snuggled closer to Jordan. They were sitting on the sofa in front of their Christmas tree. To her right a fire snapped, and the scent of wood smoke filled the room.

"Dinner was great," she said, then touched her earlobes and the beautiful earrings he'd given her. "Everything about the day was perfect. Thank you for a wonderful Christmas."

His arms tightened around her. "You're welcome."

She closed her eyes and held on to the happiness flooding her body. She wanted this day to last forever. She wanted to always be a part of him, of his world. She wanted to be able to confess her feelings and have them returned. She wanted him to love her.

A small sigh escaped her lips. There was no point in wishing for the moon. Jordan wasn't going to love her, because he wasn't going to love anyone. He feared love as she had once feared trust. He and his family had shown her otherwise, but who was there to show him?

Still, if she could have one more Christmas wish, it would be to have him want to be with her always.

"Holly, there's something I want to ask you," he said.

"What?"

He straightened slightly, shifting so he could see her face. His dark eyes were alive with emotions she couldn't read. She felt his tension, but didn't know the cause. Before she could ask what was wrong, he spoke.

"Holly, will you marry me?"

His question left her stunned and speechless. She could only stare. Marry him? He wanted her to marry him?

"I know this is sudden," he said. "But I've given it a

lot of thought. I enjoy everything about you. Being with you, talking to you, making love.''

The joy was so bright and so intense, she thought she might die right there. He wanted to marry her. *Her!*

''We want the same things,'' he continued. ''A home and a family. I have the house.'' He motioned to the room. ''Together we can be a family. I've always wanted kids. I'll take care of you, respect you.'' He touched her face, then kissed her lips. ''I think we could make it work.''

She searched his face, waiting, but he was finished. The joy faded slowly, like a rainbow disappearing into the mist. At first you weren't sure it was going, then the edges blurred and it was gone. In the end there was only the memory of how beautiful it had been.

He wanted to marry her, but he hadn't said a word about his feelings for her.

''Commitment without love?'' she asked, pleased that her voice sounded steady.

''I would honor you,'' he said, cupping her face in his hands. ''I would be a faithful and giving husband.''

Almost, she thought sadly. Almost like love, but not exactly the same thing.

''I care about you,'' he told her.

She nodded. Caring. ''I appreciate that. You like me and I'm glad. I like you, too.'' She pulled away from him, then slowly got to her feet. Her mind was spinning. She didn't know what to think. It had happened too fast.

Marriage to Jordan. She'd been dreaming of it since the moment she realized she loved him. He was offering her everything she wanted…almost. She could make love with him, share his bed, his life, have his children. She could be accepted by the loving embrace of his family. She could belong.

But he wouldn't love her. He would never know the down-to-the-bone, heart-filling emotion of love. He would never dream about her the way she dreamed about him.

"Holly?"

She laughed softly, wondering if the sound covered her pain. "You're right," she said. "About everything. We would do well together. Mutual affection and respect. Many marriages survive on less. There's only one problem." She looked at him and shrugged. "I changed the rules."

"What are you saying?"

"I'm not sure. I—" She broke off, not sure how much to confess. "I was so afraid to trust anyone. Everyone had let me down. Then you came along with your good looks and your smile. You drew me in, and I never had a chance. You offered me everything I'd ever wanted. I found myself trusting you."

His expression didn't change, but suddenly she didn't know what he was thinking. It was probably better that way, she told herself. Better for both of them.

"I've only ever asked for three things in my life," she said. "First, when I was fifteen, I asked my boyfriend to understand when I couldn't go with him to the dance because my mother was sick."

"He dumped you," Jordan said flatly. His hands tightened into fists.

She nodded. "Then I asked my father for money to help with my mom's medical expenses. You know what happened there."

"What's the third?"

"I asked my mother not to die and leave me. She did." Tears threatened, but she fought them back. "Now I want a fourth thing. I want a miracle." She drew in a steadying breath. She was probably only going to get to say this once in her life. She wasn't going to chicken out and miss the opportunity.

"I love you, Jordan. You're honorable and kind, loving, smart, funny. You're a good man. You make my knees weak and my heart beat faster. I love you, but I won't marry you. Not unless you can honestly say you love me back."

Chapter Sixteen

Holly sipped her coffee and tried to hold back her tears. She'd been up most of the night crying, and she felt as attractive and puffy as a wet sponge. If she held her head up and blinked steadily, she could get a little control, although the pain in her chest wasn't going away. At first she hadn't been able to identify the sharp ache, but she'd finally figured it out.

Jordan had broken her heart.

Oh, he hadn't meant to. His proposal had been genuine and sincere. He thought they could have a good life together. Maybe that's what made it worse. If he didn't care at all, then she could tell herself it was just a crush and she would get over it. But he did have feelings for her. Unfortunately he didn't love her. She felt as if she'd made the finals in one of life's most important events only to be told she didn't have whatever it took to win. There she was, Holly Garrett, first runner-up in the game of love.

Louise came into the kitchen. She'd reverted to her brightly colored clothes. In honor of the holiday season, she wore scarlet fitted trousers and a green patterned shirt. Three-inch plastic Christmas trees dangled from each ear.

She walked to the coffeepot and poured herself a cup. "You want to talk about it, or do you want me to leave and pretend I didn't see you?" she asked without turning around.

Holly rested her elbows on the kitchen table in front of her. "You can ignore me," she said.

Louise turned and glanced at her. "I don't think so, honey. You look a little too miserable to be left alone." She crossed the room and pulled out the chair next to Holly's. "Tell me what happened."

"I—" Fresh tears started down her cheeks. She swept them away, then tried to smile. "Christmas is supposed to be a happy time, yet here I am crying. Pretty silly, huh?"

Louise patted her hand. "Not at all. Life goes on, even if it is the holidays. Sometimes I think all the celebrating makes it worse. We're dealing with old memories, childhood dreams. You've got every right to be a little weepy."

Holly nodded. She appreciated the other woman's counsel. At times like this she missed her mother even more than usual. She, Holly, didn't understand life and men. She wasn't sure she understood all the questions, let alone had any answers.

"Jordan asked me to marry him," she said softly.

"Congratulations, child. He's not the Haynes brother I would have picked, but I know you have a soft spot for him." She looked closer at Holly and frowned. "You don't look very happy, though. Didn't you accept?"

"I couldn't. I—" She cleared her throat, then stared into her cup of coffee. "He doesn't love me."

"What?" Louise sounded outraged.

The tears started again. This time Holly let them fall down her cheeks. "He doesn't love me. He said he likes me and cares about me, that we get along well together and that we could have a happy marriage." She paused to swallow a sob. "I want more. I want him to love me with all his heart. Am I crazy, Louise? I tell myself I'm a child wishing for the moon. Jordan is a good man. He treats me like a princess." She pressed her lips tightly together and fought the tears.

"Oh, honey." Louise shifted her chair closer, then hugged Holly and drew her close. "I understand."

"I l-love him."

"I know. You've loved him from the beginning, haven't you? You came in here all innocent and lost your heart to him. I'm so sorry."

Holly leaned against Louise. The housekeeper wasn't her mother, but it felt nice to be comforted. "It's not your fault," she whispered. "It's no one's fault."

"It's mine. He knows what his father did, what he wanted, and that changed him."

Holly raised her head. "That was a long time ago."

"Jordan hasn't forgotten."

"Louise, you didn't ask Earl Haynes to divorce his wife."

"The result is the same, as if I did."

"You're blaming yourself for something that isn't your fault."

Louise was quiet for a minute. Her blue eyes darkened, and the lines around her eyes and mouth deepened. "I wish I could believe you were right, but in my heart I know the truth. Jordan was scarred that day. You forget I've known the Haynes brothers for years. I know that Craig was too responsible, that Travis worried about not being a good father, and Kyle wondered if he would ever grow up enough to care about someone else. I even know that Austin believed himself to be unlovable. And Jordan…'' She drew in a deep breath. ''Jordan is the most difficult of all.''

''Jordan believes love hurts,'' Holly whispered.

''Yes, he does. He's wrong, of course. All he has to do is look around his family and see all the good that love has brought them. But he's stubborn, like most men.''

Holly straightened and wiped her fingers across her face. ''Am I wrong not to marry him?''

''Only you can answer that.''

Holly nodded. She already knew the truth. Hearing it from Louise confirmed everything she knew. ''Since I was fifteen years old, I've been scared to trust anyone. My world wasn't secure at all. I've made my peace with that. I've learned to trust again. I trust Jordan and I love him. But if he can't trust and love me back, then I can't be with him.''

''You're very brave,'' Louise said. ''I wish I could be like you.''

Holly frowned. ''I don't understand.''

Louise wrapped her hands around her coffee mug and squeezed until her knuckles turned white. ''I keep thinking about what you said about my daughter. I want to get in touch with her. I want to give her a choice.''

For the first time since the proposal, Holly smiled. ''Do it, Louise. You've lost so much time with her already. If she doesn't want to see you, then you'll have the answer to your question. I know that would be painful to hear, but at least then you'll know. I suspect she's going to be thrilled to hear from you. Wait until she finds out she has four half brothers.''

Louise shrugged. ''I might not tell her that all at once. I wouldn't want to scare her away.'' She thought for a minute. ''You're right. I'll do it. We've lost twenty-eight years already. I don't want to lose another minute.''

Holly was pleased. At least one of them had a chance at happiness.

Jordan opened the front door and stepped inside his house. He knew right away that something was wrong. He wasn't sure if it was the absence of sound or movement, or just a sixth sense kicking in.

He started to take the stairs two at a time, then turned back and headed for the study that had been his makeshift bedroom. The closet door was partially closed. He flung it open and stared at the clean, bare floor. He didn't have to look any further. Mistletoe was gone, and with her, Holly.

He walked to the chair next to the rented hospital bed that was being returned in the morning. He sank down, rested his elbows on his knees and his head in his hands.

Gone. Just like that. Without warning. Without saying goodbye.

As soon as she'd refused his proposal, he knew he'd done everything all wrong. He should have planned his words better. But the truth was, he hadn't thought he would be proposing. He'd been thinking about not wanting to lose her when he'd blurted everything out.

He'd been a fool. Worse, he'd hurt her. Now she was gone and he didn't know what he was going to do.

''She left a note.''

He glanced up. Louise had silently entered the room. She stood in front of him and held out an envelope. He took it, then opened it and glanced at the contents.

Jordan,
I'm sorry to leave this way. It seems so cowardly, but I'm the first to confess I don't have the courage to

face you right now. I'm leaving because I can't stay.
Before it was easy to pretend I didn't love you. I can't
do that anymore. I know this doesn't make sense. After all, if I really loved you why wouldn't I jump at
your proposal? Maybe I'm being foolish and wishing
for the moon. I don't know. The only thing I am sure
of is that I want a man who can love me back. One
who trusts me enough to give his heart. I don't blame
you for not being able to do that. I wish it could have
been different.

> Much love,
> Holly.

He read the paper over and over until he'd memorized
every word. Until he couldn't breathe past the pain or focus
on anything but the ripping hole in his chest. Then he
crumpled the note in his hand.

"She's gone," he said, too stunned to realize he'd spoken the words out loud.

"This morning." Louise took a step closer to him. "I
know you don't want to hear this from me, and you're not
going to believe me, but I'm sorry, Jordan. Sorry for both
of you." She paused. "I'm leaving, too. You're back on
your feet, and with Holly gone you don't really need me."

He nodded without saying anything. She started from
the room.

"Wait!" he called, springing to his feet and hurrying
after her. "Where did she go?"

Louise's gaze saw far too much. "Does it matter?"

"Yes."

"She's rented the gate house on Kyle and Sandy's prop-
erty." She touched his forearm. "You have your reasons
for hating me," she said. "I don't agree with them, but I

understand. Even so, I'm going to give you a piece of advice. You're a fool if you let her go.''

He tightened his fist around the small ball of paper. ''It's none of your business.''

She laughed. ''You're right, it isn't. So what? Are you going to get mad at me? Jordan, you've carried a chip on your shoulder for nearly twenty years. I don't care what you think anymore. You can continue to act like a bastard, but I don't give a damn.''

Maybe it was the rawness of the pain, or the shock. For once Jordan wasn't able to hide behind a mask of indifference. For the first time since that afternoon so many years ago, he allowed himself to really look at Louise.

Her plastic Christmas-tree earrings caught the light and twinkled. There were lines around her eyes, and her skin wasn't as tight as it had been, but other than that, she was the same woman she'd always been. She had a good heart. Her willingness to put up with him proved that.

Jordan thought about how empty his world was going to be now that Holly was gone. If his father had felt a tenth of the same feelings for Louise, then maybe Jordan could understand some of his actions. He still didn't excuse them, but he could almost understand.

If he was willing to go that far for his father, the truly guilty party, then what did he owe the woman in front of him? She had made a mistake. One she'd paid for every day of the past twenty-nine years. She'd only been seventeen. He'd hated her for destroying his family, when the truth was his family had never been more than a collection of unrelated parts. Earl Haynes had made sure there was nothing left to destroy.

''I'm sorry,'' he said.

Her gaze narrowed. ''What'd you say?''

"I'm sorry. I blamed you for everything, and it was never your fault."

She planted her hands on her hips. "Dammit, Jordan, I just got this thing figured out. Don't you go confusing me again."

He shook his head. "I wanted to blame you because it was safer than blaming my father. It's been a whole lot easier to be angry with you. I've made your life hell. An apology can't change that or the past, but it's all I have."

She pursed her lips, then wiped at the corner of her eye. "I can't believe this. Now you've got me all weepy. Apology accepted."

He didn't believe her. "Just like that?"

"Would you feel better if I punished you first?"

"Yes."

"It's not my style. I have a big heart, Jordan. I can forgive. I'm not saying I won't be snippy a time or two when I remember how mean you've been, but I understand why you did it. If you're sincere, then I'm willing to forgive."

He reached out and drew her next to him. She was stiff at first, then she relaxed against him. "Now I know why my father fell in love with you."

She swatted his arm and stepped back. "You Haynes boys were always sweet-talkers. Stop wasting time with me. Go find Holly and bring her back."

Now it was his turn to be uncomfortable. "I can't."

"Figures you couldn't be good-looking *and* smart. Tell me why not."

"She needs me to love her."

"You do."

He shook his head. "No, I don't. I won't love her."

"Didn't you learn anything? You don't get a choice about loving someone, Jordan. It just happens, then you have to deal with it. Can't you see you've loved her from the first moment you set eyes on the girl?''

''No.'' He turned away. Not love. Never love. He knew the danger, the price love extracted. He'd felt the cold blade of love, and knew the damage inherent in the emotion.

''There's no fool like an old fool,'' Louise muttered, and left the room.

Jordan was alone in the silence. He listened to it and wondered how long it would take for him to forget the woman he'd lost.

Jordan felt like a fifth-grader being called to the principal's office. He stood in front of the fireplace, facing his three brothers and Austin.

Kyle threw himself on the sofa and raised his hands toward the heavens. ''You talk to him,'' he said in disgust. ''He's not listening to a word I'm saying.''

''I'm listening,'' Jordan explained patiently. ''I agree with your point. However, nothing has changed.''

Travis paced from the Christmas tree to the far wall. ''Everything has changed, Jordan. That's the point. We're all different. Ten years ago—hell, five years ago—I would have agreed with you. Loving someone was a terrifying thought. None of us knew how to have a relationship. Dad really screwed us up inside. But we've all learned to take a chance. That's what this is about. When you find someone special, you have to be willing to take risks.''

Jordan frowned. He appreciated what they were trying to do, but they didn't understand the situation. They didn't know the real truth. It had been easier for them.

Yet a small voice in the back of his mind reminded him that he *wanted* his brothers to convince him. He wanted to believe. In the seven days Holly had been gone, he'd learned that surviving without her was nearly impossible. He couldn't stop thinking about her. He needed to hear her voice, her laughter. He needed to hold her and touch her; he needed to explain how empty his world was without her. He even missed the damn cat.

"We've all let the past go," Travis said. "You've got to do the same."

"It's not that simple," a woman said.

Jordan glanced up at the newcomer. Louise entered the living room and looked at him.

"You didn't tell them, did you?" she asked.

He shook his head.

"Why not?"

"It's your secret," he said. "It wasn't mine to share."

She wore a cobalt blue blouse that brought out the color in her eyes. But her face was pale, and her mouth pulled into a straight line.

"The time for secrets is over," she said. "Travis, have a seat." She motioned to the sofas.

Austin and Craig sat in one. Travis joined Kyle in the other. Louise stood in front of the men and clasped her hands loosely together. Jordan moved behind her and squeezed her shoulders. She gave him a brief smile that didn't quite take, then drew in a breath.

"Twenty-nine years ago, when I was seventeen, I had an affair with Earl Haynes."

As she told the story, Jordan walked over and stared at the Christmas tree. There were ornaments from his childhood and several Victorian decorations that Holly had brought. He touched an old-fashioned Santa and remembered her laughing as she'd placed it on the tree. Somehow in a few short weeks she'd woven herself into the fabric of his life. Short of unraveling everything into a pile of string, he didn't know how he was going to let her go.

His brothers listened quietly. Jordan watched the different emotions play across their faces. Confusion, surprise, concern. He didn't see any anger. None of them blamed Louise.

"You're saying we have a sister?" Craig asked when she was finished.

"Half sister."

Travis grinned. "Hot damn."

Kyle bounced to his feet. "Hey, I'm not the youngest anymore."

"Where is she?" Craig asked, also getting to his feet.

"Have you been in touch with her?" Kyle asked.

Louise held up her hands. "One at a time. No, I haven't been in touch with her. I gave her up for adoption. I don't know where she is."

Travis glanced at his brothers. "We have to find her. I know a good private detective. Let's go down to the station and give him a call."

Kyle linked his arm through Louise's and headed for the door. "Do you know her name? Maybe we can trace her through the computer."

Craig joined them. "I have a couple of friends with federal agencies. They can help, too. We'll find her, Louise. Then you can invite her home."

They were still talking when the front door closed behind them.

"How do you feel about having a half sister?" Austin asked.

Jordan turned. His friend still sat on the sofa. "I thought you left with the rest of them."

Austin shrugged. "Your problem never got resolved."

"Maybe there isn't a solution."

"Maybe." The other man wore his hair long, and he had an earring in one ear. Compared to the clean-cut

Haynes brothers, he was an outlaw. But he was family, so they teased him about his wild ways and accepted him into the fold.

Austin stretched his long legs out in front of him and stared at his black cowboy boots. "You're afraid," he said flatly. "That's what this is all about."

"Bull."

"Deny it all you want, it doesn't change the truth. I know, Jordan. I recognize the symptoms." Austin glanced up. His dark eyes didn't give anything away. "I never wanted to care about Rebecca. Sure, I knew who she was. I even knew she had a crush on me. But I wasn't going to get involved. Not with an innocent like her."

Jordan thought about Holly's innocence. She'd been a virgin. Now that was gone. He couldn't replace what he'd taken.

"Then one day she was in my life," Austin continued. "Soaking wet and dripping in my garage. I couldn't turn her away and in the end I couldn't resist her."

"Do you have a point?" Jordan asked, perching on the far end of the sofa.

"Yeah, I do." Austin shifted, leaning forward and resting his elbows on his knees. He laced his fingers together. "The worst part is the unknown. The pain of being alone, the loneliness, is familiar. You've dealt with that. You understand it. But loving someone, risking everything, is unknown. There's no way to know how bad it's going to be. You barely survive the pain of being alone, so how can you deal with anything worse? So you don't bother to try."

"You don't know what the hell you're talking about," Jordan said, but he was bluffing. Everything Austin said made sense.

Fortunately Austin ignored him. "I nearly lost Rebecca because I was a fool. You're doing the same thing." He rose to his feet. "Don't. Don't let pride and fear stand in the way. Even if we'd only had one day together, I still would have risked it. Knowing what I know now, my only regret is that I held back so long. I hate to think of the time I wasted being foolish. Don't you do the same thing. You're never going to find another Holly. If you let her go, you'll spend the rest of your life waiting for the pain to stop. And it never will."

With that, he left.

Once again Jordan was alone in the silence. He sat in front of the Christmas tree and tried to figure out what he was going to do.

Austin had made sense, but he didn't know all the facts. Jordan knew loving someone was more than a risk. It was a promise for disaster. He'd seen the consequences of love and what it had done to his family. He'd seen the pain and suffering.

A thin shaft of sunlight danced off the ornaments. He remembered last year when he'd spent the day at Kyle and Sandy's while the kids decorated the tree. He remembered the laughter and joy in the house.

As he closed his eyes, he could see and hear conversations and incidents from the past few years. Husbands and wives, nieces and nephews, births, holidays, celebrations. Hundreds of disconnected events, thousands of happy moments, with one constant emotion.

Love.

For the first thirty years something had destroyed the Haynes family, but it hadn't been love. Travis and Craig had chosen poorly the first time they'd married, but then they'd figured out their mistakes.

Love hadn't torn apart his family. Love had made them whole.

Holly had offered her heart to him, and he'd turned her down. What the hell was wrong with him?

He raced toward the front door, pausing only long enough to grab his leather jacket, then hurried down the porch stairs and to his car.

Fifteen minutes later he stood in front of the small gatehouse she had rented. He raised his hand to knock, then paused. What was he going to say to her? How could he convince her to believe him and give him a second chance?

He figured the words would come or not, then rapped sharply. The door opened, and she stood in front of him.

Her long blond hair was loose around her face, the way he liked it. The silky strands hung almost to her waist. Wide blue eyes stared at him. Her mouth parted slightly, but she didn't speak. She wore a rose sweater over dark leggings. Her feet were bare. She was the most beautiful creature he'd ever seen. He wanted her as he'd never wanted any woman before. He needed her.

"Jordan?" The soft sound of her voice washed over him, healing him and giving him courage.

She stepped back and motioned for him to come inside. He did as she requested, then shrugged out of his jacket and tossed it on the sofa in the small but neat living room.

"Holly, I—" He wasn't sure what to say. He took her hands in his and gripped them tightly.

"Marry me," he said. "Not because it's sensible or because we'd be good together. Marry me because you are the best part of my world. Marry me because without you my soul is cold and dark and my heart doesn't know how to love. Marry me because I need you more than I need to draw breath. Marry me because…"

He searched her face. She glowed with happiness, and her mouth curved up at the corners.

"Marry me because I finally understand that love isn't

something to be feared. Love makes us whole. Marry me because I love you.''

A single tear trembled on her lower lashes. She blinked, and it slipped to her cheek. She brushed it away impatiently. ''Are you sure?''

''That I love you?''

She nodded.

''Yes,'' he said. ''About anything else? No. Not for a minute. I'm terrified of what's going to happen. But I'm more terrified of being without you.''

She pulled her hands free and flung herself at him. He held her close and knew that this was where they both belonged. In each other's arms.

''I love you, too,'' she said.

''So you'll marry me?''

''Yes.'' She raised her head and kissed him.

As their lips touched, he knew he'd found where he belonged. Somehow this kind, gentle spirit had seen past his protective barriers. She'd made a place for herself in the dark recesses of his being, and stubbornly insisted he let her chase the shadows away.

As her mouth parted and he dipped inside to taste her, he was vaguely aware of something brushing against his leg. He broke the kiss and glanced down. Mistletoe had bitten into his leather jacket and was dragging it across the room.

''Probably going to take it to her kittens to use as a chew toy,'' he muttered.

''What?'' Holly said as she ran her hands across his chest, then reached for his shirt buttons.

He didn't answer, because he was doing his own exploration, reaching under her sweater to cup her behind and urge her against him.

''When we get married, I want a dog,'' he murmured,

then nibbled on her neck. "I'm going to need some protection against that damn cat."

"I like dogs," she said as she unfastened two buttons and pressed her lips on his bare chest. He sucked in his breath. "Maybe a baby," she continued. "Then it can be three against one. That should be about right."

He bent over and picked her up in his arms. She wrapped her arms about his neck as he carried her toward the bedroom. He kissed her again. He wanted to have children with her. Lots of golden-haired daughters who looked just like their mother. He wasn't sure he deserved that much happiness, but he wasn't about to refuse it. With Holly, anything was possible. They'd found a miracle together and learned firsthand about the magical healing powers of love.

Epilogue

Red roses and poinsettias filled the church. Wreaths of evergreen, trimmed with red velvet ribbons, hung below the stained glass windows.

The guests were seated by the Haynes brothers and Austin, who were acting as ushers. Since Holly was new in town and didn't have any family, there was no division by bride or groom. Just as well, Jordan thought, watching the church fill up. They were going to have enough trouble fitting everyone in as it was.

What had started out to be a small wedding for just family had ballooned into an extravagant occasion that included most of the town.

Organ music filled the church, accompanied by the quiet rumble of conversation. Perhaps there were those in the crowd who questioned having a Christmas theme wedding in late January, but he didn't mind. The holiday had brought them together and would always be special to them. There hadn't been enough time to prepare a wedding for New Year's Eve, and neither he nor Holly had wanted to wait until the following Christmas to be joined as husband and wife.

As it was, her decision to stay at Kyle and Sandy's gatehouse until the wedding had sorely tried his patience. He'd barely had a taste of her lush body in his bed, then he was forced to do without. At least all the waiting would end tonight. They would spend the weekend in San Francisco, at an expensive hotel with excellent room service. Then Monday morning they would fly to Hawaii for their honeymoon.

The organ music changed to a classical piece. His brothers and Austin took their places beside him, while his sisters-in-law began their slow march down the aisle. Louise had already been seated in the front row, accepting her due as honorary mother of the bride.

The doors at the rear of the church closed briefly, the wedding march began, and the doors opened.

Holly stood at the end of the long aisle, a beautiful vision in white. Her pale gown clung to her torso before flaring out to the ground. A long veil trailed behind her. She wore her hair piled on top of her head, circled by a wreath of white roses.

Love, still a new and wondrous emotion, filled him. He wanted to go to her and draw her into his arms. Instead he waited, willing her to come to him, knowing that he'd spent his whole life preparing for this moment.

She moved slowly and confidently, her gaze never leaving his. When she reached his side, he held out his hand. She placed her palm on his. At last he was where he belonged. They both were. They smiled, then faced the minister.

"Dearly beloved," the man began.

"Wait," Holly interrupted. She looked at Jordan. "Before we say the vows, I want you to know that I love you."

He searched her face, noting the sincerity in her blue eyes, knowing his expression reflected the same earnestness. "I love you, too."

The minister chuckled. "I was going to scold you two and tell you that the loving-each-other part comes later in the ceremony, but you're right. Everything begins with love. As it should."

They exchanged vows and rings; they kissed and accepted the congratulations of their friends and family. Holly and Jordan had begun their new life with the promise of love, and that promise would last a lifetime.

*   *   *   *   *

Look for the first title in the new
MERLYN COUNTY MIDWIVES *series.*
Expecting! *by Susan Mallery*
is coming your way next month in
Silhouette Special Edition.

One Christmas Knight

KATHLEEN CREIGHTON

KATHLEEN CREIGHTON

has roots deep in the California soil, but has relocated to South Carolina. As a child, she enjoyed listening to old folks' tales, and her fascination with the past only deepened as she grew older. Today, she says she is interested in everything—art, music, gardening, zoology, anthropology and history, but people are at the top of her list. She also has a lifelong passion for writing, and now combines her two loves in romance novels.

For America's long-haul truckers, with thanks.

ACKNOWLEDGEMENTS

As anyone who has travelled I-40 through the Texas Panhandle knows, the towns of Adrian and Vega do exist, approximately where I have placed them. So does Santa Rosa, New Mexico. Beyond that, any businesses, structures or individuals in this story are pure fiction.

During Thanksgiving week in 1992, a blizzard swept down out of the Arctic and deep into Texas, creating driving conditions on Interstate 40 exactly as I have described them. Since that time, it is my understanding that the state of Texas has made tremendous improvements in its preparedness for and methods of handling such emergencies. I am certain that I join countless long-haul truckers in a heartfelt ''Preciate it.'

Chapter 1

"Lord, I hate these California turnarounds."
                                    I-40—Arizona

Like all well-brought-up Southern boys, Jimmy Joe Starr had been taught to respect both automobiles and good women. So when the lady in the shiny new silver-gray Lexus cut in front of him in the entrance to the Giant truck stop that was clearly marked Trucks Only, he didn't give her a blast from his air-horn or push his Kenworth's blue "anteater" nose up on her bumper to teach her a lesson, like some drivers he knew would have done.

But he did shake his head and smile to himself. Oh, yeah. She was a looker, no doubt about that. Just as sleek and fine and pretty a sight as you would ever want to see. And the woman behind the wheel wasn't bad, either.

Jimmy Joe wasn't generally all that attracted to redheads, but hers was a real nice color, a rich, glowing auburn. And she had a self-confident, bordering-on-arrogant tilt to her head that appealed to him—which was something else that set him apart from most Southern men of his acquaintance. Having been raised by a mama with pure applejack running through her veins, he was pretty well adjusted to uppity women.

There were a couple of other reasons why Jimmy Joe was inclined to be in an easygoing and forgiving mood. For one thing, that was just pretty much his basic nature. For another, it was the 23rd of December and he'd just dropped off a load of textiles in the garment district of downtown L.A. and picked up a shipment of piece goods destined for an after-holiday sale in Little Rock, after which he was going to be headin' for Georgia, where a little boy named J.J. was waiting for his daddy to bring Christmas home with him. The Good Lord willin' and the creek don't rise, Jimmy Joe expected to be rolling into his mama's front yard just in time for turkey and all the trimmings.

So that was why, when the redhead finally got herself sorted out and the silver Lexus pointed toward the four-wheeler parking lot, he just chuckled to himself and said, "Well, Merry Christmas, darlin'." She crossed right in front of him with a saucy little flip of her sleek auburn head, and he caught a glimpse of a California license plate.

"Figures," he muttered.

"You will never in a million years guess where I'm calling you from," Mirabella Waskowitz said to her friend Charly Phelps, in an ambiguous tone somewhere between chagrin and glee.

"Sounds like a truck stop," said Charly, much to Mirabella's disappointment. She loved Charly dearly, but the woman had no respect for a punchline.

"How did you know?"

"I can hear the loudspeaker in the background. They just called some driver for something-or-other up to the fuel desk."

"Oh," said Mirabella, who hadn't been paying attention. In her experience, voices on loudspeakers seldom had anything to say that concerned her.

"You would not believe this place," she continued after a moment, her enthusiasm undaunted. "For one thing, it's *huge*. Acres and acres of trucks. I've never seen anything like it. It's kind of awesome, actually. Oh—and they don't call them truck stops anymore. They're called 'travel stops' now—I guess so they'll appeal more to the Winnebago set. It's like a mini-mall in here. They have all sorts of stores, a post office, a couple of fast-food places, and a regular restaurant that actually has a salad bar, can you believe that? And get this—the phones are on the tables! At this very moment I am sitting in a comfy booth, one that actually has enough room to accommodate my stomach, with my decaf and a fairly decent turkey club on whole wheat in front of me."

"What?" said Charly drolly, "no sushi?"

"Mock if you must, but the rest rooms are clean. Oh—and Charly, you'd love the gift shop. What an eclectic mix. They have some lovely signed Acoma Indian pottery sitting right next to key chains made out of honest-to-God rattlesnake heads and license-plate holders that say Honk If You're Horny. Oh—and my personal favorite—there's this little bald fat-guy doll, and when you squeeze a bulb he drops his pants and moons you. I think you're supposed to put him in the back window of your car. I'm thinking of getting one for my Lexus."

Charly, who was originally from Alabama, laughed and said, "Get used to it. You know the place you're heading for is the world capital of tacky."

"I thought that was Venice Beach."

"No, no, no, darlin'—Florida! Birthplace of the pink plastic lawn flamingo. Need I say more?"

A gasp cut short Mirabella's chuckle of appreciation. She added, "Ouch…damn," and as she leaned abruptly back in the booth, her gaze collided with that of a young man, obviously a trucker, who was sitting in a booth identical to hers, just catercorner across the dining room. He was on the phone, too, but not talking, and as he listened, for some reason he seemed to be frowning right at Mirabella.

''What's the matter?'' Charly demanded. ''The little tyke giving you problems?''

Hearing the alarm in her friend's voice and knowing Charly wasn't above doing something rash, like putting in a call to the highway patrol, Mirabella hastened to reassure her. And while she was at it, she put a dazzling smile on her face for the benefit of the nosy trucker across the way.

''Oh, you know,'' she said through the smile, ''it's just these darn pressure pains. Seems like they've been getting worse the last couple of days.'' She lost the smile, though, as she shifted to find a comfortable position for her legs while a lump the size of a small grapefruit was slowly blossoming on the right side of her abdomen. She rested one hand on the lump and rubbed it with a gentle circling motion as she said through held breath and clenched teeth, ''Right now it feels like the little rascal's doing push-ups on the nerves in my groin. I get these shooting pains that go all the way down to my toes. There wasn't anything about this in the books, I can tell you that.''

''Bella, you're crazy to be doing this—you know that, don't you?''

''Hey, I'm fine.'' The young trucker had finished his phone call and was now drinking coffee and watching her intently through its steam.

Cute guy, said a voice way in the back of her mind. And then, *My God, he's young.*

It was a purely objective observation; Mirabella considered herself something of a connoisseur when it came to masculine physical attributes, having recently done some extensive research on that subject. This one was tall, lean, tan and blond— some of her very favorite flavors. In fact, if she could pick—

She gasped, gulped cold decaf and nearly choked on it.

''Bella?'' said Charly's voice in her ear. ''You okay?''

''Fine—I'm fine.'' Mirabella mopped her bulging front with her napkin. ''Spilled my coffee, dammit. Look, of course I'd rather have flown—and I don't see why they make such a fuss about it, for God's sake, my due date's still four weeks off, and anyway you'd think nobody'd ever had a baby in a plane before—but on top of that, it's the holidays, and there just wasn't anything available. It's not like I had much choice.''

''That's not what I mean, and you know it.''

''Charly…''

The sigh that drifted across the wire was suddenly contrite. ''I know, I know. I'm sorry. How's your dad doing, by the way? Have you talked to your mom?''

''I talked to her this morning. He's doing better, actually.'' She took a deep breath to calm the fear that always rippled through her when she thought about her father, and about the utterly unthinkable possibility of his dying. Pop, die? No. Not for—oh, at least twenty or thirty years, yet.

Pop, you'd better get well, and stay that way. I need you, dammit! Because, aside from the fact that she couldn't even begin to imagine a world without her dad in it, she just hadn't counted on raising this child without Pop Waskowitz for a grandpa.

Especially, she thought with a twinge of guilt she tried to ignore, if he couldn't have a dad of his own.

And with some mysterious homing instinct, like birds returning to a favorite nesting place, her eyes found the long, slender form of the young trucker in the booth across the way. *Incredible,* she thought. *Uncanny.*

''They're calling this heart attack a warning,'' she said to Charly in a tone bright with false optimism. ''Mom said it looks like they'll let him go home for Christmas, but then after the holidays they're going to want to run tests. You know how it goes—see if he's going to need surgery.''

''He'll be okay, Bella. Bypass surgery's not even a big deal nowadays.''

''Yeah,'' said Mirabella on an exhalation, not in the least convinced. ''I know.''

''He know you're coming?''

''He doesn't know I'm driving. Mom didn't want to tell

him. She's sure he'd only have another heart attack worrying about me.''

"So, you're gonna be his Christmas present."

"Let's hope," said Mirabella. "So far I've only made it as far as New Mexico."

"New Mexico! Is that all? My God, it's been two days."

"I can't help it. The problem," said Mirabella defensively, "is that I keep having to stop all the time to go to the bathroom."

"And you're still going to make it by Christmas?"

"Uh…Christmas Day, yeah, hopefully. I should be able to." But she had to shut out the little voices of self-doubt that were starting to kick up a fuss in the back of her mind, and her natural bent toward honesty made her add, "If I can make it as far as Texas by tonight. Which reminds me, if I'm going to do that, I'd better say goodbye and get on my way. What about it, Charly, shall I get you a souvenir? That Acoma pottery's nice."

"You sure you've got room? If I know you, that Lexus is probably packed to the roof with presents already."

"Just the trunk," said Mirabella with a guilty smile. "I did try to behave myself this year."

"Well, if you insist," said Charly, "I'd rather have the license-plate holder. Listen, you take it easy now, okay? Your mom and dad want you to get there in one piece. And I do mean one."

Mirabella laughed. "Oh, I'm taking it easy. Obviously."

She said her goodbyes, punched the Off button and returned the handset to its cradle on the wall next to the booth, then took a deep breath and picked up a triangle of her club sandwich. At last the baby had settled down. Maybe she could actually eat in peace.

She did notice that the young trucker across the way had picked up the phone again and was no longer paying any attention to her, thank God, but just looking out the window, watching the big trucks roll in off the interstate, one after another.…

* * *

Jimmy Joe Starr was finally getting through to his mama's house in Georgia. He listened patiently to the rings, and on the third one the voice he wanted most in this world to hear said, "This is the Starr residence. How may I help you?"

He just had to chuckle, hearing all that coming out of his eight-year-old son's mouth. J.J.'s regular greeting up to now had been more along the lines of, "H'lo, who's this?"

"Gramma been workin' on you?"

"Dad!"

"Hey, J.J., whatcha up to?"

"Oh, nothin' much. Where are you? When are you comin' home?"

Those were J.J.'s two standard questions, and they never failed to wring a twinge of guilt and regret out of Jimmy Joe's insides. And of course, never more than at this time of year. "I'm in New Mexico," he said, hoping it sounded cheerful enough. "Got a load to drop in Little Rock tomorrow, and then like I told you, I'll be headin' for the barn. I'll most likely be there when you wake up Christmas morning."

"Promise?"

"Sure, I promise—long's the road don't open up and swallow me."

"Dad..."

"Come on, J.J., you know I'm gonna be fine."

"I know, but...you know what? There's supposed to be a big snowstorm in the Texas panhandle. What if you get stuck?"

"Hey, where'd you hear about this snowstorm, huh? Gramma tell you?" He was going to have to have a little talk with his mama, is what he was going to have to do—remind her what a worrywart J.J. was.

"I saw it on The Weather Channel. They called it the Arc-Arc-tic Express. It sounds really bad."

Jimmy Joe shook his head. What was he going to do with an eight-year-old kid who watched The Weather Channel? "Hey, what'd I tell you? The Big Blue Starr'll drive through anything, right? I'll be there on ol' Santa's heels, just like I said I would. Now, quit your worryin'—you're startin' to sound like an ol' lady, you know that?'' He smiled at J.J.'s outraged denial. ''So, tell me quick, what you been up to? I gotta get back on the road. Everybody gettin' ready for Christmas? Who was that had the phone tied up so long? Your Aunt Jess, I reckon. Am I right?''

''I guess. Dad?''

''Yeah, son?''

''When can I go back to school?''

''Back to—what kinda question is that? It's Christmas vacation!'' Just as Jimmy Joe was starting to think his kid had come down with some kind of bug or other, something in the boy's tone of voice got through to him. He let his breath out and said, ''Okay, J.J., what's up? You in trouble with your grandma again?''

''It wasn't my fault, Dad, I swear! I mean, what else was I supposed to do? She *kissed* me!''

''What? Who kissed you? Gramma?''

''No! Sammi June.''

''You don't mean your *cousin* Sammi June?''

''Yeah. Right smack on the lips, Dad. Yuck!''

Jimmy Joe was trying his best not to laugh—at least not enough so it would spill over into his voice. With deep seriousness he said, ''What on earth do you suppose made her do a thing like that?''

A heartfelt sigh drifted over the wire. ''Well, *she* said it's on account of the mistletoe.''

''Mistletoe?''

''Yeah, Aunt Jessica went and hung little bunches of it all over the house. Sammi June says if you catch somebody standing underneath one of the bunches, they have to kiss you, it's a rule. Is that true, Dad?''

Jimmy Joe coughed and said, ''Well, I think it's more like a tradition than an out-and-out *rule*. So, anyway, she caught you and she kissed you. And then what did you do?''

''I socked her.'' He said it like, ''Well, of course—what do you think?''

"Oh, Lord. J.J.," said Jimmy Joe sternly, "what do you know about hittin' girls? Come on, now, I don't have to tell you that. You tell me."

There was another long sigh. "Never, never, never hit a girl. *Ever.*"

"You got it. And that *is* a rule. And don't you forget it. You hear me?"

"Yes, sir…"

"So, what'd your grandma give you for punishment?"

That patented sigh again. "No computer till after Christmas, and I have to do Sammi June's chores for a *week.*"

Jimmy Joe snorted. "You got off lucky. Times have sure changed, you know that? I'd have got my butt paddled, but good."

"I'd rather have a spankin' than no computer," J.J. said in a mournful tone. Then instantly he added, in a much perkier voice, "Dad, can we get on-line?"

Oh, Lord, thought Jimmy Joe. "Hey-hey," he said. "Wait just a darn minute—what brought this on?" Unnamed alarms were already spiking through his insides.

"Can we, Dad? It'd be so cool—there's all this neat stuff you can do—"

"Absolutely not!"

"But Da-ad…"

"Now, don't start with me, J.J. You're way too young to go surfin' around the Internet, or whatever it is they do, un-supervised. Shoot, there's stuff on there'd make *me* blush. I'd sooner let you go to the downtown bus depot by yourself."

"Dad, you would not. There's creeps and weirdos down there."

"Yeah, well, there's creeps and weirdos on the Internet, too. What put this idea in your head, anyway?"

"My friend Rocky just got on-line. He gets E-mail. If I went on-line, we could send each other E-mail."

"Yeah, and so could anybody else." What in the world, thought Jimmy Joe, was he going to have to protect his child from next? Television was bad enough, but there at least, he—or anyway, his mama—had some control over what came into the house. "I can't believe his parents'd let him do something like this, J.J. You sure Rocky isn't just puttin' you on?"

"No, Dad, honest. It's like this, see. His parents are divorced, and his mom works, so she got Rocky on-line so she can keep track of him and help him with his homework from her office. Isn't that cool? And very ed-ja-cational, too."

Jimmy Joe couldn't think of a reply to that, so he muttered something along the lines of, "Yeah, well, we'll talk about it." And remembering the mistletoe incident, he pointedly added, "*After* Christmas."

This business of being a single parent, he thought, by no means for the first time, was getting harder and harder every day. He had a lot of sympathy for Rocky's mother, even if he didn't think much of her idea of a solution to her problem. It made him sad to think about a little kid doing his homework in front of a computer screen, all by himself in a big old empty house, instead of at the table in a nice warm kitchen with his mama cooking dinner a few feet away. That was the way it ought to be. That was the way it had been for him, and the way he tried to make sure it was for J.J. Of course, he had to admit, it did help to have a whole bunch of kinfolk around to help out.

"Hey," he said, "guess I'd better get back on the road if I'm gonna get there in time for Christmas turkey. You tell your grandma I called, and behave yourself, now, y'hear?"

J.J.'s sigh was resigned. "I will, Dad, I promise. But I wish you were here *now*."

"I wish that too, son."

"I miss you, Dad. And I miss Rocky, too. There's nothin' but *women* around here."

"Yeah?" Again, it was hard to keep laughter out of his voice. "Well, all I can tell you is, there's gonna come a time that won't seem at all a bad thing."

"Uh-*uh,* Dad—no way."

"Well, we'll see. Okay, you be good now." And he added

the trucker's sign-off, like he always did when he was on the road: "Ten-four."

"Ten-four, Dad."

Jimmy Joe hung up the phone with a hollow belly and a heavy heart, which was about normal after talking to his son.

As he slid out of the booth he figured he could let himself look one more time at the woman across the way. The fact was, it had come as something of a shock to him when he'd realized that the pregnant woman squeezing her belly into that booth was none other than the driver of the silver-gray Lexus with the California plates. No doubt about that auburn hair, though. He decided he liked the way she wore it, shoulder-length and parted on the side, in a way that reminded him of the old 1940s movies Granny Calhoun liked to watch on her VCR. He thought it was kind of sexy, the way it showed her ear on one side, but dipped across her eyebrow and just barely grazed her cheek on the other. Sexy, with attitude; he hadn't been wrong about that little "So what?" tilt of her chin.

All in all, she was just plain nice to look at. She wasn't tall, which he thought might make her look further along than she was—not like his sister Jess, for instance, who was tall and big-boned and could hide a pretty good-size baby under a men's blue work shirt until the last minute if she wanted to. Obviously this lady wasn't interested in hiding anything, though, because the top she was wearing—a long-sleeved turtleneck in some kind of thick, silky stuff in a deep, dark plum that shimmered in the light—had a tendency to cling. Not in an embarrassing way; like the car she drove, the lady had class. Just enough to give a hint of the way her body might look under normal circumstances—all curves and sweet, giving softnesses, voluptuous as a Southern summer.

He would probably have looked at her a whole lot more, but he figured he'd already embarrassed himself enough, getting caught flat-footed staring at her like some kind of no-account Cracker without the manners his mama had taught him.

As it turned out, though, the booth where she'd been sitting was empty and the waitress was clearing off the table. Just as well, he thought, and tried to put the lady and some vague feelings of disappointment out of his mind.

Which was easier said than done. It wasn't about her being such a looker, either, although she sure was that. But he wondered what in the world was she doing, a California girl, way out here in the middle of New Mexico, as far along as she was. And all by herself, by the looks of things.

One thing for sure, Jimmy Joe thought, if she wasn't single, her husband ought to be ashamed of himself. And if she was… Well, it was a shame. A real shame.

He just hoped she knew what she was getting herself into.

Mirabella emerged from a stall in the ladies' room feeling not much better than she had going in. She washed her hands and blotted her face with a wet paper towel and then, since there wasn't anyone to see her, paused a moment to study her reflection in the mirror above the sink. As usual, what she saw did not please her. Her hair was okay, and her complexion, though paler even than usual, didn't trouble her; but she didn't like the dark circles under her eyes and the deep grooves, like tiny parentheses, around her mouth. She hadn't been sleeping very well, that was the problem. Just lately it seemed as if the baby had changed position, or something, and it was almost impossible for her to find a position that was comfortable— or if she did, one that would stay that way for any length of time. Small wonder—she was just so *huge.* Like a bloated hippo, she thought, eyeing her enormous and slightly pendulous breasts and bulging belly with dismay. How would she *ever* get back to her normal size and shape? Was it even possible?

Then, as she always did when such thoughts overcame her, she felt terribly guilty. I didn't mean it, she hastily assured whatever powers might be listening. *It's what I wanted. No matter what, it's worth it.*

She knew what she needed more than anything was just to lie down for a little while, maybe put her feet up. She considered with longing the lounge she'd glimpsed during her earlier explorations—a nicely darkened room with a TV and several comfy-looking couches. But it had been in the section designated Professional Drivers Only, and she didn't think it very likely anyone would mistake her for a trucker—even though from what she'd seen, some of them had stomachs as big as hers. Bigger.

Oh, well. Mirabella hadn't gotten where she was by being a wimp or a crybaby, and she didn't believe in giving in to minor inconveniences or discomforts like backaches and leg cramps. She did, however, believe in extra-strength Tylenol. So before going back out to her car, she dug the bottle she always carried with her out of her purse and shook two of the white caplets into her hand.

She was looking around for a source of water with which to swallow them when she noticed a crowd of truckers gathered around a large lighted wall map over near the ATM and the machine that sold prepaid phone cards. She'd spotted it earlier but hadn't stopped to study it, having had more pressing needs on her mind at the time. Now she deduced that it was some kind of weather map—one that displayed all the time zones, major truck routes and temperature and weather conditions for the whole Northern Hemisphere. In addition to which there were up-to-the-minute weather bulletins constantly ticking across the top of the map, like the news headlines in Times Square. She noticed that most of the assembled truckers seemed to be watching the message like it was Michael Jordan going down the court for a layup, except they didn't look very happy about it.

Mirabella had more than her share of natural curiosity, so of course right away she wanted to know what was so interesting about that weather board. On the other hand, she wasn't crazy about the idea of venturing into a crowd of fairly scruffy and rough-looking men. She felt comfortable enough with men when she was in familiar territory and calling all the shots, but this wasn't L.A. None of the men she customarily dealt with wore parts of snakes as clothing accessories or clanked when they walked.

Plus, there was nothing she hated more than being stared at, and she wasn't exactly inconspicuous at the moment. Not that she ever had been.

So she was hanging around the outer edge of the crowd, trying her best to read the message from a distance and thinking maybe it was time to get her contact-lens prescription updated, when she happened to spot the cute blond trucker from the restaurant. Since he was also busy trying to get a closer look at the board and not paying attention to anything else, Mirabella was pretty much free to stare at him all she wanted.

She couldn't get over it. It was all there—tall and lean, blond hair with just the right amount of curl, and not even a hint of a freckle that she could see. Good facial bones, strong but not heavy; nice cheekbones, straight nose, firm chin. No eyeglasses—unless, of course, he wore contacts, too. But for some reason she just knew he didn't. God, he was perfect. Everything about him was just…perfect.

No doubt about it, she could have been looking at her baby's father, in the flesh.

Right then, almost as if he'd felt her staring at him, the trucker looked around and straight at her, and she had to turn her head away quickly and try to pretend she'd only happened to glance his way by accident. Then, while she was being careful not to look at him, she was certain she could feel him watching her. Only she didn't dare look to see if he was, because if he was, then he would know she was looking at *him*.

And she wondered, Is this what it's going to be like? Every time I see a tall, good-looking blond guy walking down the street, am I going to ask myself, Is it him? Is he the one?

It wasn't, of course. She knew that. No way. Her baby's father was a student, a music major. It didn't seem likely to her that a trucker would fall into either the music or student category, even if this one was wearing a University of Georgia sweatshirt. The shirt had a picture of a bulldog on the front, and looked faded and comfortable, like an old, well-washed favorite. Maybe, she thought, letting her gaze travel on down to slim hips encased in equally worn and comfy-looking blue jeans, he just happens to like big, ugly dogs....

"Excuse me, ma'am, is there somethin' I can help you with?"

If Mirabella had been the type to die of embarrassment, she surely would have then. Fortunately, however, she'd had lots of experience dealing with humiliation, and had learned that the best way was usually just to brazen it out. Caught flat-out staring, she raised her eyebrows and said, "I beg your pardon?" in a haughty tone, as if she wasn't the one who was being rude.

The young trucker was frowning at her, but looking more puzzled than hostile. "I was just wonderin'—do I know you from somewhere?"

God, he was cute. Brown eyes, interestingly enough, not blue. Mirabella gave him a small, tight smile that said, "Fat chance," and shook her head.

"I don't think so."

"Well, hey, I'm sorry I bothered you then. I just thought, the way you were lookin' at me, like you were tryin' to figure out where you knew me from..." He had a nice, easy smile—not cocky, more sweet. Like Robert Redford. And damned if that wasn't a dimple.

Mirabella's heart did a little skip, which she knew from experience meant she was attracted to this guy and consequently in imminent danger of making a fool of herself. So of course, right away her attitude got even more haughty. "I apologize for that," she said, drawing herself up like a grand duchess. "You reminded me of someone I used to know." Then, realizing she'd been given a golden opportunity, she paused and allowed herself to melt a little. "Actually, I was trying to see that message board over there. What's going on, do you know?"

The trucker's dimple disappeared along with his smile. He sort of rubbed at the back of his neck and looked uncomfortable, as if the weather was in some way his fault. "Ah…there's a blizzard, I guess. In Texas."

"A *blizzard?*" Mirabella was a Californian, born and bred; even the word sounded foreign to her.

"Yeah, guess so. They say it's snowin' as far south as Dallas."

Geography not having been one of her best subjects, Mirabella wasn't sure precisely what that meant. She did, however, know that Texas was where she was heading. And furthermore, that she was going to have to get through it in order to reach her final destination. She drew a vexed breath and said, "Texas. Lovely."

"Yes, ma'am," muttered the trucker humbly. Then, aiming his beautiful dark brown eyes right at her and narrowing them into a frown of what looked like genuine concern, he ventured, "Ma'am, it looks like the Panhandle might be pretty rough goin'. You might want to think about headin' south—take I-25 out of Albuquerque, swing on down to ten. Whereabouts you headed?"

"Florida," Mirabella told him without even thinking whether or not she should. "Pensacola." Oh, Lord, she thought, those eyes…

The trucker nodded and looked relieved. "Oh, yeah. That's what I'd do, if I were you. Look here—" he touched her elbow in a deferential way, just enough to guide her closer to the map as he pointed "—this here is I-25, see that? Goes right on down to I-10. You'd miss all the mess that way—be a lot safer."

A lot longer, too. From what Mirabella could see, just doing a rough calculation in her head, it had to be four hundred miles longer that way, at least. A whole extra day. No way she would make it by Christmas, then. "Which way are you going?" she asked, angling a look at the trucker.

"Me?" He shrugged. "I don't have much choice. Got to stay on forty—got a load to deliver in Little Rock. But if I was you…"

"Thanks for the advice," said Mirabella, who wasn't in the

habit of taking advice from anybody, especially men—not even cute ones with big brown eyes and dimples. *Especially* not really young cute ones with big brown eyes and dimples. "But I think I'll just push on."

She was thinking, Hey, guy, if *you* can make it through on I-40, so can I.

From the look on his face, the trucker obviously didn't think so, but Mirabella was used to seeing that look on men's faces and, if anything, it only made her more determined to prove him wrong.

"Well, good luck, ma'am." He was giving her his half-frowning, concerned look, but with more intensity this time. Enough to make Mirabella's heart do that little skip again, which she really wished it wouldn't. "You have a safe trip now—drive carefully."

"Thanks," said Mirabella crisply. "I plan to."

Chapter 2

"Westbound, what's it look like back your way?"
"Eastbound, your front door's lookin' dry and dusty all
way back to the Texas line. Hammer day-yown."
                                                    I-40—New Mexico

As she pulled out of the travel-stop parking lot and back onto I-40, Mirabella's thoughts didn't dwell on the cute blond trucker with the heart-stopping dimples. She was thinking about what lay ahead of her, and feeling not nearly as confident about it as she would have liked.

Not about the weather or the road conditions in Texas—the way she figured it, people must drive around in snowstorms all the time; otherwise, life would pretty much come to a screeching halt for half the year in the northern half of the country. Besides, she had more than enough confidence in her Lexus and in her own driving skills, and if worse came to worst, she could always pull into another truck stop and pick up a set of tire chains. No way was she going to let a little old blizzard keep her from getting to Pensacola in time for Pop's Christmas.

No, what was worrying Mirabella was something a lot smaller than a blizzard and probably a lot more common, too. Although she never liked to admit to being afraid of anything, lately she'd begun to notice a queasy feeling in her stomach whenever she thought—really thought—about this business of having a baby.

She'd had no doubts about it before. None at all. After all, she'd planned this pregnancy down to the last detail, and it wasn't in her nature to second-guess herself. Besides, it had been fun, at first. There'd been the exhilaration of knowing she'd succeeded—not that she was accustomed to settling for anything less, or had ever *really* doubted for a minute that she would; but still, she'd been warned that it could take as many as ten or twelve tries, and she'd managed it in only three.

For a while after that, she'd kept it her own delicious secret. Never much of a reader, she'd devoured every baby magazine in the doctor's-office waiting room, then had gone out and bought every book she could find on pregnancy and child care. Mirabella never did anything by halves. Thus informed and prepared, she'd been fascinated rather than dismayed by the sequence of changes taking place in her body, for once not minding when her breasts suddenly grew three cup sizes. Hey, this was great—suddenly it was okay to gain weight!

The night she first felt movement, she'd called up Charly and they'd gone out for frozen-yogurt sundaes at two in the morning to celebrate.

She'd really loved putting her talent and training as an architectural interior designer to work turning her guest room into a nursery and redesigning the rest of the house to make it absolutely babyproof. She'd delighted in having an excuse to dress for comfort, which she preferred anyway. She'd enthusiastically enrolled in natural childbirth classes, having coerced a somewhat less-than-enthusiastic Charly into being her coach. After that, she'd felt confident and ready for whatever came next.

Nothing to it, she remembered thinking. This was going to
be a breeze.

But lately, in the past week or so, things had begun
to…well, change. Radiantly healthy up to now, she'd suddenly
become extremely uncomfortable. That was because the baby
had "dropped," the doctor told her. Nothing to worry about;
perfectly normal, she'd insisted. But to Mirabella it had an
ominous sound. Plus, the pressure pains in her groin really did
hurt. She wasn't sleeping well at night. And in the past couple
of days she'd noticed, to her horror, that she'd developed a
tendency to *waddle*.

It was very hard, she'd discovered, to maintain your dignity
when you were shaped like a Weeble.

And dignity was important to Mirabella, which was something few people seemed able to understand. For most of her
adult life, people—her female friends and sisters, mostly—had
been telling her how beautiful she was, and, they were sure to
add, how much more appealing she would be to men if she
would only let her guard down and lighten up more. But
they'd never understood about the dignity thing. How could
they? Eve, Mirabella's younger sister, had been blessed with
the face and body of Princess Grace, so who cared if she had
all the dignity of Soupy Sales? And Sommer, the oldest, designed more along the lines of Princess Di, seemed to have
been born with a shy and coltish awkwardness that somehow
made the whole concept of dignity irrelevant.

How could they ever understand Mirabella, who had had
the misfortune to be born short, stocky, red-haired, freckle-
faced and nearsighted, or know that there had been times when
she was sure pride and dignity were all that had kept her from
dying of humiliation?

It was just beginning to occur to her that giving birth might
be a difficult thing to accomplish with one's dignity intact.

It had also occurred to her recently that it wasn't something
she cared to go through alone. But Charly was…well, she was
a dear and loyal friend, but she just wasn't… For some reason
she just didn't have what Mirabella needed right now. Neither

did her sisters, preoccupied as they were with their own busy lives. So when her mom had announced plans to fly out for Christmas and stay until after the baby was born to help out for the first weeks and get acquainted with her new grandchild, she'd been profoundly and unexpectedly relieved.

But then Pop had had his heart attack.

"Of course, you can't leave him." Mirabella had been astonished her mother would even think of it. And with characteristic decisiveness had promptly added, "I'll go there instead."

It was only later that she'd acknowledged the squeezing sensation in her chest that had prompted her to say it, and to recognize it for what it was: pure panic.

And it was only now that she could admit to herself that the real reason she was so anxious to get to Pensacola had nothing to do with Christmas, or even her father's heart attack. She was having a baby, dammit. And like countless women before her, she wanted someone wise and nurturing to guide her through the experience. In short, she wanted her mother.

Jimmy Joe wasn't dwelling on the problems ahead, the blizzard in Texas, or even a little boy in Georgia sulking about missing his daddy. Although it didn't make him happy to have to admit it, he couldn't seem to get the uppity red-haired pregnant woman from California out of his mind.

She had to be crazy, that's what it was. Plumb crazy to think she could drive that pretty silver car of hers through a Panhandle blizzard all alone. And in her condition! What was she tryin' to do?

He thought then about that little boy waiting for him to come home, and he thought about the sweet little daughter he'd never even gotten a chance to know; and in the depths of his easygoing soul he felt the stirrings of unaccustomed anger.

What in the name of heaven is she thinking of? he wondered as he pointed his big blue Kenworth down the I-40 on-ramp, pumping his way methodically through the gears. Didn't she know how precious a gift she was carrying?

He tried hard to be fair, figuring she must have thought she had good reason to be doing what she was doing. But he could have told her it wasn't worth it. As far as he was concerned, no reason was good enough to risk a child's life. He wished he had told her when he had the chance. Now it was too late.

Once he was rolling along with the asphalt ribbon unfolding nice and smooth in front of him, Jimmy Joe picked up his mike, thumbed the button and said in his growly CB drawl, "Westbound, what's it look like back your way? What'sa story on that Texas blizzard? Come on."

He listened to static for a moment or two before he got an answer. It sure wasn't what he wanted to hear.

"Uh…looks like they gonna be closin' 'er down, here, pretty soon."

Somebody else broke in with a groan. "Ah, hell, don't tell me that."

"That's what they're sayin'. Shuttin' 'er down at Tucumcari. Ain't lettin' nobody through."

"Oh, man…"

"What I hear, ain't nobody comin' through the Panhandle."

"I just come up twenty-five," somebody else said. "Dry and dusty down that way."

"Hell, that don't do me good. I gotta get to Nashville!"

"That's just a crime, you know it? Shuttin' down a whole damn interstate for a little bit a' snow."

"Shoot, Texas don't even know what a snowplow is."

"Ain't that the truth?"

The chatter went on, but Jimmy Joe didn't join in. He hung up his mike and listened to all the bitching and complaining, which he mostly agreed with. But he was still thinking about that redhead in the Lexus, wishing he had some way to warn her. Wishing she had a CB so he could talk to her, at least let her know what she was driving into.

Mirabella couldn't see what all the fuss was about. She'd rolled right through Albuquerque without any problems, if you didn't count a couple of idiots in pickup trucks driving like kamikazis, and some bewildering lane changes in a construction zone. She did see a little bit of snow going through the mountains on the other side of the city—just a light dusting on the junipers, not even enough to look pretty. And she did feel a twinge of indecision as she came up on the turnoff to I-25 south. *Last chance.* The thought flashed through her mind. Last chance to change your mind, Bella.

But the road was dry and the skies were clear, and she was moving along normally, which is to say well over the speed limit—Mirabella preferred to think of speed limits as "guidelines," anyway. So she sailed on past the turnoff, set her cruise control at seventy-five, and popped her favorite chamber-music tape into the deck. As part of her campaign to imprint her unborn child with a taste for good music, she turned the volume up high and settled back for the long haul.

At this rate, she told herself smugly, she would easily make it as far as Amarillo tonight—maybe farther. After that it was only another thousand miles or so to Pensacola. Okay, that did sound like a lot, but hey, she had two days. She could still make it by Christmas night. She *would* make it. She'd made up her mind. And when Mirabella made up her mind to do something, she did it.

Not long after that, everything came to a halt.

Now what? thought Mirabella. According to the last mile marker she'd paid any attention to, she was still at least a hundred miles from Texas, and, it looked to her, a lot farther than that from the nearest snowflake.

Right about now she should be approaching the town of Santa Rosa—barely a speck on the road atlas that lay open on the seat beside her—where she'd planned to make a quick potty-stop. Her back was aching and her legs had developed an alarming tendency to go numb, but she'd figured on pushing ahead another fifty miles to Tucumcari before taking a real break. Which she was never going to make if it kept going like this. What, she wondered irritably, was the holdup, anyway? It had to be an accident of some kind. Dammit, just her luck.

Then she noticed that trucks were beginning to pull over and park along the shoulder of the interstate, in a long, grumbling line that stretched back toward Arizona as far as she could see in her rearview mirrors. That struck her as a very bad sign.

The traffic lanes were moving, though, still creeping slowly but steadily along. And now up ahead she could see flashing lights, and state troopers waving lighted batons like semaphores. It appeared the two lanes of traffic were being merged into one, then directed toward the nearest exit ramp. Mirabella didn't see any signs at all of an accident. She began to get a queasy feeling in her stomach.

When she got to the first state trooper she stopped and rolled down her window. Raising her voice above the oboe solo in Albinoni's Adagio, which was issuing full blast from her tape deck, she said in an imperious tone, "Excuse me, officer, what's the problem? Why is the highway closed?"

The young Native American trooper first gave her an impatient look, then did a double take and came ambling over. He leaned down to the window, started to speak, then interrupted himself and instead said loudly, "Ma'am, could you turn that down, please?" Mirabella turned off the tape player. "Thank you. Ma'am, since you haven't been listening to your radio, I guess you probably don't know. The interstate's closed at the Texas state line. They got blowing snow, icy roads and zero visibility through the Texas Panhandle."

"But that's a hundred miles from here," Mirabella protested. She couldn't believe he was serious. Snow? Impossible. It was so *nice* here.

But the trooper was straightening with an air of finality and a shrug. "Got to close it somewhere, ma'am—preferably somewhere people got a place to stay. Tucumcari's full up. Santa Rosa's the next stop down the line. Unless you have business between here and the line, I'm gonna have to ask you to exit here, ma'am. Move along, now…thank you. Exit to your right, please.'' He pointed toward the off-ramp and waved her on with his lighted baton.

Mirabella did as she was told, which was something she never enjoyed, especially when she had no other choice.

At the stop sign at the bottom of the exit ramp she was faced with two choices: she could turn left onto what appeared to be the town's main drag, where at the moment there was a traffic snarl that resembled an Orange County shopping-mall parking lot the day before Christmas. Or, she could turn right, onto a two-lane numbered highway that curved past a truck stop and disappeared into the dry hills and arroyos to the south.

South. Mirabella was chewing on her lip and thinking about that when somebody behind her gave an impatient blast on his car horn. Being a seasoned L.A. driver, she flipped him an appropriate response, then put on her blinker and turned in a deliberate and leisurely fashion to the right.

The truck stop's huge truck parking lot was already filled to overflowing with idling eighteen-wheelers. More trucks were pulling in along all the side and frontage roads on both sides of the interstate. Fortunately, there seemed to be relatively fewer passenger cars entering the truck—oops, *travel*—stop's passenger-car parking lot, and she was able to find a spot not too far from the entrance.

She was engaged in the clumsy process of extricating her bulky body and numb legs from her car when a wickedly cold wind came skirling around the open door, whistled down her collar and blew freshly up her pant legs. As she got her jacket from the back seat, she found herself remembering early mornings on the California deserts of her childhood, waiting with her sisters for the school bus, stamping the ground and blowing on her fingers to keep warm; remembering a certain smell in the air, brought on the wind from the distant Sierra Nevadas.

For the first time, snow began to seem like a real possibility.

The travel-stop store was stuffy by comparison, overheated and jam-packed with stranded motorists and ticked-off truckers all milling around grumbling and griping about the situation they were in. After making her mandatory stop in the ladies' room, Mirabella pushed her way through the crowd around the fuel desk.

"Excuse me," she said to the girl behind the counter, who was busy with a customer, "could I just ask you a question?"

The cashier—young, Native American and obviously unflappable—nodded and went on with what she was doing, which was ringing up someone's assortment of snack foods.

"That road out there," Mirabella persisted, "the one right in front—eighty-four, I think it was—does it, by any chance, go to Texas?"

Again the cashier nodded. Mirabella was encouraged by that and about to ask for further details, such as how far was it to Texas, and were there any places to stop along the way, when one of the men waiting in line broke in with a snort and said, "Not today, it don't."

There was a general rumble of agreement. Somebody else said, "Ain't nothin' goin' to Texas today. They got the whole damn state shut down."

Another voice piped up, "I heard it was even snowin' in Dallas."

The first man who'd spoken reached past her to put his purchases—a paperback mystery, a package of Twinkies and a bottle of Rolaids—on the counter. As he did he gave her a look—down, then back up again—and said in a more kindly tone, "If I'z you, I'd get myself a motel room, ma'am, before it's too late. Might as well be comfortable. You ain't goin' any further tonight."

She stood very still and didn't reply. She was, quite simply, dumbstruck.

To Mirabella, "No" had always been a challenge; the word "impossible" a spur to action, and "You can't," a gauntlet, a dare. It was her belief that there was a way around almost any obstacle, if a person looked hard enough. Right now her mind was racing in high gear trying to find a way around this one, only it just kept coming back to where she was. *"You ain't goin' any further tonight."*

She couldn't believe it. It simply didn't compute.

But she was. She was stuck. In Santa Rosa, New Mexico, for God's sake, for who-knows-how-long. And no matter what, she wasn't going to get to Pensacola in time to spend Christmas with her parents. Instead she was going to spend Christmas somewhere on the road, alone, among strangers. She was suddenly struck by a horrifying urge to cry.

Except that Mirabella *never* cried. She took a deep breath, murmured, "Thanks," to no one in particular, and pushed her way back through the crowd. At the entrance to the dining room she paused, knowing she ought to eat something, at least. But she wasn't hungry. What she was, she realized suddenly, was exhausted. The trucker was right; she should get a motel room. Then at least she could lie down.

After the overheated store, the cold outside took her breath away. Mirabella tried to hurry across the windy parking lot, but the best she could manage was a slow, ungainly, round-about kind of pace, which she thought must be like trying to walk with a basketball pressed between her thighs. Reaching her car at last, she unlocked it, heaved herself inside and sat, breathing hard and shivering, while she waited for the heater to warm up. She'd never felt so frustrated in her life.

"I don't believe this," she kept muttering furiously to herself. "I *don't* believe this."

Half an hour later she was still saying it as she drove slowly down the town's main drag, passing motel after motel, No Vacancy sign after No Vacancy sign. Other stranded motorists, equally frustrated, were zipping in and out of motel parking lots, tires squealing, engines roaring, as they raced each other in a frantic search for the last available rooms. Too late, some people shouted and banged their fists on countertops. Mirabella had banged on a few herself, and even played unabashedly on her "condition," hoping the sympathy factor might melt some adamant desk clerk's heart. But to no avail. There simply wasn't a vacant room left in town.

"No room at the inn," thought Mirabella whimsically. And then felt vaguely blasphemous, even though she'd never considered herself a particularly religious person.

In the restaurant at the 76 Travel Stop, Jimmy Joe was trying his best to have a phone conversation with his son, J.J. It wasn't easy, being as how the decibel level in the dining room was about the same as the first turn at Indy at the start of the 500. He'd turned his back to the room and stuck his finger in the ear that wasn't pressed up against the receiver, but it wasn't doing much good, and he kept having to yell, "What?" every other sentence.

"I said, you don't have to shout, Dad, I can hear you fine," J.J. was saying.

"Well, *you* better shout then, 'cause I can't hear you worth beans," Jimmy Joe hollered back. "This place is a zoo."

"How come it's so noisy?"

"Ah, it's crowded, is all. Everybody's pretty much stuck here in New Mexico for a while, I guess." He took a deep breath and broke the news. "They up and closed the road—because of that snowstorm you told me about? Looks like they're not lettin' anybody through the Panhandle right now."

"Told you," J.J. said in a know-it-all tone of voice. But his father knew him pretty well, and heard the quiver in it anyway.

For J.J.'s sake he tried to make the best of it. "Hey, don't worry, okay? They can't keep a whole interstate shut down for too long, can they? Soon as they open up the road, I'm on my way." And he would drive right on through, if he had to. The way he had it figured, it wasn't likely the weigh stations were going to be open on the holiday, so unless he got pulled over by the DOT, there wasn't going to be anybody checking his logbook. It wasn't something he would chance, ordinarily, but this was Christmas. And he'd promised J.J.

"It looks really bad, Dad. There's trucks and cars turned over and everything. I saw it on TV."

"You watch too much TV," said Jimmy Joe, "you know that? How come you're not outdoors playin' or somethin'?"

"'Cause we got rain. I gotta do something, Dad. I'm on restriction, so no computer, remember?"

Jimmy Joe chuckled. "Yeah, so how are you and Sammi June gettin' along? You two kiss and make up yet?" At that, J.J. muttered something his father couldn't quite catch. He hunched himself over the phone and yelled, "What?"

Just then there was one of those little lulls that come over a noisy crowd sometimes, kind of like everybody in the room stopped to take a breath at the same moment. But whatever it was his son was telling him, Jimmy Joe missed it anyway, because in that quiet moment he heard a soft voice, practically at his elbow, say, "Excuse me...."

He jerked around, thinking it was the waitress finally come to take his order. But it wasn't. It was about the last person he'd expected to see—none other than the redheaded pregnant woman he'd last seen a couple of hundred miles back, getting into a gray Lexus. And although she was trying her best to maintain that uppity lift of her chin, it was easy to see that it was costing her plenty to do it.

For a moment or two he just stared at her. Then he figured he must have made some kind of sound, because he heard J.J. say, "Dad? What did you say? I didn't hear you."

That snapped him out of it. He mumbled, "Hang on a minute, J.J.," then managed to gasp, "Ma'am?" as, being a well-brought-up Southern boy, he almost killed himself trying to mind his manners and stand in the confines of that booth.

She quickly put out her hand, motioning him to stay put, and said in a not-too-steady voice, "Please—don't get up. I was just wondering— I'm sorry to bother you, but would you mind if I shared this booth with you? There doesn't seem to be anyplace else...."

It occurred to Jimmy Joe while she was saying it that the way she looked, if she didn't sit down right soon, she was going to fall down. To put it mildly, she looked dead on her feet. Her face was so pale you could darn near see through it.

There were dark smudges under her eyes, and although she kept wanting to smile, what she looked like to him was somebody trying real hard not to cry. And—he hadn't noticed it before, but those eyes of hers were enormous. Dark blue-gray, like the ocean when it rained. Looking into them, he began to feel a little bit dizzy, as if he was standing on the edge of a cliff, looking down....

"Dad?"

"Oh—sure! By all means…" His natural, ingrained reflex was to get up and help the lady to her seat. But before he could get himself untangled and out of the booth, she'd already slipped in across from him with a sigh and a whispered, "Thank you."

"Dad? Who's that you're talkin' to?"

"Uh…listen, J.J., I'm gonna have to call you back after a while, okay?"

"Oh, please," the woman inserted hastily, "don't—not on my account. I didn't want to intrude."

"That's okay, I was about done anyway," Jimmy Joe assured her as he was hanging up on J.J.'s wounded-sounding, *"Da-ad…"* Then for a minute or two he had a bad case of the fidgets, while he tried to adjust to her being there and at the same time figure out how he felt about that.

One thing he felt was nervous, which was understandable; he never had been real comfortable around beautiful women. Pretty, okay. He liked flirting with a pretty woman as much as the next guy. But knock-your-eyes-out, movie-star gorgeous? Uh-uh. Women like that made him feel like he'd forgotten how to breathe. With that dark red hair and pale-as-milk skin of hers, what she reminded him of more than anything was paintings he'd seen of the Madonna. Except the thoughts he'd been having about her… Well, he would have been ashamed to think them in church—put it that way.

On the other hand, beautiful or not, she was damn well ticking him off by the way she was acting, driving across the country all by herself, taking chances with that baby she was carrying. Which was also understandable; having lost one child because of a woman's pure selfishness and irresponsibility, he had a low tolerance level for that sort of behavior.

What had him confused, though, was that now that she was sitting right there across the table from him, and he could see in her eyes how tired and scared she was, it was real hard for him to stay mad at her. Although he did mean to try. For one thing, it made it a whole lot easier for him to overlook how beautiful she was.

"Hi," she said as she settled herself, in a kind of breathless and sheepish way that for some reason made her seem more likable than she had up to now. Then she stuck her hand out and, in a more forward and businesslike way than most of the Southern women he was used to, added, "I'm Mirabella Waskowitz."

And he decided he liked that, too.

"Jimmy Joe," he said, as he took the hand she offered.

Chapter 3

"Boy, I got heartburn so bad I'd give five dollars for one Rolaid."

I-40—New Mexico

His hand felt nice. Firm and warm and strong. Just the kind of hand you hoped would be there to reach for if you really needed one.

Which was precisely why Mirabella let go of it as quickly as she possibly could without being rude about it. She didn't want a hand from anybody, especially a man. She was doing just fine without one, thank you.

But he was just so damned *adorable*. That Southern accent, that Robert Redford hair and smile, and that name....*Jimmy Joe?* Really, it was almost *too* cute.

"I can't thank you enough," she said, her relief so overwhelming she was unable to hold back a sigh. At least, thank God, she hadn't burst into tears. But it had been close. *Too* close.

He mumbled, "No problem...my pleasure."

Polite, thought Mirabella approvingly. Kind of distant, too, which she also happened to like; she despised men who presumed they'd earned the right to instant familiarity the minute they told you their names. Still, she found herself wondering about it; wondering if Jimmy Joe really was shy, or if this was an example of that Southern reserve she'd heard about, or if maybe the coolness she'd detected in his eyes was only the natural wariness of someone who wasn't about to get involved with the problems of a total stranger.

Which was fine with her and just as well, because after all, here she was just four weeks away from becoming a middle-aged, unmarried mother, and she ought to be ashamed of herself for even having such thoughts about a kid who probably couldn't even buy beer without getting carded.

It was just awkward, that's all. It was hard to get past the fact that she was sitting across from a man who was the walking-around-in-the-flesh spitting image of her unborn child.

And impossible to deny the secret delight she felt when she thought about the prospect of having a little towheaded toddler version of Jimmy Joe running around her house sometime soon—a version, of course, that would be possessed of both athletic and musical talent and an IQ in the ''gifted'' range. She was absolutely confident of that—those qualities having been even higher on her list of priorities than a tall, lean body and olive-toned skin. When Mirabella planned something, she left as little as possible to chance.

''You want somethin' to eat?'' Jimmy Joe asked, stretching around to look for a waitress. ''Let me see if I can get somebody—''

''No, that's okay,'' said Mirabella. ''I'm not really hungry. I just needed...to sit down for a while.'' The miniature-genius version of Jimmy Joe in her belly chose that moment to execute an athletic maneuver closely resembling that of a frolicking dolphin, causing her to lean sharply backward in her seat and suck in air in an audible hiss.

''You okay, ma'am?''

Since she had her eyes closed, she couldn't be sure whether

it was alarm or compassion she heard in Jimmy Joe's voice, although she thought it was probably a little of both.

She waited until the worst of the pains had gone shooting off down her legs, then nodded and let out along, slow breath. "Oh, yeah, it's just too much sitting, I guess." *If I could just lie down,* she thought. *God, please…just let me lie down.*

It suddenly occurred to her that she was teetering on the brink again. She recognized that weak, hollow feeling, the one she'd had earlier as she'd stood helplessly surveying the jam-packed restaurant dining room, just moments before she'd spotted Jimmy Joe sitting all alone in a booth big enough for two. She knew she was just one shaky step from the edge, one kind word away from tears.

Panic seized her. She couldn't humiliate herself in front of him—she *couldn't.* "Well—better go—thanks for the breather," she chirped, not even caring how ungainly she looked, frantically hitching her beachball-shaped body along toward the edge of the bench. Or how crazy she sounded, leaving so abruptly when she'd only just sat down. All she could think about was getting out of there, away from people, away from *him,* before she made a complete fool of herself.

But before she could make good her escape, Jimmy Joe's hand shot out and snagged her elbow. And there was nothing shy or reserved about the way he held on to it, or the tone of his voice when he demanded, "Hey—wait a minute. Where're you off to?"

Ordinarily, Mirabella's tolerance for being manhandled or questioned was just about zero. However, at the moment she was operating on sheer bravado, and the best she could come up with was a superior smile and a toss of her head meant to convey the impression that she was just bursting with self-confidence.

"Listen—thanks very much. It was nice of you to let me, uh, share your table for a moment," she heard herself babble. All the while she was looking anywhere but at Jimmy Joe, at anything but the strong, masculine fingers curled around her arm, or the earnest young face leaning close, now, to hers.

"But...I'm pretty tired. So I think I'm going to go out to my car and lie down for a while." *Yes—oh, yes, that would do it.* She could curl up on the back seat. That would be better than nothing. Or did the front seats recline? She had no idea; she'd never had occasion to test them. *Just...please, God, let me get out of here. Please let me lie down.*

She was standing now. So was he. Desperately, Mirabella focused her eyes on the picture of the ugly bulldog on his University of Georgia sweatshirt. She stuck out her hand, not an easy thing to do since he was still holding her elbow, and said, "Well. It was nice meeting you, Jimmy Joe." And she was thinking, Please, God, don't let me cry.

Jimmy Joe knew he was about to do something rash the minute he saw those big gray eyes of hers go wide and shiny, and realized she was about one blink away from spilling over. That panicked him; he never had been able to stand seeing a woman cry.

He coughed a little bit to loosen up the nervous knot in his chest, then said, "Look...ma'am, I've got a sleeper in my truck. It's pretty comfortable, and it'd be warm. I'm not usin' it, so if you want it, well... What I mean is, you're welcome to it."

Well. He could see he'd surprised her as much as he had himself, saying that. Because her eyes, which had been staring a hole in the middle of his chest, suddenly flew right up and smacked into his in a way he wasn't prepared to handle. Sort of made him wish he could have ducked.

Then she shook her head hard and said, "Oh, no, I couldn't. Thanks, but..."

Just like that, he didn't know why, but all of a sudden he was mad at her again. His voice got soft and polite, which, if she'd known him better, she would have known meant he was in no mood to be crossed.

"Excuse me, ma'am, but you're about out on your feet, far as I can see, and I got a perfectly good sleeper goin' wantin'. Now, I'm gonna take you out to my truck and get you settled, and then I'm gonna leave you to rest as long as you need to, y'understand? Come on, now—you need anything from your car? No? Okay, let's go, then. Come on...."

It was the tone of voice he mostly used to get J.J. to see things his way when the boy was feeling contrary and muleheaded about something, and he was glad to see it worked just as well on muleheaded pregnant women. Just when he thought he might have to tell her his personal views on women who were too selfish or too proud to do what was right for their babies, he felt her kind of relax and let out a shaky breath of surrender.

She whispered, "That's...really nice of you," then looked around like she'd maybe misplaced something, and mumbled, "I just...need to use the ladies' room first, okay? 'Scuse me...." He let her go, and she turned and headed off in the direction of the rest rooms.

As she went, Jimmy Joe saw her duck her head and brush at her eyes, and he suddenly knew she was doing her best to hold on to her pride, and hide from him how tired and grateful she really was. And he felt a softening inside, a slow melting around his heart.

He flagged down a waitress and gave her his order, along with five bucks to make sure she held his table for him until he got back. Then he got his coat and keys and went to stake out the ladies' room from a discreet distance, not really believing she would try to skip out on him, but not quite trusting that pride of hers, either. While he waited he fidgeted with his keys and paced a little, and tried to figure out why he was letting himself get so riled up over this woman.

Mirabella. What kind of name was that, anyway? Italian, that's what it sounded like. But with a last name like—what was it? He couldn't remember, except that it was hard to pronounce and definitely not Italian. Unless—well, of course, it was probably her married name. That would explain the last name, but not the Mirabella. If he'd had to guess he would have said she was Irish, with that red hair and those thick dark eyelashes, and pale as she was, in the good light in the restaurant he'd detected the faint ghosts of freckles.

Not that it was any of his business.

The fact that she wasn't wearing a wedding ring wasn't any of his business, either, but there was no use denying he'd noticed. Or that it bothered him a lot more than it should have. Jimmy Joe didn't like to think of himself as being a judgmental person, but along with everything else he'd observed so far about this woman, the fact that she'd let herself get pregnant out of wedlock couldn't help but have an effect on his opinion as to her basic good sense.

And it still wasn't any of his business.

Except that now, by offering her his sleeper to rest up in, what he was doing was butting in and *making* her his business, wasn't he? Which she hadn't asked for. And doing her a kindness didn't give him the right to pass judgment on her character. He hadn't been brought up to behave that way, and he didn't mean to start now. No, sir.

So here's what you do, Jimmy Joe, he said to himself as he made one more pass around the rack of paperback books, which by this time had been pretty well picked over, so there were mostly Louis Lamours and maybe a few John Grishams left. Sue Grafton's latest—but he'd already read that. *What you do is, you're gonna let the lady rest until they open up the road, and then you're gonna go on your way and forget about her. Ten-four.*

When he came around the rack, there she was, just coming out of the door marked Women. She looked as though she might have washed her face and taken a brush to her hair, but as far as Jimmy Joe could see, all it had done was make her look like a lost little girl.

That was when he knew the last part of that vow he'd just made might not be so easy to live up to.

To Mirabella, the walk through the truck parking lot felt like the longest of her life. It was just so damn *cold*. There wasn't any snow, but a bitter wind cut like a knife through her coat, which was a soft, lightweight leather designed for southern California winters. She wanted to hurry, but that was impossible, and for once she didn't mind that Jimmy Joe kept a firm grip on her elbow, or resent the way he patiently adjusted his long, lanky stride to match her slow, side-to-side waddle.

"Sorry I can't go any faster—I know I walk like an obese duck," she said at one point, characteristically trying to mask her embarrassment with laughter.

Jimmy Joe glanced at her and drawled, straight-faced, "Naw…more like you sat on a horse too long."

Mirabella gave a short, surprised laugh. Surprised, because he sounded so much less reserved when he said it, as if he really might have a sense of humor underneath all that politeness. And because all of a sudden she didn't feel self-conscious about the way she walked anymore. And she couldn't for the life of her figure out what it was about what he'd said or the way he'd said it that could have had that effect on her.

Then they were passing between the seemingly endless rows of idling trucks, hundreds of them, rumbling away with a sound like an oncoming stampede.

"They're so *big*," said Mirabella through her shivers, knowing it was an inane thing to say, which *didn't* surprise her, being right on a par with her usual snappy social repartee. Considered a clown in her family and a wit among her female friends, and at the very least, concise and articulate in professional situations, when it came to a conversational one-on-one with an attractive member of the opposite sex, Mirabella was generally about as eloquent as…well, a duck.

But they *were* big. Huge. Awe-inspiring, especially up close like this. Having a very literal mind, she rarely thought in poetic analogies, but the trucks made her think of great slumbering beasts—domesticated, pampered beasts, to be sure, many of whose owners had decked them out for the holidays in tinsel garlands and Christmas lights, with wreaths and red bows tied to their front grills.

"This here's the one," said Jimmy Joe, and let go of her arm while he took out his keys. When he stepped in between two of the massive machines and unlocked the door of one of them, she noticed that his truck didn't have any Christmas decorations on it. Then he pulled the door open and she could see the words Blue Starr Transport written in silver on shiny royal blue, along with a logo that looked like the star of Bethlehem, and she decided that with a name and a logo like that, he didn't really need anything more.

Shivering even harder, she said, "I can see where the Blue comes from, but Starr, with two *r*'s?"

"That's my name," he said in an offhand way as he rejoined her, pocketing his keys. "Jimmy Joe Starr. And my daddy's before me. Come on around here to the other side. That way you won't have the steering wheel to fool with."

"You sure you're not going to need a crane to get me up there?" she asked, laughing uneasily as she followed him to the passenger side. The truck had shiny chrome steps up to the cab, but it still looked like a climb, considering her limitations.

He didn't even chuckle, although she did catch a glimpse of that sweet grin before he turned away from her to open the door. "Naw, you'll do fine. Okay, here you go, now—upsy-daisy."

And before she had time to be worried about it he'd stepped around behind her and put his hands under her elbows and boosted her right up onto the first step. One more good boost and she was where she'd never in a million years thought she would ever be—sitting in the cab of an eighteen-wheeler.

"Wow," she said, looking around, "I'm impressed." She hoped he would know she wasn't just saying it, that she really meant it. She wasn't sure exactly what she'd thought he meant when Jimmy Joe mentioned a "sleeper," but she hadn't expected anything like this. The control panel just looked bewildering, complicated enough to operate a 747, but behind the seats it was like a tiny little RV, with a wide, comfortable-looking bed, no wasted space and a place for everything. Designing space for maximum use and efficiency was what Mirabella *did,* and she could appreciate a masterpiece when she saw it.

"It's comfortable," Jimmy Joe said with a diffident shrug. He showed her how to turn off the lights in the cab and where to turn them on in the sleeper, and how to adjust the heater in case she got too warm. Then he seemed to hesitate, as if he wasn't sure what to do next.

"I really appreciate this," Mirabella said with bemused sincerity. "Thanks."

He nodded and muttered, "Okay, then." He started to back out of the cab before pausing to add, "Might want to lock your doors." And then he was gone and the door slammed shut on the cold, mean wind.

Mirabella waited for a moment, then locked the doors and turned off the cab lights the way he'd told her to. She went into the sleeper and drew the curtain across the opening, then stood for a moment or two just looking, trying to orient herself to the strangeness of being in a man's private space.

She was surprised at how tidy it was. The bed was neatly made, and except for a pair of boots standing upright and together on the floor, everything seemed to be stowed away in its proper place. There was a tiny closet for hanging clothes, and drawers she didn't look in. An overnight bag, some folded towels and a baseball cap occupied a shelf above the bed; compartments at its head held paperback books, a pack of gum and a plastic bag with some change in it. He wasn't a smoker, thank God.

No bathroom, though; not even a potty. Which was too bad, because she already felt the need for one, although it had only been a few minutes since she'd left the truck-stop rest room. No way she was going back there now, though. It was just one more discomfort she would have to ignore.

She turned off the light and sank onto the bed with a sigh, curling carefully onto her side, which was the only position left that could even remotely be considered comfortable. And as the darkness and the vibration of several hundred truck engines folded in around her, it occurred to Mirabella that it felt a little like being in a womb herself...safe, warm, rocked by the throbbing of a massive diesel heartbeat.

                                    * * *

Walking back to the restaurant, Jimmy Joe caught himself looking around to see if anybody had noticed what he'd just done, as if it was something he ought to be ashamed of. It was a first for him, no doubt about that. He'd had the Kenworth almost five years now, put more than half a million miles on her, and this was the first time a woman had ever set foot inside her sleeper.

It wasn't that he hadn't had those kinds of opportunities come knocking—sometimes literally—on his door. And he hadn't said no to them when they did because he was some kind of prude, or had a religious thing about it—nothing like that. He just didn't believe in mixing recreation with work, was all. Of course, nowadays most of the better truck stops, including this one, had pretty much put a stop to the lot-lizard nonsense, which did cut down on the temptations considerably.

Not that Mirabella was anywhere near being in the same category. This was a different thing altogether. But he still felt weird about it.

Back in the restaurant he found his booth still vacant and a mug of hot coffee waiting for him. He'd just about sat down when his hot roast-beef sandwich arrived, and he was hungry enough that he put off calling J.J. while he gave his dinner his full attention. After he'd gotten that put away and his coffee mug refilled, he picked up the phone and punched in the endless string of numbers it took to connect him via calling card to his mama's house, then settled back to listen to the rings.

That was when he looked up and felt a catch in his chest as if a big bite of roast beef had gotten stuck there. Darned if it wasn't her, standing there same as before except maybe looking even more pale and peaked. He wasn't glad to see her. He especially wasn't glad about the way his stomach jumped up underneath his ribs and made his heart beat faster, kind of like the way it did sitting on top of a forty-ton load when he knew a four-wheeler was about to cut him off and he had no place else to go.

He told himself he really had hoped to have seen the last

of the uppity woman with the red hair, Madonna eyes, Italian name and no good sense, except maybe for helping her out of his truck tomorrow morning and into her own car and waving her on her way. Lord, didn't he have enough to worry about, what with the weather screwing up his schedule, and wondering how he was going to make it home for Christmas in time to keep from breaking a promise, not to mention J.J.'s heart?

He sure didn't need to be thinking about whether or not it was normal for a beautiful pregnant woman from California to have dark circles underneath her eyes, a little wrinkle of a frown in her forehead and a white look around her mouth even when she smiled.

"Hi," she said sort of shy and sheepishly, reminding him of J.J. when he was little and used to come pit-patting down the stairs on some excuse or other after he'd been all tucked in snug for the night.

Jimmy Joe put the phone up quickly—he *hoped* before anybody had picked it up on the other end, because he didn't want to have to hang up on his son twice in one evening. "Hey," he sang out, "how you doin'? Everything all right? Somethin' you need?"

She shook her head and mumbled, "Couldn't sleep," as she eased in across from him, moving like she was made of blown glass. She put her elbows on the tabletop and pushed her hair back from the sides of her face with both hands, then left them there and used them for props. "I had to come in to use the rest room anyway. Thought I might as well see if you wanted to take the bed. No sense in it going to waste."

It was a true mystery to Jimmy Joe why she couldn't sleep, because she looked and sounded to him like she was in danger of dozing off where she sat. A terrible thought occurred to him. Trying not to sound as worried as he felt, he said, "Ma'am, if you don't mind my askin', when's that baby of yours due?"

She made a vague waving motion with one hand and in the midst of a great big yawn, mumbled, "Oh, not for a month yet." Then she kind of straightened herself, making a real effort to lift up her chin. "No, I'm okay, really. It's just hard to get comfortable, you know? I get these pressure pains in my legs...."

Jimmy Joe nodded in sympathy. J.J.'s mama had had those pains, both times. He could remember times when she'd shot up out of bed like she'd been hit with a cattle prod, cussin' like nobody's mama should. He said with relief, "Maybe you ought to eat something. Might make you feel better."

She finished up another yawn, then shook her head. "I'm not hungry."

"You got other reasons to eat besides feelin' hungry," said Jimmy Joe sternly, nodding toward the part of her that was pushing up against the edge of the table. "Got to keep your strength up." He was fed up with the way she kept ignoring the needs of that baby of hers, so he didn't wait to see if she agreed with him, but just started looking around for a waitress.

Things having settled down some by that time, he was able to spot one right away. She came ambling on over and brought the coffeepot with her, probably assuming he was wanting a refill. The waitress was one he didn't know—a skinny woman with frizzy gray hair and deep lines on her face from smoking—but she looked cheerful and sort of motherly, so he checked the name tag pinned to her uniform blouse and turned on the charm.

"Hey, Dottie, what kind of soup you got today?"

Dottie looked up at the ceiling like she expected to see the menu written up there and gave it some thought. "Let's see. Tonight we got...I b'lieve it's cream of broccoli and chicken noodle."

"Well, okay. You can bring the lady a bowl of that chicken noodle, if you would. And a big glass a' milk." He grinned, flirting just a little bit, and added, "And I'll take some of that coffee, since you brought it."

Looking pleased, Dottie sang out, "Chicken noodle, comin' right up." She splashed coffee into his mug and went on her way.

Jimmy Joe sat back in his seat prepared for an argument,

but he could see right away he wasn't going to get one. He was glad to see the woman wasn't stubborn to the point of being plain stupid, and at least had the sense to recognize a lost fight when she saw it.

But...*now* what was she doing? She had her big pocketbook open on the seat beside her and was digging through it and dragging out bottle after bottle of some kind of pills.

He put his hands on the table and laced his fingers together and watched her, watched the slick, shiny red curtain of her hair swing back and forth across her face, catching the light, and tried to think whether he'd ever seen anything in his life before that was exactly that color.

Finally he cleared his throat, shifted around in his seat, and came out with, "I know it's none of my business, but..."

Her eyes flicked at him like a dog after a fly. "Vitamins," she explained shortly, and went back to rummaging.

"Ah," said Jimmy Joe, nodding. He felt unreasonably pleased. And at the same time, bothered by the notion that it did seem to matter to him whether or not this woman he wasn't ever going to see again after tonight did or did not care about her baby's well-being. It gave him a case of the restless fidgets, and after watching a moment or two longer, he reached out and snagged one of the bottles. "Vitamin K," he read off the label. "That's one I never heard of. What's it supposed to do?"

"That's for blood clotting," she said without looking up from what she was doing, which was making a neat little pile of the pills on the table in front of her. "That's to prevent excessive bleeding during childbirth."

Jimmy Joe put the bottle down in a hurry. He hadn't been present during the actual births of either of his children, through no fault of his own, and there were some images associated with the whole process he preferred not to dwell on.

"How 'bout these?" he asked, poking at some brown pills that looked big enough to choke a goat.

"Those? That's brewer's yeast. B vitamins and protein."

"Uh-huh...and this one here?"

"Let's see. That's the antioxidant combo, I think. C, E and—what else? Shoot, I can't remember—"

"What in blue blazes are anti—what did you call 'em?"

She looked shocked. "I can't believe you've never heard of antioxidants."

Well, as a matter of fact he had, but he couldn't recall exactly what it was he'd read or heard about the blamed things, and it seemed as good a topic of conversation as anything he could think of right off the bat. So he shrugged and told her half a lie. "No, ma'am, can't say's I have."

"Okay," said Mirabella, taking a breath and squaring her shoulders as if it had just become her sacred duty to educate him on the subject. Then she launched herself into a detailed explanation of what antioxidants did, which as far as he could tell involved keeping her cells' neurons from flying off to look for mates somewhere else. "In other words, oxidizing," she concluded.

"Oxidizing… Well, now I know what that is," said Jimmy Joe humbly. "I reckon that's pretty much the same as rusting, isn't it?"

To his great surprise and extreme pleasure, she burst out laughing. "Doesn't seem to be working too well in my case," she remarked, fingering a strand of hair that had fallen across her face and having to make her eyes go crossed in order to focus on it.

"Well, now, ma'am, I wouldn't say that," Jimmy Joe murmured, studying her somberly. "Looks to me like it's workin' just fine."

He was thinking about what a powerful difference a little thing like laughter could make in the way one person looked at another. For such a beautiful woman to make fun of herself like that, even crossing her eyes… Well for one thing it made him ashamed of himself. Here, just because she had a face that would tie Don Juan up in knots and happened to drive a fancy new car, he'd been judging her to be just another spoiled rich airhead from La-la Land. And hadn't his mama taught him better than to judge people by their looks? Now he was beginning to see that there might be a lot more to this Mirabella than met the eye. That for starters, she wasn't just pretty; it was turning out that she was also intelligent, funny and, doggone it, nice.

And that made him wonder all the more what she was doing out here in the middle of New Mexico, pregnant and alone, and why she wasn't wearing a wedding ring. But he was a Southern boy, and way too well-brought-up to ask.

Chapter 4

"Where'd you say that truck stop is? I'm so hungry I'm chewin' on air."

I-40—New Mexico

The bowlful of steaming chicken-noodle soup the waitress set in front of Mirabella looked good and smelled even better. Even so, she sat regarding it without enthusiasm until Jimmy Joe picked up her spoon and held it out to her and said, "Eat," in a tone that brooked no argument. Then with a sigh she took the spoon from him, plunged it into the bowl, lifted it laden with noodles and dripping broth, and blew on it, more to forestall the moment when she would have to put it in her mouth than because it actually needed cooling.

Jimmy Joe, who wasn't fooled, said, "Come on, quit stalling." Mirabella took a deep breath.

It wasn't that she wasn't hungry. That is, her *stomach* felt hungry—she just didn't seem to have any desire for food. Which was a state of affairs she would normally have relished, having spent most of her life fighting the inescapable effects of a disgustingly healthy and indiscriminating appetite. But the truth was, she simply felt too awful to eat.

She was so tired. And she had *such* a backache. Plus, she was worried about the weather, and feeling emotionally vulnerable about Christmas, just the thought of which made her throat constrict like a too-tight collar. And as if *that* wasn't enough, there was the distracting and disturbing presence of Jimmy Joe Starr.

As hard as she tried to ignore it, as determined as she was not to acknowledge it, to look somewhere else—anywhere else—and pretend a nonchalance she didn't in the least feel, she was acutely aware of him. She knew he was studying her, though trying his best not to be obvious and rude about it; watching her when he thought it was safe with a puzzled intensity she couldn't quite fathom. Why is he looking at me like that? she kept wondering. As if he had a question that was burning a hole in his tongue. If there's something he wants to know about me, she thought irritably, why doesn't he just ask? Or is he just too damn polite?

That was it. It had to be. He was so young, he probably hadn't had much experience with pregnant women, so naturally, Mirabella told herself, he would be curious. But it wasn't exactly the kind of thing you could just ask a stranger about— not without being rude—and if there was anything in the world this guy was, besides cute and young, it was polite.

Thinking about the man—boy, really—in those terms, while being careful not to actually *look* at him, Mirabella began to feel gratifyingly mature and maternal. Her confidence growing, she lifted her lashes, found Jimmy Joe's nice brown eyes and smiled.

And just like that, all the maternal feeling she'd managed to conjure up went right out the window, along with most of the maturity and confidence.

Oh, Lord, she thought, what does *this* mean? The particular intensity in that warm-as-mink gaze couldn't possibly be what it appeared to be. Of course not. *Oh, no.*

The truth was, one of the few things in life Mirabella had

never learned how to handle was male admiration. Other than in a business context, of course; appreciation of her talent and capabilities from the male-dominated world she worked in was something she not only welcomed, but considered no more than her due. But let the soft glow of admiration in a man's eyes flare into something more personal, more primitive—like lust, say—and her instant reaction was apt to be, "Who, me? What, is he *nuts?*"

Catching a glimpse of something of the sort in Jimmy Joe's eyes, her first reaction was shock: *My God, how can he? I look like a whale!* That was closely followed by dismay: *What can he be thinking of?* After that came disappointment. She concluded sadly that he must be one of those men she'd heard about who actually found pregnant women sexy. Which she considered truly disgusting.

Thoroughly unnerved, compelled almost against her will to be sure, Mirabella braced herself, then stole another look. This one was more covert than the first, slanted upward through her lashes as she dipped her head to meet the laden spoon. But now the heavy-lidded gaze she encountered held nothing more than patient amusement.

"Eat," said Jimmy Joe sternly, tapping the tabletop with a forefinger.

Okay, I was wrong, she thought. *Oh, thank God.* Giddy with relief, she feigned resentment. "I'm eating. I'm *eating,* already. You don't have to watch me, you know."

"Yeah, I do," said Jimmy Joe. But his tone was teasing, and his smile wry.

Relaxing, Mirabella tossed back the wing of hair she'd been hiding behind and smiled across the table in a friendlier way. "Seriously—I don't need a baby-sitter. I know I intruded on whatever it was you were doing—making a phone call, weren't you?—so why don't you just go on, pretend I'm not here. I won't listen, I promise." Go ahead, she thought, pretending she didn't in the least care, call your...girlfriend? Wife?

He scooted back the sleeve of his sweatshirt in order to look at his watch, then shrugged and gave her a regretful little smile. "Ah, I was just tryin' to get ahold of my son, is all. Past his bedtime back there now, though. I'll catch him in the mornin'."

"You have a son?" For some reason, that jolted Mirabella, and she halted her spoon in surprise. It wasn't that he didn't look old enough; how old, after all, did a guy have to be to make a baby? But she'd just finished convincing herself that he was only a boy himself so she could feel comfortable with him, and now fatherhood made that image somewhat difficult to maintain.

"Yeah…his name's J.J." He said it with diffidence. But something about his voice, the smile that flitted across his face like a blinding flash of sunlight he hadn't been able to avoid, caused a sudden soft prickling in the area of Mirabella's heart, rather like a bad case of static electricity.

He's so proud of him, she thought. And hard on the heels of that realization came another, much more unexpected: *I'll bet he's a terrific father.* "Tell me about him," she said mistily. "How old is he?"

Jimmy Joe kind of stretched and rubbed a hand across the back of his neck while he thought about it—which she was almost certain he didn't need to do in order to tell her how old his own child was. What it did was add a touch of winsome modesty to his already considerable charm. "Ah, let's see…. He'd be eight."

"Eight months? Oh, that's a cute age." An image flashed into her mind—a softly lit picture of Jimmy Joe cuddling a baby against his manly pecs. Which produced another of those peculiar stirrings deep in her own chest.

He grinned. "Not so cute. That's eight *years.* They tend to get pretty ornery by that age."

"You're kidding." Mirabella's spoon, halted once more on its downward arc, clattered unnoticed to the table.

His head bobbed in an affirming nod. "Be nine next July."

Lacking Jimmy Joe's Southern reserve and good manners, she went ahead and said it: "You don't look old enough."

He didn't exactly seem flattered by that, which, she thought, was in itself a measure of how young he was. Instead he shifted in an embarrassed sort of way and muttered, "Oh, I'm plenty old enough. Pushin' thirty."

Thirty. Mirabella couldn't think what to say. After a moment she picked up her spoon and calmly murmured, "Well, you don't look it." She was thinking, *Eight...almost nine years... My God.* The prickly feeling in her chest slowly dissipated.

"So," she said brightly, "where's your little boy now?" Being from California, she had none of Jimmy Joe's hesitation about asking questions when necessary, whether as a desperate attempt to make conversation, or because there was something she really wanted to know. Since the one she'd just asked fell more into the former category than the latter—just a variation on your basic "Where are you from?" gambit—the answer she got kind of took her by surprise.

"He's with his grandma—that's my mama—back in Georgia."

Mama? Well, after that there wasn't anything she could do but proceed to the next question, this one definitely in the "want to know" category. But as curious as she was, and even though tact had never been her strongest suit, she did try to make it as casual as she could.

"What about your wife?" she began confidently enough, before fumbling into stammering ineptitude. "Er...J.J.'s mother. She doesn't live... I mean, she's not..." She gestured hopefully with her empty spoon.

"His mama's dead," Jimmy Joe quietly answered, apparently taking pity on her.

Mirabella was thoroughly and sincerely aghast. For all her arrogance in business and thorny attitude toward men in general, she had a compassionate and sympathetic heart. It was, although she preferred to keep the fact a secret, a veritable marshmallow, especially where children were concerned. So it was that, forgetting her own discomforts and worries, she instantly and instinctively reached out to the motherless boy

she'd never met through the only avenue available to her—
his father.

Pushing her soup aside she lightly touched his hand—something she would never have dreamed of doing otherwise—and
then, forgetting also the dangers inherent in such contact, let
herself touch the deep sadness in his eyes, as well. "Oh, God,
I'm so sorry," she whispered.

"It was a while ago. Five years." His voice seemed so
matter-of-fact, for a moment Mirabella wondered if she'd mis-
taken the look of profound regret—as if, she thought, he somehow felt himself responsible. But then he took a breath and
went on, and she thought she understood why his feelings
might be a little bit complicated. "I didn't hear about it right
away. Hadn't seen or heard from her in years—we'd been
divorced since J.J. was just a baby. She was livin' in New
Orleans at the time."

"How did she die?" Mirabella asked softly, thinking tragic
thoughts about cancer and car accidents.

She was unprepared when he hitched a shoulder and angrily
and impatiently growled the word, "Drugs."

"Oh, God." Suddenly chilled, she pulled her fingers from
his and pressed them against her lips. She hadn't exactly led
a sheltered life, having spent a large part of it—the most recent
part—in downtown L.A., where the drug culture's human toll
called to her daily from wretched alleyways and reached out
to her from every street corner. *"Spare some change, lady?
For food…?"* But nothing in her own experience had ever
brought the reality as close to her as this.

In a low, horrified voice, she said, "You mean…an over-
dose?"

He shook his head, the brief boil of anger dissipating as
quickly as it had risen. "Couldn't say. More'n likely it was a
combination of things—malnutrition…pneumonia. Maybe she
just plain ol' gave up." He shifted again in that restless way
he had, as if talking about himself made him itch. "She'd had
trouble with it since she was just a kid. I guess I was a fool,
but I thought I could help her. I just didn't know…"

Mirabella watched him take a deep breath, the way people do when they need to make room for pain inside. "For a while I thought I had. Then, after J.J. was born... Well, I guess I wasn't strong enough. Or she wasn't. I had to give up tryin', or take chances with J.J.'s life I wasn't willin' to take. So..." He shrugged and looked away, making it clear that he'd said all he cared to say on the subject.

And Mirabella, having been in that position herself often enough to respect it, didn't pursue it.

"So," she said wonderingly after a moment, "you've raised your son on your own since he was just a baby."

The truth was, she felt humbled and chastened, and was looking at Jimmy Joe in a whole new light. He'd seemed so *young,* an impression that she now thought might have had more to do with his smile—that sweet, sleepy grin that reminded her of a tousled child just waking from a nap—than with smooth cheeks and buns that still looked good in jeans. And of course he *was* young—not even thirty!

But the impression she'd formed of carefree youth and unsullied innocence had vanished the moment she'd allowed herself to look into his eyes and recognized a certain quiet sadness in them. This was no callow, untested boy, she suddenly realized. Jimmy Joe Starr was a full-grown man—one who'd loved and married and struggled and lost; one who'd already known tragedy and failure as well as joy; one who'd unhesitatingly taken on the worries and responsibilities of fatherhood. In short, a man who'd experienced a whole lot more of life in his almost-a-decade-fewer years, than Mirabella had, by far.

A vague, indefinable sadness crept in around her heart—something like the feeling she sometimes got listening to the blues all alone late at night, or certain songs by John Lennon. If only, she thought. *If only...*

"Well, I wouldn't say alone." Jimmy Joe squirmed uncomfortably, trying to be honest about it. He wasn't sure what had just happened, but for all he'd been so disapproving of her, now that she'd handed him his chance to speak his mind on the subject of single parents raising babies, he didn't feel he had the right. The idea had come to him that maybe he ought to get to know her a little better first, find out how she felt about things, what made her tick.

It surprised him some, too, to realize how much he wanted to do that.

"My mama, you know…she helps out a lot. And my sister Jess is there, too. Lately she and her little girl have been livin' with Mama while her husband's gone overseas—he's in the military. Sammi June—let's see, I guess she'd be ten—she's company for J.J." He grinned. "Although if you were to ask him, I don't think he'd exactly agree with that right at the moment. He's feelin' just a mite outnumbered. Too many women."

Mirabella leaned her chin on her hand and smiled. "Yeah? Think how my dad felt—he had three daughters."

"No kiddin'?" Jimmy Joe blinked; one Mirabella was dazzling, but the idea of two more like her was enough to boggle the mind. He couldn't help it—he had to ask. "They all look like you?"

She made a face, and a sound that could only be described as a snort. "We don't even look like the same *species*. If you stand us up in order, we look like the letter *H*—I'm the little short piece in the middle." She sighed, then smiled in the way people do when they want you to think they aren't hurting inside. "My sisters are both tall, slim, blond and gorgeous. I'm the ugly duckling."

Well, he didn't even begin to know what to say to that. Figuring she had to be kidding, or was maybe fishing for compliments, which was a feminine ploy he did *not* admire, he just mumbled, "Come on…"

He felt a lot better when she laughed. "Oh, I don't mean *now*. I mean, well, I didn't exactly turn into a swan, but at least I think I'm…you know, an okay duck. But you should have seen me when I was a kid." Which was just what he'd been thinking, too, but he kept his mouth shut.

"Carroty-red hair," she elaborated, tweaking a rich mahogany strand across her eyes and again making a face at it. "Straight as a stick. Face as round as a Moon Pie and speckled as a turkey egg. And great big glasses. Now I wear contacts," she explained, flashing her luminous eyes at him and batting her thick dark lashes like the heroine of an old movie. "Oh— plus, I was fat. Well…plump. And short. Built like a fireplug. So naturally I was terrible at sports." She smiled the hurtin' smile again. This time Jimmy Joe felt it in his own gut. "All the necessary traits for a guaranteed miserable childhood."

"I find it real hard to believe that," he murmured, stunned.

She shrugged, still trying to make light of it. "I had the nicknames to prove it: Carrot Top…Freckle-Faced Freak… Four Eyes, to mention a few. Oh—and Firecracker. I also had one helluva temper."

And brains, he thought. And courage. And probably a great sense of humor. Hadn't anybody seen it?

"I was very popular, actually," said Mirabella, as if she'd heard his thought. "Lots of girlfriends. And the boys, well…" She made the snorting sound again. "I mean, boys just couldn't seem to leave me alone. Hey, who could blame them? I was just so darn much fun to tease. As you can probably imagine."

Jimmy Joe didn't know what to say. He wanted to tell her he wished he'd known her back then, and that if he had, things would have been different. He wanted to believe that *he* would never have made fun of her, and that he would have busted any kid who dared to do so right in the chops.

He *did* believe it, because for one thing, he knew his mama would have busted his butt if she'd ever found out he'd been teasing someone, and in a town as small as the one he'd grown up in, she would for sure have gotten wind of it sooner or later. But more than that, he believed it because he felt as a certainty in his soul that he would have *liked* that little red-haired girl—freckles, glasses and all. He would have liked her spunk, for one thing. Maybe, in his little boy's heart, he would even have secretly thought she was cute, although he would never have had the gumption to say so. But he knew for sure he would have wanted to be her friend. He just wasn't so sure he would have had the courage.

"Must've been something wrong with those boys," he finally mumbled, shaking his head. "That's all I can say. Must've been stone-blind."

She kind of half smiled at him, obviously thinking he was just being polite. "That's very sweet of you. But you weren't there. You didn't see me back then."

"Well, I wish I had been," he said with feeling. It bothered him a lot that she didn't believe him, and he knew he wasn't going to be able to make her believe him, no matter what he said. Because he could now see what he'd missed before—that the uppity tilt of her chin was there mainly because of the chip on her shoulder that had been there so long it had grown to be part of her basic nature. And that made him sad. More than that—it made him mad.

She was gazing at him now with her chin propped in her hand and a shiny look in her eyes, still smiling that little half-smile. "Jimmy Joe," she said softly, "do you know that when I was in junior high, you were barely out of diapers?"

"Come on." Shock jerked him against the brown vinyl seat, his head moving back and forth in pure disbelief. "No way!" She nodded, and he just kept shaking his head. He couldn't believe it. He had put her age at maybe twenty-six, twenty-seven, tops. "No way you can be that much older than I am," he insisted, feeling vaguely betrayed and insulted without having the last idea why. "You know, I'm older than I look— Hey, did I mention I'm almost thirty?"

"You did," Mirabella said, laughing now, but gently. She thought he looked so endearingly *affronted,* with his hair mused and flopped down across a thunderous frown, and dark eyes flashing lightning. Like one of her sister Sommer's kids passionately arguing, "But I *am* big enough! I *am.*"

Passionate. Oops! Her heart gave a little flip-flop of dismay and of warning. How had the conversation gotten so personal? What was this tension, this glow of awareness that was all of a sudden zapping back and forth across the table like a current between two electrodes?

Just then, as if in response to all the fuss and turmoil taking place one floor above, the tiny tenant who'd been peacefully snoozing beneath her ribs suddenly lurched into wakefulness. For Mirabella it was—literally—a kick from reality. The warm tingle of growing attraction vanished like campfire sparks in a cold night sky, and backache and pressure and overwhelming tiredness came to take its place.

To cover the source of her involuntary gasp, she looked at her watch and murmured, "Wow, look at the time—past midnight. I'm really sorry...I should let you go. You could be getting some rest, at least." And then she surprised herself by yawning.

Without a word, Jimmy Joe slid out of the booth, snagging the check on his way. Once upright, he pulled his wallet from a hip pocket, took out a couple of dollar bills and dropped them on the table. Then he reached over and touched Mirabella's arm. "Come on," he said in a husky voice, jerking his head for emphasis. "I'll walk you back out there. Put your coat on."

It was an order, not a subject for discussion, which ordinarily would have ticked her off royally and at the very least triggered immediate and total insurrection. But for some reason all she could summon up was a feeble and completely ineffective, "Oh, no, I insist—"

"Ma'am," said Jimmy Joe softly, leaning over and looking earnestly into her eyes as if she were a small child on the verge of misbehaving in public, "you and that baby need it more'n I do. Now, we're gonna give it one more shot, okay?"

Did he *have* to keep calling her *ma'am?*

And with that thought, suddenly Mirabella found herself in the depths of depression, weary beyond all reason and once more on the verge of tears—very much, in fact, like that contrary child. Was that why she allowed herself to be taken in hand like a helpless wimp instead of proclaiming her right to be proudly and independently miserable, as she normally would have done? She didn't know. But she did know that there was something indefinably comforting about having the reins taken out of her hands, for once; and that instead of resenting the one who'd wrested them from her, she felt a profound sense of gratitude.

As before, Jimmy Joe waited patiently while she made yet another potty stop and took her arm as they crossed the cold, windy parking lot. This time, though, there was no attempt at polite conversation. Mirabella just waddled as fast as she could, teeth clenched, hugging herself and shivering in waves, far too miserable to worry about how silly she looked or what anybody might think of her. When she saw the royal blue truck with its bright shiny star looming before her, she felt an urge to laugh out loud with sheer joy and thanksgiving, like a half-frozen wanderer stumbling onto a friendly campfire.

"Hold on, just a second…let me get 'er unlocked."

Jimmy Joe had to let go of her arm while he stepped up to the door, but he kept looking at her sideways while he did, just in case she decided to fold up on him. She reminded him of a poor little bird, standing there all hunched up, with the wind whipping her hair across her face. Like that nursery rhyme—he remembered it from years and years ago—that started out, "The north wind doth blow,/And we shall have snow,/And what will the poor robin do then,/Poor thing?"

Okay, he was starting to worry about her. He knew what she'd told him—about her baby not being due for another month—but he also knew from personal experience that babies had a way of doing things their own way and in their own good time. Either way, it was a sure bet that all this stress and strain wasn't going to be good for her *or* the baby. What she needed, he thought, was to be safe at home where there were kinfolk to look after her, somebody to make sure she got enough rest, see that she put her feet up, and rub her back for her when she couldn't sleep.

And then he told himself all over again, Jimmy Joe Starr, she's not your concern.

He got the doors unlocked, then went around to help her

into the passenger side, trying not to let out most of the warmth in the process. He had to almost lift her up the two high steps and into the cab, and once inside it seemed a natural thing to leave his arms where they were and just go on holding her. She didn't seem to mind, which surprised him some. Then again, he thought, maybe she was so cold she would have been willing to hug a grizzly bear for the heat. Shoot, that coat she was wearing was so thin it wasn't worth a nickel in weather like this. But then, what could he expect from somebody from California?

And again he told himself, Jimmy Joe, she's not your concern.

It was warm and close in the cab, and after a minute or two she pulled away from him, giving herself a little shake, like someone throwing off a blanket. Neither of them said anything, although Jimmy Joe did sort of cough and mutter, "'Scuse me," as he moved past her to turn on the light in the sleeper.

The light wasn't kind to her. He thought about what she'd told him, about how she'd been in junior high when he was still in diapers, and he still didn't believe it. He still thought she was the most beautiful woman he'd ever set eyes on in his life, but now for some reason it made his throat ache to look at her. Seeing her like this, so pale and drawn, and the glassy look of pain in her eyes, all he wanted to do was make her feel better.

And he told himself, Jimmy Joe, she's *still* none of your concern.

But this time from another part of his being a whole new voice answered back, *Yeah, she is.*

Although his overriding urge was to put his arms back around her and hug her some more, he didn't give in to it, limiting himself to a guiding touch on her elbow while he held back the partitioning curtain. "There you go," he said gruffly. "Climb right on up there, now. Pull back the covers if you want to. Be warmer that way."

"Thanks." She sat on the edge of the bed and looked up

at him, and he could see she was beginning to feel uneasy about him being there. "I'll be fine."

He knew she was waiting for him to go. He knew he ought to. But that new voice inside him had other ideas, and he wasn't all that surprised to hear himself say, with a firm, no-nonsense shake of his head, "I'm gonna just stay and make sure you're settled before I go."

"You don't have to do that." Her voice sounded breathy. "I'll be all right now. Honest."

Honest... She sounded just like a little girl when she said that, which made him smile. "Ma'am," he said as he put his hands on her shoulders, "I don't intend on goin' anywhere until I know you're resting, y'hear? Just lie right on down there, now." And as gently as he knew how, he eased her over so she was lying on her side with her knees pulled up against her belly and her head resting on her folded-up arm. "That's the way. There you go. How's that?"

She flashed him one bright, angry look that cheered him considerably, then closed her eyes without answering. He could tell by the way she was breathing through her nose—in slow, deep breaths—that she was hurting.

It came to him suddenly, gleaned from memories of suffering through two pregnancies with J.J.'s mama, what her problem might be. "Your back achin'?" he asked, sitting beside her on the very edge of the bed. She nodded, just too plain miserable to talk. "Yeah..." he said softly. "That's what I thought."

He put his hand on her shoulder, overcoming a powerful urge to reach beyond it, just to smooth the hair back from her face. With that tenderness simmering inside him, he said, "Ma'am, why don't you turn over on your other side? What I'm gon' do is rub your back a little. Make you feel a whole lot better, help you relax. Okay? Come on, now.... Roll on over."

Instead of doing what he'd told her, she suddenly squinched up her face without opening her eyes, as if she'd felt a sharp pain, and said in a sulky voice, "Do you *have* to keep calling me *ma'am?*"

That made him grin, but her eyes were closed so he didn't have to worry about her seeing it, and thanks to all those phone conversations with J.J. he knew how to keep it from showing up in his voice. "Sorry about that," he said, solemn as a judge. "I don't mean anythin' personal by it. It's just a habit—shoot, it's probably in my genes."

"Well, it makes me feel really *old.*"

Now he did chuckle, resisting again the urge to touch her face, just to run his fingertips lightly across the ivory curve of her forehead, which, as far as he could see, in spite of her concern, was completely unmarred by any wrinkles. "You have to understand, it's got nothin' to do with how old you are, just the fact that you're female."

Opening her eyes about halfway, she studied him from under her lashes. "You call your mom ma'am?"

"Oh, you bet."

"Uh-hmm. Your sister?"

"Well, now…"

"Girlfriend?"

He wanted to laugh, now that he thought he knew where she was headed. "No, don't believe I would—if I had one."

She chewed on that for a moment or two, then said slowly, "The waitress in there—you called her ma'am. Would you have done that if she was nineteen?"

"Sure would. Yes, ma'am."

"So…it's a matter of respect." She said it like, "Aha!"

"That's right." But he was beginning to feel just a little uneasy, wondering if he knew after all what she was getting at.

"So…you don't respect your sister or your girlfriend?"

Well, she had him there. He rubbed the back of his neck while he thought about it, then said, "It's kind of hard to explain—especially since I don't believe I was ever called upon to try to before. You grow up in the South, it's just somethin' you take for granted, like grits for breakfast. But I guess what it is, it's respect. But it's more like—it's formal, you know? You don't use it when it's personal, like with your friends, or your close kin—'' he paused to smile before he said it ''—unless they're older.''

''Let me get this straight.'' A little pleat of concentration puckered the skin between her eyebrows, but her voice had grown drowsy and he could see that the warmth in the truck, the lateness of the hour and her tiredness were beginning to have their way with her. ''You can't stop calling me ma'am because you don't know me well enough.''

''Yeah, I guess that'd be about right.''

''But you know me well enough to rub my back?''

So that was it. Again that tenderness wafted through him like a warm breeze over damp skin, stirring shivers of laughter that felt like goose bumps inside. Keeping it soft so as not to rile her he murmured, ''Okay, Marybell, I'll make you a deal—you quit arguin' and roll on over there, and I'll quit callin' you ma'am. How's that? Deal?''

''Deal,'' she whispered.

It was only after he'd helped her through the ponderous process of rolling over and she was once more settled on her side, this time facing away from him, that a tiny echo in her head said incredulously, *Marybell?*

But then she felt the warm weight of his hand on her lower back, on the exact spot that ached so awfully, and a firm, circling pressure that felt so wonderful she forgot everything else; so wonderful she almost wept with the sheer relief it brought her.

''Oh…God,'' she groaned, ''how did you know?''

Jimmy Joe's voice was soft and oddly muffled, as if she were hearing him through a layer of fur. ''Oh, I've done this for J.J.'s mama a time or two. It's been awhile, but I guess you don't forget how.''

''Lucky,'' Mirabella muttered with a sigh. ''How'd I get through eight months without you?''

A chuckle undulated along her auditory nerves like ripples in black velvet.

Chapter 5

"You got one of those new anteaters? Man, that is one ugly truck."
"Bet you wish you had one as ugly."
I-40—New Mexico

Mirabella was hearing voices. Mostly men's voices, but now and then a woman's, too—strange voices, mumbly and scratchy at the same time, sometimes far away and crackly, other times loud and clear, as if whoever it was talking was standing right next to her. At first she ignored them, hearing but not really registering the sounds, the way you do when you fall asleep with the TV or radio on. Gradually, though, words began to filter into her consciousness, then string together in a way that made some kind of sense.

"East a' Tucumcari."

"Couple a' county mounties come through here 'while ago with their lights on. Don' know where they was goin', but they was hurryin'."

"Dry and dusty to the Texas line."

"They gonna open 'er up sometime 'fore Christmas, or what?"

"Uh…they're sayin' maybe noon, that's what I heard."

"One helluva mess. Got more'n a hunnerd accidents 'tween here and Amarillo. Got rigs off to the side, four-wheelers ever'where…."

"Where'n hell they keepin' the snowplows?"

"Ah, hell, Texas don't waste snowplows on the Panhandle…."

Along with a return of familiar discomforts, full awareness brought the realization that, yes, she was in a bed in an honest-to-God truck, a huge blue eighteen-wheeler belonging to one Jimmy Joe Starr, a genuine Georgia redneck who happened to have healing hands and dimples and a smile like an angel's, assuming the angel spoke with a Southern accent and looked like a young Robert Redford.

And what she was listening to wasn't a TV, but a CB radio. Which meant, since she hadn't heard a peep out of it last night, that Jimmy Joe must have turned it on. And since she couldn't imagine he would turn it on without a reason, that meant he must be listening to it. Out there, right now. He was here in the truck with her, just beyond the curtain.

That thought zapped through her with a tingle that must have been adrenaline, because she felt the way you do when you've been jolted awake too suddenly—weak and trembly, heart beating way too fast. She was lying there blinking, thinking about that, trying to make sense of it and feeling scared and disoriented, when the reason for all her inner turmoil stuck his hand through the crack at the edge of the curtain and knocked on the side of the sleeper.

"Hey," he called softly, "you awake in there?"

"Yeah, I'm up," she called back in a husky, too-eager voice that betrayed that for the lie it was, struggling to get her feet around so she could at least make a stab at sitting up.

"Mornin'." The curtain was pulled back and Jimmy Joe's face appeared like a ray of sunshine. "How you doin'?"

"Okay," she responded airlessly; in her present position even sarcasm was beyond her.

He drew a small plastic bottle from a pocket in the sleeveless, down-filled nylon vest he was wearing over his Georgia Bulldogs sweatshirt and held it out to her. "Thought you could do with an eye-opener. Get your blood sugar pumpin'." He was wearing his heart-melting smile, which Mirabella, not being a morning person even at the best of times, was in no mood to appreciate.

"I don't know where I'd put it," she muttered, eyeing the orange juice with revulsion. She felt like a dead whale that had lain out in the sun too long—in other words just about ready to explode. Plus she'd slept with her contacts in, so her eyes felt like two tennis balls, and her tongue was so furry she knew she must have a horrendous case of morning breath. The last thing she wanted was a sexy, adorable guy anywhere within ten yards of her, so she was not thrilled when Jimmy Joe plunked himself down beside her, completely ignoring warning signs that were usually sufficient to send close family members diving for the nearest cover.

"Just a sip," he said, as if he were addressing a three-year-old. "Then I'll walk you in so you can wash up, if you want. Come on, now—upsy-daisy."

How does he do it? she wondered as, groaning, she allowed him to hoist her upright. *Why do I let him do it—treat me like a contrary child, or worse, a helpless female?* In her former life she would have flayed alive any man, no matter how attractive and charming, who'd dared to try such tactics with her. She'd spent most of her life perfecting the defenses and signals to ensure that those who did try were few and far between. So what was it about this man?

She sipped orange juice on autopilot while her analytical mind chewed on that anomaly. She knew it couldn't just be his kind eyes and sleepy little-boy smile; she'd never been vulnerable to that sort of thing, and in fact usually found extremely handsome men to be pretty much of a turnoff. More likely, she thought, it had something to do with him being way too young for her, and therefore no threat to her sexually—rather like a lioness's tolerance of the immature males in her pride. That, combined with her own vulnerability in her present condition, and the uniqueness of the circumstances.

Yes, she thought, satisfied with her conclusions. That would explain it.

It did cross her mind that she just might have come up against a man with a will equal to her own, but she rejected that idea. As far as Mirabella was concerned, such a man did not exist.

How does she do it? Jimmy Joe wondered, gazing at her as she drank and then licked the juice glaze from her lips. *How can she look so doggone beautiful after the night she had?*

He'd sat and watched her long after she'd fallen asleep literally under his hands, finally free to marvel all he wanted to at the old-Burgundy shine of her hair, the delicacy of her bones, the way her skin seemed to glow from inside like his mama's good china when you held it up to the light. Free to touch, with a mettlesome finger and breathing temporarily forgotten, one strand of hair that lay along the curve of her jaw and pooled in the hollow of her neck, and daringly lift and stroke it behind the fragile sculpture of her ear.

She'd stirred, then, so that his fingers had brushed against her warm cheek and intersected the flow of her breath as it sighed from between her barely parted lips, and he'd been shocked by the stirring of response in his own body.

He'd squelched it immediately. It had seemed wrong to him; a violation not only of her trust in him, but of some indefinable quality—he wasn't sure what it was—something about the way she looked with one childlike hand pillowing her cheek and the other resting with maternal protectiveness on the side of her swollen belly. *Innocence?* How could that be? Or…*purity?* And yet, he thought he'd never in his life seen anyone so overwhelmingly, breathtakingly *female*.

Which was confusing, because while part of him had been ashamed of his body's jolting acknowledgment of that femi-

ninity, something else in him had found it downright exhila-
rating.

He'd pulled the comforter over her and left her then, but
hadn't gone back to the truck-stop café, although he knew he
would have been more comfortable there. Instead, unable to
bring himself to leave her, he'd turned off the light in the
sleeper and drawn the curtain and settled into the passenger-
side seat with a book and a pillow. He'd made pretty good
headway in the new Tony Hillerman mystery he'd picked up
in L.A., even dozed some off and on before full daylight and
the comings and goings of his neighbors had roused him.

On a quick trip into the truck stop for a cup of coffee and
to use the john he'd heard rumblings about the road opening
up, so he'd made the coffee to go, picked up the bottle of
orange juice for Mirabella and hurried back to his truck to see
what he could find out from the CB. He'd expected she would
wake up, with all the noise from the radio and slamming doors
and all, but she hadn't, and he'd listened for a good half hour
before he was convinced the news coming out of Tucumcari
was more than just wishful rumors, and he knew it was time
he was going have to wake her. Wake her, say goodbye and
send her on her way.

Now, sitting beside her, watching her drink the juice he'd
brought, he felt the same protective feelings welling up inside
him that had kept him watching over her all night. Last night
those feelings had made a certain sense to him—enough so
that he hadn't thought to question them, anyway. This morning, though, they were doggone confusing.

"No more," she said, shoving the juice bottle blindly in his
direction. "I really have to go—*now*." Her eyes had lost their
unfocused, waking-up look and now held a bright glaze of
distress.

"Okay, easy now, I'm gonna get you there," he said soothingly, reaching past her to set the bottle on the recessed shelf
at the head of the bed. "What'd you do with your shoes?"

"I don't know. I kicked them off, I think."

He found them in the folds of the comforter and knelt to

help her into them, noticing that they went on easily enough. He remembered that swollen feet at this stage of the game were not a good thing, so that eased his mind in one small way.

"There you go," he grunted as he got to his feet. "What else d'you need? Your pocketbook?" She was already wrestling with the sleeves of her coat. He helped her with that, found her purse and hooked the strap over his shoulder, then bent to get an arm around her and hoist her to her feet.

"It's okay, I can make it," she protested. "You don't have to help me." To Jimmy Joe her breathlessness sounded not so much cranky as desperate. Hearing it, he did as she asked and let go of her, and after hovering anxiously for a moment, went to open the door for her instead.

"I heard the CB," she said as she eased herself between the seats, moving like a rig backing into a loading bay. "Did I hear right? Did they say the road's going to be…opening soon?"

She'd paused, apparently to catch her breath, so he pulled the door closed again to save the heat. "That's what they're sayin'. 'Bout noon, looks like."

"What time is it now?"

"Goin' on eleven. Plenty a' time, if you want to wash up…have some breakfast." He pushed the door open, stepped onto the running board and held out his hand to help her down.

But she'd spotted his pillow and paperback on the seat; he could see her looking at them with that little pleat of frown wrinkles between her eyes as she squeezed by. She transferred the frown to him as she took the hand he'd offered and asked, not with gentle concern but in a sharp, accusing tone, "Did you get any sleep?"

Jimmy Joe couldn't help but grin, she sounded so much like his mama. "I dozed some," he said, easing her down to the ground. "Mostly I just read." Then he had to laugh; the way she glared at him, you would have thought he'd confessed to spending the night in a honky-tonk bar. "It's *okay.* Hey, I like to read."

"You do?" For some reason that seemed to surprise her. Then she shook herself—or maybe it was a shiver as the cold wind hit her—and said, "Oh, that's right—I saw your books."

They'd turned and started slowly walking together toward the truck-stop café, and since she seemed to have forgotten he still had her hand, he kept it and tucked it into the bend of his elbow and covered it with his to keep it warm. Looking down at her, he could see that her nose was turning pink and her face had a pinched look to it, and he knew she would go faster if there was any way in the world she could. That high-plateau wind cut like a razor—you could smell the snow in it. To keep her mind off it he picked up the thread of the conversation they'd been having about books, asking her in a polite way if she liked to read.

Her shoulder nudged against him as she shrugged. "I've never been much of a reader. It's not that I don't *like* to read— it just seems like I always have too many other things to do."

"Yeah? What do you do when you want to just…you know, relax?"

"Relax?" She made it sound like a word she'd never heard before. Glancing down at her, he saw that she was frowning again, thinking about it.

He didn't pursue it, just shook his head and said, "I guess I can't imagine not readin'. Probably because my mama used to read to me, from the time I was too little to remember. She read to all of us kids. You know…startin' with those little picture books with animals in 'em, then Mother Goose and Dr. Seuss, all the way through the Little House books and *Tom Sawyer* and *Treasure Island*. Seems like there never was a time we didn't have a book goin'."

The wind caught her hair suddenly, and unfurled it like bright red party streamers around her face. She grabbed at it, gathered it in one hand and held it while she looked up at him, squinted an eye shut and asked, "How many of you were there? You mentioned your sister…."

"Three sisters, three brothers."

She gasped. "Seven! My God, how did she find the time?"

"I don't know," said Jimmy Joe with a shrug. "She just did."

For a few moments she didn't say anything, just walked along with her head down, her hair caught up in her hand. He felt her take a deep breath. "My mom read to my sisters and me, too. I don't know why it didn't take with me." She let go of her hair then, and shook her head as if saying to the wind, *Go on, have your way with it, I don't care!* He saw her face light up with some intense emotion he didn't know the name of—something fierce and joyful and proud—and she said, "I'm going to read to my baby though. I've been buying books, all sorts of books. Mother Goose and Dr. Seuss and those little picture books with animals in them." And suddenly she laughed.

Jimmy Joe wondered if it was the first time he'd ever heard her laugh. He knew it was the first time he'd heard her laugh that way—a sound as merry and as good for the heart as sleigh bells on Christmas morning.

It also occurred to him that it was the first time he'd heard her talk about her baby like that—as if it was a real live person and not some kind of condition. He wanted to hear more, ask her some questions, like whether she wanted a boy or a girl, and what she planned to name it, and whether the kid's father was going to be around to help her walk the floor at two in the morning. But they'd reached the truck stop's double entrance, and there was nothing for him to do but hold the doors for her, first the outer, then the inner, and he had to really hop to it to get there before she did. And he was sorry.

Inside, she left him with a distracted wave and made a beeline for the bathroom. He watched her go, then went to see if he could find them a table in the café. As it turned out, he didn't have any trouble; with the word out about the road opening, the drivers' section was emptying out fast. There was a stirring in the air, a buzz of energy like the revving of diesel engines, all those drivers itching to be on the road again—most of them, like him, heading home. He felt it too, the restlessness, the building up of energy inside him, the pull of loved ones waiting and watching for him. But for him there was something else, too; kind of an uneasiness, as if he was leaving something unfinished, something undone. Something important.

While he waited for Mirabella to come out of the bathroom, he ordered coffee—regular for himself, decaf for her—then thought about calling J.J. He still had hopes of making it home by late Christmas Day if he drove straight through without stopping. But he didn't want to get the boy's hopes up until he was safely through the Panhandle, so he didn't make the call.

He was scowling at the menu when Mirabella joined him. It was starting to be a habit, he thought, the way she would show up at his elbow, taking possession of the space around him so that suddenly even the air he breathed seemed filled with her—her presence, her scent, her energy.

She looked different this morning. She'd scrubbed her face and pulled her hair back and fastened it on top with some kind of clip in a way that made her seem even younger than she had before. Not the old-fashioned movie star now; more like a high-school cheerleader. But it was more than that. It seemed to him there was a new kind of *quietness* about her....

But it wasn't until she was easing into the booth across from him that he finally put his finger on what was different. It was her arrogance, that uppity tilt to her chin that was missing. And that worried him.

The first thing she said to him was, "How come you're not on the phone? Aren't you going to call your son and let him know you're on your way?"

Which reassured him some, being the sort of bossiness that he'd already come to understand was just her basic nature. So he smiled and said, "Naw, I'll wait a bit. Like to make it through Texas, first. Then I'll know I've got a shot at gettin' home by Christmas."

She nodded and looked quickly down at her menu, but not before he caught a glimpse of shadows in her eyes. That and the tiny quiver of her mouth made him ask, even though it wasn't any of his business, "What about you? You got folks waitin' on you?" *Like a husband, maybe?* That would explain it, he thought, if she was tryin' so hard to get to him, to be with him for the holidays. He could almost understand that.

"My mom," she said, still looking down at the menu. She swallowed and added, "And my dad," in a whisper he could barely hear.

Then he wondered why talking about her daddy made her choke up so, but poking into people's business, getting them to spill their personal secrets wasn't something he'd had much experience in or felt comfortable doing. So all he said was, "They're in Pensacola, you said?"

She glanced up at him and cleared her throat, and he could tell she was back on steadier ground. "Yes—Pensacola Beach, actually."

"Oh, man." Feeling for her, he shook his head, picked up his coffee and took a cautious sip. "That's more 'n a thousand miles. You're not gonna make that by Christmas."

She looked at him and he could see the fury in her eyes, wanting to argue with him, not ready to accept it yet. Funny, how clear the workings of her mind were becoming to him, like words and pictures printed on the pages of a book, because somehow, as if he'd known her all his life, he knew what a careful planner she was and how she hated it when things didn't work out her way.

"I thought…if I can just get through Texas—"

Jimmy Joe put his coffee mug down and reached for her hands. He took them and held them gently, making his voice gentle, too, saving all his steel for his eyes the way he did when he needed to get something straight with J.J. once and for all, and no room for dispute. "Don't you even try it. You take it easy, now, y'hear? Your mama and daddy, they'll understand. You know they'd rather have you late a thousand times than have any harm come to you or that baby."

Oh, Lord, he could feel her fighting it. Feel it in the tension in those small-boned hands, see it in the anger burning dark in her eyes. How she did hate to give in! But then he saw the fire in her eyes cool behind a glaze of tears he knew she would die rather than shed, and she took a breath with a quiver in it and let it out along with the words, ''I know.''

He waited a moment more before he released her hands. As soon as he let them go she straightened and used them to smooth invisible strands of hair away from her face, which he knew was just a way for her to get her poise back. It seemed to work, because her voice was steady when she went on, ''I really wanted to spend this Christmas with my dad. He just had a heart attack—''

''Oh, Lord,'' said Jimmy Joe. ''I am sorry.'' He was thinking of his own daddy, dead long before his time, and the second heart attack that had been his last. It was not an uncommon way for a man raised on Southern cooking to go.

''He's going to be okay,'' said Mirabella firmly. ''But he can't travel, obviously. My mom was going to come and stay with me until after the baby…but she can't leave my dad, so that's why I thought I'd go there instead. But I couldn't get a flight on such short notice, so then I figured I'd just drive. Plenty of time, right? Or so I thought. And now…here we are.'' She held out her hands, gamely smiling. ''Looks like it'll just be me and Junior this Christmas.''

Jimmy Joe laughed, although his heart was hurting for her. ''Hey, you know, this kinda reminds me of a movie I saw once—funny as the dickens—about this guy tryin' to get home for…Thanksgiving, I b'lieve it was.'' He kept on talking— glib as a traveling preacher, telling her about all the crazy things that happened to the poor guy in the movie, wanting only to make her feel better somehow—until the waitress came to take their order.

While they waited for the food to arrive they tried talking about movies some more, but it was hard to find enough common ground to base a good discussion on. Jimmy Joe liked action movies and slapstick comedies, the kind Mirabella called ''brainless.'' She went for the type of films critics cooed over and nobody else had even heard of, until somebody in one of them got nominated for an Academy Award. That, and

movies based on Shakespeare's plays and Jane Austen's novels, which always put Jimmy Joe straight to sleep. Then they
found out they'd both seen every Walt Disney film ever made,
and got into an argument about which was the greatest cartoon
feature of all time that lasted all the way through breakfast.

The waitress came and refilled their coffee cups, slapped
down the check and hurried away with a distracted, "You
folks have a safe trip, now." Silence fell. Jimmy Joe reached
for the check, but Mirabella got there first.

"Let me buy you breakfast," she said, although she didn't
sound nearly as bossy as he'd grown accustomed to. "It's the
least I can do, after all you've done for me." She watched
him with quiet, unreadable eyes.

Every Southern-bred instinct in him wanted to refuse, but
he could see it was important to her, so even though it caused
him embarrassment to do it he gave in and let her take the
check. He sipped his coffee in uncomfortable silence while he
watched her fish in her pocketbook for her wallet, then haul
out a bottle of Tylenol and shake a couple into her hand. She
swallowed them down without looking at him, but she didn't
have to, or say a word, either, for him to know she was hurting
again. He was starting to recognize the signs.

She opened up her wallet and took out a couple of dollar
bills and tucked them neatly under her coffee cup, then gave
him a bright look and said, "Ready?"

Jimmy Joe said, "Let's roll," and scooted out of the booth
ahead of her so he would be ready to give her a hand—if she
would let him. He had a funny feeling in his chest as if he'd
gotten a wad of food stuck way down deep in his esophagus,
right under his breastbone. It was the kind of lump he got
when J.J. was sick and he had to leave him anyway; the same
lump that had been there when he'd left the hospital after
visiting his daddy for the last time. He told himself the lady
really wasn't any of his business, that she was just a passing
stranger he'd happened to lend a helping hand to, and now it
was time to go his way and let her go hers.

He was a little surprised when she took the hand he offered

her and let him help her out of the booth. She let go of it in a hurry, though, and tugged the silky sweater down over her belly and fooled with her hair and her pocketbook in nervous little gestures as she said in a voice as bright and false as her smile, "Well, I guess this is goodbye."

He shook his head. "I want to see you to your car."

"I, uh, have to make a stop first."

"That's okay, I'll wait."

He tried to avoid it, but she pressed some money into his hand and went off to the rest room one more time, leaving him no choice but to wait in line at the cash register. In a way, though, he was glad to have something to do so he wouldn't have to watch her walk away from him, moving as if every bone in her body hurt.

When she came out he was waiting for her near the main entrance. He gave her her change, then held her pocketbook for her while he helped her on with her coat. He thought how natural it was beginning to feel to help her like that, and how she seemed to be getting used to having him do it.

They made the slow walk to her car without saying anything. It was still cold, with a slate-gray overcast that looked like snow. But the wind smelled of fuel and the air vibrated not with thunder but with the indescribable roar of several hundred big diesel engines growling through their gears as they headed out onto the highway like giant beasts joining a vast migration. Hearing that sound, seeing the rigs moving slowly past him, Jimmy Joe could feel his heart begin to beat faster.

She unlocked her car with a little gadget on her key chain that chirped like a cricket when she pressed on it. He reached past her and opened the door for her and then stood so he was shielding her as well as he could from the wind while she eased in under the wheel, stuck the key in the ignition and fired it up. All this, while he was being careful not to touch her and she was being just as careful not to look at him, and both of them were wondering who was going to be the first to say it.

"Well," she said, her voice sounding dry and breathless, "at least it started, huh?" She looked up at him then, with dark, fierce eyes, almost as if she was angry with him about something. Funny how he knew that wasn't it at all.

"You got enough gas?" he asked, dragging it out even though he was restless and anxious to be on his way.

She glanced at her gauge. "Half a tank. I thought I'd fill up in Amarillo."

He nodded and straightened, looking out across the roof of her car. "Well, then. Guess you're all set to go." He took a deep breath and ducked back down like somebody bobbing for apples in a barrel of water. "You take care now, y'hear? Drive safely." His voice sounded garbled to him, as if maybe it *was* coming from under water.

"I will." She sounded impatient, a little annoyed with him for doubting her. Then she gripped the wheel with both hands, and as if it was the hardest thing she'd ever done, looked up at him and croaked, "Ah…thanks. For everything. For…you know, letting me use your sleeper, and…everything. It was really nice of you."

"No problem." He cleared his throat. "My pleasure…" And he could tell by the ghost of a smile that quivered the corner of her mouth that she knew how close he'd come to saying "ma'am."

She squinted up at him, still thinking about smiling but not quite doing it. "I hope you make it home to your little boy in time for Christmas."

"Yeah," said Jimmy Joe. "Me, too. And I hope your daddy gets to feelin' better real soon."

She laughed on a shaky breath. "Yeah, me, too." Then, reaching out for the door handle, she said, "Well…okay. Thanks. Again. See ya. Oh—and Merry Christmas."

"Yeah, you have a Merry Christmas, too." After that there wasn't anything to do but stand back out of the way and let her shut the door. He hung around while she fiddled with the radio and heater controls, then gave him a wave through the window to show him she was on her way. He waved back and watched her head out across the parking lot toward the four-wheeler exit and the highway beyond.

It was when he'd turned to walk back to his truck that it occurred to him that after all that, neither one of them had said it. Neither of them had said goodbye.

Chapter 6

*"I got me four big boxes a' tapes here, and there's not
a one of 'em I feel like listenin' to. I'm just runnin'
through the radio, lookin' for a station."*

I-40—New Mexico

One radio station on the whole dial, and it had to be playing
Christmas music. Then Mirabella remembered it was the day
before Christmas—Christmas Eve. What else would they be
playing?

She just didn't want to believe it was Christmas Eve. How
could it be? It didn't *feel* like Christmas Eve. On the day
before Christmas people were supposed to be snugged up in
their houses frantically wrapping presents and stuffing themselves with popcorn and eggnog, or at the very least fighting
their way through the mall for some forgotten-till-the-last-
minute gift or other, half-deafened by the din of the crowds,
canned Christmas carols on the loudspeakers, and those Sal-
vation Army Santas jingling away in every doorway. Who had
ever heard of a Christmas Eve spent slogging across a cold,

lonely desert along with a lot of other poor hapless pilgrims....?

A shiver went skittering down her spine. Okay, she thought, this is just a *little* weird.

But there *was* something almost biblical about the vastness of the landscape, where the Rockies melted gradually into juniper-studded plateaus and twisting arroyos before disappearing completely in the flat, treeless prairie. Out here the horizons seemed to stretch forever and the leaden sky came down to touch them, and somewhere out there in the deep lavender haze where they met she could almost imagine a pyramid or two, and yes, perhaps even a caravan of camels plodding slowly eastward.

"'We three kings of Orient are;/Bearing gifts we traverse afar,'" Mirabella sang lustily in her off-key baritone, attempting with sheer volume to dispel the loneliness and depression that was slowly but surely creeping in around her heart. "'Field and fountain, moor and mou-oun-tain,/Following yonder star./*OO*, star of wonder, star…'" *Starr…Jimmy Joe.* Her voice fizzled into silence just as the music critic in her belly began expressing his outrage.

"Sorry, sweetheart," she said with a soft and rueful laugh, rubbing at the mushrooming bulge just below the right side of her rib cage. "Bad idea, I know. Wish I'd brought along some James Galway or Pavarotti tapes, but I didn't think about it. So I guess the best I can do is…" She pushed a button and the radio's automatic tuner settled on the only available station, which blared forth a lush and throaty, "Blu-blu-blue Chriss-mas." She settled back in her seat and sighed. "Elvis."

Although really, she told herself, things could be a lot worse. After all the fuss, the road was "dry and dusty," as she'd heard the truckers on Jimmy Joe's CB radio call it, with not so much as a flake of snow or a smidgen of ice that she could see. Traffic was heavy but moving right along, and she was sure that whatever problems they'd been having through Texas—well, they must have gotten them cleared up or they wouldn't have opened the road, would they? Of course not.

Plus, she was feeling much better after Jimmy Joe's back rub and a good night's rest, and the Tylenol seemed to be helping because her back didn't ache nearly as much.

At this rate, she told herself optimistically, she would be in Amarillo in three hours, and maybe, just maybe, she could find a flight going…anywhere. Somewhere *south*. She wouldn't even have to tell them she was pregnant—if she kept her coat on maybe they would just think she was fat. She would fly standby, if she had to. Then, if she could get to someplace even *close* to Pensacola, she could rent a car, and… *Yes,* she could still do it, by God. She could still get there on Christmas Day. And she *would*.

When Mirabella put her mind to something, she didn't give up easily.

Jimmy Joe was glad to be back on the road. It felt good, even knowing what he was heading into, watching those miles roll by, knowing every mile marker he passed put him that much closer to J.J. and home.

Home. He thought about that, focusing his mind on what it felt like to be there, walking himself one by one through the rooms of the big old white frame, two-story house he'd grown up in. Remembering what it smelled like—the smell of canning tomatoes in his mama's kitchen in the summertime, the wet-dog odor of the back porch when it rained, the sweet, warm fragrance of honeysuckle. He thought of the pantry door where his growth and that of all his brothers and sisters had been charted from the time they were big enough to stand straight and tall, and rooms filled with shabby furniture and cluttered with books and magazines and children's artwork in crayon and poster paints. He thought of the old tree house, and the silk spider that had spun her web in its doorway.

And he thought about his own house—a real nice house about a mile down the road, solidly built of red brick, with a big front porch and white trim and a nice big sunny kitchen, and great old oaks and pine trees for shade. He'd done a pretty good job with it, too; made it nice and homey for J.J., filling up the rooms with books and pictures and things he'd brought back from his trips, interesting things from all over the country. Navajo rugs and Acoma pottery, and a big old bed he'd found up in the Blue Ridge Mountains, hand-carved from four-hundred-year-old walnut trees.

He was happy there, and so was J.J. And when he had to leave, well, there was the old place and a grandmama right down the road, and you couldn't ask for better than that. No, sir.

He said to himself, Jimmy Joe Starr, you're a lucky man. Couldn't ask for more than you've got, and that's a fact.

When it came to families, he'd always thought it was too bad everybody couldn't have one like his. They weren't perfect, nowhere near it, with his daddy dying so young; and his mama could be tough as nails sometimes. And there was his sister Joy Lynn's two divorces, which was something of a family record, and brother Roy who liked his beer a little bit too much, and his youngest brother Calvin who'd dropped out of high school and never had learned how to work a lick or hold on to a job.

But there was a lot of love in the family in spite of nobody being perfect. And when the holidays rolled around, or somebody's birthday, and the whole bunch got together—and there would be babies crying and kids running underfoot, and the womenfolk gathered in the kitchen all talking at once, and the men outside arguing politics or throwing a ball around if the weather was good, and the older kids playing hide-and-seek or hunting turtles in the woods behind the house—then he knew how good he had it.

Then he knew—oh, how he knew—that he was lonely.

Much as he hated to admit it, it was the truth. No matter how much he loved his kid, or how great his mama was, or how much he enjoyed his brothers' and sisters' company, there were times when it wasn't enough. Times when he would come in off the road and walk into his house and hear his footsteps echo in a kitchen that smelled of nothing but "empty," and his big old hand-carved bed seemed cold, and

way too roomy for one person. Times he would even feel
envious watching his brothers and sisters bicker and squabble
with their mates. It had been a long time since he'd had anybody to argue with over breakfast about something as foolish
as Walt Disney movies.

I'm going to read to my baby....

Suddenly, clear as a bell, he could hear Mirabella saying
that, hear the fierceness in her voice, the joy in her laughter.
He could see her face, too, the sparkle in her gray eyes, her
nose turning pink, and the wind in her hair....

His heart went *bump* against his ribs. He muttered, "Christmas," under his breath and reached over and turned on the
radio to see if he could find some music to take his mind off
things he had no business thinking about.

He was lucky. On the only clear station in that part of New
Mexico he caught Brenda Lee just finishing up "Rockin'
Around the Christmas Tree," and right after that Elvis started
in with "Blue Christmas." He left it there and turned the
volume up loud so he wouldn't have to listen to all the talk
coming in on the CB about the mess waiting for him up ahead
in Texas.

For one of the few—the very few—times in her life, Mirabella was feeling uncertain; she would never admit to being
afraid. But as she clung to the wheel of her Lexus and dog-
gedly followed the taillights of the big rig in front of her, she
felt a chill that had nothing to do with the snow blowing past
her windshield.

Everything had been fine until about ten miles into Texas,
when all of a sudden both lanes of traffic on the interstate had
slowed to a crawl. A few miles farther on she'd come to know
why. Snow—not from the threatening black clouds overhead,
but blown by the wind across that flat, unbroken plain—had
reduced visibility to nearly zero. Packed down by the tires of
hundreds of eighteen-wheelers, it had turned the road surface
into a narrow track of bumpy, rutted ice. The double line of
trucks became one, an endless train creeping fitfully eastward

at a pace slower than a man could walk. With very good reason. If Mirabella needed more dramatic evidence of the need for caution, there were the dozens of cars stuck in roadside drifts and even a few big rigs jackknifed on the median to remind her.

Oh, God, she thought as she crept past yet another disabled vehicle, what if I...

No. Ice trickled down her spine, and she shivered. No, she wouldn't even think of such a possibility. It wouldn't happen to her; she wouldn't let it. She wasn't an idiot; she knew enough not to make stupid mistakes. She knew the rules: *Don't brake or accelerate suddenly. Always turn into a skid.* She would be okay if she kept her head. She wouldn't panic. Of course not—Mirabella never panicked.

Oh, but how long could this go on? It was only fifty miles to Amarillo, but at this rate, that would take hours. *Ten hours.* It would be dark in three. And—oh, God, she had to go to the bathroom *now.* How was she ever going to be able to wait that long?

She knew the answer, of course. She would simply have to. Because there was absolutely no way she could stop, even if there had been a place to do so in that vast, unending whiteness.

To make matters worse, the Tylenol she'd taken this morning at breakfast had worn off, and now she couldn't even reach for her purse to get some more. She didn't dare take a hand from the wheel, not for an instant. But, oh, how her back hurt. The pressure was worse than ever, too. She felt as if she were being squeezed in a giant vise.

In fact, Mirabella was absolutely certain she had never been so miserable in her life, and that things couldn't get much worse than they were right now.

A few minutes later she knew how wrong she was.

Suddenly there was a soft *pop,* and she felt a flood of warmth and wetness, a simultaneous release of pressure. She gasped. No—she felt as if the air were being sucked from her lungs.

For the first time in her life her mind went completely blank, as if someone had pushed a button and instantly wiped her data banks clean of every rational thought and all common sense. In short, she panicked.

And then she hit the brakes.

The next thing she knew she was clinging uselessly to the steering wheel while the world outside her windows passed by in a dizzying white blur. There were horrifying lurches and teeth-jarring crunches and explosive popping sounds and things flying at her from all sides. *Air bags!* Thank God—she was engulfed—all but smothered—in air bags. Then there was stillness…and silence, except for a soft whimpering, which Mirabella realized with utter horror was coming from her.

She was no longer uncertain. Nor was she afraid. Now she was positively terrified.

She knew what had happened. The impossible. The unthinkable. *Her water had broken.* And it had shocked her so badly she'd done just what she knew she shouldn't have, which was tromp on the brake, and as a result her car had skidded off the icy road and was now stuck in a snowbank, like those of all the other poor souls she'd passed and pitied. And now she and her baby were in big trouble. *Desperate trouble.*

Oh, God, she thought, what am I going to do?

Get ahold of yourself, Bella. Don't panic.

All right, it was a little late for that last bit of advice. But she did need to get ahold of herself, stay calm, and *think.*

Okay. The first thing she had to do was get help. *Please— somebody help me!*

But she couldn't just sit here and wait for someone to come along. There was no telling how long that might be, and she had to get to a hospital *now.* So there wasn't any way around it; she was going to have to get out of the car and try to flag someone down. Someone…someone in one of the endless caravan of trucks that continued to growl slowly by, only a few yards and a whole world away.

Jimmy Joe had lost the New Mexico radio station, which was just as well. He had no business listening to the likes of

"Grandma Got Run Over By a Reindeer" when he had enough to do just to keep his rig on the road. The CB was really cracklin', too, what with a few hundred drivers all stuck in the same place and all trying their best to relieve the tedium and tension.

"Eastbound, you got a four-wheeler on the side at mile marker…"

"Yeah, you got two more down here…."

"Hell, you got 'em everywhere! I quit countin'."

"Federated, you okay down there?"

"Yeah…think I got me a little problem…."

"Man, I mean, this is criminal."

"Can you believe an interstate in this condition?"

"Anybody got any idea what it's like in Amarillo?"

"S'pose it's like this all the way to Oklahoma?"

"Oh, man, I sure do need to pee."

"Well, you better open up the door, then, 'cause you ain't gonna find no bushes out here!"

"Uh…eastbound, on that four-wheeler on the side…looks like you got somebody out of the car, trying to wave somebody down. Ah, hell…looks like a lady—you believe that? What's she doin' out here, anyway?"

When he heard those words Jimmy Joe felt a jolt that went right through his insides. *What's she doing out here?* Wasn't that just what he'd said to himself the first time he'd set eyes on that crazy red-haired pregnant lady from California? The one he hadn't been able to get his mind off since.

A four-wheeler on the side and a woman trying to flag somebody down—he sure didn't like the sound of that. How many women could there be, out here all alone in conditions like this? He picked up his mike, thumbed the Talk button and growled, "Uh, what's the twenty on that four-wheeler with the lady wavin'? Come on…"

He waited through some crackling and muttering, counting his own heartbeats, before the answer came back. "Uh…cain't

see the mile sticks…. Make it 'bout a mile past the grain elevators at the Adrian exit. That'd be…what, twenny-two?''

Jimmy Joe watched the grain elevators at the Adrian exit
crawl past his windows and swore out loud, which was something he didn't do often, having had his mouth washed out
with soap more than once in years past for that offense. He
did so now because he knew it was a good twelve miles to
the next exit, which at this pace was going to take him more
than two hours, and that meant there wasn't going to be any
way he could get off the interstate. And there sure wasn't any
place to pull over to the side. So it looked like, if he was
going to stop and pick the lady up, he was going to have to
do it the hard way, which was to stop the whole blamed line
of traffic.

Picking up his mike again, he thumbed it on and growled,
''Breaker…this is the Big Blue Starr. I'm gonna be slowin'
down here in a little bit. Gon' try an' pick up the lady. Just
don't want anybody crawlin' up my back door.…''

From all up and down the line the responses and assurances
came crackling back at him. And then, loud and clear, one
that made his blood run cold:

''Oh, Lordy, looks like she's got one in the oven, and from
the looks of 'er, she's 'bout to pop, too. *Somebody* better get
'er, quick.''

''I'm on it,'' Jimmy Joe said grimly into the mike as he
checked his mirrors once more and then turned on his four-
way flashers. ''Hey, yellow truck—J.B. Hunt, that you on mah
back door?''

The answer came back—a woman's voice, calm and confident. ''I got you, Big Blue. You got lotsa room…go for it.
Ten-foh.''

''Thank ya kindly… 'Preciate it.'' He hung up the mike as
the word was being passed back up the line.

A strange calm settled over him, the way it did sometimes
when his way, though difficult, seemed clear and certain. Outside his windows the white crept by, yard by yard, while inside
the cab he counted off the seconds with his own heartbeat and
the chatter on the radio faded into a tense and waiting silence.

In his mirrors he could see the J.B. Hunt truck's headlights dropping back. How much longer? he wondered. A mile past Adrian—that would make it ten, maybe fifteen minutes. Seemed like an hour already....

At last he saw her, a tiny figure standing hunched and forlorn beside her disabled car, too dispirited now to even wave. There was no mistaking the silver Lexus or that red hair, either, although the rest of her didn't bear much resemblance to the Mirabella he'd come to know. Nothing very uppity about her now, that was for sure. Not a trace left of that know-it-all tilt to her chin. She looked cold and scared, plumb done in and all alone. *"And what will the poor robin do then, poor thing?"*

Carefully manipulating brakes and gears, he eased his truck to a gentle stop. Behind him, in an unbroken line that stretched clear back to New Mexico, one by one the other drivers did the same. Then, while a thousand rigs sat idling on the icy interstate, Jimmy Joe set his brake, opened the door and stepped out into the teeth of that freezing wind. It just about took his breath away.

He made his way around the front of the Kenworth, holding on to the bumper and slipping and sliding on the unevenly packed ice. When he got around to the other side, Mirabella was just struggling through the ridge of filthy black snow thrown off by all the truck tires. She was bent over, half crouching, with both hands held out to keep her balanced, and through the wind-whipped ribbons of her hair her eyes reached for him like prayers. In all that whiteness, the palest thing he could see was her face.

"Jimmy...Joe," she gasped, clutching at him. "I have to...get to..." And now he could hear what he couldn't before. She was sobbing.

"Easy...easy, now," he said, soothing her the way he did J.J. when he'd had a bad dream. "It's okay...I gotcha. You just hold on now.... Here, put your arms around my neck."

She did as she was told, her big, scared eyes never leaving his face, and somehow he got his arms under her and lifted her up like a baby. Praying that the Lord would guide his feet because he sure couldn't see where to put 'em, he carried her through the rocklike frozen sludge to his truck, set her down on the first step while he got the door open, then braced himself and levered her up and into the cab.

"Stay there," he told her—unnecessarily, for sure—as he slammed the door shut. Plowing back through the snow to the Lexus, he got the keys out of the ignition and her pocketbook from the front seat, then popped the trunk. After he'd locked up the car again, he grabbed what looked to him like an overnight case out of the trunk, slammed it shut on a mountain of Christmas presents and ran for his truck, thinking he might just about make it there before he plumb froze to death.

Back in the Kenworth's nice warm cab, he found Mirabella still sitting in the passenger seat where he'd left her, shivering so hard he could just about hear her bones rattle. "Hey there, Marybell," he said with forced cheerfulness as he heaved her luggage into the sleeper, "aren't you s'posed to be in Florida?"

Her big, terrified eyes followed him. "I have...to get...to the...ha-ha—" But the shudders racked her and she couldn't get the words out.

"Come on back here—let's get you warm." He took her by the shoulders and gently eased her around and then to her feet, guiding her like a sleepwalker.

He knew he didn't have much time, that he had to get the rig rolling again, but he couldn't very well leave her the way she was, either. Silently asking his brother and sister drivers for patience, he began to talk to her in an easy, soothing voice while he shucked off her worthless coat and sat her down on the bed, then knelt down and took off her ruined shoes. The thin, calf-high stockings she was wearing were soaking wet too, so he hiked up her pant legs and peeled them off. Then he opened up his locker and got out a pair of his nice thick winter socks.

"Here ya go," he said gruffly. "Put these on—get those feet warmed up." But she just looked at him.

After a moment it became clear to him that she wasn't up to putting the socks on alone, so once again he skinned up her damp pant legs and did it himself. He couldn't help but notice how cold her feet were, and how small and defenseless they looked. The socks came clear up to her knees. He told himself it wasn't all that different from helping J.J. get dressed on those winter mornings when the boy didn't feel like waking up and going out in the cold to catch the school bus. But as small as her feet were, they weren't a little boy's feet. They were a woman's. And the way he felt when he touched them wasn't anything at all like he felt when he was dressing J.J.

He got her eased down on the bed and the blankets tucked in nice and snug around her, then left her and slipped back into the driver's seat. For a moment he sat and listened to the living, breathing, waiting silence coming over the CB radio. Then he picked up the mike, thumbed it on and drawled, "Uh...this potty stop was brought to you by the Big Blue Starr. Hope y'all enjoyed it.... Ten-foh."

He grinned as the radio erupted with whoops and hollers and crackling static, with everybody within earshot trying to talk at once. A few nearby drivers cut loose with blasts from their airhorns. Then he hung up his mike and put the Kenworth in gear, and slowly, slowly the line began to move again.

When he was pretty sure things were going along okay, nobody taking any unscheduled side trips into the median, he glanced around and called hopefully, "Hey, you doin' okay back there?"

He thought he heard her whisper, "Fine..." But through the open door of the sleeper he could see that she was still curled up on her side with the blankets cuddled close, and that her eyes were closed. She was still shivering, too. He turned up the heat another notch and went back to concentrating on keeping his rig on the road, but worry was beginning to gnaw at his insides.

The channel 19 airwaves were pretty much back to the normal chatter, drivers bitching and moaning and looking out for one another, just generally doing what they could to keep their spirits up. Jimmy Joe listened to it while another couple of miles crawled by, then once again picked up his mike. He thought a minute, then thumbed it on.

"Uh…anybody seen any bears lately? Come on…"

That got him some guffaws and some rude remarks.

"Hell, there ain't no bears out here. Ain't no place for 'em to hide."

"I ain't seen a smoky since yesterday. Cain't say's I miss 'em."

"Westbound…anybody out there?"

"Ain't no bears gonna be movin' westbound. They do, they ain't gonna get back to Amarillo, not unless they can fly."

"How come there's never a bear around when you need one?"

Jimmy Joe let a breath out, taking his time about it. It was pretty much what he'd expected, but he didn't like it. After thinking about it another minute or two, he punched the mike button again. "Breaker…this is Big Blue Starr again. I'm gon' be switchin' channels here for a while, gon' try and raise somebody over on nine. Uh…I could use a little help. Got a lady here in need of transportation right quick, that's 'bout the…twenty-four-mile yardstick. If you got any bears in your neighborhood, I'd appreciate it if somebody'd flag 'em down. Ten-foh."

He didn't wait for a reply. When he had channel 9, the emergency channel, tuned in, he listened to nothing for a few seconds, then thumbed on his mike once more. He spoke in a low voice with only a trace of his trucker's drawl.

"Mayday…Mayday… This is Blue Starr Transport. I'm eastbound on I-40, about three miles east of Adrian…got an emergency situation here. Repeat—this is an emergency. Come back…" He listened hopefully, then tried once more. "Mayday, Mayday…anybody out there listenin'?"

There was only silence.

"Jimmy Joe?"

Oh, Lord. He held the mike against his thumping heart

while he cleared his throat, then sang out, "Well, g'mornin', sunshine. You feelin' better?"

She crept in between the seats, wrapped like an Indian in the comforter from the bed—an old quilt he'd borrowed from his mama's house—and eased herself into the passenger seat. He knew he ought to tell her to fasten her seat belt, but a quick look over at her, the way she was holding herself, made him think…maybe not.

"Jimmy Joe…" She took a deep breath and pulled herself up straighter, and he could see that she was trying hard to recover some of the dignity she'd lost back there in the snowbank. "I think you should know…. My, uh, my water broke."

Oh, Lord, he thought. Lord, no.

But she took another breath, shakier than the first, and went on with it like somebody scared silly but determined to make a full confession. "Back there. It…startled me. That's why I lost control of my car." Her voice, which had started off calm and strong, got gradually fainter until she finished in a whisper, "I have to get…to a hospital. I think I'm going to have my baby…now."

Chapter 7

"Eastbound, you got your ears on?"

I-40—Texas

Well, Lord, Jimmy Joe thought, if you're listenin', this would be a real good time for a miracle....

Because he knew that all the "Maydays" and all the prayers in the world weren't going to get an ambulance out on that track of rutted black ice, and if one did manage to get here, there wasn't any way in the world for it to get back to Amarillo with Mirabella—not with a solid line of trucks plugging up the road. Not unless it could fly. And until the wind died down and the snow quit blowing, there wasn't much chance of that, either.

The best he could hope for was to keep going, keep heading for Amarillo, and hope he got there before the baby did. Amarillo...no more than fifty miles, now. At this rate that was ten hours. *Ten hours.*

He didn't know why he wasn't more surprised. Scared, yes, but not surprised. Icy sweat filmed his upper lip and ran in a trickling trail from his armpits and on down his ribs. Maybe we'll make it, he thought. Sure, we will. Babies, especially the first one, can take a long time.

"Jimmy Joe?" Her eyes were dark, beseeching.

"Yeah," he said, and cleared his throat, wondering how long he'd been sitting there in frozen silence. "I heard what you said." He realized he was still holding his CB mike pressed against his chest and reached out to hang it up, stretching his arm slowly...stalling.

"I'm sorry."

I'm sorry. He glanced at her, then transferred his scowl to the left-hand mirror instead, where beyond the endless line of headlights he could see streaks of red in between the layers of black and purple clouds. Somewhere out there behind him the sun was going down. It was going to get dark soon.

"Hey," he said, "let me ask you something."

Hearing the hoarseness and the edge in his voice, Mirabella caught her breath and waited. She wanted him to look at her with the calm, reassuring eyes she remembered—eyes the warm, comforting brown of teddy bears and chocolate. But he kept his face turned away from her, and the angle of his head and the set of his jaw had a tense, angry look.

"You said your back's been hurtin' you. That a steady kinda hurt, or more off and on?"

She closed her eyes and leaned her head against the back of the seat. "Off and on, I guess. I just thought it was the Tylenol taking effect. I thought I was aching because of too much sitting. I thought I was just tired. I never thought—"

Jimmy Joe was muttering under his breath. He broke off to ask, "How long has this been goin' on?"

Wretchedly, Mirabella whispered, "Since yesterday, I think."

Then he did finally look at her, with eyes that were more black than brown and in no way comforting, and exclaimed, "Good *night,* woman, what's the matter with you? Don't you know enough to know when you're in *labor?*"

She flinched at the word—an appalling thing to do, but she

couldn't help it. Even though she knew she'd earned his anger, it seemed so unexpected, so incomprehensible, more frightening than anything that had happened to her so far. To her utter dismay she began to tremble, and then to cry. "It wasn't supposed to *be* now!" she wailed. "It's not supposed to be for another month. I just thought…I was, you know… uncomfortable. I never dreamed… It's not supposed to…"

Another month. Oh, Lord. He remembered now; she'd told him that. Lord help us, he thought. A month early—a preemie. Oh, hell. Oh, damn. Anything but that. He felt himself go icy cold, then numb.

But not too numb for it to occur to him he'd forgotten who he was dealing with, to know he'd lost control of himself, and as a result now he had a very upset woman on his hands. Not too numb to feel like a bully, and thoroughly ashamed of himself.

He took a deep breath and stretched his arm slowly across the space between them, gripping the back of the seat, near enough to her to touch the quilt she'd wrapped herself in. "Easy… You just take it easy, now," he muttered. A tremor went through him as he felt the slippery warmth of her hair against his fingertips. "It's gonna be okay…it's gonna be okay."

She bowed her head so that her hair pulled through his fingers like a shuttle full of silk floss through a loom. It slithered forward across her cheeks and his hand found her neck instead. In a voice he could barely hear she whispered, "Jimmy Joe, I'm scared."

Scared? He wanted to tell her he was scared, too; as scared as he'd ever been in his life before. *Lord,* how scared he was. He wanted to tell her—and God, too—that he didn't want any part of this.

No, Lord, I don't want ever again to hold a too-tiny baby in my hands and watch it slip away before it even has a chance to live. Not again, Lord. Not again.

"It's gonna be okay," he said for the third time, trying to

make himself believe it. His voice sounded like the scratched 78-rpm records Great-granddaddy Joe Doyle used to play on his windup phonograph. "We're only fifty miles from Amarillo."

He could feel her turn to look at him, with a gaze both direct and solemn. "How many hours?"

Since he never had been any good at telling lies, instead of trying to think one up he gave her neck a little squeeze and then took his hand away. In his scratchy gramophone voice he said, "I put a call out on the emergency radio channel. We'll get you some help out here, don't you worry."

Then he had an inspiration. Taking his mike down from its hook, he held it out to her and showed her with his thumb how to work the speaker button.

"Here," he said, "why don't you give 'em another call right now? You just mash on this right here when you want to say somethin', then let 'er go so you can listen. See there? Go on, give 'er a try." If nothing else, he thought, it would give her something to do, make her feel, if not better, at least maybe not so helpless.

One of her hands crept from the folds of the quilt and took the mike from him. It came as a shock to him to feel how cold her fingers were. He heard a soft sniff, a throat-clearing cough, and then in a low voice, "What do I say?"

"You probably oughta start with 'Mayday,'" he said dryly, trying out a grin to see if it had any effect on his spirits. It didn't, and his words came out with an impatient edge. "Then, I don't know. Tell 'em it's an emergency. Tell 'em where you are. Then…shoot, just tell 'em what the problem is."

"I've never done this before." She gave a nervous, hiccuping laugh. "I feel funny."

He looked over at her, saw her trying to smile, and the sheen of fear in her eyes. His voice gentled. "No trick to it," he said softly, dragging his eyes back to the road. "Just hold it up to your mouth, mash the button and talk. Nothin' to be bashful about."

"Okay, here goes.…" He heard her take a breath, clear her

throat. "Okay... Mayday, Mayday. This is an emergency. Uh...I'm in a truck—Blue Starr Transport—on I-40. Let's see, that's about fifty miles west of Amarillo. We're stuck in traffic, and I'm, uh, well, I'm in labor. And, uh, we need help. So...please send someone. Please. Help..."

"What now?" she whispered after a tense little silence. "Nobody's answering."

"Did you remember to let go of the button?"

"Oh...shoot." She swore under her breath. Another few minutes of silence went by. "Still nothing. Shall I try again?"

"Sure, might as well." Then he had to smile as this time she jumped right in with a self-confident singsong. He had to hand it to her—the lady did learn fast. Sounded just like a born trucker.

"Mayday, Mayday, this is an emergency. Repeat, this is an emergency. I am in a big rig owned by Blue Starr Transport, stuck in westbound traffic on I-40 about fifty miles west of Amarillo. I am in labor and in need of assistance. Please respond. Mayday."

Together they listened to crackling static and breathing sounds. Then in a flat, expressionless voice she said, "Well. So much for that." From the corner of his eye he could see her hand reaching toward him.

Wordlessly he took the mike from her and hung it back up, wishing he could have taken her hand instead, just because sometimes when there wasn't anything to say, it was kinda good to have a hand to hold on to. But the mike was there in the way, and by the time he had it taken care of, the moment had gone by. So all he could do was try and find some words.

"We'll keep 'er on that channel," he said gruffly. "Just keep on tryin'. Sooner or later we're bound to raise somebody. Meanwhile, maybe you oughta go on back there and lie down for a while. Seems to me if you keep quiet, things might slow down some. Get out of those wet things, too, while you're at it. I know I've got some clothes back there you can wear. Couple of sweatshirts, some long johns..."

"Jimmy Joe..." Just that.

The way she said it, the way she was breathing, got his attention real quick. He looked over at her, his heart jumping right out of his chest. "You havin' a contraction?"

She nodded rapidly, clinging to him with eyes suddenly gone dark and scared. "I guess it must be."

"Okay…okay." He gripped the wheel and stared a hole in the windshield, hoping he didn't sound as scared as he felt, hoping he didn't drive right up the tailgate of the reefer truck in front of him. "Now…"

What now? It had been a long time since he'd attended those childbirth classes with Patti—J.J.'s mama. All he could remember about them was a lot about relaxation, and something called "cleansing breaths." Which, judging from the sounds she was making, Mirabella already had down pat.

Finally getting up enough courage to look over at her, he saw that she had her eyes closed now and was concentrating on those breaths for all she was worth. It gave him an odd, lonely feeling to watch her, as if she'd gone away somewhere, to some place he could never follow. Nothing for him to do but keep his mouth shut and drive, until finally she let out her breath in a long, slow hiss and finished it up with, "Oh, boy."

"Bad one?" he asked awkwardly, fully aware of the fact that no matter how she answered him, he would never really understand. Nothing like childbirth to make a man feel totally useless, he thought. Probably why in ages past at times like this the womenfolk were always sending the men out to chop wood or boil water or hunt buffalo, just to make 'em feel like they were good for something.

"Not so bad." She said it with a relieved chuckle, like a kid finding out that the punishment he'd been dreading wasn't so terrible after all. "If they don't get any worse than that, I can handle it."

"How often you havin' 'em?"

"I don't know." She shifted restlessly. "I guess we'd better start keeping track."

"Okay, say we start—" he pulled back the sleeve of his sweatshirt and got a good look at his watch, adding a couple of minutes for the time they'd been talking ''—now. Okay, now, you tell me the minute you feel the next one comin' on, y'hear? And right now before it does, you best get on back there and lie down.'' He jerked his head in the direction of the sleeper. ''Get some rest.''

Then he caught a replay of himself. He shook his head and made a sound that was full of all the self-disgust and help-lessness he felt. ''I beg your pardon—don't mean to be givin' out orders. I just do it so I'll feel like I'm doin' somethin'.'' He gave her about half a grin, which was the best he could muster.

''That's okay.'' After a moment she gave a soft laugh and added dryly, ''You probably ought to get in some practice while you can. Looks like you're going to be my childbirth coach.''

With that she got up and eased herself between the seats. The quilt got hung up on the gearshift and he reached auto-matically to unhook it for her, taking more time than he needed, fussing with the dragging end like a bridesmaid with a bridal train while he tried to get some spit flowing in his mouth again. He'd never known his mouth to be so dry. Fear. That's what it was.

But he couldn't let Mirabella know. That was why he scraped up a little laughter and kind of a confident, know-it-all tilt to his head and drawled, ''Childbirth coach… Oh, yeah, I sure do remember that. Those classes, now… I reckon that's what they're for, don't you? Make the father feel like he's actually doing something worthwhile, even if all it is is prop-ping his wife up and yelling at her to do what she's already doing anyway.''

''You went to childbirth classes?'' He heard the surprise in her voice along with the soft grunts and scuffles she made as she settled herself back in the sleeper. ''Really?''

''Sure did. Went with my wife when we were expectin' J.J. It was a while ago, though—don't know how much of it I remember.'' Traffic having stopped for the moment, he twisted around to look at her and then had to laugh out loud at the pure disbelief on her face. ''Why, what's that for?''

''What's what?''

''That look. What'sa matter? You don't think I've been to childbirthin' class?''

''Well…it's kind of hard to imagine.''

''Yeah?'' His eyes were bright, teasing. As uncomfortable as she was with the way the conversation had turned, Mirabella was glad to see his smile again. ''Why's that?''

''Oh…well, uh…'' she faltered, realizing that as usual she'd put her foot in her mouth, and there wasn't going to be any way she could answer that without it sounding like a put-down. And the galling thing was, she had the feeling he knew it, and didn't mind.

''Doesn't fit my image, huh?''

''I guess it just seems like a Yupppie thing,'' Mirabella hedged lamely. *Not a truck-driver thing.* How awful it was, to discover that she was a snob.

''What, you don't think we got Yuppies in Georgia?'' His eyes were attentive, his smile gentle and off-center.

''Oh, I'm sure.'' Shame made her snappish. ''But *you're* not.''

''Now, how do you know what I am?''

The two things Mirabella hated most were, number one, being teased, and number two, being bested in a verbal battle. The first of those usually brought on an urge to stamp her foot and scream. Fortunately, determination not to succumb to the second almost always gave her a strong enough incentive to resist that urge and hold on to her temper.

''I'm from L.A.,'' she said dryly. ''If there's anything I know, it's Yuppies, and believe me, you're not one. Anyway—'' She broke it off, suddenly both furious and panic-stricken, because she'd just discovered that the last thing she wanted to do was try to define Jimmy Joe—even to herself, much less to his face. ''I didn't mean anything by what I said. It's just—I never would have thought Southern men were into that kind of stuff, that's all.''

"Now, there you go," Jimmy Joe said, overdoing the vexation just enough so she knew he was kidding. "Where do you get your ideas about Southern men? I bet every single thing you know about us Southerners you got from redneck jokes and country music."

"I don't listen to country music," she said stiffly; she considered the very term an oxymoron. "And I think redneck jokes are…" His sudden laughter and her own latent sense of good manners stopped her.

"Hey—not all of us Southern men are rednecks."

"I never thought you were!" But she could feel her face warming. There it was—the *R*-word, the one she'd been trying to shut completely out of her mind. She didn't want to admit to herself that she'd ever thought of him that way. But she had, at first—okay, sure, cute as the dickens, but a redneck nonetheless. And now she felt ashamed of that.

"Now, what do you think a redneck is?" he persisted, his eyes bright and teasing, his drawl exaggerated. "Pert' near anybody that talks with a Southern accent, right?" He shook his head, making a "Shame on you" sound with his mouth. "That's prejudice, you know that? You Northerners think anybody talks with a Southern accent has got to be ignorant, otherwise we'd a' learned to talk 'right.'"

"I do not," said Mirabella stiffly. But she'd already begun to perk up, stimulated by the promise of a good argument, by which was about anything that didn't touch her on a personal level.

"Sure you do. Take 'ain't.' You Northerners think sayin' 'ain't' is bad grammar, but I'll tell you somethin' I bet you didn't know. 'Ain't' was considered perfectly fine grammar in Shakespeare's time. That's right. That's the thing about Southern grammar—you Northeners might think it's bad grammar, but that's not necessarily true, see? What it is, it's just Southern, is all."

Mirabella could never, but never pass up a chance to be right. So she couldn't resist reminding him, "*You* don't say ain't."

Jimmy Joe let her see his grin before he shifted gears and turned to face the front again. "Yeah, but that's because my mama was a schoolteacher. She'd skin me alive if I ever did."

"Aha!"

"Aha, nothin'. She never did let me take the Lord's name in vain, either, and lots of educated folks do that—includin' Northerners."

"Including me," she had to admit.

Jimmy Joe was plainly on a roll. "You want to know what's ignorant?" he said, smacking the steering wheel with an open palm. "I'll tell you what, you get these people tryin' to talk like Southerners, sayin' 'y'all' when they're only talkin' to one person—now that's ignorant."

Mirabella suddenly realized that she was smiling. And that she wasn't afraid anymore. And that she no longer knew whether this discussion had a point to be made, or cared whether she won or lost it. It was just…fun. Fun to be with him. Fun to listen to him. Arguing with him was less a matter of winning than stoking a fire, just so she could bask in the stimulating warmth of his voice. It was a totally new experience for her, and one that for the moment, at least, seemed to have taken her mind completely off the *other* new experience she was caught up in.

"Hey—I'll tell you what a redneck is, if you want me to." Jimmy Joe's accent was suddenly thick as molasses. He looked back at her and she saw that although his face was perfectly straight, his eyes were liquid with laughter. She held her breath, keeping back her own.

"Now, you know, what rednecks enjoy doin' more'n anything in this world is to lay around in the woods amongst a bunch a' hounddawgs, old washin' machines and cars that don't run, and drink Red Dog beer and shoot at things… occasionally one another."

Mirabella let out a snort of laughter. Jimmy Joe held up a finger, paused as if to give it some thought, then continued in a nasal singsong. "Then, one step up from there you got yer good ol' boys. Now a good ol' boy reveres his dogs. In his esteem, his dog ranks above his wife and kids, but probably somewheres below a good huntin' rifle and his pickup truck, which he likes to decorate with replicas of the Confederate battle flag. Don't laugh—'' Mirabella, who was trying not to wet herself more than she already was, made a strangled sound. ''Miss Marybell, I swear to you—'' he solemnly made a crisscross on his chest and held up his right hand in a ''Scout's honor'' sign ''—I am not a redneck. Never in my life have I used an old tire for a planter or called anybody 'bubba'—oh, well, except for Bubba Johnson back in junior high school, but you can't hardly count that, bein's how Bubba was his given name.''

I know what he's doing, she thought. Somehow, in spite of her desperate snorts and giggles, he must know about the quivery, achy, tear-filled reservoir inside her that was ready to overflow without warning. And obviously he was no more eager than she was to have that happen—although whether it was a matter of gallantry on his part, or whether like most men he was simply chickenhearted when it came to a woman's tears, she couldn't decide.

Either way, she was grateful to him. Grateful for the arguing and the laughter, grateful for the distraction, for the opportunity to recover some of the dignity she'd left back in that snowdrift. Grateful for the chance to forget, for a little while at least, what lay ahead of her, and how grave her situation was. It wasn't easy to do under the circumstances, but since he seemed to be trying so hard to help her, she did her best.

''Speaking of given names,'' she said after the laughter had run its course, making a poor job of smothering a yawn as she curled on her side on the sleeper's wide bed and snuggled the quilt around her—discovering that through the curtain of her lashes the back of his head and neck looked surprisingly mature, the spread of his shoulders broad and powerful. ''Jimmy Joe—is that really yours? Or is it a nickname, like…short for James Joseph?''

His chuckle seemed to stroke her auditory nerves, soothing as a caress. ''Just Jimmy Joe—that's it.''

"Huh. Nobody ever calls you Jim?"

"Jim was my daddy's name. *His* daddy was James, and I think the Joseph came from another granddaddy—that'd be Joe Doyle. To avoid confusion, I got Jimmy Joe. Does beat the heck out of Junior. Hey," he said with another of those caressing chuckles, "it was good enough for the president of the United States."

She murmured, "Jimmy just seems—" *Right.* That came to her balanced on the edge of sleep, and she felt an odd little flare of surprise. And then a flutter near her heart.

"Hey, you know, you can call me anything you want to." For some reason his voice had grown husky. "Shoot, call me Jim if you want to."

She smiled and murmured, "Too late—I've gotten used to Jimmy Joe, now." She would have a hard time calling him anything else. *Jimmy Joe.* What a sweet, gentle sound…

"How 'bout Mirabella? How'd you ever get a name like that? Especially with a last name like—"

"Waskowitz? Yeah, I know—awful, isn't it? My dad's family was Polish—I think they shortened the name somewhere along the line. My mom—she was a teacher, too, by the way— she's just kind of this unique person—part English, part Irish, but I think she picked our names based on whatever her kick happened to be at the time. My sisters are Sommer and Eve. Don't ask me how I got Mirabella." She yawned unbashedly. "I looked it up one time. It means—"

The word evaporated in a puff of air that blew every last vestige of sleep fog from her brain and left her senses blasted and cringing. The nagging ache in her back, which up to now she'd been able to ignore, sort of like a radio turned down low, had suddenly intensified as if someone had given the volume knob marked Pain a wrenching twist to the right.

"Mirabella…that's a mouthful. Everybody always call you that? Your family…friends?"

When he didn't get an answer, the first thing Jimmy Joe thought was maybe she'd finally dozed off. He wasn't sure what made him look back, but when he did he could see that even though she had her eyes shut, she definitely wasn't sleeping.

"Focus," he barked, which was the first thing that popped into his head as his heart gave another one of those bad leaps, banging against the wall of his chest. *"Breathe."*

Damnation, he thought. *Damn.* He could hear her begin to whimper, making a sound like a hurt puppy that had to be about the worst thing he'd ever heard in his life.

He just did remember to check his watch. "Nine minutes," he yelled. Was that a good thing? He wasn't sure, but he thought it must be good, because didn't the pains have to be a whole lot closer together before things really got serious? Maybe they had more time than he'd thought. Maybe the road would improve. What he ought to do was get back on the radio again and find out what was going on up ahead. Maybe they would make it to Amarillo, after all.

But then, he thought, what if they didn't? It was almost dark now. At the rate they were going, it was still a good many hours to Amarillo. And then, what if somebody jackknifed and blocked the road? Meanwhile, Mirabella was back there all by herself, having those pains, which were only going to get worse. She needed somebody to be with her; somebody to make her do those breathing things she was supposed to do. Dammit, he couldn't very well help her and drive at the same time!

What should he do? If he was going to help her, he was going to have to pull off somewhere. But if he did that... Everything inside him went cold and quiet. Because he knew that if he did get off, he wasn't going to get back on again. He would be committed. Unless by some miracle help did arrive in time, whatever happened, it was going to be just him and Mirabella. Him, Mirabella, and a baby that was bound and determined to show up four weeks ahead of schedule.

Oh, Lord, help me, he thought. *What should I do?*

It was right then that his headlights picked up the sign for a rest area that was coming up, next exit, just one mile ahead. A rest stop—that was a whole lot better than one of the crossroads, with their overpasses and uphill off-ramps, where he would stand a good chance of jackknifing his rig. And there would be a rest room, water, maybe even a phone. He let out a breath that was almost relief, figuring if that wasn't a sign of some kind, he didn't know what was. Almost as if the decision had been taken out of his hands.

"Bella…" It came from the sleeper on a soft cushion of air, much like a sigh.

Jimmy Joe, who was busy changing radio channels, glanced back and said, "I beg your pardon?"

She was sitting up straight, rocking back and forth slightly. Her face was pale, her eyes dark and calm. She gathered her hair away from her face with one hand and took a quick breath, then smiled. "Bella. That's what my family calls me. And most of my friends. You want to hear a joke? It means—"

Channel 19 came crackling in, drowning out the rest. He unhooked the mike and held it while he waited for a lull in the chatter, but when one came he didn't hit the Talk button right away. Instead he looked back at Mirabella and got her eyes for just a moment, and he said softly, "Means 'beautiful'—I know that much Italian. And I never heard a more fittin' name."

He grinned at the stunned silence he got in reply as he thumbed on the mike and intoned, "Breaker, one-nine… This is Big Blue Starr. I'm gon' try an' get off here at this rest stop east of Adrian. Uh…I got a lady havin' a baby here, so if any a' you drivers happen to run across any help out there, I'd 'preciate it if you'd send it my way. I'm gon' be listenin' to channel 9 for a while…. Anybody knows anything about delivering babies, I'd sure like to hear from you over there… Ten-four.'

He hung up the mike and got the channel changed just as the rest-stop exit sign was picking up the glow of his headlights. He flashed his running lights and switched on his turn signals and sent up a prayer.

"Hang on," he muttered to Mirabella as he turned the Kenworth's nose onto the snow—and ice-choked ramp.

Chapter 8

"Gotta make a change here. Got a' alligator in the road."

I-40—Texas

While the big truck churned slowly along the exit ramp, carving its own tracks in the frozen, unblemished white, Mirabella focused on its driver's hands. They looked so strong and sure, so steady on the wheel. And she thought, We'll be okay in those hands, my baby and I.... Everything will be all right.

The truck came to a lumbering stop. There was an explosive hiss of air through the brake lines and then, except for the quiet grumble of the idling diesel engine, silence. Jimmy Joe set the brakes and flipped switches, then turned in his seat to grin at her. "Well," he said with a little half-shrug, "here we are."

She arranged her own lips into a smile for his benefit, although there was still a hollow feeling in her chest, and asked, "Where, exactly, are we?" It looked pretty much like nowhere to her—eerie in its emptiness, without so much as a light showing in the distance.

"We're at a rest stop." He let out a breath and stood, leaning across the passenger seat to peer out the side window into the darkness. "Not much of one—pretty much just picnic tables and potties. I expect the rest rooms're gonna be a mite chilly—"

"Rest rooms! Seriously?" That right there was enough to pick up her morale. "Oh, God—where?"

He gave her a doubtful look. "You sure you want to go out there? I was thinkin' maybe I could rig up somethin'…you know…" He paused, coloring a little. "Portable, or somethin'."

"Over my dead body," said Mirabella through her teeth. At some point, modesty was probably going to become optional, even for her. But not yet. Not yet. "I can walk. Let me out of here—now. Open the door."

He made an exasperated noise as she looked ready to bowl right over him, but he managed to get a good firm grip on both of her arms. "Okay, now hold on, wait a minute," he said as he steered her backward into the sleeper. "At least put a coat on first, okay? One of mine—that one a'yours isn't worth a darn…." As he spoke he was opening a door, at the same time taking the precaution of maintaining a hold on one of her elbows as if he expected her to make a break for it as soon as he let go. "Here," he said, pulling out a Levi's jacket lined with sheepskin, "this oughta do it—put this on."

"It's my bottom half that's wet," she told him as he held the jacket for her and guided her hands into the sleeves as if she were a three-year-old.

And suddenly hearing herself, she thought, *I can't believe I told him that. A man and a stranger, and I told him as easily as if we were best friends and I'd known him forever.*

It just didn't seem real to her. None of this did. The world she lived in—her carefully planned, controllable universe—had vanished. Everything was different. All the rules had changed.

"What's the matter?" Jimmy Joe's body had gone tense and still. "You havin' another one?"

She shook her head rapidly and tried to explain. "I just…don't believe this is happening. It's not… Nothing's the way I planned.…"

"Hey."

He turned her toward him, his brow furrowing as he watched his hands tug the two halves of the jacket together just below her chin, slip inside the collar and under her hair and carefully lift it free, then return to fuss unnecessarily with the lay of the collar and lapels. Only when he had them smoothed to his satisfaction did his eyes finally move upward to her face, while his fingers, left on their own, slipped back into the warm places along the sides of her neck as if they belonged there.

The warmth, the feel of them there, made her want to close her eyes, but he cradled her head as if it was something precious and tilted it slightly so that she had nowhere to look except into his eyes.

"Now, you listen," he said, his voice gone soft and growly. "Everything's gonna be okay, you hear?"

She nodded, but the gentle movement of his sensitive fingers along the cords of her neck made her shiver. So he repeated it: "Everything's going to be okay." Then he closed his eyes and pulled her gently forward. She felt the tickle of his exhaled breath in her hair as his arms came around her, and then her eyes were closing, too, and she was leaning into him, holding on to his strong, hard body as she accepted with a sigh the support and comfort he offered.

How wonderful this feels, she thought, her skin, her cells, her being soaking up the unfamiliar sensation of masculine hands drawing gentle patterns on her back. As if even they knew…

I wish I could stay like this…forever.

Knew that for her, forever would be counted in minutes…seconds…fetal heartbeats. And measured in the tolerance of a tiny but independent creature for being squashed between two large and inconsiderate bodies.

They both felt the kick at the same time and drew apart, laughing. Jimmy Joe coughed and said, "That's some little slugger you got there," and hooked a thumb in his pocket and shifted his feet in endearing awkwardness.

"Tell me about it," said Mirabella, gasping at the continuing convulsions taking place in her belly.

"Well," he said, "I reckon that's a good sign."

She gave a short, soft laugh. "Yeah, I guess..." And then, frowning: "Jimmy Joe?" As it often did, unguided by thought, her hand had come to rest on the quivering bulge just above her navel, where it moved in gentle, circling strokes. Emotion crept up on her, stealing the words, but still somehow she managed, "I, uh...thanks. For stopping...for picking me up. For...you know. Being here." And although she didn't want it to, the wobble in her voice added, *And for everything we both know is still to come.*

As clumsy as it was, he seemed to understand, murmuring huskily, "Shh...no problem." And all the while his eyes followed the movement of her hand on her belly, his own hand hovering in the space between them as if he very much wanted, but wasn't sure he had the right, to touch.

Seeing that, all at once Mirabella's heart felt swollen, and something very much like grief stung the backs of her eyes and throat. Why couldn't it have been? she thought. Oh, *why* couldn't I have found someone like this *before?* I wouldn't have given up! It wouldn't have had to be like this! *Dammit, where were you?*

She forced a laugh to explain the unexplainable tears, then sniffed, drew a breath and in a high, distressed voice, said, "Uh...can we go to the bathroom now? *Please?*"

He jumped as if she'd startled him out of a doze, lifting the errant hand and using it to push a fallen lock of blond hair back from his brow, letting out a breath with a sound not unlike the truck's air brakes. "Oh—sure. Just let me get a flashlight...."

From yet another of the sleeper's storage compartments he produced a battery-powered lantern, the kind you can either carry or set down on its base. He kept a light hold on her arm as he edged past her and reached across the passenger seat to open the door. Then, guiding her carefully after him, he backed out into the darkness.

The wind was brutal. The instant it touched her, she swore and began to shake uncontrollably. All she could say was, "Oh, God. Oh…God."

Jimmy Joe switched on the flashlight and set his teeth and concentrated on not shivering so much himself, and also on resisting the strong temptation to lift Mirabella into his arms and carry her. It probably would have been faster and easier, and a darn sight warmer for both of them if he had. But a lot of stuff from those childbirthing classes was coming back to him, and one of the things he remembered was that laboring women were apt to be funny about being handled; that sometimes they liked to be touched and sometimes they didn't, and that it wasn't always easy to know what kind of mood they were in. He figured he and Mirabella had lots of time ahead of them to get to know each other's ways, and he didn't want to take a chance on messing things up before they'd gotten started.

Hugging her, now. Holding her. That had been nice. He thought about it as he crunched beside her through the frozen snow, supporting her with one arm hooked across her back and under her arm while she hung on to his hand with a grip like a vise. Yes…she'd seemed to like that. He'd liked it, too. Probably a lot more than he should have, considering the circumstances.

The fact was, he didn't know quite what to do with the thoughts and feelings that kept coming over him where Mirabella was concerned. He kept thinking—and telling himself—that he ought to be ashamed. But he wasn't. For one thing, what he felt for her wasn't the usual kind of lust or desire for a beautiful woman's body, which likely *would* have been shameful. It seemed to him it was more a kind of "connectedness'' that had been growing on him for a while now, ever since he'd put her to bed in his truck and sat beside her and rubbed her back and watched over her while she slept.

Maybe even before that. When he'd ordered chicken-noodle soup for her. Or when he'd first offered her his bunk.

But whenever it had started, what it had grown into was a sense of closeness, a degree of familiarity he couldn't remember having had with any woman since J.J.'s mama. Not even then. It was probably something to do with the drugs and alcohol and all that, but there had been a big part of Patti he'd felt closed off from; a part—maybe the most important part— that he could never reach.

What was even stranger to him was that in the years since their divorce he hadn't met a woman he'd even wanted to get that close to. And he couldn't for the life of him figure out why, when he finally did, he'd picked one about as different from himself as it was possible for two humans to be.

It didn't make much sense to him. He didn't know what it all meant or where it was going, and to be honest, he didn't even want to think about it. Tonight, whatever happened, it looked as if it would be just the two of them, and a baby to be brought safely into the world. Right now he had to concentrate on that.

The rest-room building was dark and as cold as he'd thought it would be. If there was any power in the place it was evidently out—lines were down somewhere, probably. Any ideas he'd had about calling for help from here were fleeting; the phone was dead, too.

It made him think maybe it was time he got one of those cellular phones for his truck, which up to now hadn't seemed like a high-priority expense to him. Between the radio and the table phones in truck stops, it just hadn't been necessary— plus, he had a real strong dislike of people, mostly four-wheel drivers, he'd seen goin' down the road with phones in their ears instead of payin' attention to their driving.

Against her wishes, he helped Mirabella into the ladies' side of the cinder-block building and got her situated in a stall.

Then, although it made him uneasy to do it, he put the flashlight down on the cold concrete floor for her and left her there.

There was enough reflected light from the snow for him to see by as he made his way around to the men's room, although inside it was so dark he had to take care of his own necessities pretty much by feel. The water in the lavatory was flowing, but the way it felt to him, it wasn't much more than a degree or two above freezing. That made him think about that porta potty and microwave oven he'd decided not to have installed in the truck when he'd had the cab customized, but he'd figured he would never have much occasion to use 'em and it was just going to be a waste of money and space, so why bother?

Goes to show you, he thought. You just can't predict where life's gonna take you.

He had plenty of time to think about that while he huddled in the lee of the rest-room building shivering and stamping his feet and trying his best not to freeze to death while he waited for Mirabella to come out. *You can't predict life.*

"I can't believe this is happening," she'd said, which was her way of saying the same thing, he supposed.

Except that in his life so far, he figured he'd seen just about everything, and what he hadn't seen he'd probably heard about, and the fact was, there wasn't much about life that surprised him anymore.

He did still have a sense of wonder, though, which was a whole lot different than surprise or disbelief. And it was definitely wonder he felt as he stood there in the snow with a Panhandle wind blowing right through him and all around him a black sky full of cold, bright stars coming down to touch the edges of the whirling snow. There was a strange, desolate beauty about the night, and something more than that. A shivery kind of feeling. A sense of excitement. Anticipation, maybe.

He wondered if it had more to do with it being Christmas Eve, or the fact that just inside those cinder-block walls there was a woman about to give birth to a baby. What an incredible thing that was, when he really thought about it. And what a strange way to spend Christmas.

He thought about how it would have been, how it usually was: his family all gathered together—Mama, J.J., Jess and Sammi June, Granny Calhoun and his other sisters and their husbands and kids, and his brothers and probably a few odd aunts and cousins and neighborhood strays. Right now they would most likely be gathered around the old upright piano, Mama bangin' out the accompaniment while everybody sang carols out of the hymnbook—"O Little Town of Bethlehem," "Away in a Manger" and "Silent Night."

"Away in a manager,/No crib for a bed…"

That was when it occurred to him that maybe this Christmas Eve wasn't so strange after all. And he wondered if this was how Joseph must have felt, pacin' up and down outside that stable, all those years ago. And whether Joseph had felt the same kind of awe, excitement and fear.

It had been a long time since he'd thought much about praying. He'd been about Sunday-schooled to death when he was a kid, and through all the troubles and bad times with Patti he'd given up on the whole notion of religion; these days he left that aspect of J.J.'s education pretty much up to the boy's grandmama.

Now, though, standing there all alone in the cold looking up at those stars, thinking about the woman and child who were depending on him, he suddenly felt more than a little bit overwhelmed. He figured what he needed now was some help, and it wasn't the kind that was going to come in a chopper or with flashing lights and a siren. He also knew there wasn't any way he was ever going to find the words to say what he wanted to say, or to ask what he needed to ask. So in the end he just stood real still and quiet and prayed that the Good Lord would know without being told.

With that taken care of, it began to seem to him like Mirabella had been in the rest room a long time. He was just thinking maybe he'd better chance it and go and see if she was okay, when he saw the shadows shift and the lantern light

come splashing out onto the snowy walkway. He went to her
and put his arms around her and hustled her back to the truck
as fast as he could, neither of them saying anything until they
were back inside, and shivering and shaking and rubbing
themselves warm.

"I'm…sorry…I took…so long," she said as soon as she
could get the words out. "I had…a contraction…in there."

It was pretty much what he'd thought, and concern made
his voice harsh. "You okay?" She nodded, and he drew a big
breath.

"Okay, let's see…." He looked at his watch and tried to
figure how long it had been between that one and the one
before, but with everything that had been going through his
mind, he'd lost track. Near as he could tell, though, the interval
seemed shorter.

"It was really strong," Mirabella said with a shudder.
"Stronger than the others. I think…" She paused, hiccuped,
and finished thoughtfully, "It might have something to do with
gravity."

"Gravity?"

"Yeah, because I was standing up. You know…the weight
of the baby…more pressure."

"Yeah, well, maybe you ought to be lyin' down," said
Jimmy Joe uneasily.

"What for? I was thinking, maybe if I walk around—well,
move around anyway, just in here, like this—it'll go faster."

"Faster?" His voice rose to a squeak he'd never heard before. "Don't you think we ought to be tryin' to slow things
down? I was thinkin', if we can hold off until daylight, maybe
the wind'll die down enough by then, they can get a chopper
out here…."

But he realized as the words were coming out of his mouth
how selfish of him it was, to want her in pain that much
longer, and that it was pure-and-simple panic making him say
that.

So he wasn't surprised when she gave him a dirty look and
said with a snort, "That's easy for you to say—you're not the
one in labor."

Then, in spite of everything, he just had to grin. It was such a Mirabella thing to say—the old Mirabella, the one with the uppity chin and the California brass. The cold had put color in her cheeks and the wind had played havoc with her hair, and she looked wild and sort of magnificent sitting there glaring at him with that spark of anger in her eyes.

"Yes, ma'am," he said contritely, and was rewarded with another dirty look. Only this time he could see by the quiver at the corners of her mouth that she knew he was teasing her, and he had an idea she'd already forgiven him.

After that an odd little silence fell, a moment of comfortable friendliness of the kind that happens between people who know each other well, just sitting there in the truck's front seat with the armrests folded up, knees almost but not quite touching, facing but not looking at one another, heads turned instead toward the dark windshield. They both drew breath to speak at exactly the same moment, then laughed.

Mirabella said, "Go ahead," and Jimmy Joe gestured toward the radio and muttered, "Ah, I was just thinkin' maybe I ought to try callin' again."

She nodded. "Good idea. I was thinking I should go and put on some dry clothes while I've got the chance."

But while she knew her voice was gratifyingly brisk and businesslike, she also knew her actions definitely weren't. Getting up was a slow and ponderous process—in her view, much like an elephant rising from a mud wallow. Jimmy Joe, of course, was instantly there trying to help her, but she waved him off, saying through clenched teeth, "It's okay, I got it," as she finished the job herself. A small victory, but she felt immeasurably stronger for it.

The fact was, she'd had some time to think, sitting alone in that frigid toilet stall, counting her way through a contraction bad enough to make her sure she didn't want to experience very many more like it. And what she'd decided was that she didn't like feeling lost and scared and helpless. She wasn't used to it. It wasn't *her*. What she wanted was to feel like herself again—strong, capable and in control.

She'd reminded herself that she'd planned this thing from the very beginning, every aspect of it, and just because fate had decided to step in at the last minute didn't mean everything had to fall apart. So this was the way it was going to be? Fine. So she was having her baby in a truck? Big deal. People had babies in worse places—like taxicabs, for instance—all the time. So nobody was coming to help? At least she'd been through the whole course of childbirth classes, so she knew what to expect.

And she wasn't alone. She had Jimmy Joe. There was no reason why things shouldn't be fine. Of course not. All she had to do was stay strong and keep a clear head.

She was running all that through her head, making her way between the seats when she felt it—first the tension in her back, then radiating pain that coiled around and under her belly like a saddle girth, stopping her in her tracks. She clutched at the seats for support and her right hand found Jimmy Joe's shoulder instead.

He didn't say a word, but was suddenly there behind her, his body warm and solid against her back.

"Easy, now…I got you." His voice was a calming murmur, a soft vibration against her temple as his arms gently encouraged her to lean into him. "You just relax now. *Relax*. Don't hold your breath. Breathe easy, now…. Let 'er go…let 'er go."

Relax…yes. I'd forgotten. That's what I have to do. Relax.

But it was easier said than done. "I *can't*," she gasped, and was instantly furious with herself. Ordinarily, "can't" was simply not a word she allowed in her vocabulary.

"Sure, you can. Close your eyes, now, and lay your head back. 'Atta girl, just like that. Think about something else. Water, now… Yeah, water's good. Just float…."

She did as he told her. The words blew softly past her ear, tickling. She smiled, and the pain seemed to grow smaller, as if she were drifting away from it.

The humming in her ear became singing. "'Row, row, row your boat/Gently down the stream….'"

That struck her as funny. She giggled, and seemed to drift even further away from the pain, leaving it behind....

Then it was gone. And it felt so good. "It's over," she announced on a long exhalation, almost trembling with euphoria, as if she'd just won a tremendous battle. She didn't want to open her eyes; it would be so nice, she thought, to stay right here and float like this forever.

But Jimmy Joe was saying something to her, shifting her weight, easing her back into her own axis. Her legs and body felt odd, as if she really had been on a boat and was now having to accustom herself to solid ground again.

"That was much better that time." A tremor crept into her voice as she felt the shock of separation, the chill of air where his body had been. "It really helped. Thanks." And suddenly she was laughing. "'Row, row, row your boat'?"

"Well, shoot," Jimmy Joe said with a shrug and an abashed grin, "it was the only water song I could think of. Tell you what, I'll try an' see if I can come up with somethin' better next time." He looked at his watch and frowned, fiddled with it for a moment, then flashed her his smile again. "Okay, we'll see how that does. Supposed to be a stopwatch—don't think I've ever had occasion to use it before. If it works right, we're gonna know just how far apart those pains are coming."

"Right," said Mirabella staunchly.

She realized she liked the way he kept saying "we."

Which was a new and strange feeing for her, accepting a partnership when she was so accustomed to going it alone. And even more strange to feel so overwhelmingly grateful for someone's presence. She, who had always valued her privacy above all else and guarded her independence so jealously. But right now, standing close to this man who should have been a stranger still, so close her belly almost brushed his belt buckle, she found that she wanted nothing but to lean against him and lay her head on his chest and feel his arms around her and his warm breath in her hair. And she wondered how it could feel so comfortable and right.

"You aren't havin' another one already, are you?"

She blinked Jimmy Joe's face into focus and found that he

was frowning at her in alarm, and realized only then that she'd
been gazing at him—with God only knew what sort of dopey
expression on her face.

"No," she said quickly, looking away. Swallowing hard.
Telling herself, *It's just the circumstances. As soon as this is
over he'll be gone. And I'll be glad, won't I?*

"That's good." His frown eased into something else—
something she couldn't read. Then he reached unexpectedly to
touch her face, rubbing his thumb over the place between her
brows where tension gathered. "We want to be ready for the
next one so it doesn't sneak up on us again. Get you relaxin'...breathin' right."

"Right," Mirabella whispered. His eyes were so dark and
warm...as bracing as coffee on a cold morning. She wanted
to hold on to them, wrap herself around them and drink in
their strength and certainty.

His smile blossomed slowly, almost without her noticing...until, like a finger of sunlight reaching into a dark corner,
it touched something deep within her, and she felt stirrings
like the fine tremblings of a moth's wings—like the first tiny
movements of the new life inside her.

"We're gonna do okay, you and me," he said in a husky
voice, drawing a feathery line across her forehead with his
fingertips like someone leaving stroke marks in velvet. "Don't
you worry now, y'hear? Everything's gonna be just fine."

She nodded, and her hand rose unguided to touch his where
it cradled her cheek—touch, then catch and hold it there. She
made what was for her an unprecedented sound, a laugh so
saturated with emotion it sounded almost like a sob. Embarrassed by it, she closed her eyes...and felt the soft brush of
his mouth on hers. Just that, there and then gone, so quickly
she might have imagined it, if his next words hadn't blown
like a whisper of breath across her lips.

"You'd best go now...get outta those clothes while you
can."

Dazed and disoriented, she let him turn her and guide her
into the sleeper.

"I got that out of your car for you," he said, pointing to

the navy blue overnighter that she'd somehow failed to notice sitting in the far corner of the bed compartment. "Don't know what all you got in there—hope it's somethin' you can use. If you need anything of mine, just go on and help yourself."

She murmured her thanks, and heard the curtain slide across the opening. A moment later she heard the crackle of radio static, and his growly CB drawl saying, "Mayday, Mayday, we got us an emergency here...anybody out there listenin'? Come on..."

My overnight bag. She reached for it and pulled it toward her, smiling mistily and shaking her head even though she knew she ought to be used to Jimmy Joe's ways by now. But she wasn't, and she didn't think she would ever get over being a little bit awed by him—and grateful. At least she hoped not. People like him shouldn't ever be taken for granted, she thought. Like roses and robins, and the Grand Canyon.

Mostly her overnight case held cosmetics and toiletries, her hair dryer and changes of underwear, none of which she was likely to be needing anytime soon. This trip, however, she had thrown in a nightgown, for convenience during one-night motel stops. It was her favorite, an enormous T-shirt with a picture of a glowering cat on the front and the words, I Don't Do Mornings. Made for comfort rather than modesty or style, it did absolutely nothing to camouflage her swollen breasts and bulging belly. It wasn't very warm, either, but it was long enough to cover her legs to mid-calf, and since she wasn't going to be wearing any bottoms, that seemed a big plus. For warmth and modesty she could always wear one of Jimmy Joe's shirts on top of it.

No bottoms... A little spasm of queasiness gripped her. I feel like a virgin preparing for my wedding night, she thought. And then the irony of that struck her and she had to sit down, holding her stomach and hiccuping with silent laughter.

"How you doin' in there?" Jimmy Joe called from the front.

She jumped guiltily and began to shuck off clothing as fast as she could, managing to answer with a muffled, "Fine...just about done."

After a pause, his voice rode in on a ripple of laughter. "Hey, I thought of a good water song."

"Yeah?"

"Yeah…how 'bout 'The River'? Garth Brooks."

Preoccupied with peeling off her wet pants, she had to confess she'd never heard of either the song or, "Garth…*who?*"

Which clearly appalled Jimmy Joe. "Come on, now. You don't mean to tell me you never heard of Garth Brooks? One of the biggest country singers the last couple years. Songs've been at the tops of the charts— Where you been, woman?"

Mirabella sniffed. "Oh…well. I told you, I don't listen to much country music."

"Huh." There was a little silence, then, on a note of curiosity, "What've you got against country music, anyway?"

"I don't have anything against country music. I just consider it a contradiction in terms, is all." But she was smiling, exhilarated by the prospect of a new battle. Arguing with Jimmy Joe was such *fun*.

He gave a loud disdainful snort and to her delight countered with, "Don't know why that surprises me, comin' from a woman who thinks *Pinocchio* was Walt Disney's best movie."

"What?" She swept back the curtain with a grand gesture. "Oh, not again. How can you even argue that? It's common knowledge Pinocchio was Disney's masterpiece. All you have to do is look at the artistry, the animation, the characterizations, the themes…. What?" Jimmy Joe was solemnly shaking his head. "Okay, why not? Just give me one good reason."

"One's all I need," he said, watching her with his soft, unreadable eyes, smiling a quirky half-embarrassed smile she'd never seen before. "And I'll tell you what it is. It hasn't got a romance in it."

"What?" Mirabella blinked, then laughed. "*Romance?* What's that got to do with anything?"

He shrugged, then got up and came around the seat. Disconcerted, she took a step backward. "It has to do with everything, that's what. Don't you know that? Pretty near every great story's about love. You notice every other Disney movie has one? *Cinderella* has one, *Snow White* has one—even

Bambi has one. Only *Pinocchio* doesn't. Shoot, the only female in it's that fairy.''

She sat on the edge of the bed and stared at him. ''I can't believe it. You're a romantic.''

He accepted that with that same half-serious, half-embarrassed little smile. ''And you're not,'' he said thoughtfully.

The sleeper felt crowded and too warm, and she didn't know whether it was because of his presence in it, or the subject under discussion. ''As far as I'm concerned,'' she said tightly, ''the whole business is overrated. I've never met anybody in love who was happy about it. It just seems to make everybody miserable.''

''You ever been in love?''

She just looked at him; opened her mouth to answer, then closed it again and gripped the edge of the mattress with both hands.

Another one. He'd been half expecting it. He was puzzled, though, and a little disappointed because now he didn't know whether it had been the contraction coming on or the mention of love and romance—particularly the question he'd asked— that had made her tense up like that.

If it had been the latter, that might explain a lot, he thought as he thumbed his stopwatch, glanced at it, then set it again. Say she'd got her heart broken, the baby's father had run out on her—now that was a possibility that hadn't even occurred to him, but it sure would explain her being where she was and the situation she was in. Not to mention the attitude.

Hard to imagine any man doing that, though. Especially to her. If she'd been his...

He squelched the thought, but it lingered in his voice as he coached her with a fierce kind of tenderness. ''Don't tense up on me, now. Breathe...''

Chapter 9

"How you doin' back there?"
"I'm droppin' back a little, but I'll make it."
I-40—New Mexico

"Why do you always say that?" she asked in a strained and testy voice. "You and Charly—always the same thing: *Breathe.* I *am* breathing, dammit. Otherwise I'd be dead. Oh—*ow.* That hurts."

"It hurts," Jimmy Joe scolded, "because you're not breathin' right. And you're all tensed up. Look at you." Although he couldn't exactly blame her, considering the knot his own insides were in. "You gotta relax, now."

He peeled one of her hands off the mattress and sat down beside her. Holding it with both of his, he began to delicately manipulate the small bones in her palm, gently bending each finger, lightly stroking along the tendons in the back of her hand as if he were fine-tuning a musical instrument or an intricate piece of machinery.

And all the while his jaw was clenched tight and his mind was screaming, *Charlie? Who's Charlie?*

"Charlie—that your husband?" he casually asked as he watched his fingers work their way from the base of her palm to the incredibly fragile bones of her wrist. He told himself it was to get her mind chewing on something else besides the pain she was in.

But it was hard to overlook the way he felt when she replied, with a funny little snort of laughter, "She's my coach." He felt light-headed and sort of goofy, like he wanted to smile but knew he shouldn't.

"Well, she's right. You should listen to your coach." He crooned the words with a perfectly straight face. But inside, his heart was singing like a set of jakes on a downhill grade. *She. Not a husband. Not even a boyfriend. She.* "Here, why don't you lie over there, now. Let me rub your back…get that breathin' goin' right."

She shook her head rapidly, emphatically. Her eyes were closed and he could see that she was in that other place now, the place he couldn't go, concentrating hard on the breath she was taking. The hand he was holding had gone limp and boneless and the other appeared to have relaxed its grip on the edge of the mattress, so he kept his mouth shut and rode it out with her. Which was all he could do.

"It's going," she whispered on a long exhalation, slowly rocking herself back and forth. And finally, "There." And she smiled and opened her eyes. "Gone." She looked triumphant.

He noticed then the nightgown she was wearing, the outlines of her body clearly visible beneath the cartoon character on the thin T-shirt material—the fullness of her breasts, the pert little button of her turned-out navel. Her bare arms and her feet swathed in his thick white socks looked oddly defenseless, almost childlike.

"You warm enough?" he asked her, lightly brushing her arm with the backs of his fingers, frowning when her skin suddenly roughened with goose bumps. "Let me get you somethin' to put on.…" His voice thickened in his throat.

He loosened his hand from hers in a hurry, heart thumping, and got up to rummage through his closet. He found a plaid flannel shirt, one of his favorites, nice and soft with some blue and green in it that he thought would look nice with her hair.

"Here you go," he muttered, the words crowding his chest, getting mixed up with air he seemed to have forgotten to exhale. "Put your arm in here."

It smells like him, she thought as she pulled the shirt around her. She inhaled deeply, closing her eyes as she took in his scent, letting her mind drift, free to follow paths and currents of its own choosing. She saw—no, *felt*—a beautiful shimmering spring, its water warm and clear and life-giving; felt it surrounding her, bathing her in comfort and security. And then somehow the water wasn't there anymore and instead it was Jimmy Joe, and for a moment it was he who held her, safe and comforted, in his arms.

"That's good," she heard him say softly. "You're relaxin' better already."

She felt his fingers on her forehead, on the spot between her brows where the tension knot would be. And for some reason his touch made her face ache and her sinuses burn with an overpowering urge to cry. She let the breath out abruptly and pushed herself erect, compelled by a confusing combination of fear and birthing instincts to stand, to move, to flee.

"Let me out—I want to go to the bathroom," she said, querulous and demanding, knowing she was being unreasonable. And not caring.

A chuckle came from close behind her, near enough to stir the hair behind her ear. "You'd freeze to death out there, dressed like that. Come on, now…settle back down here."

His hands brushed her upper arms. She pulled away from him like a contrary child, insisting, "But I have to *go.*"

"No, you don't. You just think you do. You just went not ten minutes ago, you know that?" His voice was gentle, patient. "Wait a little bit. Then if you want, I'll wrap you up in a quilt and take you."

"You're not going to carry me!" Mirabella rounded on him, raw and furious. "I'll walk, or I won't go at all."

"Suit yourself," he said with a shrug. And to her added fury, she caught a fleeting glimpse of a dimple.

Suddenly she felt smothered, as if she was being buried beneath an avalanche of emotions. Confusing, conflicting, overwhelming emotions. "How am I supposed to do this?" she demanded, gesturing wildly. "I can't do this!"

"What is it you can't do?" Jimmy Joe's eyes were soft, his voice tender. She wanted to hit him.

"*This!* I can't have a baby here. There isn't any room. I can't even walk around. How am I supposed to have a baby if I can't walk around?"

She hardly heard her own words, but it didn't matter. They weren't what she wanted to say anyway. She didn't know the words for what she was feeling—frightened beyond imagination, utterly overwhelmed by what was happening to her; and not just to her body, but to her heart and soul. And the most incredible thing was that Jimmy Joe seemed to understand it all.

"Shh," he said. And again, "Shh…hush, now."

And she felt his arms come around her, wrapping her in his own special scent, his warmth and comfort, just as in her vision. She felt his heartbeat thumping against her cheek and his hand stroking her hair, and the trembling and fury inside her cleared away like storm clouds before a fresh spring wind. She felt her breathing calm and time itself to his…she felt warm again, and safe.

"I'm sorry," she whispered. "I'm sorry."

"I know…I know. It's okay."

"I'm not really… This isn't your fault. I know it isn't. I'm just being…" She paused and gave a small, liquid laugh. "I suppose this is normal, isn't it?"

His chuckle rumbled softly against her ear. "I imagine it is."

"I guess you've been through all this."

"How's that?"

"With your wife."

"Oh." He coughed, and she felt him jerk slightly; his hands moved restlessly over her back. "Yeah...well. To tell you the truth...."

It was coming again. She could feel it. Feel it lurking like something dark and terrifying just beyond the reaches of her consciousness. It was coming, and there was nothing she could do to stop it.

"Jimmy Joe, it's starting again."

How calm her voice was. But he knew. He could tell by the way her muscles went rigid beneath his hands and her breathing suddenly seemed to drag as if even her lungs had stiffened.

"Don't tense up on me now.... *Relax*." His voice growled in his throat. Calm... Stay calm, he thought. How you gonna keep her calm if you're not?

He clicked his stopwatch, then cleared his throat and asked, "You want to lie down?"

She shook her head, too busy coping with the pain now to answer. He took a breath. Closed his eyes. "Okay." He heard himself sigh. "Hold on to me now. Let it come...let it come." And he felt her weight come against him and her breathing time itself to his, while he held her and rode it with her, all the way up the long, dark climb...and down the other side.

All the time he was thinking, Oh God, how am I gonna tell her? Here she was depending on him, counting on his knowledge and experience. How was he going to tell her he was as much a novice at this as she was? God knows, he didn't want to tell her; she was scared enough as it was. But he knew he had to, because sooner or later he was going to let her down. Better now, he figured, than later, when she was apt to be going to pieces anyway.

"It's going," she said on an exhalation, telling him what he already knew.

Then for a while neither of them spoke. He felt her skin quiver beneath his hands and her breath flow warm and easy against his throat, and he thought how much like the aftermath of sex it was; the sweet, fragile time when bodies grow quiet and whispers of secret fears, drowned out by the drums of passion, are heard from again.

Presently she stirred and said, "They're coming faster, aren't they?"

He nodded without looking at his watch. Faster, longer, harder. Just like it was supposed to. He wondered how much time they had—half of him wanting things to hold off as long as possible, preferably until help arrived; half wanting it to be over so she wouldn't have to hurt anymore. He just wished they had some way of knowing. In a hospital, he knew, they would have ways of telling how far along she was. But he didn't, and all he could do was stay with her and try to make her as comfortable as he knew how, and when the time came, pray to the Good Lord to help them both.

"You know what?" she said, straightening and pulling away from him, restless again. She pushed into the space between the seats, stared for a moment through the windshield, then turned and came back again. He could see the tension between her brows, like the pleats in a tiny accordion. "Is there anything to eat in here? I'm hungry. And thirsty. Really thirsty."

"Shoot," he said under his breath, thinking hard. The truth was, he'd never been one to carry much with him in the way of food and drink. Truck stops being as plentiful and convenient as they were these days, if he had his druthers, he preferred to do his eating in something that didn't vibrate. And as far as fluids were concerned, well...he'd learned the hard way that whatever he took in, sooner or later he was going to have to find a place to get rid of it, so unless the weather was hot and dry and he had to be careful about dehydration, he was apt to go real easy in that department.

Then he remembered the orange juice he'd brought her— was it just this morning? Yes, it was still there in the little alcove at the head of his bed where she'd set it down. She hadn't drunk much of it. He reached for it and at the same time grabbed the plastic bag he kept his pocket change in.

He gave the orange-juice bottle a shake and held it out to her, smiling as her face lit up and she came for it like a hungry lamb. "There you go," he murmured, guiding her until she was sitting on the bed again, "you stay here and sip on that. I'm gonna go see if I can find us some vending machines."

Eyes closed, already drinking, she made wordless sounds of acquiescence and gratitude while he found the lantern, checked the beam, then braced himself, opened the door and stepped once more into that strange, unearthly night.

He was struck at once by the stillness. The quiet growl of the big diesel engine behind him, the constant rumbling of the trucks passing in endless procession just beyond seemed to have no connection with the land or the scene spread out before him. The wind had died down, leaving a quiet cold that burned like fire in his lungs. In the east there were clouds, lit to shades of indigo and silver and milky white by the rising moon, while under the light of the shrouded moon and brilliant stars the snow lay like a pale blue blanket across an empty land.

"Silent night! Holy night!/All is calm, all is bright...."

To take his mind off how cold the night was and how alone he felt in it, he sang the words of the carol in his mind as he made his way to the cinder-block shelter that housed the vending machines, keeping time with the crunch of his footsteps in the frozen snow.

"O little town of Bethlehem,/How still we see thee lie...."

He fed coins into the machines until he couldn't feel his fingers, stuffing the pockets of his vest with packets of cheese and peanut-butter crackers, Oreo cookies and cans of 7-Up.

"Above thy deep and dreamless sleep/The silent stars go by...."

The coins were gone. Breathless with cold, hugging his goodies-filled vest and feeling like Santa Claus, he retraced his steps to where his truck sat patiently grumbling, giving off welcoming plumes of vapor like smoke from a farmhouse chimney. Halfway there he slipped on an icy patch and almost fell on his butt, interrupting his silent singing to utter aloud a

cussword so inappropriate in that context it made him whoop
with laughter.

He was still chuckling, singing, "Here comes Santy Claus,/
Here comes Santy Claus," under his breath as he climbed into
the cab, but the song and the laughter both fizzled out when
he saw Mirabella sitting in the front seat, looking wide-eyed
and clutching the CB mike in both hands as if it were a wild
bird she'd just captured.

"Someone was there," she said in a hushed and excited
voice. "I was going to turn on the radio. I thought I'd try to
find some music. Then I heard crackling, and I think...a voice.
But it was so faint. So far away. I tried to answer, but I don't
think they heard me. Oh..." She broke off to wipe a furious
hand across her eyes and nose, and he took the mike from her
gently, ever mindful of emotions so perilously near the surface. Well aware that some of them were his.

He slid into the driver's seat and shut the door behind him,
then eased on over into the space between the seats, pulling
cellophane packages out of his vest pockets with one hand
while he thumbed the mike on with the other. Mirabella
watched him hungrily until he grinned and handed her a packet
of cheese crackers.

"Mayday, channel 9, Mayday... Come on." He listened to
silence broken only by rustling paper and munching sounds,
then fiddled with the tuner and tried again. "Mayday, Mayday,
anybody out there listenin'?" He heard a faint crackling and
caught and held his breath while he listened with every nerve
cell in his body. But whoever it was trying to reach him, the
signal was too weak and too far away.

"Jimmy Joe..."

He felt something lightly touch his face and realized only
then that he'd been listening with his eyes shut. When he
opened them he felt as if his heart was turning clear over inside
his chest, because he could see then that it was her hand that
lay along his beard-stubbled jaw, her fingers stroking back the
hair just above his ear. He couldn't remember exactly but he
thought it was the first time she'd touched him like that, of

her own accord. And when he looked at her he knew everything he was feeling must be right there in his face for her to see.

"Jimmy Joe, it's all right," she said, and stopped a tiny, silent burp with her hand. She shook her head and went earnestly on, smelling rather touchingly of Ritz crackers. "Even if nobody comes, I know everything's going to be okay. You're here...."

He shook his head and had to look away from her, the back of his hand, clutching the CB mike, pressed hard against his lips.

"I mean it," she whispered earnestly, "I'd rather have you for my coach than anybody. Promise you won't leave me."

"Lord help us, I ain't goin' anywhere!" he exclaimed, his voice raspy and full of bumpy laughter.

"Um, shame on you, you said 'ain't.' What would your mama say?" She was laughing, now, too, but stopped when she picked up her own thread again. "I mean...even if somebody comes. Please don't leave me. Promise you'll stay with me until my baby is born. Please, Jimmy Joe."

He grabbed at her hand, but it was going to be a little while before he could bring the words up out of the jumble inside him. He waited, head bowed, holding her hand while he worked at it, and when he was pretty sure he had his own voice back he cleared his throat and said, "Marybell, there's something you've gotta know." He lifted his head and looked straight at her then, facing up to the truth like a man, like his daddy had always taught him. And because he knew he was going to let her down, it was one of the hardest things he'd ever done. Especially with those big trusting eyes of hers gazing into his.

He took a breath. "I didn't lie to you. I did go to those childbirthing classes with Patti—my wife. I just... See, I never got to go through the actual birth with her. It was just the way it happened. Both times I was out on the road. The first time—"

"Contraction," she gasped, and then went right on breathing like that, way too hard and too fast.

He yelled, "Slow down!" just to get her attention, but she stared at him and didn't ease up on the breathing even a little bit, and he knew she was caught up in it and didn't know how to stop. He took her face in his hands and felt her skin growing clammy to the touch.

"Breathe with me, dammit," he said between clenched teeth, hoping he wasn't going to start hyperventilating himself.

She shook her head frantically. He could feel that her jaw had gone rigid, see her eyes darken with panic. Lord, he thought, forgive me. He took a deep breath. And then he kissed her.

As kisses went, he supposed it wasn't much. On a thrill scale, he would have had to rank it somewhere below an electric toothbrush and a fresh stick of cinnamon chewing gum. But it did what it was supposed to do, which was to stop her breathing long enough for her to get control of it again. To shock her enough to break the grip of her panic, like a slap in the face or a bucket of cold water. That was the way he meant it, and he hoped she would know that and forgive him for it.

The trouble was, his *body* didn't know it. All his mouth knew was the shape and texture of hers, and the messages that got sent along his nerves to his brain were all about how sweet and good it tasted, how warm and soft it felt. And so of course his brain—not the thinking part of it—had to go and put the word out to other parts of his body: happy, joyful, excited messages, clanging Christmas bells and choruses singing "Hallelujah."

It might not have been so hard if she'd stiffened up and pulled away from him like he'd expected she would. But instead, after the first frozen moment, the first shocked gasp, she leaned into his mouth—hard, and then harder, as if she couldn't help herself, as if in some strange way there was a connection between the kiss and the cataclysm that was taking place in her body. It almost made a kind of sense to him, although he couldn't have explained why or how. He only knew it affected him deeply—more profoundly than any kiss ever in his life before.

It ended when the contraction did, but for both of them the shock of it seemed to linger, so that their first words were whispered across an airless space of only inches.

"What did you do that for?"

"You were hyperventilating."

"Oh."

"I'm sorry."

"No—that's okay."

"I didn't mean—"

"I know."

He felt her grip on his forearms ease; until then he hadn't noticed how her fingers were digging into his muscles. She sat back, widening the space between them. He watched her draw in a breath, long and deep, then slowly let it out, at the same time lifting both hands to sweep and hold the hair back from her face. He noticed that she still looked horribly pale—almost greenish. The residual effects of the carbon-dioxide imbalance, he was sure.

He smiled at her and lightly touched her cheek. "You gotta watch that, you know? Next time, you keep your eyes on me, you hear? Breathe with me. That's assumin' *I'm* not hyperventilating."

She didn't smile back; her eyes had a glazed, distant look. But as he watched, he saw them darken and focus on his face, and she nodded gravely. "I will. I'll try. You have to help me, Jimmy Joe." He nodded, and she took his hand and held it in both of hers. "We didn't have much time to practice this, did we? We barely had time to get to know each other."

"We still got time," he said, his voice husky. But she shook her head.

"I didn't tell you—I had two contractions while you were out there. *Two*, Jimmy Joe. Hard ones. It seems like there's hardly any time between them. I just feel like one big raw nerve." She said the last words with a kind of breathy desperation, then paused as for a moment or two she struggled to regain control. She cleared her throat and continued in a low voice, clinging to his hand. "So, I guess it's getting serious. Isn't it?"

There had been a couple of other times in his life when he'd wished and prayed for something to be different from the way it was, and he'd never wished or prayed any harder than he was doing right now. But he knew from past experience that in the end all a person could do was accept what was. So he nodded and said, "Yeah, it is."

And now she did smile, a little crookedly, with her head tilted to one side. "So, it's true? You've never done this before, either?"

He ducked his head and made a rueful clicking sound with his tongue. "It's the truth. Missed the big event completely." Lifting his eyes back to hers, he forced himself to smile. "So I guess I'm as much a novice as you are."

"I kinda doubt that," she said dryly. Then after a moment, "Jimmy Joe? A while ago you said—" she frowned, and his heart began to beat faster "—both times. What did you mean? You told me about your son—J.J., right? So, what…"

Impulsively he lifted his hand, the one she was holding, and added his free hand, enfolding both of hers in the process. Closing his eyes, he pressed them, his and her hands together, against his lips. His throat had locked up tight, but she waited in patient silence, not rushing him but not letting him off the hook, either. And presently he swallowed past the pain and began to push words against their tightly clasped fingers. Eventually they came more easily, and to make room for them he let their hands fall to the space between his knees—though he didn't let go even then, and neither did she.

"J.J. was my second baby," he said. "My first was a little girl. Patti—my wife—was pretty heavy into drugs and alcohol then. She'd promised me she'd quit, you know, but she lied about it, and I was gone so much, what with tryin' to get my business goin'—my daddy had just passed away not long before, and I was out there on my own for the first time… Ah,

hell.'' He stopped, shaking his head. He'd made the same excuses for himself so many times. ''The fact is,'' he said, ex-
haling in a rush of guilt, ''I didn't keep as close a watch on
her as I should have. She had the baby early…way too early.''
He heard Mirabella's soft sound of distress—he'd been waiting for it—and pushed past it before she could say anything.

''My little girl was born so tiny and sick, I reckon she never
had a chance. I was out on the road. When I got there, they
had her on life support—just this tiny little scrap of life, all
hooked up to tubes and wires. Patti, she didn't want to have
anything to do with her, wouldn't touch her, wouldn't even
come to see her. I guess I couldn't blame her, really. They
told me my little girl couldn't live without those machines,
wasn't ever going to have a chance for a normal life. And they
asked me if I wanted to hold her. So they unhooked her and
wrapped her in a little pink blanket and put her in my hands.
It seemed like she hardly weighed anything at all. They had
this rocking chair…and I sat there and rocked her and sang
to her until she left me.…''

His words became whispers, then nothing. It hurt too much.
His chest, his throat, his whole body, like an old wound torn
open again, raw and fresh as if it had happened yesterday. But
how could he tell her about that when she was in so much
pain herself? He had no right!

His face was wet. He knew some of the moisture and
warmth he felt was his own tears, but there was something
else there, too. Something miraculous. Somehow there was the
soft flow of breath, *her* breath, issuing from her lips as they
gently brushed his cheeks, his eyelids, his brows. And her
fingers, stroking through his hair.

''I'm sorry.…'' It was a whisper of sound—no more—
breathed against his temple. ''Another contraction… Please
hold me.''

Nothing had ever seemed more natural to him than to do as
she asked. He pushed his fingers through her hair and cradled
her head in his palm and drew it gently down, tucking it into
the hollow beneath his chin. And it felt to him as if he'd been

keeping that place for her for all of his life; a special nest, just for her head. Her arms came around his neck, not frantically clutching, but holding fast with complete and unquestioning trust. His hands stroked down her sides and around to her back to find the place where the pain was sharpest and the tension lurked, and as he began a kneading, circling pressure, he felt the breath gush through her in a sigh of sheer relief.

They rode it out that way, facing each other across the space between the seats, arms wrapped around each other, legs comfortably sandwiched, breathing almost as one being.... Entwined like lovers.

How natural it seemed. How sweet and easy.

Chapter 10

"I'm gonna start noddin' off, here, pretty soon. Talk to me...talk to me."

I-40—Texas

"What was her name?" Mirabella asked, her voice muffled and dreamy.

Still dazed, Jimmy Joe mumbled, "Pardon?" and she lifted her head from his chest and gazed at him with an earnest-but-unfocused smile.

"Your baby girl. Did you name her?"

"Oh." He coughed and cleared his throat as he straightened. At the same time she took her arms from around his neck and let them slide through his hands, until that was the only part of them still touching. "Amy," he said, without taking his eyes from their clasped hands. "We named her Amy."

"Amy... That's pretty." She said it absently, then rose abruptly, breaking even that small physical contact.

He watched as she moved away from him, rubbing at her

back, distracted and restless again, and was conscious of a sense of loss and regret. He had an idea it was the way she would be from now on, becoming more and more introspective and closed off from him as her time grew nearer and she concentrated all her energy, mind and body, on the job ahead of her. She would be focused on that, wrapped up in it, consumed by it, deaf and blind to everything else, including him.

Which was normal, he told himself. Just as it should be. And which made what had just happened between them—her compassion and concern for *his* pain—seem so miraculous to him.

He hadn't meant to get in her way. The way he saw it, his job was just to be there for her even when she didn't know he was, to lead and guide her like a blind person through a swamp, to keep her safe from harm, to keep her from feeling lost or scared. Thinking about the responsibility of it all made him feel awed and humble. He just hoped he was up to it.

"You got a name picked out for your baby?" he asked.

"Hmm?" She turned like a sleepwalker, frowning. Already it was becoming harder to distract her. "Oh—yeah." A smile flickered across her face, sure and confident, for an instant a touch of the old Mirabella. "Eric. His name is Eric. It means, 'all-powerful.'"

He nodded. "Nice. How 'bout if it's a girl?"

She shook her head emphatically. "It won't be. It's a boy."

It had been so long since he'd seen that little lift of her chin, he couldn't help but smile. "You know that for a fact? I mean, did they do the tests and all?"

"I've seen the ultrasound. The doctor says he's sure it's a boy. Anyway, I hope…it is." She hiccuped, and distress flitted briefly across her face.

Automatically, he reached behind him, found one of the cans of soda he'd brought back from the vending machines and popped it open. "Why's that?" he asked as he handed it to her.

"Why do I want a boy?" She lashed him with a dark and furious look, snatched the soda from him and gulped heedlessly. "How can you even ask?" She waved the can like someone who's maybe getting tipsy. "Because it's still a man's world, dammit. And I don't want my child…to have to *struggle*…like I did. Ow…*dammit*."

He rescued the soda can and found a safe place for it on the floor in front of the driver's seat, then turned his attention back to Mirabella. But when he reached for her, she squirmed away from him with a furiously hissed, "Don't touch me!"

And then, before he could even decide whether it was okay to ignore that or not, she cut loose with a belly-deep wail, a growl, almost, that seemed to come from the depths of her soul.

"Noooh!" Shaking her head. Fighting it. Denying it. "No. Not now. It's too soon. I'm not ready. I want to rest. I can't…*do this!*"

Somehow he got his arms around her. Somehow he managed to still her thrashing and get her leaning against him, get her to breathe with him, slow and steady, the way she was supposed to. And all the time he was crooning to her, telling her yes, she *could* do it. Telling her how strong and brave and beautiful she was. Meaning every word.

By the time it was done she was sobbing, "I'm sorry, I'm sorry," over and over, and he was stroking her temple with his chin and growling, "It's okay, it's okay…. Nothing to be sorry about…"

He felt lost…helpless.

He wanted to tell her it was happening too fast for him, too. That he wasn't ready, either. He wanted to tell her he wished he'd had more time with her, time to get to know her better. A lifetime of time. Time to get to know her ways, her body's tender secrets—where she hurt and how she liked to be touched, and the mysterious feminine noises she uttered when she made love. There was so much about her he wanted to know. So many things he wished he'd asked her when he'd had the chance.

Mostly, he wanted to know why. Why, on Christmas Eve, was she here with him, a stranger, having her precious baby in a snowbound truck when she should have been in a warm, comfortable place with people to take care of her, and a husband to hold her and stroke her and tell her how much he loved her—the baby's father, sharing it all, the whole wonderful miracle of it, with her? *Why?* He thought it had to be a tragedy of some sort—he couldn't imagine any other explanation. He really wanted to know.

But she'd moved beyond him now. She was out of his reach, and he thought it was too late to ask her.

She'd pulled herself together and moved back a little, lifting her eyes to his, eyes that were filled with questions of their own. "Jimmy Joe?"

"Yeah, I'm here," he murmured, pretending he knew the answers.

She drew a bright and hopeful breath. "I really do need to go to the bathroom. I know I'd feel better if I could just—"

But he stopped her there, firmly shaking his head, wishing he didn't have to see the entreaty in her face. "I can't let you go out," he said as gently as he could. "It's not just cold, it's icy and dangerous. What if you hurt yourself—or your baby?"

He brushed her cheek with the backs of his fingers, wiping away a tear she probably didn't even know about. "Tell you what, though. I'm gonna find you something, so you can go...." Now she was shaking her head—wildly, frantically. He saw the fear in her eyes and somehow knew that what she was most in dread of at that moment was the thought of losing her privacy—her dignity.

Mindful of that, he caught her chin and held it still, and leaning close, whispered his instructions in her ear as if they were in a room full of strangers and it was the most intimate of confidences he was sharing with her. So softly she had to catch her breath, still her breathing in order to hear him. When he was finished, she shivered like a child with a secret and whispered an airless and mollified, "Okay."

He guided her into the sleeper compartment with a deferential touch, as if he were escorting a duchess to the dinner table, reached up to take down the pile of towels from the shelf above the bed and presented them to her without a word.

From another compartment he took out a plastic trash bag with a drawstring top and his first-aid kit. He left the bag on the bed, tucked the first-aid kit under his arm and backed out of the sleeper, pulling the curtain closed as he went. Then he slid into the driver's seat, dialed in channel 19 on his CB radio and turned the volume up loud. Static and chatter filled the cab, drowning out all other sound, even the sigh of his own exhalation and the drumming of his rapidly beating heart.

For a while he just sat and listened to it. He felt curiously drained, felt a need to rest and rebuild his store of energy, not so much from what he'd already been through, but for what was still to come. Because this was only the beginning. He knew that, just as he knew she was going to need everything he had to give her.

The radio blared suddenly with a crackly, tinny rendition of Tennessee Ernie Ford bawling, ''O Come, All Ye Faithful,'' somebody evidently trying to share his own particular brand of Christmas cheer through his open mike. Takes all kinds, Jimmy Joe thought as he picked up his own mike and thumbed it on, grinning. Even among truckers.

''This is the Big Blue Starr— Hey, shut that thing off, will ya? I got a lady havin' a baby over here. Need to talk to somebody.... Come on.''

''Hey, Big Blue!'' The voice was nearby, loud and excited. '''Bout time you put your ears back on. Good to hear from you, buddy. How you doin' over there?''

Jimmy Joe chuckled. Already the sound of other drivers' voices had lifted his spirits, made him feel hopeful, not quite so alone. ''Doin' okay, so far. Could use a little help, though. Anybody seen any smokies lately?''

''Hell, no— 'Twas the night before Christmas and not a bear stirrin'—''

''Hey, Big Blue, they're talkin' 'bout you all way back to New Mexico. How's the little lady doin'?''

''Hangin' in there,'' said Jimmy Joe. ''Listen, we'd sure

'preciate it if you'd pass the word along to Amarillo. Tell 'em we need some help out here."

"Already been done, Big Blue."

And from farther away: "Uh…that's affirmative. Word got there—oh, been a while ago. Word now is, they're, uh, tryin' to set somethin' up, tryin' to patch through a relay, or somethin'. Got a buncha phone lines down, so it's takin' awhile, but they're workin' on it. You'd best go on over there to channel 9 and wait for 'em.…"

"Thank ya kindly, 'preciate it," said Jimmy Joe. He was about to turn the dial when a woman's voice broke in.

"You tell the lady we're all prayin' for her."

And from all up and down the line the voices of lonely, snowbound drivers chimed in.

"Yeah, you hang in there, now."

"We're pullin' for ya.…"

"Y'all have a Merry Christmas!"

"Take care…"

"We're with you, Big Blue!"

"God Bless…"

"Thanks," said Jimmy Joe. "I sure do 'preciate it. Y'all have a Merry Christmas, now. Safe trip… Ten-four." He signed off with a lump in his throat and tears in his eyes.

For a moment he just sat there holding the mike while all that flood of emotions and feelings just sort of rolled over him like a great big wave, and when it receded, he felt calm again. Peaceful. As if somebody had put out a hand and touched him and said to him, "Son, everything's gonna be okay."

He took a big breath and huffed it out, then dialed in channel 9 and went through his "Mayday, Mayday!" thing once more. He thought he heard some faint mumbles and crackles in response, but since it wasn't clear enough to be any use to him, he hung the mike back on its hook and left the channel open with the volume turned up loud.

There wasn't any sound coming from his sleeper, so he turned on the regular radio and found a pretty clear station playing Christmas music, which he left on low just to provide some cover noise in case Mirabella still needed the privacy.

Then he started going over in his mind what she and the baby were going to need, making sure he had everything ready. Thank God, he thought, for his comfortable sleeper and for the reliability of his good ol' diesel engine. They had the most important things—warmth and shelter and a comfortable bed. Towels and bedding for her; soft, clean flannel shirts to wrap the baby in. The first-aid kit, with scissors and disinfectant and all kinds of stuff to tie off the cord. Even a plastic squeeze bottle that held eyewash—which he dumped out—in case he needed something to suction out the baby's nose and mouth.

As far as he could see he had everything except water for boiling, but what the heck—he always had wondered what all that hot water was supposed to be for. So it looked like he was ready. Ready as he was ever going to be.

On the radio Garth Brooks was singing "Silent Night." Jimmy Joe smiled a little, remembering what Mirabella had said about never having heard of him, and turned it up some more so she could hear it.

"All is calm, all is bright...."

This is the calm before the storm, he thought, rubbing his eyes.

Then for some reason he remembered that Mirabella had mentioned she wore contacts. He wondered if she'd thought about them, and whether she might want to take them out and put them away for safekeeping. He wondered just how blind she was without them. There was so much about her he didn't know.

He reached through the curtain and knocked lightly on the side of the closet. "Hey, how you doin' in there?" He listened, and when he didn't hear any urgent orders to keep out, went ahead and pulled back the curtain.

She was lying on her side with her back to him, knees drawn up slightly and her head resting on her arm. He could see the pale curve of her cheek, and her hair pooling like spilled wine on the pillow behind her. He thought for a moment she might be sleeping, until he saw that her hand was moving over her belly in slow, caressing circles. He went to sit on the mattress beside her, being careful not to jostle her too much, and reached over to smooth back the wisps of hair from her face. He felt dampness, but didn't know whether it was sweat or tears. Either way, he felt his throat tighten.

"Everything okay?" he asked huskily. "Feelin' better now?"

She sniffed and nodded, moving her head slightly so he could see she had her eyes closed. Then she whispered something, and he had to lean closer to hear. "Make a mess..." was all he caught. He didn't know whether to laugh or to strangle her.

"Marybell," he said with an incredulous snort, "you really are the limit, you know that?"

The exasperation in his voice startled her enough so she opened her eyes and craned her head around so she could look at him, frowning. "Why?"

"You always this hard on yourself?"

The frown turned into uncertainty; she looked as vulnerable as a scolded child. "What...do you mean?"

With restraint and tenderness he brushed his knuckles across her eyebrows, using his thumb to smooth out the worry-creases between them. "Look at you—here you are, doing probably the most fantastic and wonderful thing it's possible for any human being to do, and you're worried about makin' a *mess?* Woman, what am I gonna do with you?" She drew a quivering sniff and didn't say anything. He cocked his head to one side and teasingly asked, "Tell me the truth—did you seriously think you were gonna have a baby without makin' a mess?"

"I sure did mean to try," she muttered.

It felt good to laugh.

While he was doing that, he also had a strong desire to gather her into his arms and kiss her, but he was pretty sure it was the last thing she would have welcomed. Instead, he remembered to ask her about her contacts.

"I already took them out," she told him, struggling to sit up. "They're in my overnight bag." She paused to glare at him. "And don't you dare lose them."

"Yes, ma'am," he said humbly, and was delighted when she socked him right smartly in the arm.

By the time he'd helped her get herself turned around so her legs were dangling off the edge of the bed, though, he could see the shine of sweat on her skin. He watched her as she sat gripping the edge of the mattress and breathing hard, slowly rocking herself, and then he reached out and gently wiped her forehead with the palm of his hand.

His throat ached when she sighed and murmured, "That feels good."

"Wish I had some cool water," he mumbled.

She took a breath and then surprised him with a soft laugh. "Do you know…that I planned to have this baby in a tub full of water?"

"A *what?*"

"It's called a birthing tub. It's the latest thing. It's supposed to make it a lot easier for…both them the mother and the baby. I had it all…planned. Oh…*damn.*" Her breathing had gotten faster and her voice more guttural, until it ended in one of those belly-deep groans. He could see her teeth clench as she tried to stifle it.

"Why don't you go ahead and holler?" he grunted when he'd gotten his arms around her and her weight settled against his chest. "I don't mind, and it might make you feel better." He doubted she even heard him.

Later when the crisis had passed, though still in pain, she tried again to tell him—almost, it seemed to him, as if she were compelled. As if it was terribly important to her, as if he wouldn't know she hadn't meant it to be like this.

"I had it planned," she whispered. "I did…everything right. Everything."

Not everything, he thought. And because it had been making so much noise in his head for so long, and because he didn't think she was really going to hear him anyway, he went ahead and asked it, in a harsh and raspy voice that wasn't even his.

"What about the father? He have any part in this plan of yours?"

Her head pumped wildly back and forth. "No—he's not supposed to. That's not the way it works—" Her breath gushed from her in a cleansing torrent. "Oh…God. They're starting again. They…sort of slowed down for a while, when I was lying down. Now it's like…there's no time in between. I can't rest. It doesn't stop. I can't…do this!"

What could he do then but soothe her and calm her and get her settled down and focused again? But he was left feeling confused and guilty, and his questions were still unanswered.

He lost track of time. Or rather, to be more precise, he stopped letting himself think in terms of time. Instead, he started thinking about what they were doing as sort of like climbing a mountain, a great big mountain that was made up of a lot of little mountains. All he had to do was keep climbing the little mountains, one at a time, all the time keeping his eye on the big one, which a lot of the time seemed like it wasn't getting any closer. But he knew if he just kept climbing the little ones, sooner or later he was gonna get to the top.

He tried sharing his mountain image with Mirabella, but she wasn't in any frame of mind to appreciate it. She was having about all she could handle just getting over the "little hills"— although when he used that phrase to describe one of her contractions, for some reason, she tried to hit him.

He did his best to keep her relaxed, touched her when she would let him, massaging her back or her legs, rubbing her neck or her feet, depending on the mood she was in. He tried telling her not to think about the contractions, but to think instead about nice things, like good smells and bright colors and her favorite food, which she told him was chocolate-covered cherries. He told her his was macaroni and cheese, but didn't think she was listening.

When she got cranky and fed up he told her to cuss him if she wanted to, and she took him up on it a time or two. Again he told her to yell, really cut loose and holler, but as much as he knew she wanted to, he couldn't get her to do it. He didn't know if it was because she didn't want to upset him, or because she was afraid of making a spectacle of herself. Maybe, he thought as he began to know some of her ways, a little of both.

He was sorry about that, because he had an idea it would have made it easier for her. It seemed like such a natural thing to do. Like making noise during sex, he thought. And then he wondered why that idea didn't shame him. But the truth was, he'd been thinking for quite a while about how sometimes it seemed what was happening here and now—this birthing business—was a lot like making love. Only more so. Bigger. A whole lot bigger. Lovemaking to the ultimate degree. It made so much sense to him, because after all, this was what sex was supposed to be about, wasn't it? Two people in love makin' a baby.

Yes, it seemed right. Right that he should be holding this woman between his thighs, cradled against his body, her breathing so perfectly timed to his, her breasts heavy against his arms, and feel the tightening, the pulsing, the cataclysmic tremors deep within her body.

So profoundly right.

"Yeah…" he growled as he felt the pressure and the need inside her build. "Yeah, let it go. That's the way, darlin'. It's okay…let it go.…"

His eyes closed, his lips brushed her ear, his heartbeat rocked him like a boat caught in the ripples of a wake.

"Don't be afraid," he whispered hoarsely, wanting so badly to break through her barriers that he hurt inside. "It's just like loving…like making love when there's nobody to hear you. Think about it. Makin' love on a warm summer night in a cabin way out in the woods…with the frogs chirpin' and the whippoorwill callin' and the air so soft and sweet…and nobody in the world to hear you but the man who loves you more than life. Let him hear you love him. Come on, darlin'…let me hear it.''

She was so close…so close. He could feel her body arching, feel it building inside her like a cresting tidal wave. He heard the first sounds, like a rusty gate opening—and then suddenly it burst from her in an anguished, gut-wrenching wail: *''I ca-a-an't!''*

His chuckle was sympathetic but insistent. ''Sure, you can…sure, you can.''

But he'd already broken the dam, and the vocalizations he'd wanted came pouring out, complete with words. ''I don't know…I don't know…. I've never…made love before….''

He laughed softly, thinking how funny she was, how sweetly confused. Stroking her damp hair back from her forehead, he murmured tenderly, ''Darlin', what in the world are you talkin' about?''

''I mean,'' she growled, ''I've never made love before. Can't you understand English?''

Sweating and muttering furiously, she subsided, leaving him bewildered, to ponder what she could possibly have meant by such a statement. He could think of a couple of possible explanations, none of which made him feel good. The unanswered questions sat in his chest like an anvil.

After that, when the contractions got to be too much for her, he told her to think of her baby. Her sweet, precious baby boy, and how good it was going to be to hold him in her arms soon. Think of that, he told her. Don't think about the contraction. Think of your baby.

Himself he told to think of nothing at all.

It seemed to Mirabella as though she'd been existing in a nightmare—or rather, in a sort of twilight world between wide-awake and dreaming. What it reminded her of was a time long ago in her childhood—the last and possibly the only time in her life that she'd been sick. Really sick. She remembered being in bed, having a terrible, terrible headache that seemed to go on and on. A second had seemed like an hour when it was happening, but then she would find that hours had passed in what she'd thought were only seconds. She remembered hearing people talk to her, hearing herself answer, knowing she was doing things—drinking water, taking medicine, eating soup, and getting up, trembling, to go to the bathroom—but having no real control over anything that happened to her. Right up until the moment when she'd opened her eyes, gazed into her parents' worried faces and said in a loud, clear voice, "I want *waffles*."

She was in the waning moments of a contraction, coming down the back side of the mountain—that had been Jimmy Joe's idea, those mountains. How many more of them were there, she wondered, before she reached the top? Hundreds, probably. Hundreds and hundreds.

She felt an urge to hiccup, or perhaps to burp. But when she gave in to it, the ripples in her stomach seemed to want to go down toward her pelvis, rather than up toward her throat. "Oh," she said, startled.

"I want to push," she announced.

Jimmy Joe's face hovered above her. He looked exhausted. "Well, that's good," he said huskily, smoothing back her hair. "Real good. Looks like you're gonna be havin' a baby pretty soon."

For some reason he looked much older than she remembered—at least ten years older. She reached up to touch his face, trying to rub away a deep crease that had appeared near the corner of his mouth. With deep pity she said, "Oh, no, not yet. I still have all those mountains to climb. Lots and lots of mountains…"

There it was again—that strange, upside-down hiccup.

"No more mountains, Marybell."

She opened her mouth to argue, but instead of words, what came out was a low, growling sound. Was that *her?*

"That's it, you just go right ahead and push."

"I'm not…pushing," she gasped stubbornly. "Can't have this baby yet. Still…have…mountains…*oh!*"

"No more mountains." She felt Jimmy Joe's body behind

her, lifting and supporting her. "Just a great big sheer rock cliff. Now you gotta pull yourself up to the top, you hear? Pull yourself up, hand over hand, one pull at a time…. Way to go…good girl. Now you rest a minute…just rest…."

Rest? That's easy for *you* to say, she thought resentfully. First all those mountains, and now he wanted her to pull herself up a cliff? What kind of a superwoman did he think she was? Here, her body was trying its best to turn itself wrongside out, and on top of that, now somebody—some strange man with a Texas accent—was yelling at her to, "Come in…*come in!*"

Jimmy Joe jumped up like he'd sat on a pinecone. Laying Mirabella back against the pillows as gently as he could, he lunged for the CB mike and got his thumb on the button.

"I'm readin' you loud and clear!" he shouted. "Come on back."

"Ah…this the fella with the lady havin' a baby, out there on the interstate?"

"That's me!" yelled Jimmy Joe. "Sure am glad to hear from you." And that, he thought, had to be the biggest understatement he'd ever uttered in his life. He was so relieved, his insides felt like jelly. "Hey, where are you? Baby's on its way. Right now. We could sure use some help!"

"Ah…well, we're gon' try our best. Listen, I got me a gas station over here, just west of Vega—my power and phone's been out pert' near all day, just come back on a little while ago, an' looks like it's a good thing it did. Didn't have my radio on, it bein' Christmas Eve, an' all. Anyways, I got a telephone call from the state police. They got a chopper standin' by, but they not gonna be able to get it in the air until the weather clears. So what they done is, they got me patched through to the hospital in Amarillo. Got a doctor here on the line right now. Wants to know how far along she is."

With the realization that that excited voice on the radio was all the help he was going to get, Jimmy Joe felt the terrifying sense of responsibility settle once more onto his shoulders. He closed his eyes briefly, then shrugged it off and spoke into the mike with a calm and confidence he was a long way from feeling. "She's wantin' to push. Ask the doc if it's okay to let her, or if she ought to be pantin', or something."

There was a pause, then, "Doc says don't let 'er pant, it'll just wear her out. Says, let her push, but not too hard. Don't let 'er hold her breath, or turn purple, he says. Just little pushes, if, ah…if that's what her body wants to do."

"Gotcha," said Jimmy Joe, with a glance over at Mirabella, who looked as if she was trying to lift the back end of a truck. He was about to put the mike down and get over to her when the voice spoke again.

"Uh…the doc here's got a couple questions for ya. Wants to know, can you see the baby's head yet?"

Jimmy Joe's stomach gave a lurch and nearly jumped into his throat. He broke out in a cold sweat and just did manage to mumble, "Don't know…. I'm gonna have to get back to you on that."

"Okay…he says check and tell him what you see. Then he wants to know if you've got somethin' to catch the baby with."

"Yeah," said Jimmy Joe, "I got that." He took a deep breath and felt better. "Tell him I think I've got everything ready. Got plenty of clean towels. Got a pretty good first-aid kit—antiseptic and bandages, scissors, stuff like that. Ask him if there's anything else I oughta have." Besides an ambulance and a couple of experienced paramedics, he thought.

There was another pause. "Doc says sounds like you got it pretty well covered. Wants you to check her and get back to him."

"Right… Ten-four." He pulled the mike cord out as far as it would go and draped it over the back of the seat so he would have it within arm's reach when he needed it, then eased himself back into the sleeper and sat down on the bed beside Mirabella. "How you doin'?" he asked, his throat husky.

She rested, propped on both elbows, and glared at him. "How do you *think* I'm doing?"

"Guess you heard all that." She nodded, watching him. "I'm gonna have to look." And again she nodded.

And then she closed her eyes and groaned, "Well...be quick about it, dammit!" as another powerful contraction overtook her.

Funny, he'd been dreading that moment so. But she didn't seem to mind it when he gently and carefully drew her nightgown up and eased her legs apart—barely seemed aware of him at all, in fact. Instincts a lot more compelling than modesty were driving her now.

A moment later he was back on the radio, his heart beating like a jackhammer. "Can't see anything yet," he panted. Behind him, all inhibitions apparently forgotten, Mirabella was making all the noise he could ever have wanted, and more.

Pause. "Okay, doc says get back to him when you see the head. Oh—and he says, don't let her lie on her back. Says you should get her as upright as possible—get gravity workin' for you."

"Right." Back to Mirabella. He settled himself behind her, supporting her with his body, and whispered in her ear, "You're doin' fine, darlin'. Just got a little bit more work to do.... That's right...just a little bit more."

How much more could she do? he wondered. He'd never in his life seen anybody work so hard. Her hair was soaking wet with sweat, and he knew his arms would bear the imprint of her fingers for a long time to come. He began to get scared again. It seemed such an impossible thing she was trying to do, and it didn't do any good at all to remind himself that it had been done a few billion times before. What if she couldn't do it? What if...

And then...there it was.

"I see it!" he shouted into the mike. "I can see the head." He was laughing, crying a little, too, maybe. Trying to hold on to the mike and Mirabella at the same time.

"Doc says, you sure it's the head?"

"Yes, I'm sure... Hey, darlin', you hear that? We got a head!"

"I...hear...you!"

"Doc wants to know, is it facin' up or down?"

"Can't tell yet.... One more push, darlin'...one more...one more..."

"If you...say that...one more time...I'll kill you!"

"Down! It's facing down!"

"Doc says—"

"No, wait—it's turning! It's turning to one side!"

"Doc says that's okay—that's good."

"One more..."

I will kill him, Mirabella thought. If I survive this.

She was on fire. Burning. Splitting in half.

And then—suddenly there was relief.

"The head's out! Darlin', you hear that? The head's out!"

I know....

"Just a little bit more—let's get the shoulders out—come on, now, one more good one..."

One more...one more...

"Doc says you gotta clear the airways!"

Silence.

"Hey—what's happenin' out there? Talk to me...talk to me!"

What's happening? Jimmy Joe? Oh, God...my baby...

And then she heard it. A faint gurgling, then a tiny, rasping cry. As the cry grew louder and stronger, a sob struggled up through her exhausted body. More sobs...laughter and sobs. She struggled to sit up, reaching for the purplish, squirming thing in Jimmy Joe's hands.

It was so tiny, slippery wet, all waving arms and frantic wails. He held it for a moment, then laid it carefully, almost reverently on her belly. She touched it—oh, God, what an incredible thing! Soothed and cradled it with her hands. And the wails quieted to soft mewings.

Jimmy Joe knelt beside her, and she felt his body quaking as his arms came around her, helping her, holding her up so she could see better.

"Merry Christmas," he whispered brokenly. "Say hello to your baby girl."

Chapter 11

"Okay, big truck, ya missed me.... Come on back."
"Thank ya kindly... Think I'll stay out here awhile."
I-40—Texas

"I can't believe it," Mirabella whispered as she gazed down at her daughter's tiny head, dwarfed by the breast she was so eagerly nuzzling—so tiny and yet, so utterly perfect. "A girl…"

She thought of the waiting nursery she'd decorated in primary colors and Disney characters. Thank God she didn't believe in genderizing, and had always hated pastels. But still…

She shook her head and laughed softly. "Here, all this time I'd been planning on a boy—"

"Yeah, well, my daddy had a saying," Jimmy Joe murmured, lightly stroking the baby's head with a wondering finger. "You want to make God laugh?" He glanced up at her and for the first time in a long time she saw his dimple. "Just make a plan."

"Huh," said Mirabella absently, and smiled. She wondered

briefly that it didn't seem at all strange to her, that juxtaposition of her baby's head, her naked breast, and Jimmy Joe's hand, or even that it had been he who'd shown her how to get the baby to nurse. But then it was a night for wonders.

She didn't remember very much about the immediate aftermath of her baby's birth. In a fog of exhaustion, exhilaration and awe, she'd been only dimly aware of Jimmy Joe…tying and cutting the cord, wrapping the baby in one of his own shirts, following instructions shouted over the radio. She thought there'd been some bad moments when he'd worried about bleeding, and it seemed to her that was when the voice on the radio had told him to try to start the baby nursing. And he'd shown her how, by tickling one tiny cheek so that the baby had turned her mouth instinctively, like a baby bird, toward the waiting nipple.

Then Mirabella had felt the most amazing, excruciating tingling sensations, tingles that radiated from her nipples outward and through her entire body. There had been more contractions, but not too terrible or lasting too long. The placenta had been delivered, the bleeding stopped, and soon after that the voice on the radio had gone away. She'd been vaguely aware of someone wrapping her in clean towels and warm blankets, of her sweat-damp nightshirt being pulled gently over her head, and her arms being guided into the sleeves of a warm flannel shirt. How strange and wonderful it had felt to be fussed over and coddled.

She remembered saying, "Look at us—we match," gazing at the incredibly beautiful, absolutely perfect little face nestled in a bunting of farmer's plaid and laughing tearfully, and that Jimmy Joe had laughed too, the same way, and had kissed her on the tip of her nose.

But she'd begun to shiver uncontrollably then, in spite of the warm shirt and all the quilts and blankets he'd been able to pile on her. So he'd stretched out on the bed and wrapped his arms around her and held her until the shivering quieted.

"Rest," he'd crooned to her, as if *she* were a baby. "Rest now."

Exhausted as she was, she'd been too full of fear and wonder to rest, afraid to take her eyes from her tiny daughter even for a moment. "I can't believe it," she'd said, and was still saying. "I can't believe it."

"Yeah," said Jimmy Joe in a groggy drawl, "I don't think Eric is gonna suit 'er. Guess you're gonna have to call her Erica."

Mirabella glanced at him, but he was still gazing down at his finger, watching it brush back and forth across the baby's downy head. She could see his wavy, dark-blond hair and matching eyebrows, his thoughtfully furrowed brow and dark cresents of eyelashes, the strong, straight bridge of his nose. Lips that were curved in an utterly besotted smile. And suddenly her chest seemed to swell, and for the first time in her life she understood what the phrase, "a full heart" meant. Her heart was so full she felt as if it would burst. So full it had to overflow—with the tears she'd been saving all her life and now seemed to have in endless supply.

"No." She paused and drew a quivering breath. "Her name is Amy." There was a moment of utter stillness, and then through a rainbow shimmer she watched his lips tighten and his lashes quickly drop in a vain attempt to hide the shine of moisture that had caught him unawares. Shaking with emotion, she leaned across the tiny bundle in her arms to kiss his temple, and then with her lips against his hair, to finish in a choked whisper, "Amy…Jo."

It was, finally, too much for Jimmy Joe. Unlike most Southern-raised boys, he'd never been indoctrinated with the taboos against men's tears; his uppity mama's opinions had been every bit as radical on the subject of rights and privileges for the male of the species as they were for her own sex. But he'd grown up in the real word, after all, and while he wasn't ashamed to shed a tear in private if the occasion warranted, breaking down and crying like a baby wasn't something he enjoyed, or felt comfortable doing in front of other people. The events of the night had already stretched the limits of his self-control just about to the breaking point; dazed and raw, he'd been sagging on the ropes trying to catch his second wind. And now this. He felt as if he'd suddenly been stripped naked. Enough! he wanted to cry. *Enough!*

For a few moments he couldn't move, couldn't speak, just sat rigid and vibrating with his arms locked in a protective circle around Mirabella and her baby, with Mirabella's cheek pressed tight against his forehead. But no male animal tolerates such vulnerability for long. Self-preservation messages sang along his nerves and shouted in his brain: *Protect yourself! Take cover! Flee!*

Heart hammering, muscles surging, he "fled" to the limits of available space, which in his case was only as far as the front of the cab—to his own realm, his domain, where he'd always been in supreme control—to his driver's seat. But it was enough. In that familiar space he felt his heartbeat slow and his panicked breathing ease, and a sense of humility and calm settled warm and soft around his shoulders. He looked over at Mirabella, propped upon the pillows, eyes shining in her pale face like silver stars as she gazed back at him, then down at the baby cradled against her breast. He thought he'd never seen such a beautiful sight in all his life. The Madonna herself couldn't have looked so lovely.

He huffed out air, smiled sheepishly and rubbed at the back of his neck. "Wow," he said. "Amy, huh?" And then again, "Wow."

"Would you like to hold her?" she asked softly.

His heart stumbled; his chest quaked. He nodded.

She leaned forward, holding the baby toward him in her outstretched arms, swaddled in his own favorite, his very softest blue plaid flannel shirt. He took her like the precious gift she was, with suspended breath, with gratitude and awe, and held her up so he could see her face-to-face…eye-to-eye. "Hello, Amy Jo," he whispered. *Welcome.*

She gazed back at him with her unfocused newborn's stare, one tiny fist curling and uncurling against one perfect, petal-like cheek. And suddenly it seemed to Jimmy Joe that he heard tiny, silvery tinklings and loud, rumbling crashes, the sounds of things falling and breaking all around him. Soft and miraculous as the sound of raindrops falling on flower petals—the sound of a heart falling in love. Mighty and powerful as an avalanche—the sound of the earth shifting beneath his feet, of his life changing forever.

My God, he thought. *My God.*

He thought how different this was from the way he'd felt when he'd first set eyes on his son, J.J. He'd been so proud, of course. Sorry he hadn't been there to see him born. And relieved the baby was healthy and strong, glad his own long vigil was finally over, hopeful Patti would stay off the dope this time, and sad because deep in his heart he'd known she wouldn't. It was only later that he'd come to love that little boy more than his own life.

But this—he'd never felt anything like this before. He felt awed and humbled, yes, but also strong and powerful, invincible and mighty. For this little girl he would slay dragons, move mountains, swim oceans. He would guard and protect her, lay down his life for her, and love her without condition until the day he died.

Behind him, the CB radio gave a little belch of static. He'd forgotten—he'd left the channel open in case the doctor in Amarillo or the state troopers needed to get ahold of him. Now, though, it reminded him of something.

"Somethin' I need to do," he muttered. And it pleased him, as he tucked the bundled baby neatly into the crook of one arm, that it felt so natural and easy, and how quickly it all came back to him.

He reached to unhook the mike he'd left dangling across the passenger seat and looked over at Mirabella. She smiled sleepily back at him and nodded. He glanced down once more at the baby nestled against his heart and then, using the hand with the mike in it, he tuned in channel 19.

Only the rush of the open channel filled the cab; in the lonely hours of Christmas morning, it seemed, even the tired truckers had run out of something to say.

Elation filled him. He was grinning from ear to ear as he

mashed the button and calmly intoned, "Breaker, one-nine…
Merry Christmas, all you drivers out there on I-40… This is
the Big Blue maternity ward. Thought you'd like to
know…we got us a little Christmas present here. Mama and
new baby daughter are both doin' just fine. Folks…say hello
to Amy Jo.…"

Well, the minute he said that, he knew it was a mistake.
The radio just about exploded with whoopin' and hollerin' and
everybody trying to talk at once. He got the volume turned
down as quick as he could, but it didn't help much. From the
sound of things, every driver within hearing distance of his
broadcast was cutting loose with his airhorn. At the unaccustomed noise, Amy Jo's eyes, instead of staring with searching
intensity at his face, squinched up tight, and her fists started
waving and she began to make unhappy squeaking noises.

"Uh…sure do 'preciate all your good wishes," he said as
soon as he could reclaim the channel again. "Let me tell you,
it's been a long night, and I think mama and baby could both
do with a little peace and quiet, so, uh, we'd 'preciate it if
you'd use your lights instead of your horns to say hello while
you're passin' us by.… Thank ya kindly, an'…y'all have a
Merry Christmas, now. Ten-four."

After that things got quiet, except for an exuberant toot
busting loose now and then. Jimmy Joe put away the mike
and gave his full attention to the baby, who by this time was
getting warmed up pretty good. Out of the corner of his eye
he could see Mirabella, riled and worried as a mama bear
hearing her cub squall, but instead of handing the baby over
to her, he cuddled her closer and gently joggled her while he
crooned, "Shh…it's okay, sweetheart. Hush, now…hush."
And he began to sing to her the way he always used to sing
to J.J., and just once in her too-short life, to another precious
little girl.

"Bye baby bunting,
Daddy's gone a-hunting,
Gone to get a rabbit skin
To wrap the baby bunting in.

From the nest he'd made for her in his sleeper bed, Mirabella watched him rock and sing to her newborn baby and didn't once think about how politically incorrect the lullaby was. Strange shivers and tingles ran about beneath her skin like pulses of electricity; a lump she couldn't identify sat in her chest—was it panic? was it fear?—and no matter how many cleansing breaths she took, she couldn't ease it. She wanted to cry—what else was new? She wanted to laugh.

Oh, God, what is this? she wondered. Could it possibly be normal? Something she'd missed in all those books she'd read, some kind of postpartum high, perhaps. It would certainly explain why she seemed to see him as a blur in a wash of shimmery golden light.

But it wouldn't explain the desolation and longing she felt, seeing him over there in his seat, so far away from her. *So far away.* The emptiness in her arms where her baby should be— that she understood. But what was this chill all around her where *his* arms had been? Why did she feel so lost without him near her, so lonely without his body next to hers? *Come back!* she wanted to cry. *Please come and hold me again.* Her face ached with the pressure of her longing.

He must have seen something in her expression, because he rose slowly and came to lean over her, crooning as he settled the once-again-peacefully-sleeping baby in her arms. Crooning to *her,* not the baby. "There now…it's okay. Here she is…here she is. Yeah…see there? Everything's okay now."

And as she gazed down at her daughter's face—so perfect, so lovely—a sob shuddered through her. *No, it's not okay. We're not enough, Amy and me. We need you. Please stay. We're not complete without you!*

"Hey, now," he said huskily, sitting on the edge of the bed. She felt his fingers under her chin, gently lifting it. Felt his thumb brush at the wetness on her cheek. "What's all this, hmm? Come on, now, Marybell, don't cry."

She raised her eyes to his face, able to see it clearly now that he was close to her again, even without her contacts. She could see his kind, warm eyes, his sweet, familiar smile.

Oh, God, what am I doing? she thought. *What am I thinking of? After everything he's done for me. After everything I've put him through...*

She sniffed and said in a low voice, "I'm okay. It's just...I think I'm just really tired."

"Sure you are." He stroked the hair back from her temples, and she tried, really tried not to find anything but his own natural compassion in the tenderness. "You just lie back there and sleep. I'm not gonna let anything happen to your baby."

She nodded, but couldn't tell him how she felt inside—trembly and wired, her nerves jumping around inside her like popcorn in a popper. "You must be exhausted, too," she said huskily. "Jimmy Joe, I don't know how I'm ever going to be able to thank you—"

"Oh, hey—" he began, but she put her fingers to his lips.

"For everything you've done. I know I must have put you through hell."

He kissed her fingertips, then shook his head, eluding them. "Naw, you were great," he said in a gravelly voice. "You were fantastic. Beautiful."

She smiled ruefully at him. "I don't think so. I seem to remember I hit you a couple of times."

"'S okay...I had it comin'." His dimples flickered on and off, like signal lights.

"I know I yelled mean things at you."

"Hey, I told you to, remember?"

She allowed herself a brief ripple of laughter, throaty and precarious. "Well, anyway...I just want to apologize, okay? For the god-awful mess I've made of your truck, for any really weird and embarrassing things I might have said or done..."

He winced as if she'd poked him and made an exasperated clicking sound. "Now there you go again. You worry about the doggonedest things, you know that? Woman, you just brought a brand-new life into this world! You got nothin' to apologize for, understand?"

"Yes, sir," she said meekly, and he laughed and leaned over and kissed her. So naturally, so easily, as though he'd done it many times before. And her heart stood still.

"Although…" he said thoughtfully as he drew away from her. She blinked and struggled to focus on the teasing glint in his eyes. "Now that you mention it…"

"Oh, no," she groaned, closing her eyes. "I knew it. What did I do?"

"Well, now, there was one thing you said was kinda cute—really had me goin' there for a while." He paused for dramatic effect, showing his dimples.

"Tell me," she breathed. "I can take it."

"You told me you'd never made love before, and since that's not very likely to be true, I was kinda wonderin' if you could tell me what you mighta meant by that."

"Oh, God." Heat flooded through her, rose from her belly and chest and rushed up into her cheeks. She tried to cover her face with her one free hand, desperately wishing she had something bigger—like a grocery sack, maybe. "I can't believe I told you that," she whispered. "I never tell anybody that. *Ever.*" Her deepest, most closely guarded secret. Oh, God. Oh…damn.

"Yeah? Why not?" His voice was light, and she didn't notice, then, how still he'd gotten.

She took her hand from across her eyes and glared at him. "Well, how would *you* feel?" she asked hotly. "If you were pushing forty years old and still a virgin, would you go around admitting it? It's not like I planned it that way, you know. It's not like that's what I wanted. It just *happened.*"

"Are you tryin' to tell me…it's *true?*"

Humiliated beyond bearing, she couldn't look at him, could only hear the shock and utter disbelief in his voice. "Well, technically, I don't suppose I am anymore. But…yeah, it's true. I've never made love before. Ever."

There was a gust of incredulous laughter. "Marybell, I don't know how to tell you this, but unless I just witnessed the Second Coming, that just ain't possible."

She flicked him a pitying glance, then fastened her mortified glare on the front windshield. "What century are you living in? Of course, it's possible. Didn't you ever hear of artificial insemination?"

After a stunned silence, he repeated it. "Artificial… insemination?" The words seemed to hang in the air like an accusation. He rose from her side, moving slowly and stiffly, and paced the two careful steps to the front of the cab. Standing there facing the windshield, rubbing mechanically at the back of his neck, he said hoarsely, "Are you telling me…you did this by yourself? You went and had this baby…and you've never— Oh, man. I mean…I don't believe this."

"It's not what you think," Mirabella said in a low voice. He was looking at her now, and in his blanched face, his eyes seemed almost as black and cold as the night outside the windows. Looking into them she suddenly felt desolate and afraid. Words tumbled urgently from her. "I'm not…gay, or anything. I just always wanted children. I always took it for granted I'd have them someday—the usual way—you know, meet somebody, fall in love, get married. But that didn't happen. I never met the right one." *Until it was too late. Until…tonight.*

She took a deep breath and went on, looking down, now, at her baby's face. Her voice grew calm and soft. "I thought, maybe it was never going to happen. And meanwhile, the years were going by, and I was getting older. I didn't have forever, you know? Maybe I could have settled for something less. Settled for *anything*. Anyone. Just so long as he gave me children. But…" She shrugged, and her lips curved into a smile that ached all through her tired body. Mirabella had never "settled" in her life. "I thought this way was better."

And it was. *It was.* She'd seen enough of her friends suffer in bad relationships to know that. Her way was better. She was right. She knew she was right. Don't you dare judge me, her heart cried. I have my baby, and it was worth it. *It's worth it.*

Jimmy Joe suddenly realized that she was waiting for him to say something, watching him with a wry and weary smile that was going to haunt him from now on. Not the smile so much as the pride and disappointment he could see in her eyes. But he didn't have any words to give her. He never had been one to spend them freely, and the ones he did, especially at important moments like this one, he generally liked to think about first, to make sure they were the right ones and a true indicator of what he was feeling. Right now he didn't know what he was feeling, and he couldn't think. So he stayed silent.

He'd taken a deep breath, then didn't seem to know what to do with it. The air in the cab already seemed too dense, charged with tension and cluttered with emotions. He thought suddenly that he was going to suffocate if he didn't get out of there and get some fresh, uncrowded air.

"I, uh, think I'm gon' go use the rest room," he mumbled, and grabbing up his sleeveless, down-filled vest, yanked open the door and dived out into the night.

The door slammed. Mirabella winced involuntarily and closed her eyes.

She felt bewildered and abandoned, but at the same time vindicated, never more sure of the rightness of her decision than at this moment. Relationships were just too hard. Men and women never really understood one another. They were like alien species, struggling to cohabit on the same planet, each believing they'd figured out how to speak the other's language when in reality neither of them had a clue. And while it was true that some people did seem to find ways to make it work, those relationships always seemed wonderful and miraculous to her, like stories of scientists cohabiting with chimps, or gorilla mothers rescuing human children. As far as she could see, most marriages—even seemingly happy ones like her own parents'—were quiet daily struggles just to understand and be understood.

I don't understand, she thought. *What did I do to make him look at me like that?*

It couldn't be the fact that she'd had a baby—a moment

ago he'd told her, with glowing softness in his eyes and tenderness in his touch, what a wonderful thing she'd done. And if he didn't particularly approve of the way she'd done it, why on earth should it matter so much to him? What could possibly make him look at her with such pain and disappointment in his eyes? As if, in some indefinable way, she'd betrayed him.

It was one of the few times in Jimmy Joe's life he wished he'd had the courage to go against his mama and take up smoking. Then at least he would have an explainable excuse for what he was doing, stomping up and down in the bitter cold, trying to keep his extremities from freezing. Funny how nobody ever seemed to think it was crazy to risk a case of frostbite just to grab a few puffs of a cigarette.

But he couldn't think of any kind of reasonable explanation for not wanting to go back inside his nice warm truck just yet. He was just so...well, *hell.* He didn't know what he was, that was the problem. He didn't know if he was mad, or disappointed, or what. He for sure didn't know why it mattered so much.

Well, yeah, he did, too. He just didn't know what to do about it.

He thought about how he'd felt when he'd first run into Mirabella back there in New Mexico; how he'd judged her selfish and irresponsible for doing what she was doing, making a trip like that all alone; how angry it had made him to see her putting her child at risk. He hadn't known what to do with those feelings then, when she'd been no more than a stranger to him. And he sure didn't know what to do with them now that there was so much more at stake.

And that was the crux of his problem. Because somewhere along the way he'd gotten to know her, even thought he was beginning to understand her.

Somewhere along the way he'd fallen in love with her, even though she was as different from him—with her sophisticated big-city ways—as night was from day. And not only with her, but with her baby, too. And now he just couldn't figure out how in the name of heaven he could have done such a thing. How could he love a woman when her beliefs and her whole way of thinking and living were completely different from his?

You just do.

The answer didn't come to him like a revelation or anything, with beckoning stars and singing angels. It had been in his heart all along, and what he was doing out there freezing his butt off in the Panhandle wind was trying to get used to having it there. Trying to get used to the pain it brought him. Because yeah, he loved the woman, in spite of all the ways she was different from him. No doubt in his mind about that at all. And even if she loved him back—which was by no means a given—there wasn't any way in the world it was ever going to work out between them.

So, what was he going to do? What *could* he do?

Well, he knew the answer to that one, too. What he was going to do was go back there to his truck and keep the woman he loved and her new baby girl warm and safe until somebody came to take them away from him forever. And while he was doing that, he would be trying his best to understand how a beautiful, bright, funny woman could think it was okay to have a baby without ever knowing what it was like to make love to a man, and how she could do something so selfish as to deliberately deny her child the chance to grow up in a home with both a mom and a dad in it.

And, he thought, remembering the pain and disappointment in her eyes when he'd left her, if that didn't work, he would do his best to pretend it didn't matter.

An apology was sitting primed and ready on his tongue when he climbed back into his truck, but he never got a chance to give it to her. She'd gone to sleep at last, with the baby snuggled on her bosom, cozy as a bunny in a nest. And again he thought he'd never seen a more beautiful sight.

He went and knelt beside the bed, feasting his eyes on the two of them, mother and child. He picked up a strand of Mirabella's hair and let it run like silken strands through his fingers. "Ah…Marybell," he whispered. He'd never felt such a fullness inside. He touched the baby's head with a single finger, wondering at the incredible softness of it, like the velvet fuzz on a butterfly's wing. *Amy Jo*… He'd never felt such sadness. He wondered why it was he seemed destined to hold his sweet baby girls only once—just long enough to fall in love with them—and then lose them forever.

Mirabella awoke to the loveliest sound. Someone was singing "Greensleeves"—or rather the Christmas version, "What Child Is This?"—in a very nice tenor voice. Could it possibly be Jimmy Joe? No—the radio, of course. But what were such a nice voice and such a beautiful song doing on a country-music station? It had to be a country-music station, there wasn't anything else out here in the middle of the Texas Panhandle.

Then she realized that she *was* hearing something else. Something amazing. For the first time in her life she was awakening to the sound of a man snoring in her ear. She listened to it in sleepy bemusement, finding it oddly pleasant, thinking how surprising that was. She'd always thought she would hate sleeping with a man who snored. She turned her head slightly…and felt the tickle of hair on her lips. Her heart lurched and warmth burst inside her. Oh, God, she thought. *Oh, God…it's true. I do love him.*

And her logical mind quickly responded, *Nonsense! It's the circumstances. You only think you do because you were in trouble and he came to your rescue, dummy. Like a knight on a big blue charger. In fact, wasn't that what they used to call truckers? The Knights of the Road…?*

The baby nestled below her breast stirred, arching her tiny body and shooting out one fist like a miniature pugilist. So that's what she's been doing, her mother thought, gazing down in teary adoration. No wonder her legs had been going numb.

She moved her legs experimentally and was pleased to find that they seemed to be in working order, although they felt as though they each weighed several hundred pounds. Conversely, the middle part of her seemed light as a feather, if a little loose and jiggly, like half-set gelatin. And, when she laid an exploratory hand on it, it was not nearly as flat as she'd hoped. The lower part of her torso, the part diapered in thick layers of towels, it seemed wisest not to disturb.

Soon, she thought. It was getting light. Help would be coming soon.

She watched the light turn from blue-gray to mauve, and to a beautiful shade of rose...and then to gold. And suddenly streaks of blinding radiance shot across the sky and frozen landscape, splashed like molten fire over the dashboard and front seats and onto the bed where she lay with her baby in a sleeping man's arms.

She gasped at the sheer glory of it, and Jimmy Joe's snoring instantly stopped. He lifted his head from the pillow beside hers, his eyes going first to the baby then to her face. Reassured, he propped himself on one elbow and frowned at the light.

"Wha' time is it?"

"Morning," said Mirabella huskily. "That's all I know. Christmas morning."

"Everything okay?"

She nodded, unable to take her eyes from his face. For a long, seemingly endless time he gazed back at her without speaking. Then he leaned down slowly and kissed her.

She'd never been kissed like that—never. His mouth was so firm and warm and soft; strength and sensitivity wrapped in satin. It felt so wonderful. It made her feel like crying—like a beautiful sunset, a touching movie, a sad song, tiny children singing. It was nourishment—food and drink—and warmth and shelter and loving arms all rolled into one incredibly sweet, impossibly lovely touch. She wanted it to last forever.

But of course it couldn't. Her cheeks and eyelashes were wet when he lifted his head. She gazed at him through a silvery blur, trying to read the messages in his glowing brown eyes, finding tenderness and puzzlement and wonder and fear, knowing they must be reflections of hers. Her lips trembled as she waited for him to say something. Anything.

Her heart was hammering so loudly she could hear it. Or was it his?

But he'd suddenly gone still, listening as she was. And she knew it wasn't thundering pulses she heard. They both closed their eyes and their bodies relaxed together as the silent beauty of the morning, and that fragile and precious moment, were shattered forever by the clatter of a helicopter's rotors.

Chapter 12

"Attention, K mart shoppers, there's a blue-light special at mile marker…"
"We got a bear convention goin' on—bears in the bushes, bears ever'where!"

I-40—Tennessee

The helicopter threw a long blue shadow across a sheet of unblemished white as it hovered above the rest-stop parking lot. The snow was frozen so solid even the chopper's rotors couldn't stir it up, and it set down like a dragonfly alighting on a sheet of frosted crystal.

Jimmy Joe watched it from the wind-sheltered side of his truck, squinting into the just-risen sun and puffing out clouds of vapor. Being a Southern boy through and through, he was convinced air that cold could kill you, and he was trying his best to figure out how to extract enough oxygen from it to live on without actually letting it into his lungs.

When the chopper's rotors had slowed to a lazy thunk-thunk beat, the door opened. Two men—one of them the pilot, wear-

ing orange coveralls and a knit ski cap and carrying a paramedic's kit, and the other an older guy in a fur-lined parka, a
Stetson hat and earmuffs—jumped out and headed for the
truck with their heads down, walking fast, half jogging. Both
were wearing sunglasses. Jimmy Joe stepped forward to meet
them, wishing he'd thought to put his on. The cold and the
glare were making his eyes water.

The guy in the parka stuck out a mittened hand. He had a
large cold-reddened nose and a thick brown mustache that
seemed to spread across his face when he grinned. "Howdy.
Mr. Starr—it sure is a pleasure to talk to you face-to-face for
a change." He laughed at the "Beg your pardon?" look on
Jimmy Joe's face. "Dr. Austin—I was on the other end of that
phone relay last night. How's ever'body doin' this mornin'?"

"Good—doin' just fine," Jimmy Joe mumbled. He nodded
at the paramedic, who told him his name was Travis, shook
his hand, then gestured toward his truck. "Been waitin' for
ya."

He went to the passenger side and opened the door, stepped
up and called softly, "Marybell? You ready for company?"

She was sitting up, swaddled from the waist down in his
mother's old quilt, the baby cradled in her arms. He saw that
she'd brushed her hair and fastened the top and sides back
from her face with a clip of some kind. She looked about
sixteen years old, radiant and a little apprehensive, like a little
girl getting ready to take her first trip on an airplane.

"Okay," she said breathlessly. But her eyes clung to him
as if for reassurance, pleading with him—for what, he didn't
know.

He stepped down and gestured for the doc and the EMT to
go on in, wondering as he politely held the door for them why
it was resentment he felt more than relief. As if they weren't
rescuers, but intruders. He felt like there was a primitive being
inside him that wanted to be standing in front of that door
snapping and snarling. Like a wolf, guarding his mate and
their young in his den. *His mate. His woman.*

He heard the doctor sing out, "Well, hello there, little lady, how are you doin' this mornin'? Let's have a look at this pretty girl, here. You two all ready to go for a ride?'' Then he slammed the door shut and turned away with his chest aching and his heart pounding.

He was pacing up and down alongside his truck, grinding his teeth and swinging his arms, too cold to think about anything except how to keep from freezing to death, when the door opened up again and Travis, the EMT, hopped out.

''You wanna give me a hand with the stretcher?'' he called out as he loped off toward the chopper.

Jimmy Joe grunted, ''Sure thing,'' and took off after him.

''That's one tough little ol' gal,'' Travis said as they were wrestling the basket stretcher out of the helicopter. ''Sure is pretty, too.''

Jimmy Joe grunted. ''Yeah, she is.''

''This your first baby?''

Jimmy Joe didn't know quite how to answer that. He stammered around and finally decided it wasn't worth explaining, so he mumbled, ''Uh…no, I got a little boy—''

''No, I mean first one you ever delivered.''

Then he felt a little sheepish and had to grin. ''Oh. Yeah, it sure is.''

''Yeah, well…it's always a thrill. Always a miracle.'' Travis bent down and picked up one end of the stretcher and Jimmy Joe got a grip on the other and they headed back to the truck at a jog-trot. Travis threw a look over his shoulder. ''Must've been quite a night for you.''

''Yeah,'' Jimmy Joe panted, ''it sure was.'' *Quite a night.* One he wondered if he was ever going to be able to get over. One he sure as heck knew he would never forget.

The cab of Jimmy Joe's truck had suddenly gotten terribly crowded—full of noise and way too many strangers. Mirabella felt lost in all the confusion. She longed for the soft sounds of Christmas songs on the radio, Jimmy Joe's snoring, the tiny squeaks Amy made when she nursed. She wished they could go back to the way it had been; just the three of them together, cocooned in the truck, isolated from the world and swaddled in intimacy and warmth, magic and—daringly her heart whispered it—*love*.

Now all of that had been lost, the peace shattered, the cocoon stripped away. She felt jangled and panicky, lonely and unprepared. The world seemed to be spinning too fast, out of her control. She was bundled and lifted and settled and strapped, more like a parcel than a person. People talked around her and over and about her, never *to* her. She found herself retreating into dazed isolation, cloaked and protected by the paranoia of her newly awakened maternal instincts, clinging to her baby with primal ferocity, her eyes daring anyone to take her from her. Perhaps understanding, no one tried.

She looked for Jimmy Joe, desperately needing the reassurance of his sweet smile and kind eyes, his soft Georgia drawl saying, "There now…everything's gonna be fine." He was there, or at least his body was, helping to wrap her in layers of blankets and tuck her into the stretcher, bustling around collecting her belongings, making sure she had everything— her purse, her clothes, her shoes and overnight bag. She followed him with her eyes, silently begging him to look at her, to touch her, to reach out to her in some way that would let her know that the bond that had grown between them through that long, miraculous night was still there.

But he wouldn't look at her. She couldn't find him—the Jimmy Joe who'd held and stroked her, guided and sustained her, laughed and cried with her as he'd placed her newborn daughter in her arms. Where was he? Oh, God. *Please, Jimmy Joe, I need you.*

They were taking her to the waiting helicopter, Jimmy Joe at her head where she couldn't see him, the man in the orange coveralls at her feet, the big man in the cowboy hat alongside. It was cold, so cold, but Mirabella hardly felt it. Amy was safe and warm, snug in her arms in a thick nest of blankets, and Jimmy Joe was there with her. She knew as long as he was there, she and her baby would be safe.

She felt the stretcher tilt as it was lifted into the helicopter. The doctor climbed in beside her, the man in the coveralls moved up to the pilot's seat, and the air filled with wind and noise. Jimmy Joe was backing out of the open doorway.

Panic seized her. Struggling frantically, she managed to free a hand from the straps and blankets and fastenings and grab his shirtsleeve. *"Jimmy Joe—"*

"Yeah, I'm right here." He wrapped her hand in both of his and she held on to him with all the strength in her body, as if she were dangling over a void and he was the rope. "Everything's gonna be fine. You'll be in Amarillo in a little bit."

"Please—" she gasped. "You're coming with me, aren't you?"

His inverted face hovered above hers, lined with strain and pinched and reddened with cold. But for the eyes, with their familiar glow of kindness, she would hardly have recognized it. His fogged breath mingled with hers as he smiled. "Sorry…wish I could. Gotta stay with my truck. I'm gonna be along in a little while. Listen, you're gonna be just fine. You just take good care a'that baby, now, y'hear?"

"Jimmy Joe—" *Don't leave me!*

"Safe trip." He leaned down and kissed her, quick and hard. She felt his hand slip from her grasp.

The helicopter door clanged shut. A mittened hand patted her shoulder and a kindly Texas voice said, "You just hold tight, now, honey. We'll be there soon."

Mirabella closed her eyes as her stomach gave a dreadful lurch. *Don't…leave…me….*

Jimmy Joe stood and watched the helicopter lift off. Watched it until it was just a speck in the sky. He felt as if a great big piece of himself had just been ripped off him and was flying away from him. And if he lived to be a hundred, he wasn't ever going to be able to forget the look in Mirabella's eyes when he'd left her alone in that chopper.

A truck crawling by on the interstate saw him standing there and blasted an airhorn greeting. Jimmy Joe lifted his hand and waved, then started walking back toward his big blue Kenworth, still idling faithfully away as it had through that long, cold night. She looked a mite road-weary, he thought, covered with grime and snow sludge, mud flaps crusted with frozen mud. He promised himself the first truck wash he came to after he got out of this mess, he was going to pull in and give her a nice bath. Himself, too, while he was at it.

And they were both going to be needing some fuel pretty soon; the Kenworth's tanks might have a few more miles left in them, but he was running on empty. The snacks he'd gotten from the vending machines were all gone, except for a half-eaten package of peanut-butter crackers. He ate those and washed them down with warm 7-Up, then tidied the sleeper as best he could and disposed of the trash. After a safety check of his rig and a last visit to the rest stop's freezing-cold toilet facilities, he was finally ready to roll.

First, though, he turned up the volume on his CB radio and took down the mike, then waited until he got a lull in the conversation. "Uh...this is the Big Blue Starr," he drawled. "I'm over here at the rest stop at the twenty-eight-mile stick.... Gon' be joinin' you here in a minute. I'd 'preciate it if you'd give me some room.... Come on."

As it seemed to be more and more often these days, it was a female voice that came back to him. "You got it, Big Blue. Sure am happy to hear from ya again. How's the lady and her baby doin'? Ever'body okay?"

"Doin' just fine. Chopper picked 'em up this mornin'. They're headin' for Amarillo as we speak."

"We sure are glad to hear that. We been prayin' for ya. My husband Tom, here, and me, we're drivin' team. Got two little babies ourselves, over there in Enid, Oklahoma. We're still hopin' to get home in time to hug 'em and tell 'em Merry Christmas, but...I don' know. If this don't clear up pretty soon..."

"How's it lookin' over that way?"

"Uh...pickin' up a little, they tell me. Looks like they finally got the overpasses sanded, anyways. Sun's gettin' up there now, though. Gon' start gettin' slick, here, pretty soon."

"Thanks," said Jimmy Joe. "I'll watch it."

"You do that. Pass on our good wishes for us, if you see the lady and that little baby again, would ya? 'Preciate it."

"I'll do that. Y'all have a safe trip, now."

"Back at ya. Ten-four."

Jimmy Joe hung up the mike and put his rig in gear, sending up a little prayer as the first of eighteen wheels bit into unbroken snow. He churned down the on-ramp and a hole opened up for him. He eased the blue Kenworth into it and once more became part of the long caravan of trucks ploughing steadily eastward.

It felt real good to be on the road again, and heading for home at last. But for some reason, without Mirabella and the baby in it the cab seemed awfully quiet to him. And empty.

It was past midday by the time Jimmy Joe rolled into Amarillo. He'd made one stop, at a gas station on old Route 66 just west of Vega, where he'd bought a few gallons of diesel and shaken the hand of the man whose voice, coming through on the radio emergency channel, had guided him through the long night just past.

Turned out the fellow, whose name was Riggs, had a pretty good garage and a tow truck besides, so he'd given him some money and Mirabella's car keys and asked him to go pick up the silver Lexus as soon as the roads cleared up enough. Riggs had wanted him to stay and have a bite of breakfast, but hungry as he was, he was even more anxious to be on his way. So he'd settled for a cup of coffee and a quart of chocolate milk, and then he was on the road again.

On the outskirts of Amarillo, the going got a little easier. The bright sunshine hadn't warmed things up much—just enough to melt a thin coat of water on top of the ice that made it about as slick as grease. But at least the overpasses and the on- and off-ramps had been sanded. And the streets leading to the hospital had been well plowed. It looked like about half of the parking lot had been scraped clear, too, and the snow pushed up in a pile over to one side.

He parked his rig next to the pile and set the brakes, and

was indulging in a good stretch when he noticed that the parking lot seemed to be an awfully busy place, considering it was Christmas Day. He noticed several TV-news trucks and vans with satellite antennas sticking out all over them.

"Wonder what's goin' on?" he muttered to himself as he climbed out of the cab. He hoped it wasn't some sort of disaster or other. Happening on Christmas—that sure would be a shame.

The hospital's front entrance and main waiting area were all a-tangle with people, quite a few of them carrying video cameras, the rest standing around drinking coffee out of plastic cups and looking out-of-sorts. Several of them kind of stared at Jimmy Joe when he walked in, which was a reminder to him that it had been a couple of days since he'd showered and shaved. He was glad he'd put on a clean shirt and his good boots and changed his trucker's vest for his fleece-lined Levi's jacket, but he knew from the glimpse he'd caught of himself in the glass doors coming in, with his two-day beard and bloodshot eyes, that he was no prize. On the other hand, it was Mirabella he'd come to see, not a bunch of strangers, and he had an idea she would forgive him if he looked a little rough around the edges.

He eased his way through the crowd with a few "Beg your pardons" and "'Scuse me, ma'ams" and made it up to the reception desk, where a sweet-faced, gray-haired lady wearing a pink pinafore was trying her best to ignore all the hustle and bustle.

She flicked him a glance and said, "May I help you?" in a tone of voice that warned him she would rather not.

He cleared his throat and leaned as close to her as he could across the countertop so he wouldn't have to shout his business to the whole world over the noise. "Uh…yes, ma'am, I'm lookin' for the maternity department?"

The lady in pink folded her hands together as if she was about to say her prayers and gave him a look that wasn't much warmer than the temperature outside. "Of course you are. And the patient's name?"

"Uh…yes, ma'am. That'd be Mirabella…" Damnation, what was it? "Uh, Waskowitz. She and her baby were brought in this morning."

"Yes, sir, and are you a member of the family?"

Whew, thought Jimmy Joe, if that voice had been any colder it would have given him frostbite. A moment later, when he thought about it, he knew what he should have done was lie— just say, "Yes, ma'am, I'm her brother," or something like that, and be done with it. But the habit of honesty was so ingrained in him, by the time the inspiration came to him, he'd already blurted out the truth.

"No, ma'am, I'm not. I guess you could say I'm a friend." He saw right away that wasn't going to get him anywhere, so he shuffled around and cleared his throat some more, and then jumped back in with, "But I know she'll want to see me. My name's Jimmy Joe Starr, and, uh,… Well, see, I was with her when she had her baby. In fact, she, uh, had it in my truck. And…well, I promised her I'd come by and see her, soon as I could. Just to say hi, you know, make sure she's okay…"

Somewhere along in there, it came to him that the people around him had gotten real quiet. In fact, he figured he could have heard a pin drop. He kept lowering his voice and leaning closer to the lady in pink, trying his best to keep his business private, but when he did that, it seemed to him that everyone in the place sort of leaned with him.

Then all of a sudden it was like a dam had burst. The whole roomful of people surged in around him, everybody trying to push everybody else out of the way, people shoving microphones and video cameras in his face and shouting questions at him, all talking at once.

"Mr. Starr—Mr. Starr!"

"Over here—"

"How did it feel—"

"Are you the trucker—"

"What do you think about being called a Good Samaritan?"

"When did you know you were going to—"

"Had you ever delivered a baby before, Mr. Starr?"

"Mr. Starr—Mr. Starr!"

"How does it feel to be a hero, Mr. Starr?"

Oh, man. Once when he was a kid, Jimmy Joe remembered, he and his oldest brother Troy had hooked a hornets' nest while they were fishing. That was pretty much the way he felt right now, like he wanted to cover his head and make for deep water.

But they had him cornered, and it looked like there wasn't much hope he was going to be able to make a run for it. Out of the corner of his eye he spotted the lady in pink making her escape; all he could hope was that maybe she'd gone for reinforcements.

In the meantime, he had to try and make the best of it. And one thing he wasn't going to try to do was outshout everybody. Neither was he going to shuffle his feet and look like some dumb Cracker—his mama had taught him better than that. In fact, it was his mama's methods he called on, particularly the one she used to always use to get the attention of a classroom—or a kitchen—full of kids all squabbling and hollering at once. He raised one hand, bowed his head, closed his eyes, and then…just waited. He waited until everybody got quiet again, which didn't take as long as a person might think. When he wasn't hearing anything except some rustling around and nervous coughing, he opened his eyes. And it seemed like everybody drew in a big breath and held it.

He pointed to a woman standing right in front of him, with sleek dark hair pulled back in a French twist and a familiar look about her, although he couldn't place her. He took a breath, hesitated a moment, then let it out in a rush and said, "Who *are* you people?"

Then everybody laughed, and it seemed like he'd made a whole roomful of new friends.

The woman he'd pointed to waved her microphone but this time remembered her manners and didn't poke it in his face. She said, "I guess you've been a little out of touch, Mr. Starr. This is a great story—Good Samaritan trucker delivering a baby on a snowbound interstate, on Christmas Day. It's a wonderful story. The whole country's been following it, ever since word started coming in last night. It seems you've become quite a hero. What do you think of that?''

Jimmy Joe looked at all those microphones and video cameras pointed at him—at a respectful distance, now—and for a few moments he didn't say anything. He was thinking about Mirabella. Remembering…so many things. Like the images in a kaleidoscope, fragmented and rearranged into images of unimaginable beauty.

Terrified eyes, shivering voice… "I think I'm having my baby.…"

"I'm sorry…I'm sorry.…"

"Can't…make a mess!"

Furiously… "Can't you understand English?"

"I ca-an't!"

The imprint of her fingers on his arm…the feel of her mouth.

"Too many mountains…more mountains…"

"If you say that one more time, I'll kill you!"

"Amy…her name is Amy."

"I've never made love before.…"

"Please…come with me!"

"Don't leave me.…"

He had to cough, clear his throat and take a couple of deep breaths before he could speak, and when he did his voice was still so raspy it didn't even sound like him.

"Well, first off, I'm no Good Samaritan, and, uh…I'm sure not a hero. What I did wasn't any more'n any other person I know of woulda done, under the same circumstances. The only hero here is that lady lying up there in that hospital bed. She's—'' And then he had to stop and cough some more. "Well, she's just about the bravest person I ever saw, is all. And, uh…well, that's all I've got to say. Now, if y'all will excuse me…"

He turned blindly, thinking he knew how a trapped wolf felt just before he started gnawing his leg off, and there was a big burly fellow in a rent-a-cop uniform reaching out to him and saying in that quiet, no-argument cop way, "Sir, you want to come with me, please? Right this way."

Beyond the security guard Jimmy Joe could see the lady in the pink pinafore hovering, holding open a door marked, Hospital Personnel Only. From the pink in her cheeks and the smile on her lips, it looked like she might have warmed toward him quite a bit since she'd spoken to him last.

The security guard touched Jimmy Joe's elbow and raised his voice and said, "Okay, folks, that's all. You want to step aside and let us through, please?" He ushered Jimmy Joe through the door and the pink-pinafore lady closed it smartly after them. Jimmy Joe could just imagine her glaring in frosty triumph at the thwarted reporters left on the other side.

Left alone with the security guard, he didn't know exactly what to expect—whether he was about to be hustled out the nearest exit, or what. It sure wasn't to have the guy clap him on the shoulder and say, "Son, I'd sure like to shake your hand. That was a wonderful thing you did. God bless ya."

Feeling too dazed and confused to argue, Jimmy Joe muttered some sort of thank-you and shook the guy's hand, which was about the size and texture of an old fielder's mitt. For some reason that made him think of his dad, and that brought a lump into his throat.

Maybe it's just being in a hospital again, he thought as the guard whisked him past offices and through storerooms and up an echoing concrete stairway, through clanging steel doors and then down polished corridors that smelled the way hospitals always do. Like most normal healthy people who don't actually work in one, Jimmy Joe wasn't fond of hospitals. Which wasn't surprising, considering that with one exception, his associations with them, starting with having his tonsils taken out when he was seven, were all pretty bad. The arm he'd broken playing football hadn't been serious enough to get him past the emergency room, but then there had been his dad's first heart attack, and then the last one. He remembered the long night in the waiting room, he and his brothers and sisters sprawled and draped over every available piece of furniture, and at dawn, the doctors coming with headshakes and expressionless faces. And the worst shock of all had been watching his mama's face turn old before his eyes.

Not very long after that, there had been Amy—the first Amy. And then, for a while, regular visits to a different kind of hospital, where patients shuffled aimlessly through the corridors or sat and looked out the windows with blank faces and empty eyes. Then there had been the exception—J.J.'s birth. But even that hadn't exactly been a happy time in his life. That had been almost eight years ago, and he'd done his best to avoid hospitals ever since.

"She's been askin' for ya," the security guard told him as they turned down a corridor painted in cheery shades of rose pink and aqua green. Jimmy Joe could hear trays clanking and people laughing. And mixed in with the regular old hospital smell was a new one, one he remembered well—diapers. "We've been tryin' to keep that horde downstairs away from her until she's had a chance to rest up a bit. Here ya go—you can go on in."

And suddenly there he was, standing outside a closed door that he knew Mirabella was on the other side of, and he didn't have a single idea in the world what he was going to say to her once he opened it. He felt like it had been days, maybe even years, since he'd seen her, instead of just a few hours. In his truck, it had seemed as if they were the only two people in the whole world, and that somehow the two of them and Amy Jo and everything they'd been through together had gotten woven into one whole cloth, like a beautiful tapestry, or one of those Navajo rugs he'd brought back from his trips. For some reason he'd thought they would be that way forever.

But from the instant that helicopter had set down in the rest-stop parking lot, he'd known it hadn't been real, and that the world didn't belong to just the three of them, after all. This was somebody else's world, and he, for one, didn't feel real comfortable in it. In this world, Mirabella and her baby girl were a media event, and everybody was trying to make him out to be some kind of hero. Well, he sure didn't feel like a hero. What he felt like was a man who'd just lost something precious to him—something so rare and beautiful he was afraid he wasn't ever going to come across it in his life again.

The security guard waved to him and moseyed off down the corridor, nodding to a couple of nurses along the way. A nurse bustling by did a sort of double take when she saw Jimmy Joe, and smiled, her face lighting up like a Christmas tree.

"It's okay," she chirped. "You can go on in. She's been waiting for you."

He nodded his head, took a big breath, and tapped on the door. A voice—like Mirabella's, and yet not quite hers—said breathlessly, "Yes—come in!"

The wide hospital-room door swung open and a woman he didn't know stood there beaming at him. She had shiny brown hair cut short but in a way that nicely suited her features, and greenish-blue eyes that crinkled at the corners. And although the two didn't have one single feature in common that he could see, he knew this woman was Mirabella's mother. In some strange way he couldn't put a finger on, she just reminded him of her.

In a hushed and excited voice, like someone trying not to wake a sleeper, she said, "Hello—you must be Jimmy Joe. The front desk phoned to let us know you were on your way. Oh, I'm just *so* happy to meet you. Bella," she called softly over her shoulder toward a partly drawn curtain, "you have a visitor." And then back to Jimmy Joe again, taking his hand and towing him inside. "Please, come in. I'm Ginger, by the way—Bella's mom."

"Ma'am," Jimmy Joe mumbled politely. As the door whisked shut behind him it occurred to him that he'd never felt so awkward in his life, or more conscious of the quarter-inch of stubble he was wearing on his face. Why hadn't he thought to bring something—flowers, maybe, or a baby gift?

And then Ginger was pulling back the curtain, and there she was. And he suddenly remembered how he'd thought her the most beautiful woman he'd ever seen in his life before. And forgot he'd ever held her naked body in his arms, massaged her feet or whispered love words into her sweat-damp hair. It was all he could do to unstick his tongue from the roof of his mouth long enough to mutter, ''Hey, there, Marybell, how're you doin'?''

Chapter 13

"Man, that is a sight for sore eyes."
I-40—Texas

"Other than the fact that my insides feel like jelly, I'm fine," snapped Mirabella, and she could just see her mother's eyebrows arching at the way she sounded, so brusque and cranky. So typically Mirabella.

She didn't mean it, of course; she almost never did. No one knew that sometimes it was simply the only way she could get a word out without her voice shaking, or how important it was to her pride and self-esteem that she always appear calm and completely in control.

Even more so now, considering the state of near panic she'd been in the last time she'd seen Jimmy Joe. And considering that not ten minutes ago she'd been in a similar state just because she couldn't shower and wash her hair.

"What am I going to do? I look like hell!" she'd hissed in a burst of tearful hysteria that was completely foreign—and consequently utterly bewildering to her. "Mom—quick—let me have your brush! Do you have any lipstick? Oh, no...I've lost my hair thingy. I look like a wet cat. Oh, God, I can't let him see me like this!''

''Bella,'' her mother had said, laughing in amazement, ''since when do you *care?* Besides,'' she'd added dryly, ''I imagine the man has just seen you looking a lot worse.''

''That was *different,*'' Mirabella had snapped, feeling free to behave like an unreasonable and obstinate child as long as there was no one but her mother to witness it.

It was only now, looking up at Jimmy Joe's face, that she knew how right she'd been. It *was* different. Unavoidably and inevitably, everything had changed.

He hadn't, of course; he still looked like a young Robert Redford—an unshaven one, to be sure—lean and blond, dimpled and adorable. His eyes were just as kind and his smile every bit as sweet as she remembered. It wasn't he who had changed, she realized; or her, either, for that matter. What was so different was the way things were between them.

They were like...strangers. It was hard even to remember now, the closeness, the incredible bond they'd shared. She hadn't imagined it—she knew she'd been pretty much out of it for a lot of the time, but she wasn't wrong about that. It had been real. Never in her life before had she known, or even imagined she could know, such a sense of *oneness* with another human being. It was as if she'd found a part of herself she hadn't even realized was missing. But now the piece was lost once more, and how would she ever again be able to delude herself into believing she was whole?

They were like strangers, but worse than that—strangers with memories in common of time spent together in abnormal intimacy, both physical and emotional; of things said that could not be unsaid; of secrets revealed that would never be forgotten. It was only natural that there should be awkwardness between them, Mirabella told herself sadly. She should have expected it.

What she couldn't have expected was that it would hurt so much. She ached inside in places that didn't have anything to do with having just given birth to a child. She ached as though her heart had been torn in two.

"What's all this?" he asked with a frown, waving a hand at the plastic bag dangling above the head of her bed, at the tube leading from it to a needle stuck into the back of her hand and held in place with a crisscross of white tape.

She glanced down at it and dismissed it with a shrug. "Nothing—some fluids and antibiotics. I guess I was a little bit dehydrated. The antibiotics are just as a precaution."

"Where's the baby? She doin' okay?"

Mirabella smiled; it had become a reflex, automatically triggered by any mention of her daughter. "Amy's fine. They've got her in the nursery, doing all the tests they usually do on newborns. But yeah…she's fine. Weighs five pounds six ounces. In another month, she'd a'been a chunky little seven-pounder."

"Like her mother," Ginger added, smiling smugly. "All my babies were seven pounds plus."

"Well," said Jimmy Joe. "I sure am glad to hear that." He shifted and cleared his throat, looking even more uncomfortable, if that was possible, rubbing at the back of his neck in that embarrassed way he had. "Uh…hey, listen, I'm sorry I didn't bring anything. I meant to get you some flowers, but…"

"Oh, that's okay," Mirabella murmured, feeling her face grow warm. God, how awkward this was. "You didn't have to do that."

Then for a moment there was silence, as both of them struggled to find something else to say. She felt as if she was suffocating.

"They say how long they're gonna keep you here?"

She lifted the hand with the needle in it. "I don't know. I guess until this is done. I think they might want to keep Amy overnight, just to be on the safe side. I don't know what I'm going to do, though. I mean—"

Her mother interrupted with, "Now, honey, I told you not to worry about that."

"Mom flew in this morning," Mirabella explained. "So I guess Amy and I'll just go back with her, as soon as the doctors say it's all right. But I don't know what I'm going to do about my car...all the Christmas presents.... Everything's still out there in that damn snowbank." She gave a strangled gurgle of laughter; she was damned if she was going to shed another tear—not while *he* was here.

Jimmy Joe was rubbing his neck again, looking ashamed of himself the way he always did, she was beginning to realize, when he'd done something to be particularly proud of. "Don't need to be worrying about that. Got it all taken care of." He lapsed into hopeful silence. When he saw he was going to have to do a little more explaining, he coughed and looked pained.

"You maybe don't remember it, but the fella helped us out on the radio last night? Guy's name is Riggs. Anyway, he said he had a service station. I figured I'd stop in, you know, just to say thank-you to him for everything he did. Turns out he's got a nice little garage out there on old 66 just west of Vega— has a wrecker, too. Anyway, I gave him your keys and told him to go pick up your car, soon's the road clears up some more. He'll keep it for you until you can get back here for it, no problem." He patted his pockets, reached into one and pulled out a business card, which he handed to her with another of those embarrassed little coughs of his. "So—you can just give him a call when you feel like it. It's all taken care of."

Mirabella usually hated it when people—men especially— tried to take charge of her life. But instead of feeling resentful, she felt a curious melting sensation inside. Fighting against an urge to weep and sniffle, "Oh, Jimmy Joe..." like a swooning belle, instead she scowled fiercely and demanded, "What about all my stuff? All my Christmas presents are in the trunk of my car."

"Oh, for heaven's sake, Bella!" her mother exclaimed, throwing up her hands. "You and that new granddaughter are all the Christmas presents your dad and I need! What is the matter with you?''

It was a question people asked her a lot, for some reason. But now it brought her even more dangerously close to tears. What *was* the matter with her? She should be just about the happiest woman in the world. She'd just had a baby; a beautiful, healthy baby, the baby she'd always wanted—she'd already convinced herself she'd really wanted a girl all along. So why was she still wishing for something she *didn't* have? Especially when it was something she'd come to terms with long ago.

Thoroughly ashamed of herself now, she made a gallant effort to brighten up, although faking cheeriness wasn't something she excelled at. ''Thanks... 'Preciate it,'' she said grudgingly, and felt her heart bump when Jimmy Joe grinned at her use of the favorite truckers' acknowledgment, as if it was a private joke they'd shared.

She took a deep breath and pushed herself up on the pillows. ''You going to see Amy before you leave?''

His smile grew tender. ''Sure am. Yeah...thought I'd stop by on the way out.''

Her world darkened, as if a cloud had drifted across the sun. ''So...I guess you're anxious to be on your way.''

''Yeah... J.J.'s waitin' for me. Still got a load to deliver, too. You know how it is....''

''Yeah...'' Her smile flickered, then went out like a snuffed candle when she met his eyes. She grabbed a desperate gulp of air and said, ''You talked to J.J.?''

Jimmy Joe suddenly frowned. ''Haven't had a chance. I'm gonna call him after I get out of here, I guess. That's *if* I get out— Did you know there's a whole crowd of reporters downstairs? They tell you about that? TV, newspapers, I don't know what all.''

He sounded so incredulous, she had to laugh. ''That's what I heard. So...I guess you're a hero, huh? Did you talk to them?''

''Hero...'' he muttered under his breath, then gave a disgusted-sounding snort. "Didn't have much choice. They pretty much had me surrounded. Those media people sure are somethin' else. Damn—oh, 'scuse me, ma'am—darned if I didn't feel 'bout like General Custer at Little Big Horn. Course…" He smiled and reached out as if he meant to touch her, and her heart skipped a beat. But he let the hand drop to his side and then made sure it stayed there by hooking the thumb in his jeans pocket. "They only talked to me because they couldn't get at you. You know that, don't you?"

"Me?" She tried to laugh at the absurdity of it, at the same time shrinking back against the pillows. Because having lived most of her life in a media-crazy town like Los Angeles, she knew exactly how an ordinary, unremarkable story could catch fire in the public's imagination, especially when fueled by a hungry media trying to fill a slow news day. *This* story— Christmas Day, lady stranded on snowy interstate, giving birth in a truck, handsome trucker-driver hero—oh, God, it would be like manna sent from heaven!

Oh, God. Everything in her cringed at the thought. How stupid she felt. How humiliating it was. To have everyone know…the people she worked with… And worse than the humiliation was the thought that the specialness of her time with Jimmy Joe, the beautiful intimacy they'd shared, might be taken away from her to become just more fodder for the newsmagazine shows.

"Oh, God," she whispered "Oh, no…"

"Marybell, I'm afraid you are about the biggest thing to come along since Madonna had her baby," said Jimmy Joe, smiling crookedly down at her. There was a look in her eyes she couldn't quite fathom, a certain sadness, perhaps. Could he possibly regret the loss of what they'd had together as much as she did? Her throat filled. "The hospital's doin' a pretty good job of keepin' 'em away, so far," he went on, "but soon as you leave here, you know they're gonna be waitin' to jump you. Probably be best if you just faced the music. Hold a press conference, or something, get it over with right here."

"I'd hate that," Mirabella snapped. She felt like a cornered animal. I don't want to deal with this, she thought furiously. Not now. Now when I feel so vulnerable, so not myself. So alone. "I can't do it."

She saw her mother and Jimmy Joe exchange looks. Then he shrugged and touched her cheek with the backs of his fingers, lightly, as if brushing away tears. "Well, now…" he said in a soft, soothing tone, "you sure don't have to, not if you don't want to. Hey—I'll just go talk to 'em for you, how's that? Sure…listen, I'm gonna take care of it, don't you worry about a thing."

Okay, great, she thought resentfully. Now what does he think I am—a helpless wimp? Just because he saved my life, just because I needed him last night, does he now think I can't get along without him?

"You don't have to do that," she muttered, shifting around against the pillows. *I don't need you, Jimmy Joe Starr. You, or anybody else. Amy and I will be just fine!* She glowered first at Jimmy Joe, then at her mother. "Okay—okay. Tell the hospital I'll talk to them. Just once, though. *After* I've had a chance to shower and wash my hair!"

"Marybell, are you sure you want to do this?" Jimmy Joe asked, bending over her, his eyes dark and concerned.

"Of course I am," she snapped. "I'm not a child."

"Well, okay then." He ducked his head and planted a kiss on her forehead, then straightened and looked across at her mother. She heard her mother give a tiny gasp, quickly stifled, then a laugh that sounded both surprised and pleased.

"What?" she demanded, her paranoia prickling.

"I think I'd better be rollin'," said Jimmy Joe in a husky voice as he leaned down to kiss her again. Not on the forehead this time, but on the lips, and with such tenderness she instantly forgot all her suspicions, forgot she'd just vowed she didn't need him. Maybe she didn't need him, but she wanted him. Oh, yes, she wanted him. Wanted him kissing her like this again—often—for all the rest of her life.

Then he straightened and she felt his fingers, briefly, in her hair. "I'll stop by the nursery, see if they'll let me say goodbye to Amy Jo. You take care a' yourself, now, you hear? Ma'am—sure was nice meetin' you.''

And just like that, he was gone.

Mirabella stared after him, feeling stunned…like a hollow, aching shell. I can't believe it, she thought. *He's gone. I'm never going to see him again.*

"Well," her mother said when the door had closed silently behind him, letting her breath out in a rush of laughter. "I certainly can see why you feel about him the way you do."

"Oh? And what is that supposed to mean?" Mirabella's voice was light and breathy, cheery and fragile as a soap bubble.

"Oh, honey, anyone can see you're crazy about him."

"That's ridiculous," said Mirabella with a snort. "Just *look* at him, Mom."

Her mother's eyebrows rose. "I did. He's an absolute joy to look at. I also saw the way he looked at you, my dear. Those eyes…"

Mirabella rolled hers in exasperation and leaned back against the pillows. "Oh, brother. Don't read anything into it, okay? He just has kind eyes, that's all. And cute little dimples and a sweet, sexy smile. So what? He's not even thirty. That's eight years younger than I am, Mom. *Eight years.* So, forget it." She sniffed and threw an arm across her eyes. "Just forget it, okay?"

There was silence for a moment, and then Ginger said with a soft laugh, "Well, all I can say is, for somebody so young, he's awfully wise. He certainly managed to figure *you* out in a hurry."

Mirabella uncovered one eye. "What are you talking about?"

Her mother was wearing that arch, Moms-know-everything look that always annoyed her so. "I'm talking about that nifty little piece of reverse psychology he just pulled on you. Boy, how did he get your number so fast? That's what I want to know."

"Reverse—that was no such thing!" said Mirabella hotly. "I simply—"

"Bella, he *winked* at me."

"He what?"

"He winked at me—right after you'd 'knuckled under' to his demand for a press conference."

"He didn't."

"Yes, dear, he did. He saw you crumbling like a wet cookie, and somehow he already knows you well enough to realize that the best way to get you to do something you don't want to do is to tell you you can't do it, or offer to do it for you."

"Yeah, well, if he knows me so well," Mirabella sobbed angrily, "how come he didn't stay, huh? Tell me that!"

"Oh, for heaven's sake, the man had things to do! Besides, with all those prickles of yours, how was he supposed to know you wanted him to? Oh, my dear," her mother said huskily, "you have so much pride. But I'll tell you this—if you let that beautiful young man get away, you are absolutely crazy. Do you hear me? *Crazy*."

And she said no more. Because like the terrific mother she was and always had been, she knew when it was time to ignore all the prickles, and simply…hug.

A nurse bustled in, strewing cheer before her like flower petals. "Oh—having a little cry, are we? We certainly know how that is! Well, I have someone here who's going to make you feel a lot better!" She held back the door and wheeled in a tiny plastic bassinet with a practiced flourish. "Here you go—this pretty little girl wants her mama, don't you, sweetie pie? Yes, you do…."

Mirabella sat up straight, sniffling, and wiped her eyes on her hospital gown as she searched avidly through her tears. "Oh," she cried, laughing when she saw the tiny bundle tucked in a bright red Christmas stocking, a tiny red stockinette cap on her fuzzy pink head. "She looks just like an elf!"

"That's just what she is," cooed the nurse. "A li'l ol' Christmas elf. And she's all nice an' clean an' sweet, an' she's even had a visit from her handsome daddy, and now she's *hungry,* aren't you, darlin'? Here you go, mama.''

And she scooped up the baby, red stocking and all. Mirabella held out her arms, and as the nurse placed her daughter into them, she wondered again in utter awe how something so tiny could rouse such enormous feelings in her.

''Oh…'' she whispered, and a moment later she wasn't even astonished to hear herself doing something she'd vowed she would never, ever do. But she was. She—intelligent, sensible, no-nonsense Mirabella—was talking baby talk. Cooing like a besotted dove. ''Hi, there… How's my widdle girl? How's my sweetie—little-lov'ums, huh?''

Oh, it was awful. It was glorious. It was…Amy. Her baby. Her miracle.

The nurse hovered, ready to help with the breast-feeding, until she saw that Mirabella didn't seem to need any help. She laughed and said, ''Well, I see somebody's taught you right. I'll just leave you to it, then. Y'all just give me a buzz, now, if you need anything.'' She parked the bassinet beside the bed and went away.

''Who was it?'' Ginger asked softly. ''Jimmy Joe?''

Mirabella nodded, her head bowed as she gazed intently at her hungrily nursing daughter. She rocked herself slowly back and forth, awash in prickles and weighed down by an ache deep, deep inside her.

''Oh, look—Bella, look! She has *red hair!*'' her mother cried, just as a tear rolled off the end of Mirabella's nose and dropped onto the baby's downy head.

It took Jimmy Joe another four hours just to get out of Texas, and he was never so glad to see anything in his life as he was that Welcome to Oklahoma sign, or the smooth, dry blacktop beyond it. Something in him sure did want to put the old hammer down and not ease up until he hit Little Rock, but he knew that was just plain stupid, considering he hadn't had much sleep in more than two days and was already running on raw nerves. So the first Motel 6 sign he saw, he pulled off. His sleeper was going to need some clean bedding before he would be able to use it again, but it was a hot shower he wanted more than anything. He didn't stop to eat—he'd filled his belly before he'd left Amarillo, anyway—just got his rig buttoned down and himself checked in, then headed for his room, and a shower so long and hot it made his pulse pound. He didn't even remember falling into bed.

He woke up to early-morning light pouring in through the window he'd forgotten to draw the curtain across twelve hours before. He showered again, and shaved this time, then dropped off his key and hit the road. First truck stop he came to he pulled off again, this time to fill up the Kenworth's fuel tanks, and his own, too, while he was at it.

He thought about calling J.J. again, but decided there wasn't much point in it, since he'd already told everybody at home he was on his way. He'd made the call from the hospital, right after he'd left Mirabella and said his goodbye to Amy Jo. The pink-pinafore lady had been real nice about letting him use a phone in one of the administrative offices, out of sight of the pack of newshounds out in the front lobby.

He remembered how he'd worried about it, thinking it was worse than getting a tooth pulled, having to explain to an eight-year-old boy why he'd broken his promise to him. He remembered the way his stomach had tied itself in knots as he'd stood there with the receiver mashed up against his ear, listening to the rings.

It was picked up on the fifth ring, and he'd had to shout to be heard over the racket in the background. And a moment later he'd heard his son's excited voice yelling, "Dad! Hey, guess what, I saw you on TV!"

"Naw," said Jimmy Joe. "No kiddin'?"

"No kiddin', Dad. It's on CNN—we all saw you. Is it true? Did you really deliver that lady's baby? Just like on *Emergency 911?*"

"Well, yeah…sorta. Hey, listen, how're you all doin'? What's all that racket I hear? Everybody havin' a good time?"

Before J.J. could answer, there was a click and his mother's voice said, "Hello, son. Merry Christmas."

"Merry Christmas, Mama. What's everybody doin'? Sounds like you got a houseful, as usual."

"Oh, yes, everybody was here for dinner. Al and Tracy left a little while ago—they had to get back, Al's on duty tonight. Pretty much everybody else is here, though, just relaxing—you know how it is. They've got the football game on now, I think. The girls are still cleaning up in the kitchen...."

"Hey, Dad," J.J. interrupted. "You know that new computer game you got me? It is so cool. Oh, yeah—and I like the remote-control truck, too, only I haven't had a chance to play with it yet, hardly. Uncle Roy's been playin' with it all day, and he won't give it back."

Jimmy Joe was laughing when his mama said quietly, "Well, son, I guess you've had quite a time of it this Christmas."

His laughter turned soft, and he took a breath and said, "Yeah, Mama, I sure have."

"Well, you can tell us all about it when you get here. Where are you now? You headin' home?"

"I'm 'bout to. I got this load to drop off in Little Rock tomorrow, so it's gonna be late—sometime the next mornin', probably—before I get there. Don't you wait up, now, y'hear? You can save me some of that turkey and sweet-potato pie, though."

J.J. yelled, "We will, Dad!" while his mama was laughing in a way that told him she was probably wiping away some tears, too. Then she called out, "Hey, it's your brother—come and wish him Merry Christmas!" And then there was so much yelling and hootin' and hollerin' Jimmy Joe could hardly hear himself think, so he wished everybody a Merry Christmas and said his goodbyes laughing.

When he was hanging up the phone, he found that there was a lump in his throat, and a few tears in his eyes, too. And since there wasn't anyone around to see them, he figured this was one of those times he didn't mind letting them fall.

After that, he hadn't been able to think about very much

except how badly he wanted to be home with his family, which made it easier than he'd thought it was going to be to leave Texas and everything that had happened there behind him. What with Christmas homesickness and road conditions that required all his skill and concentration just to keep his rig on the road, he thought he managed pretty well to keep his mind from dwelling on Mirabella and her baby. But that was yesterday.

This was another day, and after a good night's rest, it seemed like his mind just wanted to gnaw on the situation like a dog on a fresh bone. He went over everything that had happened—every minute, every word, from the first moment he'd set eyes on the lady in the silver Lexus, way back there in that New Mexico truck stop. And the conclusion he came to was that he was making way too much out of the whole thing.

It was something his son had said to him, about it being like the TV show *Emergency 911,* that had really pulled him up short. Shoot, it happened all the time—people delivering babies in taxicabs and snowstorms, saving people's lives and all that stuff—cops, firemen, EMTs, and sometimes even plain old ordinary guys like him. It stood to reason a man might feel some sort of bond between himself and a woman whose baby he'd helped deliver, or somebody whose life he'd saved, and that she might feel grateful and tender toward him, too. Sure, that would just be natural. But did these people go around falling in love with the ones they'd helped, or getting all involved in their lives? Uh-uh. That just didn't happen, except maybe for remembering birthdays, cards at Christmas, things like that. Mostly, though, their worlds were separate, and once all the excitement died down, everybody went back to their own world and got on with their lives. That was the way it was supposed to be.

And all for the best, too. At least that was what he told himself over and over again on that long drive home. He told himself he had J.J. to think of, a family that loved him and a trucking company to build, and that ought to be enough to keep him happy and occupied. He told himself just about the last thing he needed in his life was a headstrong and independent career woman from L.A. who hated country music and thought it was perfectly reasonable to go and have a baby without even knowing what it was like to make love with a man. It took him close to a thousand miles, but by the time he got home, he almost believed it.

Two days after Christmas, at four o'clock in the morning, Jimmy Joe's mama came downstairs and found him sitting in her living room in his daddy's old favorite chair, watching television in the dark. She stood in the doorway with her glass of antacid fizzing in her hand and watched with him for a while, then said, "Son, you're gonna wear out that remote."

He looked over at her. "H'lo, Mama, sorry I woke you up."

She shrugged and waved the glass. "Oh, I was up anyway. Always eat too much of that rich food over the holidays, then I have to take a few days and get my stomach straightened out." She came and sat on the couch and put her feet, which were clad in slippers that looked like a pair of pink lapdogs, up on the coffee table. "How long ago'd you get in? I didn't hear your rig."

"It's down at my place. I parked it and drove the car over. Didn't want to rouse everybody." He spoke absently, his eyes following the images on the screen. Images of a mother with burgundy hair with her newborn baby. The baby was dressed up in a Christmas stocking like a little bitty elf.

"Which one is that?" his mother asked, then answered herself. "Oh—*The Today Show*. I think CNN's after that one."

"Yeah, I know. I've already been through 'em once." Actually, he was on his third go-round, but he didn't tell her that. Or that he hadn't been able to bring himself to turn the tape off. Or what a shock it had been to him to see Mirabella's face, hear her voice again, and how turning it off had seemed worse than leaving her all over again, and how lonely he'd felt in the silent darkness of that cozy and familiar living room.

"Son," his mama said quietly, "are you in love with this woman?"

A laugh burst from him. "Trust you, Mama." But he knew from long experience she wasn't going to leave it alone, so he tried to joke her out of it, which was a tactic that never had worked with her very well. "Do you know how ridiculous that is? Now, how in the world am I gonna fall in love, huh? I got a child to raise, a trucking company to build, a house to take care of—"

His mother interrupted him with a sigh. "Yeah...sometimes I forget you're not my oldest child. Son, you're not even thirty, and you're older than any of them, you know that? I don't think you ever were a kid—you've been saddled with so many responsibilities all your life. There you were, taking on the responsibility for Patti when you were just in high school, then your daddy dying and you taking over the business, and trying to raise J.J. all alone. Tell me something—are you ever gonna think about yourself sometime in your life? Do what makes *you* happy?"

Jimmy Joe pressed the Pause button, freezing Mirabella's face just as she was looking down at the baby in her arms. Pain punched him in the gut. "I am happy, Mama."

"Yeah," Betty Starr said with a snort. "A happy man sits all alone in the dark watching a tape of a beautiful woman over and over."

His thumb moved on the remote and the image sprang to radiant life. His heart lifted. "Yeah," he breathed. "She is beautiful, isn't she?"

His mother chuckled softly. "So, I'll ask you again. Are you in love with her?"

He sighed and scrunched down farther on his tailbone. "I don't know. Sometimes I think I am, and sometimes I'm sure, and then other times...I'm sure I'm crazy."

"Well, good, you're confused. That's a good sign you are in love."

Jimmy Joe snorted. "I'm not confused, Mama. I know right well when a woman is out of my league."

The lapdog slippers hit the floor and the empty glass hit the top of the coffee table. "Now, you just stop that right there. I know I raised you to be humble, but I sure never raised you to be ashamed of who and what you are."

He sat up straight and raised a calming hand; grown-up or

not, all of Betty Starr's kids knew to steer clear of her temper. "Now, simmer down, Mama. It's not a case of being ashamed of who I am. You know me better'n that. It's a case of knowin' who *she* is. We're from two different worlds. We're just—" he took a deep breath to ease the ache in his chest "—too different."

"Well, now," said his mother thoughtfully, "you know that's not necessarily a bad thing."

With one savage gesture Jimmy Joe shut off the VCR and slapped the remote down, then got up to pace in the restrictive area in front of the coffee table. He felt restless and jangled, overloaded with feelings he didn't know what to do with, and like any overloaded child needing to blow off some steam, he knew he was safe with his mama. "I'm not just talking likes and dislikes," he said with controlled fury. "Different politics and opinions, things like that—that's nothin'. What I mean is, we don't even think alike. We don't believe in the same things."

"You know this for a fact?" his mother said mildly. "That's an awful lot to know about somebody in just two days."

"She's a Californian, Mama, through and through." He paused to put up a hand, holding off what he knew she was going to say next. "I'm not judging—I'm not. But I've been around those people out there enough to know they don't think like anybody else in this world." He shook his head and blew out air in a breathy whistle. "She's got some strange ideas." *You don't know the half of it, Mama. She's a virgin at thirty-eight—a virgin! And she's just had a baby—a baby she made herself from a damn test tube. What kind of woman does that?*

Betty Starr watched him for a moment, then settled back on the sofa cushions, once more installing the lapdogs in comfort on the coffee table. "I don't know. I saw her on that interview, and she sounds like a real nice woman to me."

"Well—" he lifted his arms and blew out another exasperated gust of air "—sure, she's *nice.* She's intelligent and funny and fiesty and opinionated, and she can be a real pain in the butt sometimes." *And a whole lot of fun to argue with.* He looked sideways at his mama and grinned. *A lot like somebody else I know who's near and dear to my heart.* He leaned over to kiss her.

She patted his cheek and smiled at him. "Well, then?"

He pulled away, exasperated again. "Okay. So, say I do love her. Say I love her enough to get past all the differences—what about *her?* What's a woman like that gonna do out here? She's a city girl. She's got a career, friends, family...."

"If I heard right, she said her parents live in Pensacola."

"Yeah, yeah, they do, but she's got a couple sisters, some friends out there in L.A. The point is, she's got a life there. You think somebody like that's ever going to be happy living in a place like this, a hick Georgia town—"

With a sly smile, she finished it for him. "With a bunch of Crackers and rednecks?"

"You said it, I didn't."

They both laughed, and his mama sighed and said, "Oh, Jimmy Joe..."

After a forgiving silence, she said gently, "Let me ask you this, son. Who do you think you are to make that decision for her? Did you even ask her how she feels about it?"

He went back to his daddy's old chair, sat in it, and leaning earnestly forward with his elbows on his knees, began to shape pictures for her with his hands, the way he sometimes did when he had something complicated to explain.

"It's like this," he said patiently, ignoring his mother's broad smile. "There's ducks, and then there's chickens. Ducks live in the water, and chickens live on dry land, and there's no way they're ever gonna find a way to live happily together. Now you take the chicken—that's me—and throw him in the water—that's the big city—and he's just gonna sink like a stone. The duck, on the other hand, she can go and live in the chicken yard, all right, but is she gonna be happy there?" He sat back with a fat sense of satisfaction, figuring he'd made his point about as well as anybody could make one. "Now, I ask you, can you think of anything in this world sadder than a duck who's never going to see a pond again?'' He couldn't understand why his mama was just sitting there laughing.

"Oh, Jimmy Joe—'' she chuckled, reaching over to pat him on the knee ''—you know, I think you read too much.'' She paused to wipe her eyes, then gave a deep, amused sigh. "Son, I don't know how to tell you this, but people aren't chickens or ducks. People can live anywhere, adapt to anything, if they want to. Depends on their priorities, what they want out of life, what's important to them.'' She paused again, this time to let the seriousness in her voice settle in around them, and then continued, "And the only way you're ever going to find that out about a person is to ask.''

Jimmy Joe stared at the floor and said nothing. He was suddenly aware of how tired he was. Out of the corner of his eye he saw his mother's lapdog slippers slide off the coffee table as she stood and gathered up her antacid glass. He felt a lump settle into his throat as she leaned down to kiss him.

"I'm just so glad you're home safe and sound, son,'' she said huskily. She gave his shoulder a squeeze and shuffled off toward the kitchen. In the doorway she paused and turned. "You know,'' she said. And he thought, Uh-oh. He knew that sly tone of voice. "J.J.'s still got a week's vacation left. Why don't the two of you go on down to Florida, spend some time together? I'll bet Pensacola Beach'd be pretty nice this time of year.''

He cleared his throat and waved his hand and tried his best not to sound like he was making excuses. "Ah, well…you know I sorta promised J.J. I'd take him to Six Flags. It's open just for the holidays. And then I got to service my truck…get ready to make another run out to California.…''

"Son,'' his mama said sternly, "I never raised you to be a coward.''

Chapter 14

"Westbound, you got a smoky comin' your way with his lights on—don' know where he's goin', but he's in a hurry."
"'Preciate it."

I-40—Oklahoma

The way Jimmy Joe saw it, it wasn't a case of being a coward. There was a difference between being a coward and being sensible. And he didn't think he was being stubborn and muleheaded, which his sister Jessie accused him of, either. What he was, he told himself, was patient. Patient and sensible.

All he needed was time. Time to forget. Time to forget everything that had happened to him out there in that Panhandle blizzard, and all but the haziest memories of a selfish and uppity redhead from California and her tiny pink scrap of a baby girl.

If only, he thought, she hadn't gone and named her Amy.

Still, he was sure it was just a matter of keeping busy and letting enough time go by so that the memories would start to fade. So he wouldn't keep thinking he heard Mirabella's voice talking to him above the highway hum and the growl of a big diesel engine. So he wouldn't keep waking up alone in his hand-carved walnut bed remembering the way her body had felt in his arms. Then, if he could get those memories out of his head, maybe the feelings that went with them would go, too—the aching sense of longing, and loss.

The problem was, it didn't seem to be working. Instead, it seemed the more time that went by, the more vivid the memories got. And the stronger the feelings. Sometimes he would tiptoe downstairs in the dead of night and plug the interview tapes into the VCR and run them over and over until his eyes smarted; the feel of her skin, wet and slick against his cheek, the smell of her hair, the salt taste of her sweat vivid in his mind, and every nerve in his body feeling as if it had been rubbed with sandpaper.

He couldn't even remember anymore how he'd felt about her back then, when he'd been handcuffed and hog-tied by the knowledge that she was a pregnant woman, a woman in labor, and almost certainly someone else's woman besides. All he knew was the way he'd come to feel about her since; the way he felt about her *now,* which was a way he hadn't felt in so long he was astounded to discover he still could.

The last time he'd felt like that he'd been—oh, about sixteen, grappling and groping with Patti in the back of his oldest brother's car, unable to think about anything in the world but how good her breasts felt in his hand, and how if he didn't get himself inside her he was going to blow apart into a million pieces. She'd been a virgin, too. They both had been— he, too randy and dumb to know that she'd lied to him about the bruises he'd found on her body, or that because of them there were blacker ones on her soul, and that he was about to make the biggest mistake of his life.

That was what those kinds of feelings did to a man, he thought. Made him forget everything he'd been taught about what was right and what was wrong, everything he knew about common sense, everything he believed in. He might have had some kind of excuse back then, being just sixteen. But he wasn't sixteen anymore. He was a grown man with a child of his own, and a future to make for him. And no matter what his mama had told him, going after something just because it would make *him* happy was a luxury he couldn't afford. If, in his longing for Mirabella, he sometimes felt like an addict at the end of his tether, well…too bad. He'd gotten over worse. He would get over this, too.

I'll get over you, Marybell.

No. Marybell had been *his* name for her, *his* fantasy. But that was just what it was…fantasy. Mirabella…that was who she really was—a woman as exotic and foreign to him as her name.

But…why did she have to go and name her baby Amy?

The week after J.J.'s Christmas vacation ended, Jimmy Joe hit the road again. It was a pretty good trip—a long one, which was okay with him—another load of textiles headed for L.A., after which he was supposed to go out to San Pedro to pick up a bunch of electronics components just come in off a boat from Taiwan and run them up to Boise. He planned it so he would take the southern route out and the northern route back, and that way avoid I-40 and the Texas Panhandle altogether.

But when he called in from Boise, his broker told him there was a load of designer-label beer down in Denver, if he wanted it, headed for Fort Worth, so he wouldn't have to dead-head it all the way home. He couldn't very well pass up an opportunity like that, could he? So much for well-laid plans.

The weather was downright balmy for January as he dropped down out of Denver and headed into New Mexico. He hit a little rain in Albuquerque, but none of the frozen stuff. In fact he couldn't see any traces at all left of the blizzard that had paralyzed the whole midsection of the country just a few short weeks ago.

Butterflies began to stir in his belly when he rolled past the Santa Rosa truck stop where Mirabella had spent the night in his sleeper, and he remembered how he'd rubbed her back and fed her chicken soup, and that they'd argued about Walt Disney movies.

From there, with the road dry and dusty, it was only two hours to the rest stop east of Adrian. It seemed incredible to him now, rolling along with his tires singing and the radio placidly droning on about the whereabouts of any bears in the vicinity, to recall that the last time he'd driven through there it had been in a single-file convoy creeping along at no more than walking speed.

The pounding of his heart didn't ease up after he passed the rest stop, either. Still to come was Vega, and Riggs's gas station where he'd left the keys to Mirabella's car. He wondered if she'd picked it up yet, or if it was still there, waiting for her.

He wasn't going to pull off and see. He'd sworn to himself he wouldn't. But suddenly there was old Route 66 and the sign that said Riggs's RoadSide Service, and the next thing he knew the Kenworth was heading up the exit ramp, and he was turning left onto the overpass, all the while cussing himself and calling himself several kinds of fool.

Riggs was tickled to death to see him; had to tell him all about how he'd seen Jimmy Joe on TV, and how he'd become something of a hero himself around those parts, and asked half-jokingly for his autograph. He took Jimmy Joe out to his garage and showed him the Lexus, all washed and polished and covered up with a nylon tarp to keep the dust off.

"Don't know how long she plans on leavin' it here," said Riggs. "Guess she's gonna be stayin' with her folks down there in Pensacola for a few more weeks, anyways."

"You talked to her?" Jimmy Joe asked, his heart flapping against his ribs like a tire going bad.

"Oh, yeah, she called me here, couple weeks ago, now. Right after New Year's, I guess it was. Wanted to know if I'd send her stuff to her, UPS. She had all her Christmas presents for her folks in the trunk, you know. She said she'd send me some money to do it, but, ah, you know, I went on ahead and sent 'em for her. I knew she'd be good for it, and she was—the money come just a few days later. Say, you know, she is just the nicest little ol' gal—sure am glad everything turned out okay for her.''

"Yeah," said Jimmy Joe. Funny thing—it seemed like all of a sudden he couldn't get enough air to breathe. "You, uh, you say you shipped her things to her UPS? You, uh…" He gulped oxygen and plunged. "You wouldn't happen to still have her address, would you?"

"Well, now, I sure do." Riggs looked at him sideways, kind of sly. "You thinkin' about gettin' in touch with her? Saw her on TV—my, she sure is pretty, ain't she?"

"Aw, you know," said Jimmy Joe, shuffling his feet like a teenager facing down his prom date's daddy, "I just thought I'd maybe drop her a note, or something. Find out how she and that little baby are doin'…."

"Well, sure 'nuff—I would," said Riggs, and added casually, "You can give her a call, if you want to. I got her phone number, down there in Pensacola where she's stayin' at her folks' place. Come on in where it's warm and let me find it for ya."

Ten minutes later Jimmy Joe was back on the interstate, heading east with a trailer-load of beer and a grin on his face, as his daddy would have said, "Like a possum with his paws full a' paw-paws." He felt jangled and so weak in the knees he didn't know how he was going to shift gears. "You're an idiot," he said to himself. "You know that, don't you?"

He did. But that didn't keep him from wanting to blast everybody he met with his airhorn and shout to the heavens, "Hallelujah!"

In Amarillo he left I-40 and headed down to Fort Worth on Highway 287, which was a long, straight shot, and once he'd left the little Panhandle towns and their speed traps behind, about as fast a one as a driver could ask for, for not being an interstate. He drove most of the night, pulling over on the outskirts of Fort Worth to catch a few hours' sleep, then slipped on into the city ahead of morning rush-hour traffic.

When the wholesaler's warehouse opened up, he was there at the loading dock, waiting.

He unloaded, then pushed on down to I-20, to a truck stop he liked where he knew he could always find clean towels and plenty of hot water, plus a fairly decent cup of coffee. After a shower and a shave, and with a good hot breakfast under his belt, he screwed up all his courage and made a phone call.

Not long after that he was on his way again, heading east on I-20 in a cold, misty rain.

"I have this theory," Mirabella said, on the phone to her friend Charly Phelps in Los Angeles. "What I think is, that it's all just a matter of chemistry."

"No kiddin'," said Charly in her dry Alabama drawl.

"No—I mean actual brain chemistry. To be more specific, oxytocin."

Laughter bubbled against her ear. "Oxytocin?"

"Yeah, remember? They talked about it in childbirth class, It's this chemical that's released naturally during pregnancy, also during touching and during nursing. They call it the bonding chemical. It's what triggers contractions—also triggers orgasm, by the way."

"Oh, that's good to know."

"Yeah, well, I've been reading up on it in my childbirth books since I got my stuff back last week—did I tell you the man with the service station shipped them to me UPS? The one that talked us through the delivery, and then Jimmy Joe gave him my keys and had him pick up my car? Turns out he's the nicest guy. Anyway, when you consider all that oxytocin oozing around inside me, then all that close physical contact—he was always touching me, Charly, rubbing my back, my legs, my feet, even my face..." *And he kissed me— don't forget that. I'll never forget that.* "Then you throw in a whole bunch of endorphins on top of it, and I must have been a walking chemical love potion. It's no wonder my emotions were so susceptible."

"So what you're saying is, it wasn't that this Jimmy Joe guy was so wonderful, just that he was *there?*"

"Charly, at that point I'd have probably bonded with a BarcaLounger."

This time Charly's hoot of laughter held the derision that is completely permissible between old and trusted friends. "Bella," she said fondly, "you are such an idiot." And then, after a brief pause to see if she would deny it: "So that's your theory, huh? Tell me this—are you buyin' it? Because I'm not."

"I'm working on it." Mirabella sighed and kissed the top of the downy head nestled like a sun-ripened peach against her heart, then leaned her head back against the crocheted afghan that lay draped, as it had for as long as she could remember, across the back of her mother's old rocking chair. "Right now it's too soon to tell. I mean, I'm nursing, you know? And that oxytocin is still flowing, so…it stands to reason I'd still have all those feelings and memories."

Just as strong and clear as if it had been yesterday we were together in that truck…Christmas carols playing on the radio, and Jimmy Joe's arms holding me and his voice yelling in my ear, "One more…one more!" And his face when he laid Amy on my stomach and said, "Marybell, say hello to your new baby girl…" so vivid in my mind I feel sometimes he's just in the next room, and if I call to him, in the very next moment he'll be here beside me, smiling his sweet, Jimmy Joe smile….

On her chest, Amy stirred and uttered a tiny squeaking sound, and Mirabella's hand began a slow stroking and patting rhythm to counteract the effects of her own rueful laughter. "Anyway, I'm hoping it will all go away once I get my body back to normal—like a bad dream, you know?"

"How's that coming, by the way? I know you, you're probably thinkin' you ought to already be wearing your regular clothes by now, and driving yourself nuts if you're not. Are you working out?"

It was Mirabella's turn to snort—but softly, so as not to disturb Amy. "I'm not *that* compulsive." But she smiled when she said it, because she knew full well that a few months ago she *had* been, about her physical self, anyway, and especially about her weight.

But now...she didn't think she could have explained it, certainly not to Charly, but since Amy's birth she'd noticed, well, a distinct *difference* in the way she viewed her own body. Where once she'd focused on and criticized its every flaw, now when she looked at her body she felt what could only be described as pride. *Yes,* the feelings seemed to say, *what a wonderful, marvelous body you are, to have done this miraculous thing!* Instead of her usual restless dissatisfaction, her constant drive to improve herself, she felt a kind of complacency that was almost catlike, bordering on smugness.

And something else—something she'd never known before, and so couldn't begin to explain. It was as if something sleeping deep inside her had been awakened, like jillions of tiny seeds sprouting where everything had been barren before. As if all those tiny new shoots and buds were pushing, straining, reaching for warmth and light, because like all newborn things, they demanded nourishment. She felt a new restlessness now—not of dissatisfaction, but of longing; an itch not of compulsion, but of desire. Having a child had fulfilled her, as she'd known it would; fulfilled the caring, giving, loving and nurturing woman she'd always known herself to be. But at the same time it seemed to have awakened a strange new woman, one she'd never met before. One who *needed* nurturing. One who needed, one who yearned, one who deserved to be cared for...given to...touched...loved.

"It's coming pretty well," she said, drawing a shaken breath. "I feel really good—I think the nursing's helping me get back in shape, if you don't count my chest, which of course is still enormous. I've been walking—not today, though. It's raining, and it's cold."

"It's beautiful here," said Charly with typical California smugness. "Just your basic January in L.A. After all the lousy weather in December, suddenly the sun's shining and the hills are green. So, when are you coming home? I miss you, and I'm dyin' to see Amy.''

Home? Mirabella gazed at the rain-drenched Mandevilla vine growing up the trellis beside her parents' patio door and wondered how she was ever going to tell her best friend that Los Angeles didn't seem like home to her anymore. It seemed as far away to her as the moon, and about as hospitable. Sometimes her life there seemed like a rapidly fading dream.

But if my home isn't there anymore, she thought with a vague sense of bewilderment and sadness, then where is it?

''I'm not sure—'' she began, just as a truck's air brakes hissed explosively out in the street. Her heart jumped and the hand holding the phone jerked so violently it startled Amy, making her tiny body jerk, as well. What is this? Mirabella thought. Am I going to leap out of my skin every time I hear that sound for rest of my life? Suddenly furious, she swore under her breath.

''What's the matter?''

''Nothing—just some truck making noise out in the street. One of my mom's neighbors is probably having something delivered, repaired or hauled away. This is a retirement community—there's a lot of that going around. Listen—I'll be home soon, I promise. I'm planning on it. Pop's doing a lot better. I think they're going to schedule him for a bypass in a month or two, and Mom would probably have an easier time of it taking care of him if Amy and I are out of her hair.''

She paused to chuckle. ''She made him go grocery shopping this morning, can you believe that? Said he needed to get out and get some exercise. They've been gone quite a while— Oh, now what? *Damn.* Someone's at the door. Looks like I'm going to have to get that. Hold on a minute while I get out of this chair—''

Supporting the sleeping baby with one hand and juggling the cordless phone with the other, she pushed herself awkwardly upright.

''Uh, Bella, maybe I should let you go.''

''No, no, that's okay, it'll just take me a minute to get rid of whoever it is. It's probably just somebody collecting for the Heart Association—there's a lot of that around here, too. Hold on—'' She had to use the hand with the phone in it to open the door.

''Yes? I'm sorry, but the Wasko—'' The words flew away on an exhaled breath, like whispers in the wind. The cordless phone fell to the floor with a clatter as, in a purely instinctive reaction, her hand flew to cover her baby's head. Her lips moved, soundlessly forming his name: ''Jimmy Joe.''

No smile, no dimples, although one corner of his mouth twitched slightly upward, obviously trying. The light in his eyes was uncertain and brooding as he stood with one thumb hooked in the pocket of his Levi's, one hip and shoulder canted higher than the other, raindrops sparkling on his skin and beginning to drip from the spiky-wet ends of his hair. Dangling from the other hand as if forgotten was a bouquet of pink roses wrapped in cellophane.

''Hey, there, Marybell,'' he said with a rueful sniff. ''Guess your mama must not a' told you I was comin'.''

She looks like she's seen a ghost, he thought, which was about the way he felt. Her hair was even brighter and her skin more translucent than he remembered, and she seemed tinier, too, somehow. She was wearing white cotton pants and a long-sleeved button-up-the-front shirt in some sort of gauzy material that draped gently over her voluptuous breasts and nested the sleeping baby's cheek like thistledown. The soft, sea colors of the shirt made him realize something he hadn't before— that in certain lights and moods, her eyes were more green than gray. Standing there in the rain and gloom of January, she seemed to him all sunlight and flower-scented freshness, like a spring breeze that had come without warning to snatch his breath away.

''Mom knew you were coming?'' Her voice was an airless whisper of disbelief.

His heart was pounding so hard he couldn't think straight, but he managed a little half-smile of apology. ''Yeah, I called yesterday from Dallas. Tried to again, a little while ago when I got into town, but your line was busy.''

He stepped up onto the doorstep, and she sucked in air in a startled gulp. Cautiously, with a light touch on her arm and a raised eyebrow to ask permission, he leaned past her to pick up the telephone she'd dropped. Without taking his eyes from her face, as if she were some rare wild creature that might vanish in a blink if he did, he mumbled into the phone, "'Scuse me, but can she call you back? 'Preciate it,'' then laid it carefully, along with the roses he'd brought, on the little table that was there in the entryway behind her.

Even with the rain coming down, he could hear the small, sticky sound she made when she swallowed. As dry as his own mouth was, he wasn't surprised that her voice would still only come in a whisper. "Jimmy Joe…what are you doing here?''

Ah, you know, I was just passin' through— That was what he started to say, until somewhere in the back of his mind he heard his mama's voice saying, "Son, I never raised you to be a coward.'' So he took the deepest breath he could and in an adolescent's cracked and terrified voice, told her the truth.

"I came to see you. And because…there's something I've been wantin' to do.''

In a world gone suddenly silent, Mirabella watched his hand float across the space between them and come to rest on Amy's head, a touch as sweet and reverent as a benediction. She didn't breathe; her heartbeat rocked her as the hand rose and she felt that same touch on her own cheek. The warmth of it flowed like oil into her neck, and when his other hand came to cradle her head she gave a sigh of gratitude, for it had grown too heavy for her own muscles to bear. The warmth poured downward into her shoulders and chest, into her belly and farther yet—deep, deep down. Her breasts tingled and her legs grew weak, and all the hungry new shoots inside her lifted and swelled with joy.

"Oxytocin…'' she murmured.

"Pardon?'' His breath misted her lips.

"It's just…chemistry."

"You got that right," he growled, and brought his mouth the last sweet distance.

Their lips met like lovers who have traveled a lifetime and ten thousand miles to find each other—with yearning and gladness and thanksgiving and joy; with breathless awe and trembling disbelief.

"I *can't*," gasped Mirabella.

"Why not?" His mouth hovered a suspenseful whisper above hers.

"I can't do this—I can't," she breathed, moving her head back and forth just slightly, as if fighting a hypnotist's powers. "It won't work. I'm much too old for you. It's not—"

"Hush." With one word and a gentle shake of her head he silenced her. Then he pulled back, but only far enough so she could see his eyes. And there was no gentleness in them now; they were brooding and dark, with a fire in their depths she'd seen once before. When he spoke, the tone of his voice was familiar to her, too—the same firm, unyielding voice she'd clung to through a long, dark night, and that had calmed her fears and brought her safely through the birth of her child.

"I'm gonna ask you one question, and I want you to answer me truthfully, and then we're gonna be done with this, you understand? I want you tell me—in all that time we spent together in my truck, did it even once enter your mind to think about how old or how young either one of us was?"

"But that was—"

His mouth stopped her there. Then once again he drew back to gaze down at her, the fire in his eyes banked to a tender glow. "Marybell, I do enjoy arguing with you, and I expect we're gonna be doin' a lot of it, about a lot of things. But this ain't one of 'em. We're done with this now, y'hear?"

She was conscious only of mild astonishment as she heard herself answer meekly, "Yes, sir."

Overriding every other thought and feeling was the most intense hunger she'd ever known. She watched his mouth descend to hers as though it were the only drop of water, the last crumb of bread, the only blade of grass in a barren and thirsty world, feeling as though she would die if she couldn't taste it again—just once more. She actually felt a sharp pain when he suddenly halted, still a tantalizing, tormenting hairs-breadth away.

"Oh—" she cried, a sound somewhere between a laugh and a whimper. On her chest Amy was stirring and making impatient snuffling noises.

"Looks like she's wakin' up," said Jimmy Joe, one hand dropping, lightly as a falling leaf, to the baby's bobbing head. He looked at Mirabella and his eyebrows rose. "May I?"

"Oh—of course."

She watched, breath suspended, an aching knot of warmth growing inside her as she recalled the last time those strong, sensitive hands had cradled her daughter's tiny body—slippery wet with gunk and warm from her own body, attached to her still by a pulsing cord, kicking, punching and squalling with outrage at the shock of cold on her skin and the intrusion of air in her brand-new lungs. How gently he'd held her, then placed her on Mirabella's belly and guided her frantically searching hands to take the place of his.

"She sure has grown," he said huskily. In response to his voice, Amy's head turned slowly from side to side like a radar scanner as she searched for the face that went with it. Homing in and locking on, she studied it with infant intensity, her mouth pursing and stretching as she ran through her entire repertoire of facial expressions for this new and fascinated audience.

"Red hair?" He touched it with a fingertip and smiled. "She looks just like you."

And suddenly as if in response to his words, Amy's eyes crinkled up and her mouth popped open and then stretched wide, and the corners tilted upward. "She's smilin'," he said, looking up at her mama, all but thunderstruck. He felt as if his heart was going to burst.

"She sure is," Mirabella murmured, moving closer so she

could see it, too. "That's a first." She looked oddly misty to him, like a flower in the rain.

"That's no gas pain, either. Look at her—she just won't quit." He thought he could have drowned in that smile. Then he felt like maybe he *was* drowning, the way his chest hurt and it was so hard to breathe.

"Okay, now she's got her priorities straight," Mirabella said with a tender snort, as one of the baby's waving fists found its way to her mouth and she began to suck avidly on it.

Jimmy Joe chuckled. "Looks like she's hungry."

"She's *always* hungry. Which is another way she's just like her mother. Yeah...funny, isn't it?" Her smile was blurred and soft as she gazed down at her daughter and tickled her cheek with a finger. Mirabella's eyes flicked up at him and her smile grew wry. "If you want to make God laugh, just make a plan—isn't that what you told me? All I can say is, He must really be holding his sides right now. I mean, here I had it all planned, picked out the perfect set of genes. I was going to have a tall, slim, blond little boy with a sweet, beautiful smile and..." Her voice caught, and she looked quickly back down at her baby with her face so full of adoration, watching her was like looking into the sun. "Look what I got—a round, roly-poly redhead with an appetite like Pac-Man...."

"And just as pretty as a little wild rose," said Jimmy Joe, in a voice so fierce and raspy he felt as if he might have swallowed a whole bush's worth of those rose thorns himself. "And I wouldn't mind..."

His breath ran dry, and he stared at her, realizing he was on the verge of blurting it all out, everything he'd come to say to her—that he not only wanted her and Amy to come and live with him and share the rest of his life with him, but that he would be tickled to death to have several more just like her, eventually, Lord willing. Just like that, without any warning or leading up to it, without telling her all the reasons he thought he could make her happy, without presenting any of the arguments he'd thought up to answer the doubts she was sure to have. Just clobber her with it, before he'd even had a chance to woo her— Lord, he hadn't even given her the flowers yet! And then if she said no, *then* what?

He was staring down at her, with the baby held between them like a vow and his heart hammering in his throat, feeling as scared and helpless as he had the night Amy was born, and Mirabella was staring back at him, looking so beautiful he wondered if maybe he ought to chuck his whole game plan and just kiss her again, and go on kissing her until she didn't have any breath left to say no.

He was about to embark on that new strategy when a voice behind him sang out, "Oops, home too soon!"

He turned, heart pounding like a guilty teenager's, while Mirabella said, "Hi, Mom...Pop," in a breathy, little-girl voice he didn't recognize.

"Pete," her mama was scolding as she bustled up the walk with her hands full of plastic grocery bags and a plastic rain-bonnet on her head, "I *told* you we should have eaten lunch first."

"The hell with that," growled the barrel-chested man beside her, waving around the umbrella he was holding so it wasn't doing much to keep the rain off anybody. "I told you I want to meet the man—shake his hand. And that's what I'm gonna do."

He heaved himself up the steps, furling the umbrella as he came, his chin jutting out ahead of him in a way that reminded Jimmy Joe so much of Mirabella, he almost forgot his manners completely. He had to fight hard to contain his smile when he saw the traces of rust mixed in with the thick, straight, iron-gray hair.

Mirabella gamely murmured introductions, which her father mostly drowned out with his crisp and authoritative, "G'mornin', son. I sure am glad to meet you...glad to meet the man that brought my granddaughter into the world. Come on in here, now. No sense in lettin' all the warm air out." He dragged Jimmy Joe into the house, pumping his hand.

Behind her husband's back, Ginger caught Jimmy Joe's eye and winked. "Ohh, look—roses!" she cried, spotting the bouquet he'd left on the table. "Aren't they gorgeous? They need to go in some water. I'll just take these groceries into the kitchen—"

"Let me carry those for you, ma'am."

"Now, let me see, how's my little ol' baby girl?"

"She just woke up, Dad. She needs her diaper changed. She's hungry again, too. I was just going to—I better go feed her...."

"You do that, honey. Son, you're plannin' on stayin' and havin' lunch with us, aren't you?"

"Well, sir, ah..." With his hands already full of grocery bags, there wasn't much Jimmy Joe could do but follow Mirabella with his eyes as she fled down the hallway with Amy in her arms.

In the kitchen with her parents, he had an attack of claustrophobia. The cheery room seemed too crowded with just the three of them in it, and yet he felt Mirabella's absence so profoundly, it almost bordered on panic. He couldn't shake the feeling he was losing her, that he was about to let everything he'd hoped for slip through his fingers, just when he'd had it in his grasp. Because he *knew* her. He knew exactly what she was doing right now, in there alone with her baby and her thoughts. Right now her rational, reasonable planner's mind was telling her all the reasons why things wouldn't ever work out between them; and in another minute, her stubborn, muleheaded, opinionated mind was going to set it all in concrete. And he knew that once Mirabella had made up her mind, there wasn't anything on earth, short of a force of nature, that was going to change it. So if he was ever going to try to do it, he had better do it now.

He set the bags of groceries on the kitchen table as gently as he could, and with a muttered, "'Scuse me, sir...ma'am," dived through the doorway and headed off down the hall in the direction Mirabella had taken.

He found her in a back bedroom—the guest room, by the

look of it, since he didn't think Pete Waskowitz would have tolerated all those flowers, or the white priscilla curtains at the windows. There were a few of Mirabella's clothes and lots of baby things lying around, a white bassinet beside the bed, and a baby blanket spread out on the comforter. The room smelled of baby powder and a just-changed diaper, which brought back all kinds of memories for him.

She was sitting in a chair near the windows, so engrossed in the baby at her breast, she didn't notice him for a minute or two. He watched her—watched the play of rain shadows in her hair, the creamy-soft curve of her cheek as she bent over her child, the gentle smile no one else would ever see—and knew that he'd been right, and that he would love this woman and this child until he drew his last breath…and beyond that, until the end of time. It strengthened his resolve for what he had to do.

She gave a gasp of outraged modesty when she saw him, and yelped, "Jimmy Joe—go away!"

But he ignored her, and instead went to sit on the edge of the bed right opposite her, and leaned forward to watch her somberly with his hands clasped between his knees. Her eyes followed him, darkening with wariness, at first. But once she knew he wasn't going to run blushing at the sight of her naked breast, she relaxed and accepted his presence, it seemed to him, with a kind of quiet pride. They sat like that in silence for a while, listening to Amy's squeaky gulps and the whisper of the rain on the windowpane.

Then she shook her head, just slightly, and he saw her eyes fill with tears. "Jimmy Joe," she said in a broken whisper, "what are you doing here?"

He'd had a thousand miles to prepare for this. He'd probably thought of a thousand different ways to say what he wanted to say—clever, intelligent ways. Every one of them went right out the window. With his heart in his throat and in his eyes, he finally looked at her and said it: "Marybell, I've come to take you home with me."

Chapter 15

"That home cookin's smellin' awful good right now."
I-40—Texas

He knew from her silence and sadness that she'd probably expected it, that she'd already guessed what he wanted to ask her. And that the tears in her eyes were there because she'd already convinced herself it wasn't going to work.

Funny thing—he never once thought it had anything to do with her maybe just not feeling the same way about him that he did about her. Somehow, he knew she did. It was just a feeling he had, something to do with the way she looked at him, the way her lips clung to his when he kissed her, the way she trembled when he touched her. And then, she'd named her baby Amy.

"Jimmy Joe," Mirabella whispered, "I can't." The ache inside her was so vast that she wondered as she gazed down at her daughter's fat, contented little cheek, how she could not feel it, too.

"You say that a lot," he said matter-of-factly. "So far you've been wrong every time."

Since normally there was nothing Mirabella hated more than being told she was wrong, that should have been enough to launch her headlong into an argument with no holds barred. But now, since deep in her heart she wanted nothing more than to be wrong, all she could do was snap, "It wouldn't work," then clamp her mouth shut again and glare at him in stubbornness and confusion.

He took a deep breath and for a moment didn't say anything, while she watched his eyes roam the room, touching briefly on her, on the baby at her breast, the rain-streaked window, the bassinet, as if searching for something that lay just...*there*—so near but always beyond his grasp.

Then his gaze came back to his hands, clasped between his knees, and he cleared his throat, lifted his eyes to hers and smiled his sweet, Jimmy Joe smile and said, "I've never been much good with words. I mean, I *know* a lot of words. I read— my mama tells me too much—and the words are all up there in my head, and I hear them sometimes when I'm drivin' and I don't feel like listenin' to the radio or one of my books-on-tape. Words just flow along so easy, then, like a river. But when there's something important I want to say, I don't know, it's like somebody throws up a dam, or somethin', and all those words back up inside me, and the only ones that come through is just my usual trickle."

He paused to grin, then shake his head and look down at his hands again. "See, I knew you'd have to argue with me. And I had about a thousand miles to think how I'd answer you. All the good reasons why, different as we are and crazy as it seems, I think I could make you happy. Now that I'm here, though..." He looked up at her, his smile slipping awry. "The minute I saw you, I knew I wasn't gonna have the words. So I figure the best way is just to show you. So...Marybell, that's why I'm askin' you to come home with me to Georgia. So you can see for yourself who I am and what I've got to offer you. And then you can decide if it's anything you want, or not. It's up to you. So…what do you say? Will you come with me?''

Come with me…. It's up to you. Oh, God, what was happening to her nice, controllable, well-planned world? It was as if he'd suddenly come to her and said, ''Hey, you want to fly to the moon? Here are the tickets—we leave in an hour!'' The wild, the crazy, the impossible, was suddenly there within her reach—and she felt confused, terrified, paralyzed, her heart racing and her mouth as dry as sandpaper. She opened it, but no sound came out. The silence grew tense and viscous. And then…

''Oh, for heaven's sake, Bella,'' her mother said, ''don't be an idiot.''

They both turned to see her standing there, Amy's infant carrier car-seat in one hand, the diaper bag slung over her shoulder. Jimmy Joe rose instantly, mumbling, ''Ma'am,'' as good manners dictated. Mirabella simply sat, dumbstruck, as Ginger dumped the baggage onto the rug and advanced with arms outstretched.

''Here—I'll take that baby. You go get your coat.''

''But…she hasn't been burped—''

''I'll do it. Go and get yourself ready—now. This instant.''

Mirabella drew a sharp, reflexive breath as she saw her baby lifted from her arms, an instinctive preparation for battle. Then she caught Jimmy Joe's quiet gaze and the exhalation sighed softly from her lips. ''Yes, ma'am,'' she murmured humbly.

They rolled into the front yard of Jimmy Joe's mama's place late in the evening, long past the usual suppertime. He'd thought about whether he should take her home, first, but then he'd figured that might not be fair to her, and that he couldn't really expect her to make a decision until she'd had a chance to see what she was getting into. And that meant his whole family—at least the part of it he lived with on a regular basis, which was to say, Mama and Granny Calhoun, Jess and Sammi June, and of course, J.J.

His heart did a little double-skip when he thought about

Mirabella and his son meeting for the first time. He wasn't worried so much about J.J. liking Mirabella right off the bat—how could he not?—and even growing to love her like the mama he'd never had.

On the other hand, he had to face the fact that his son had pretty much outgrown the cute-and-adorable stage, and that he could be a real pistol, sometimes. He knew it was asking a lot of a woman with a brand-new baby of her own to take on someone else's eight-year-old kid, besides.

But whichever way it was going to go, he knew he wouldn't have to be in suspense for long, because the minute J.J. heard the rumble of his diesel and the hiss of those air brakes, he would be out that front door like a shot, just like he always was.

With one ear tuned to the slamming of the door and the familiar cry, "Hey, Dad!" he turned to Mirabella, who'd come quietly to stand between the seats and was peering through the cab windows at the house, which for some reason was all lit up like Christmas. "We'll stop here a minute, if that's okay," he said, just a little out of breath. "Just want to pick up J.J., have you meet my mama. My place is just down the road."

She didn't say anything, but nodded and began to unbuckle the belt that held Amy's infant carrier securely in place in the passenger seat. He got out and went around to open the door and lift the carrier down for her. Then he offered her his hand to help her down the steps, remembering what a climb it had been for her before, wondering if her independent nature would let her accept. When she gave him a look but took his hand anyway, he thought it was a good sign.

They were standing together beside the truck, sort of straightening themselves out and shaking the road stiffness out of their legs, when he finally heard the door. Not a slam, though, and without the exuberant shout of welcome that usually went with it. He turned and saw that his son had come onto the porch. But instead of running on out to meet him as he always did, he was just standing there with the light from the windows behind him shining in his hair, so he looked like he was wearing a halo.

Jimmy Joe touched Mirabella's elbow and they started across the yard, last fall's dead leaves crackling and crunching underfoot. When they reached the front walk, J.J. started slowly down the steps and came toward them, holding himself straight and tall, as if he was walking down the aisle of a church, fixing to light the candles on the altar. Wondering what had gotten into his son, Jimmy Joe set the baby carrier carefully on the ground, cleared his throat and said, "Hey, son, there's somebody here I'd like you to meet."

That was when he got his first look at Mirabella, who had stopped dead-still in the middle of the walk. He didn't know how to describe her expression, except to say she looked...stunned. Then as he watched, her face began to take on a kind of glow, as if she was witnessing a miracle. She glanced up at him, and her eyes—again there was only one way to say it—her eyes were *dancing.*

"God does have a sense of humor," she murmured as she moved up beside him, her hand going out toward the boy standing so tall and stiff before her. Thinking she meant to ruffle his hair, Jimmy Joe held his breath, knowing how J.J. hated that sort of thing, but she stopped just short of it and instead said briskly, "Hey, how are you doing? I'm Mirabella."

Then, while J.J. solemnly shook her hand, his father let his breath out in silent thanksgiving, knowing it was going to be all right. He'd seen that look on Mirabella's face before, as she watched her baby while she slept.

"You're a lot prettier in person than you are on TV," J.J. said, studying her with his head cocked to one side.

"Thanks—I think," said Mirabella, laughing shakily. She still felt jangled after the shock of seeing her fantasy child in the flesh, right there before her eyes.

In the boneless way of all eight-year-olds, J.J. dropped to his knees beside Amy's carrier. "Boy," he said in an awed voice, "she sure is little."

"Can I hold her?" asked a tall, slender girl with long blond hair pulled back in a ponytail, who had just joined them.

"This is J.J.'s cousin, Sammi June," Jimmy Joe said. "Sammi June, say hey to Mirabella."

"Hey," said Sammi June dutifully. "Can I hold the baby?"

"Well—" Mirabella looked over at Jimmy Joe and caught his reassuring nod "—sure, you can. As soon as we get inside."

"I get to hold her first," J.J. hissed, glowering possessively.

"Uh-uh. I'm the oldest, so *I* get to hold her—"

"Uh-uh, do not! I saw her first!"

"Sammi June!" yelled a tall, slim, dark-blond woman from the doorway. "You get in here, now, and help Gramma put the food on the table."

"That's my sister Jess—Sammi June's mother," said Jimmy Joe, then muttered under his breath as he bent to pick up Amy's carrier, "Sure am glad everybody's just bein' their usual selves."

They went up the steps together, Mirabella thinking, Oh, God, is *everybody* in this family tall, thin and blond? Then she saw the woman standing behind Jimmy Joe's sister, waiting for the confusion to clear. A small woman, shorter even than Mirabella, with a neat cap of hair in a rich, natural-looking shade of brown, and a body that was still youthful, though definitely on the voluptuous side.

"Mama," said Jimmy Joe, sounding slightly breathless, "this is Mirabella."

"Betty," his mother said firmly, as she held out her hand.

She doesn't look anything at all like Jimmy Joe. That was the first thing to sort itself out of the mess in Mirabella's mind. Then she saw his mother's eyes—warm, brown eyes, with a golden gleam of fire lurking in their depths. And she thought, with a sense of familiarity that was almost like a homecoming, *Yes...*

"I'm just so happy to finally meet you," Betty Starr exclaimed, dragging them all through the doorway and into her house with the sheer force, it seemed to Mirabella, of her personality. "Let me see this little one, now. Oh, she's sound asleep, isn't she? Well, that's good. Just bring her on in, we'll set her right down beside the table. Y'all come on, now, food's on the table. We waited supper for you. Would you like to freshen up? No? Well then… *Mama…?*" Her voice rose to a melodic bellow. "Supper's ready, Mama. Company's here and food's gettin' cold."

In a kind of daze, Mirabella followed her into the large, informal dining room that adjoined a rather old-fashioned kitchen, with appliances that probably dated at least from the sixties. She was reassured by the light pressure of Jimmy Joe's hand on her back, and in a strange way by the children, fidgeting and hissing at each other as they came along behind. Children, at least, were the same everywhere.

While Jimmy Joe's mother directed everyone to their places and his sister Jess bustled off to the kitchen to see to last-minute preparations, they were joined by a tiny wraith of a woman, no taller than the two children and bent and gnarled as a tree root with osteoporosis.

"Hey, there, gorgeous," said Jimmy Joe, bending over to kiss and hug her, handling her as though she were made of blown glass.

The old woman beamed and reached up to pat his cheek, then clutched his arms and peered around him like a child playing hide-and-seek. "Where is she?" she croaked, her old eyes gleaming, and Mirabella knew that, frail though she might be, here was a woman who still held the reins of life firmly in her hands.

"Granny," said Jimmy Joe, "this is Mirabella."

"Yes…yes…it's nice to meet you." She peered intently up at Mirabella, who felt her hand clutched in a grip of surprising strength. Then Granny Calhoun announced to nobody in particular, "She's a lot prettier than she looks on TV."

My family… Jimmy Joe watched them assemble around the table, squabbling and bickering and bossing one another as they always did and always would, and felt the familiar feeling that always came over him when he'd just gotten home after being gone awhile. A sense of thankfulness for them all, a rueful acceptance that they weren't perfect, and acknowledgment that he loved them in spite of—maybe even because of—that.

He wanted to look at Mirabella and smile at her with his eyes in a way that said, Yes, I know, but they're part of me. A big part. And a big part of what I brought you here to see. So what about it? Do you think…?

But he couldn't look at her then, too afraid of what he might see.

They all took their places—Mirabella, with Amy in her carrier at her feet, at the end closest to the living room in case, she was told, she needed to get up and tend to the baby during dinner. Jimmy Joe was down at the other end—miles away, it seemed—at the head of the table, with Granny Calhoun and the two children on one side and Betty and Jess on the other. The food—roast chicken and mashed potatoes and gravy, and boiled greens and corn bread—all smelled delicious, even to a semivegetarian like Mirabella, but she didn't know if the twinges she felt in her stomach were hunger pangs or butterflies.

On her right, Jimmy Joe's mother held out her hand. After a moment's uncertainty, Mirabella placed hers into it. Then she noticed that everybody was joining hands all around the table, so she looked over to her left and sure enough, there was Jess holding out her hand, too. *Oh, God,* she thought, not even aware of the propriety of that as everybody bowed their heads for the blessing.

She felt cold, suddenly. Lost and alienated. Not unusual, surely, for somebody thrust abruptly and unexpectedly into the bosom of a strange family. But this was Jimmy Joe's family. He'd brought her here in the hopes that she might want to become a part of it, too. *Could she?* Maybe she wanted to. But how would she ever make it work, when everything was so…different?

She felt so…*lonely.*

Then, while Sammi June did the honors in a singsong, recitative voice, Jimmy Joe suddenly lifted his head and looked down the length of the table at Mirabella and smiled his sweet, special smile. And she felt a strange stirring, like the rustling of the wind through the pine trees outside....

Later, when supper was finished and they'd collected J.J. and everybody had said all their goodbyes and y'all-come-backs and they'd gone on home, Jimmy Joe got J.J. settled down and then went looking for Mirabella. He found her out on his front porch, wearing his Levi's jacket and hugging herself against the cold, just standing and listening to the sounds of the night.

He went to her cautiously, not knowing quite what to make of her stillness. He felt calm and confident now, as he mostly did when he was here in his own place, but wired and restless, too, in a way he couldn't remember ever feeling before. With J.J. all tucked in for the night in his bedroom upstairs, and Amy Jo sound asleep again in her carrier, suddenly it was just the two of them—him and Mirabella, alone in the quiet of the night for the first time since that Christmas, more than three weeks ago. It seemed like a whole lot longer—another time, another place.

"Chilly out here," he said.

And she nodded and murmured, "Yes."

And then after a moment she went on, drawing a deep, quick breath, "I like it, though. It feels so crisp...so fresh. Reminds me of when I was growing up. We lived in the desert, then. I don't think we ever had snow, but it could get cold, and I remember the sky being like this, so black and clear and full of stars."

Hope filled his throat. He coughed and said, "Yeah, it's real nice in the summertime." He made a little gesture toward the two rocking chairs he kept there, side by side. "Sometimes I like to sit out here in the evenings and watch the night come in—you know, the air feels soft on your skin and the honey-suckle smells so sweet, and the fireflies twinkle on and off in the trees...."

"I've never seen fireflies," said Mirabella wistfully. And then he could hear a smile in her voice as she added, "Except at Disneyland—fake ones."

"I've seen those. They look awful darn close to the real thing." He went and sat in one of the rockers, and after a moment, she took the other. "If you sit here long enough," he said after a while, "the whippoorwill'll start to sing, somewhere out there in the trees. Just sings his little ol' heart out."

"I've never heard a whippoorwill." Her voice sounded far away. "What do they sound like?" She caught her breath and flicked him a quick, delighted smile when he cleared his throat, pursed his lips and whistled the three-note song. Then she turned her head away again, but not before he saw her smile go soft and wry. "I remember…you told me about the whippoorwill. The night Amy was born."

Warmth rose in his cheeks, and he laughed. "I'm kind of surprised you remembered that."

"Oh, I remember everything about that night." She sounded wistful again. Almost sad, he thought. "I remember you held me, and you told me it was like making love. And then…"

"And then, you told me…"

"I'd never made love before."

"I didn't believe you," he said softly.

She gave a dry snort of irony. "*You* didn't—I couldn't believe I'd said it. It's not something I go around telling people, ordinarily."

"I didn't believe you," he said again in a muffled voice, talking to the boards between his feet. "How could I? There you were, havin' a baby."

"And then…" Her breath sighed and the rocker creaked softly as she leaned back. "I told you I'd been artificially inseminated."

His short, dry laugh was an echo of hers. "*Then* I believed you. I figured nobody would make up somethin' like that."

"You were so shocked." Her voice was gentle; not accusing, just stating a fact. "I know it…changed things. Between us. The way you felt about me.'' He shifted uncomfortably, wishing he could deny it, knowing he owed her the truth. Knowing she wouldn't let him deny it, even if he'd tried to. Her eyes were steady on him now, the light from the living-room windows shining in them like moonlight on water. ''I know it did, Jimmy Joe. I felt it. What I couldn't understand was *why?*''

He looked at her for a long time without answering, trying to pick apart the knots of feeling inside him. He was discovering that knowing something in your gut was one thing; trying to reason it out so you could explain it was something else. Finally he shook his head and began, ''I never meant to judge—''

''But you *did.*''

He looked down at his clasped hands. ''Yes, I guess I did, for a while.'' He paused, then went on in a voice he kept low to hide the intensity of the emotions inside him. ''I *know* what it's like, you know, raising a child all alone—I've been doin' it for eight years, now. And dammit all—I can't help it if I have strong feelings about a kid needin' *two* parents. Me, I know I'm one of the lucky ones, because of Mama and Jess bein' so close by, so even when I'm gone I know J.J.'s always got somebody around to love him and care for him. But I've seen what happens to kids, left alone with the TV or some computer for a baby-sitter.''

He left the rocking chair, propelled by the tension he couldn't keep to himself any longer, paced to the railing and stopped. Leaning his hands on it, he stared into the darkness and said quietly, ''I know things happen to people they can't help, and when they do they've got no choice but to make the best of things. But I thought, for somebody to do that to a child on purpose, that it was kind of...'' He looked over at her, hating to say it to her now, because of the way he felt about her, but knowing it was best to get it said and over with right up front, too. So he took a breath and murmured, ''Self-ish.''

She sat hunched forward in the chair, rocking it slightly,

making faint creaking sounds, not saying anything. He watched the way her hair shone warm in the light, like polished cherry-wood, and thought again of the nursery rhyme about the robin.

"Selfish…" She whispered it, then shook her head and said slowly, "And yet, you brought me here."

His feelings burned inside him like fire. He wanted so much for her to understand. "But that's just it," he said with gravel in his throat. "I know you're not selfish."

"No—maybe I *am* selfish." She left the chair rocking, empty, and came to the railing, her chin lifted in that uppity way she had. And he caught his breath, filled with a sudden burst of pride and delight in her, so it was all he could do to keep himself from bursting out in smiles and dragging her into his arms then and there.

"I wanted to be a mother," she said, roused and angry. "That's pretty selfish, I know. And I had a good job, plenty of money, a really nice home, and all this love and warmth and security—everything a child could want or need, right? Except for one thing—oops, no father! Bummer. But then I thought, so what? The important thing is the *love,* not who it comes from, or how many. I know lots of kids with two parents who'd be a helluva lot better off with one—or none at all, if you want to know the truth. So I thought, I've got enough love for two people, and I knew I'd make one terrific parent, so I decided to do it. I planned to try it this way first, and if that didn't work, I'd adopt. But it did work. And if you want me to say I'm sorry I did it—well, I'm *not.*"

He listened to the angry rhythm of her breathing and felt his own pulses quicken in response, and his body heat with a passion to match hers, although he knew it was a different kind. He meant to change that as soon as he could. He didn't move toward her, though, but said in a slow, soft drawl, "Well, Marybell, like I said, I know you're not selfish. And I won't say you're wrong about anything you just said, especially the part about the love bein' what's important, and you bein' a terrific mama. Which I guess just leaves me with one question.'' He turned his head to look at her. ''Why? Why did you have to do it this way? I mean, look at you—you're smart, funny, warm, a whole lotta fun to argue with, and probably the most beautiful, the sexiest woman I've ever seen in my life!''

Her breath caught, and surprise flashed like summer lightning in her eyes. His own heart stumbled, then began to pound like answering thunder. He whirled away from her, not trusting himself so near her, heat pumping through his body. Struggling with it, searching for a way to say it without being crude, he finally burst out with, ''Woman, there must have been men fallin' over themselves to be the father of your child!''

Behind him, she laughed softly and unevenly, as if someone had taken her by the shoulders and shaken her. ''Maybe so. But not the *right* one.'' Silence pulsed between them.

Then she said in her brisk, businesslike Mirabella voice, ''I guess you want to know how come I'm a virgin at thirty-eight. Well, like I said, I didn't exactly plan it that way. My problem has always been, you see, that I don't look anything like who I really am. I told you what I was like as a child. Well, there was a poem I remember—it was about this little girl who was a tomboy on the outside, but inside she was something completely different. That was me. It still is. When I was fat and homely, I kept waiting for some little boy to see how funny and smart and generous I was.

''By the time I got prettier, I'd developed this enormous chip on my shoulder. So now I looked like this cute, sexy little airhead, when actually I was an angry, resentful witch. And…I kept waiting for some guy to see how funny and smart and generous I was in spite of all that.''

Remembering the thought that had come to him way back in that truck-stop diner in New Mexico, Jimmy Joe wanted to burst out with, '*I* would have! *Me!*'' It took all the patience and good manners he had in him not to interrupt her.

''Guess what? Nobody ever did. Oh, I had crushes, of course—always on somebody who didn't have a clue. Guys who were attracted to me because of my looks—which was pretty much all of them—got turned off as soon as they found out who I really was. They just weren't expecting somebody who looks like I do to have a brain, I guess. They thought they'd be getting this adorable little someone they could dominate and control, and when they found out I was bossy and independent and headstrong and just as capable as they were— if not more so—boy, did they back off in a hurry.

"So…" She gulped, and suddenly there were tears in her voice. She lowered it to a whisper and went on, hurrying now, determined to get it all said. "I kept waiting for some guy to come along who would see how smart and funny and generous, and headstrong and independent and capable I was, and love me anyway. And no one ever did. I could have settled for just…someone, I suppose, but I've never been much good at compromising." She stopped there for a short huff of dry laughter, then finished in a flat, matter-of-fact tone. "For me it was the right man, or none at all. Eventually, I realized that the right man wasn't going to come along in time, and if I was going to have a child, I'd have to do it without one. So I did."

"Maybe," Jimmy Joe said hoarsely, "you just gave up too soon."

Chapter 16

"I'm gon' be rollin' into home 'bout twelve, one, to-night. My wife's gon' be lyin' in bed a-waitin' for me."

I-40—Texas

"Oh...Jimmy Joe."

He turned to her then, all primed and ready to take her in his arms, but when he saw the way she was looking at him he froze, a terrible fear prickling his skin. Her eyes were huge and dark with tears; he could see them glistening, too, on her cheeks.

"Don't you see?" she said, her voice so gentle and sad it just about broke his heart. "You don't know who I really am, either, any more than they did. You don't know me—how could you? You've only seen me...what—when I was in labor. Weak and helpless and scared to death and vulnerable. And now with Amy, when I'm such a soppy, sentimental fool. That's not *me*. I'm not at all like that!"

He would have reached for her right then, pulled her into his arms and murmured reassurances into her mouth, but she put up both hands to ward him off, and continued in a rapid, breathless voice.

"I'm an impossible person to live with. I'm moody, and I really need my privacy, my own space. I'd organize you to death—I'm frighteningly efficient. And a compulsive planner. I always have my Christmas shopping done—and everything wrapped—by mid-October. I'm bossy and argumentative, and I always have to be right. I stick notes on things, and underline in magazines. I…I'm a health nut. I don't eat red meat. And I really do hate country music!"

He studied her as she wound down through the laundry list of her shortcomings, saying nothing to derail her. But as he listened and watched her, he felt the fear slowly leave him, and the quiet joy of certainty come to take its place. He knew he could have kissed her then, and in a very short time thereafter had her in his bed. But it wasn't about that. It never had been. It was more important than that. There was a lot more at stake here than a few passion-filled hours. This was about the rest of his life. Except for the issue of her virginity, he couldn't see how taking her to bed was going to solve anything important.

He didn't think arguing with her was going to solve anything, either. He thought about it—about finally making his pitch like a traveling salesman and telling her all the ways he'd figured out that she could have a life with him here in Georgia and still do the things she liked to do out there in L.A.; how she could start her own business, if she wanted to, and go to Atlanta for shopping and concerts and plays, or to Athens, even to the university.

But he knew this wasn't the right time for that, either. She was right about a couple of things—she did dearly love to argue, and she did hate being wrong. At the moment she was on a roll, and he had an idea if he tried to argue with her she would just dig her heels in and get stubborn about it, more than ever determined to prove she was right.

"Reminds me of one of the great movie lines of all time,"

he drawled, when he saw she'd finally run down. He paused, shrugged, and delivered it: "'Oh, well...nobody's perfect.'"

She blinked, then let go a misty gust of laughter. He saw a look of confusion flash like a bird shadow across her face.

"Gettin' cold out," he said gently. "Gettin' late. Come on, let's go inside. I'll show you to your room."

He put his hand on her back to guide her through the door he was holding open for her, and felt her tremble. He almost lost it then, all his resolve and patience and self-control. Okay, he thought, so maybe making love to her wouldn't solve anything important between them, but it sure as heck would take care of her trembling, not to mention the hunger that was burning up *his* insides.

He was starting to worry about that, too. If things kept building up in him the way they were, he was afraid that when he finally did make love to her, he might have trouble being as gentle with her as he knew he was going to need to be. This whole thing, in fact, was turning out to be a lot more complicated and difficult than he'd thought it would be. It was going to take just about all the patience and self-discipline he had in him to get it to work out right. But he never doubted that it would. Or that she was worth it.

I really hate this, thought Mirabella. Here she was, all primed to have it out with him once and for all, and he'd left her flat, with nobody to fight with. Now she felt frustrated, and a little foolish.

Also confused. She didn't understand him. She'd seen the way he'd looked at her, the way his eyes had seemed to glow with some deep, inner fire. Everywhere they'd touched her she'd felt hot—as if the sun itself was burning her naked skin. And yet at the same time, she shivered. Chemistry, she thought, then scoffed at herself. *Chemistry, hell. Call it what it is, girl. It's just plain old desire.*

Desire. Oh, yes, she was awash in it, on fire with it. Her body pulsed with it. She wanted him. She could taste him on her tongue. He was in the air she breathed. Her legs felt like melted wax.

And now…he was going to say good-night?

Cold, confused, and wobbly with uncertainty, she picked up Amy's carrier and watched him while he locked up and turned off lights. She offered no objection when he took the carrier from her, but moved ahead of him to the stairs, feeling his hand like a knifepoint at the small of her back. She climbed slowly, breathlessly, wondering if her legs would support her to the top.

"This is my room," he said softly, opening a door at the top of the stairs. He turned on the light, then stood back out of the way so she could see.

It's nice, she thought. Tidy, like the sleeper in his truck; wholly masculine, but with touches of gentleness and beauty, too, in the shelves full of books and Indian pottery, the Navajo rugs that covered the floor, and in the magnificent, hand-carved four-poster bed.

"What a beautiful bed," she murmured, meaning nothing more than that.

Jimmy Joe glanced at her and nodded. "Bought it from a man up in North Carolina. He told me he carved it from the wood of four-hundred-year-old walnut trees." He waited while she admired it, then said quietly, "It's too big for a man alone. I'd like to share it with you…when you're ready."

But I am ready! She wanted to shout it at him. Why couldn't he see that? Why couldn't she tell him? She suddenly felt as though she were enclosed in glass, walled up inside herself; that there was a door between them that hadn't been opened yet. He held the key—she knew he did. But for some reason, whatever it was, he hadn't used it; not yet. *Please, Jimmy Joe. Please say the words that will make it right.*

He touched her elbow and smiled, just the faintest shadow of his sweet, Jimmy Joe smile. "The guest room's this way," he said.

Jimmy Joe lay awake on the living room sofa listening to his house creak and groan in the stillness of night. It sounded to him like the wind was picking up outside; the rain he'd driven through from Texas to Pensacola would be here by tomorrow. He thought about that, about the rain and the trip and his truck, and all the little things he had to do now that he was home. He thought about them hard, as if they were big problems he had to solve, trying every way he could to keep his mind off the woman sleeping upstairs.

It occurred to him that some of those creaks and groans had taken on the rhythm of footsteps. He thought it might be J.J. looking for him, or getting up to use the bathroom or get himself a drink of water. He waited for the boy to come down the stairs. When he didn't, he pulled on a pair of sweatpants and went to investigate.

The door to his bedroom was open. When he looked inside he saw Mirabella standing beside his bed, framed in a rectangle of light from the yard lamp outside. She was wearing her nightgown—something long and slim and white—and he thought she looked a little like a candle standing there, with her hair the gleaming flame.

"I was looking for you," she said, her voice soft and faraway sounding. She threw a bewildered glance toward the quilt that covered his bed, still smooth and undisturbed. "You haven't been to bed?"

He moved toward her, feeling his heartbeat grow stronger with every step he took. He made a gesture, a small throwaway with his hand. "I don't sleep here much. Told you, it's too big for one person. Just makes me feel lonely. Usually I sleep in the guest room. Tonight—" he smiled and shrugged "—I'm on the couch downstairs."

She shivered when he came up behind her. With a sigh, he wrapped his arms around her and brought her warm and snug against him. "You said you were lookin' for me," he murmured into her hair. "How come?"

He felt her soften in his arms as she let out the breath she'd been holding. He could barely hear her whisper, "I wanted…to tell you I'm ready. I want…you to make love to me. I want to share this bed with you."

"For tonight?" he asked, holding himself still, "Or from now on?"

She didn't answer. His heart knocked heavily against her back.

He shifted his arms, nestling her more securely against him, and drew a breath. "I have to tell you about this bed," he said. "I told you I bought it up in North Carolina, in the Smoky Mountains, from an old man who'd carved it from the wood of four-hundred-year-old walnut trees. He told me about it, told me it was something special, not just for sleeping in. A marriage bed, he called it. Said it was a bed to last a lifetime, and that I probably wouldn't understand that then, but I would someday.

"Well, I remember thinking, who is this old coot, and who does he think I am—a kid, or something? Shoot, I knew what a marriage bed was for—didn't I already have a child of my own? I thought he was talkin' about sex, of course. But he wasn't. I understand that now.

"See, I always thought I had marriage figured out. When I was a kid, I saw my parents—Daddy always away workin', Mama takin' care of the house, runnin' everything including us kids—and I thought that's what it was—kind of a division of labor, I guess you could call it. Then I got to be in my teens, and the hormones kicked in, and all I could think about was gettin' some girl into bed. And of course there was everybody tellin' me that was wrong, that was supposed to wait for marriage, right? Big revelation—*now* I knew what marriage was really all about. Marriage was so you could have sex without goin' to hell."

He rocked her gently, as they laughed and trembled together. "Then…I got Patti into trouble, and we got married, and I found out there was a whole lot more to it than just sex. Hoo boy, was there ever! All of a sudden, marriage was about responsibility, and providing, and taking care of somebody, and when it's your child, that means *forever*."

"I know," Mirabella whispered. "I know."

"After Patti…well, I dated some, went to bed with a few. I was looking, I guess. But there was always something missing. I was lonely—sometimes even when I was with somebody. Usually, in fact. And I never knew exactly what it was I was lookin' for. Until you.''

He was shaking harder now, so he held her tighter, too, and laid his cheek against her hair. ''That's when I knew that what I'd been lookin' for was my *mate*—you know, like half of a pair. And that the reason I'd been so lonely was, half of me was missing. And then I found you, and all of a sudden I wasn't lonely anymore, because now I was…whole.''

He turned her suddenly, his hands on her shoulders holding her away from him so he could look into her eyes. Through the blur of her own tears Mirabella saw his face—not just its beauty and sweetness, but also its intelligence and strength, and she thought she was seeing him clearly for the first time.

''And it doesn't *matter* if we're different,'' he said in a voice gone hoarse with passion. ''Night and day, black and white—it doesn't matter, you understand? It's like this rug we're standin' on. Black and white can make one real beautiful whole, when you weave 'em together right.''

She could only nod; tears rolled freely down her cheeks, and she made no move to wipe them away. His hands slipped from her shoulders and down her arms, and he took her hands and held them clasped tightly between both of his.

''Marybell…Mirabella, I know I'm not a sophisticated man, or very exciting, and I'm sure never gonna be rich. But I will promise you this—that I will love you and that little girl in there with all my heart and soul until the day I die, and spend every day of my life makin' sure you know it. And I will tell you so again with my last breath. I told you, I'm not good with words—''

''You didn't need many!'' It burst from her on the crest of the sob she could no longer contain. ''Just those three would have done it!''

''Just—'' He looked bewildered for just an instant, and then his smile blossomed. '' 'I love you,' you mean?''

''*Yes!* I kept waiting for you to say it…dammit.'' She snatched her hand from him and swiped furiously at her nose, and when that proved futile, sniffed loudly instead. ''I love you too,'' she said soggily.

"Oh, I know that." He took her wet face in his hands and turned it up to his.

"How could you?" She sniffed again. "I didn't know myself. I thought it was just another stupid crush—you know, because there you were, riding to my rescue on your big blue charger, scooping me out of a snowbank and sweeping me up in your arms and saving my life—how could I not fall in love with you? And then I thought it must be chemistry, or hormones, or something. I never dared believe—"

"*Believe,*" he growled, and lowered his mouth to hers.

And suddenly she did. Believed in him absolutely, knew with utter certainty that her heart would be safe forever in his keeping, and that she could grow old with him and never have to fear that he would love her less, even when she looked like Granny Calhoun.

"I'm sorry about this virginity thing," she gasped, when his mouth had left hers to travel by slow, melting degrees down the side of her throat. It seemed to her the only relevant issue still unresolved, and it loomed like a mountain in her consciousness. "Of course, technically—"

"Don't worry about it," he murmured. "Not a problem…"

All at once, she believed that, too. *Of course,* she thought, weak-kneed with relief and desire. For some men it would have been, but not Jimmy Joe.

And it wasn't.

She, who had always been envious of the tall and the slim, and secretly ashamed of her own body's voluptuous curves, now stood dazed and compliant while for the first time in her life the man she adored slowly drew her nightgown over her head. She watched his eyes feast hungrily on the sight of her, and when he told her she was beautiful, for the first time in her life she believed it.

He laughed, and chided her gently for her embarrassment at the predictible response of her nursing breasts to his touch, and lightly, tenderly, lovingly covered them with a towel. "We'll save that for later," he promised huskily. "We have all the time in the world. A lifetime…"

But her legs gave way when his lips brushed her stomach. The melted-wax thing again…

So he drew back the quilt and the blankets and laid her down on the marriage bed that had been carved from the wood of four-hundred-year-old walnut trees, and stretched himself out carefully beside her. He kissed her mouth, deeply and thoroughly, until he felt her body begin to squirm and yearn unconsciously toward him, searching for him in its own natural way. And then he kissed her belly and her thighs and, parting them with gentle stroking, the damp and silky places between.

He heard her gasp, ''I…can't,'' just once, and breathed a smile against her skin. Then he told her with his hands and mouth and tongue that she *could*.

She, who had never believed in anyone but herself, believed now in him. With complete confidence and trust, she gave herself into his hands. How easy it was, then. Like dying, she thought. And shattering…overwhelming…wrenching, too. Like being born.

Contractions, small cataclysms rocked her, then slowly receded. Jimmy Joe held her and murmured to her, telling her how wonderful she was, how sweet and beautiful. And yes, she believed him.

She stroked her hand over his tight, flat belly, pausing when she came to the drawstring of his sweats. He held her hand there for a moment, and asked huskily, ''Are you sure you're ready? It's only been three weeks.''

''I'm ready,'' she said firmly. *It's been a lifetime.*

''I'll be careful.''

''I know.'' She found one end of a drawstring tie and pulled it.

He smiled at her, lazy and sure. ''You know what you're doin'?''

''I'm a virgin,'' she replied, ''not an idiot.'' The ties slid through her fingers. Breathless, she lowered her mouth to his belly and slowly drew the sweats over his hips.

''Marybell,'' he gasped, ''what is this?''

''Dessert,'' she whispered. And then there was silence.

He stood about a minute of it, then grasped her wrists and

rolled her over with one swift twist. "If you want me to be gentle," he murmured, pinning her with his legs, "you're gonna have to stop that, right now."

She didn't answer, just gazed at him, her eyes all sleepy and soft. Then she closed them and smiled. Her legs came around him. He whispered her name once more. *"Bella..."* He lowered his head and kissed her and kissed her and kissed her. And while he was kissing her he slipped into her body like a cat burglar and stole her virginity away.

"There, now," he said tenderly. "That wasn't so hard, was it?"

Shaken and relieved, she laughed. And deep inside her he felt it, and with her felt all the newness, wonder and excitement of the very first time. *Her* first time. His, he would always remember as a Christmas night in the sleeper of his snow-bound truck. Shaken himself, he thought of miracles; frightened, he thought of his life if he'd never found her, and with his heart pounding, bowed his head and sought her mouth and kissed her until his world had righted itself again.

He rocked her gently, so gently. Her tender body enfolded and caressed him and he felt every muscle and tremor, every pulse beat, the tiniest flinch and spasm. He knew when she tensed and tightened, and when she relaxed and softened, and when her body began to swell and throb to its own rhythms; when it was time to take them over and make them his...and then theirs. And when he could take them both to the limit—and beyond. And finally...finally, he knew when to let them both go, so that they spun wildly, deliriously out of control, overwhelmed and laughing with the sheer joy of living, and of making and being *in* love.

Quietness and peace came slowly, like twilight settling down after the sun has set in a blaze of glory. In the stillness between sighs, Mirabella heard it—the snuffling, snorting sounds of a baby waking.

"Oh, boy," she murmured, laughing. "Perfect timing."

"I'll get her," Jimmy Joe said. He was already pulling on his sweats, padding across the room in his bare feet.

A few minutes later he was back with Amy tucked expertly

in the crook of his arm, a fresh diaper and dry blankets in his other hand. Her heart turned over as she watched him spread out the blankets and change her daughter's diaper while she stretched and gurgled and made faces at him in the soft light of the bedside lamp. When he finished, he scooped Amy up and placed her gently in her waiting arms, then quickly piled up pillows, climbed back into bed and drew Mirabella against him and pulled the blankets around them all.

"I think," said Mirabella drowsily, "I know what the old man meant. About this bed being a marriage bed—a bed for a lifetime. It's this, isn't it? For being together…"

He nodded. "For making love, and just talking…"

"For making plans…"

"Reading out loud to your kids…and grandkids…"

"Cuddling on Sunday mornings…"

"Reading the paper…"

"Making love…"

"Making babies."

"Making babies?" she asked, craning to look at him. "Are you sure?"

"Well," he said, "of course, Amy Jo's mine already, but I wouldn't mind makin' a couple more—long as we do it the old-fashioned way."

She was quiet for a moment. Then she said slowly, "You do realize, don't you, that if I hadn't done what I did, I'd never have met you? If it hadn't been for that idiotic thing I did, I wouldn't have been out there on that interstate, pregnant, in labor, stranded. Then you couldn't have rescued me, and then where would we be?" She shivered suddenly, and his arms tightened around her.

"I don't know," he said, dazed. "I guess you might be right."

Mirabella laughed softly. "Of course I am," she said triumphantly. "I'm always right."

"Okay, eastbound, I'm headin' for the barn."

"Happy trails, westbound. Ten-four…"

* * * * *

SILHOUETTE®

*Super*ROMANCE™

proudly presents
a brand-new series from

KATHRYN SHAY

Serenity House

They'd grown up at Serenity House—a home for girls.
Now they're coming together for the first time as
adults. Childhood friends who'd shared difficult times,
who'd shared hopes and fears, laughter and tears—
and perhaps most important of all...secrets.

Practice Makes Perfect
October 2004

A Place to Belong
November 2004

Against the Odds
January 2005

1004/SH/LC94

SILHOUETTE®

*Super***ROMANCE**™

proudly presents
a brand-new series from favourite author

Anna Adams

THE
CALVERT
COUSINS

A few Calverts may have flown the nest, but
somehow they always find their way home...

The Secret Father
January 2005

The Bride Ran Away
February 2005

The Prodigal Cousin
March 2005

0105/SH/LC100

THE TRUEBLOOD
Dynasty

Isabella Trueblood made history reuniting people torn apart by war and an epidemic. Now, generations later, Lily and Dylan Garrett carry on her work with their agency, Finders Keepers.

Book Eight available from 17th December

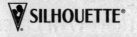

SILHOUETTE®
SPECIAL EDITION™

AVAILABLE FROM 17TH DECEMBER 2004

ISN'T IT RICH? Sherryl Woods

Millionaires' Destinies

Tycoon Richard Carlton suspects that his aunt has more than business matters on her mind when she insists he meets Melanie Hart. Melanie might be beautiful, but Richard won't open his wounded heart…

EXPECTING! SUSAN MALLERY

Merlyn County Midwives

Pregnant and alone, Hannah Bingham came home and met tall, dark and devastating Eric Mendoza. Devoted to his career, could the sexy executive be persuaded that he would prefer the position of husband and dad!

PRINCE OF THE CITY Nikki Benjamin

Manhattan Multiples

Bill Harper might be the mayor of New York, but there was no way Eloise Vale was going to let him close down Manhattan Multiples, and if accepting her old flame's invitation to a ball would help her cause, then she would go out with him, dance in his arms and begin to believe in fairy tales!

THEIR BABY BOND Karen Rose Smith

Rugged and handsome hostage negotiator Jake Galeno returned to Santa Fe to Tori Phillips—and the chemistry they shared was combustible. But Tori was about to adopt a baby boy and *he* was the only male she had room for in her life!

HIS PRETEND WIFE Lisette Belisle

When a logging accident landed loner Jack Slade in hospital, Abby claimed to be his wife to keep her promise to him. Jack needed her and she was determined to stay until he was well. But would her heart be broken when it was time to leave?

THE BEST OF BOTH WORLDS Elissa Ambrose

At a wedding a few months ago, Becky Roth and Carter Prescott had indulged in a little too much cake…and lovemaking. But now that he was going to be a father, Carter was suddenly a man on a mission—marriage!

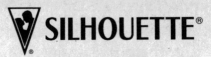

M398

Published 17th December 2004

TESS GERRITSEN
BARBARA DELINSKY

Two emotionally compelling novels by international
bestselling authors in one special volume

Family Passions

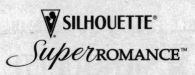

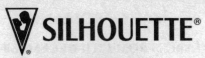